The Acts
Of Life

Copyright © 2021 Kristin Mulligan

To Stacy. Who read everything I ever wrote.
Even if she had no choice.

Table Of Contents

ACT I – SAM

CHAPTER ONE

———— ♦ ————

My vodka tonic sits in front of me as I sit at an empty table. With each sip and passing minute, I hope the vacant chairs will be occupied by Jake and Diego, my tardy friends.

The bar is overflowing with people, all waiting like vultures to scoop up the next empty table.

I'm the asshole at a four top drinking alone.

The waitress comes around to check on me. I'm three drinks in and if Diego and Jake don't arrive soon, I'm closing my tab.

Five minutes turns into ten and I realize they're standing me up.

I flag down the waitress, ask for my bill, and shoot back the rest of my vodka tonic.

When I swallow, I spot a brunette searching the crowds. I can only assume she's looking for a table. She locks eyes on me and I decide it's her lucky night. She can take my table as soon as I sign the receipt.

But when she finally gets closer, she asks, "Are you Matthew?"

She's even more appealing up close. Her dark hair fans out past her chest, exposing a perfect amount of cleavage. Her tight black dress is so complimentary against her curves. Who is this lucky bastard Matthew that she's meeting tonight?

"I can be Matthew?" I flirt.

"I've been looking for him all night."

"Blind date?" I predict.

She squints at me like I'm psychic.

"Wow, good guess. Yeah, but I think I got stood up. Assuming you aren't him?"

"I wish I was, but no, I'm Sam."

She exhales with impatience and leans down to grab her phone in her purse. The cleavage busting out of the deep V garners a glance or two.

This mysterious woman has sprinkles of light freckles against her tan, flawless skin and I can't help but stare. A buzz of electricity filters down to my dick and I'm jolted with arousal.

"Gonna call it quits?" I ask, suddenly hoping she'll sit with me instead. She caught me on a lonely night and I could use the company.

"Yeah I guess so."

"Have you called him?" I suggest, unsure why I'm giving her options because I'd rather her stay and indulge me for another hour. I'm not ready to go home anymore.

"He's not answering my texts." She says, embarrassed. "I think I can take a hint."

"Well hey wait a minute!" I say as she turns to leave. "Have a drink with me. I have this entire table to myself. Let me buy you a drink. Not all men are assholes like Matthew."

Celestial hues of green and hazel encircle her dark pupils. They interrogate me with purpose, wondering if I'm a serial killer.

"I'm a nice guy, promise!"

She bites her lower lip, her perfect white smile pinching the ruby red flesh that I, too, want to sink my teeth into. Damn, this girl is a knockout. She's stunning in an unconventional way. I'm guilty of *almost* overlooking her. Had she not approached me first, her face might have gotten lost in the crowd. She deserves a second glance. She's exquisitely different from the typical women in this city. Her curves are molded from an hourglass and her dress hugs her perfect, well developed shape.

"You're not waiting for your girlfriend?"

I chortle, "No, I can assure you, I do not have a girlfriend."

Her lips tremble for the quickest second, but she says, "…Sure! Why not? I got all dressed up. Would be a waste going home now."

She parks herself across from me and sets her Louis Vuitton purse on the empty chair next to her.

"I'm Sam, in case you didn't hear me earlier."

She reaches out a hand and says, "I'm Harper. Nice to meet you!"

Her bracelets and breasts jiggle when we shake and I stupidly let my eyes linger for a few seconds too long.

She catches me staring and I wish I had been quick enough to avert my eyes.

"Shit, I'm sorry. I'm not doing too well with this whole 'I'm not an asshole' thing."

She laughs and admits, "What do women expect when they wear a dress like this? At least I know it's working."

A wide grin stretches across my face from her direct honesty.

The waitress comes by with my bill but instead we both order a new drink.

Another vodka tonic for me and a Cosmo for her.

"So, Harper," I begin. "What do you do in San Francisco?"

"Well aside from being stood up by strangers," she laughs at her rejection. "I'm a book editor. I actually moved here a month ago. And to be honest, the city hasn't been so great to me."

"Why's that?"

"It's hard meeting people. I grew up in Maine and I'm not used to the big city life yet."

"I can see that. I grew up in LA so it's similar enough."

"What made you move from LA?"

Instead of admitting the honest yet depressing reality, I tell her a half-truth.

"I went to law school in LA and I needed something new. My best friend opened his own law firm out here and I decided I'd help him out. I only work part time so I have plenty of time to have fun while I'm still young."

Our eyes connect and she releases a nervous laugh.

"Well gosh, you're handsome, you're a lawyer. How are you still single?"

Instead of drowning myself in my water, I ignore her hair-raising question. "Trust me, civil law is the least exciting career choice. It's comprised of four branches: tort, contracts, property, and family. I don't deal with drug dealers or murderers. Usually the people I help are seeking compensation, money, or damages. It's not fun like the movies portray. If your HOA is screwing you, maybe you slipped in a Starbucks and broke your leg, need a temporary restraining order, child support is unpaid, I'm you're guy."

"Now that you mention it, my ex *has* been behind on child support for a while…"

I swallow hard, looking for a wedding ring tan line and wait for the inevitable "just kidding."

It finally comes when her lips part and she dips her head backwards.

"I'm kidding! Oh my god I'm so sorry. No ex-husband. I've actually been single for a while."

I release a nervous chuckle and immediately it's stifled when she places her hand over mine. Harper squeezes my fingers with compassion, her laugh lasting longer than mine.

"I'm so sorry." She gathers her composure as the waitress brings our drinks.

Perfect timing, I need to loosen up. She's making me nervous for some reason.

My phone buzzes against the table. Incoming texts.

"Excuse me, one minute." I request, grabbing my phone.

Jake: "Sorry guys, I got held up at the office."

Diego: "I can still be there if you're there Sam."

Sam: "Forget it. I met a girl."

Diego: "Bastard."

"Well hey, if it makes you feel any better, my friends stood me up, too!"

"To being stood up." She agrees.

I clink my glass to hers and we both sip.

"You sure you weren't meeting a girl? If I see

some poor, helpless thing looking for a handsome man like yourself, I'll feel terrible."

"I haven't had a girlfriend in a while." I clear my throat, wanting to talk about anything else but my previous disasters. "Tell me about this guy you were going to meet."

"A coworker set us up. She knew how hard it's been for me meeting new people. Her boyfriend recommended this friend of his, and she reassured me he was 'beyond sexy.' So naturally I started looking for the hottest guy here and then I saw you."

That's like the third comment she's made about my appearance within a few minutes, not that I'm counting. One more subtle hint and I'll consider this a done deal.

"I see this as fate."

"Looks like it is." She smiles at me again, one of her eyebrows rising as if on cue.

I gulp my drink, feeling more confident as she gives me playful smiles and teasing glances. Her foot brushes against my leg every time she crosses her legs under the table. Our mutual attraction is palpable. The low lighting and loud atmosphere create an invisible partition.

"So how is book editing? I assume you read a lot?"

"I grew up around books my entire life. My parents owned a bookstore so I would spend all my days reading while they worked."

"That's so cool. Do they still own it now? Back in Maine?"

"No, unfortunately they passed away when I was young. I used some of my inheritance to buy a condo here in the city. Otherwise I'd never be able to afford to live here."

"Seriously? My parents passed away when I was a teenager. That's actually the real reason I couldn't be in LA. It was too hard."

I'm very guarded about the loss of my parents. Many people know they aren't around, but the details are hazy. A girlfriend of one month wouldn't even get the information Harper is hearing, and we've known each other less than an hour. It's remarkable I'm able to be so honest.

"Oh Sam, I'm so sorry. That's awful."

"Well here's to our parents as well." I cheers her drink again, mine practically empty.

"Hey that's bad luck!" Harper tells me. "You shouldn't cheers with an empty glass!"

"Uh oh, what's going to happen to me?" I tease.

"You might go home alone." She teases back.

"Well let me rectify that."

———— ◆ ————

I'm on my fifth drink of the night while Harper's on her second. I'm loosening up and she's definitely getting there. Provocative comments and playful jokes are being tossed back and forth. I keep the topics of conversation innocent and steer clear of politics and religion, but would love to bring up sex.

"So Samuel, how old *are* you?"

"How old do I look?" I hate when women ask that follow up question, but I'm curious to see if I've still got it.

I furrow my eyebrows and give her the sexiest pout I can muster.

"Hmm… thirty… nine?"

"What!" I exclaim. "39? I look that old?"

Harper has a flat, thin smile as she sips from her cocktail glass.

"You're fucking with me?" I assume.

"Your skin looks way too perfect to be nearing 40."

"Well thanks." I say, "I'm 18."

Her head flies backwards again as she shrieks, loud. It's a contagious laugh that sends a weird buzzing inside my stomach.

What the hell is going on? I'm blaming the alcohol currently controlling my nervous system. This playful banter has me wanting to reach across the table and take her here and now. That smile, her laugh, it's melodic. One of my downfalls is a woman's smile.

"I'm 33." I confirm. "And you?"

"I turned 30 a few weeks ago actually."

She looks a lot younger and I'm immediately smashed with a torrent of guilt. Mid 20's seems to be my weakness. I'm not used to mature, sophisticated women.

"So you moved out here because of a job offer?" I ask, stunned someone would be so bold to uproot their life like that.

"Yep, there was nothing for me back in Maine except my ex and a dead end job. It was one of the easiest decisions I ever had to make."

"Good for you." I say, hoping she doesn't bring up her ex again.

Harper is engaging and easy to talk to, but if I'm being honest, I'm ready to see what comes after drinks.

———————◆———————

The night is winding down. Our conversation is becoming shorter and words are scarce. I get the impression Harper is waiting for me to suggest leaving. With or without her is what's circling my mind.

"Hey, maybe that's Matthew." I point to a guy alone at the bar.

"Oh my gosh stop, don't point! What if it is? I don't want to talk to him now." She's turning her body in the other direction hiding, pretending not to enjoy my teasing.

"Here give me your phone, I'll text him."

She playfully smacks my hands away as I grab for it.

"Sam, don't you dare!"

"Well maybe we should get out of here?"

She nods, a gleam in her eyes that screams, "It's about time you asked."

My second bill of the night arrives and Harper amazes me again. She actually tries to give me money for her drinks; a gesture I appreciate more than she knows. It's the fact that, while I did originally offer, she doesn't expect it like she's royalty.

"My treat, for making my night better than it would have been." I confess.

"I'll buy the drinks next time." She says, getting off her chair.

It's brave of her to assume I want to do this again and I immediately feel like a jerk. While yes, I had a great time, I had no intentions of seeing her again after tonight.

We squeeze out of the crowds of people and saunter to the door outside. I let her go ahead while I place my hand on her lower back. Harper leads the way, my touch claiming her as mine to any men wondering if she's here alone.

"Where to?" I ask, wondering if she'll choose another bar or ask me to walk her to her car.

"Your place."

———◆———

The front door of my sky rise condo opens a crack when Harper locks her wrists around my neck, bringing my face to hers.

We're lingering halfway in my door frame and halfway out in the hallway, kissing as if it's just us in the world.

In reality, it is not just us in the world. My next-door neighbors are also coming home from a night out and remain entranced by our gritty make out session. They stare as if they've never seen anything like it.

Two drunk, horny adults going at it with zero apprehension is not something you see every night.

Giving them both a sideways smirk, I lift Harper at the inner thighs and wrap her legs around my waist, guiding us both into my condo for more privacy.

Normally, I don't bring women back to my place. But at this moment, I'll give Harper a set of my keys just so I can feel what it's like to be inside her.

Her lips are soft, plush pillows that contradict the hard erection in my pants. We're past the threshold when I get a giant handful of her ass.

When she moans in my mouth, I nearly drop us both to the floor.

I kick open my bedroom door and drop her to my bed, her dress rising past her thighs. Her legs spread, wanting me.

I'm unable to contain my excitement as I unintentionally rip off my shirt and throw it to the floor like a male stripper. My dick is ready to rip through my pants. She scoots to the edge of the bed, her face level with my increasing bulge. She unzips my pants and takes me into her mouth.

It's heaven. I'm in heaven. Harper's lips were made from God and I'm experiencing nirvana.

Her mouth ravages me as she dips her head, lips and tongue sliding along my shaft so she can taste all of me.

She teases me, slowing down her movement as I grip her hair in my fist. I control the speed and she keeps up perfectly as I build closer and closer to finishing.

And as much as I love this foreplay, I need more.

I bring her up to my face, our lips connecting again as I slip her out of her dress. I'm ungraceful and messy, saving my torturous, sexy moves for another night, maybe another woman. She's left standing in a red thong and I practically shred it to pieces.

I step fully out of my pants and boxers, completely nude and exposed.

Her fingertips graze over the contours of my abs, as if she's never seen something so stimulating.

"You're fucking amazing." She compliments. Hearing her say "fuck" makes my cock even harder and I didn't think that was possible.

I'm ready to bust right now as I take her all in.

Harper is unreal. She has the most flawless breasts I've ever seen, and I've seen a lot. The shape and silhouette are too perfect; they can't be real, but they are. I know this because they are now in my mouth.

They are soft, yet firm. I'm guessing a solid D cup that fits the palm of my hand to perfection.

I gently shove her backwards onto my bed, her body enveloped by the feather filled duvet. I hastily put on a condom.

I grip my hands under her knees and yank her to the end of the bed. She's lying beneath me, her feet dangling off the edge, back flat on the mattress as I tower over her.

As I admire every part of her, I confirm she's not too drunk she'd regret this later.

"Do you want this?"

She nods her head aggressively.

"Tell me you want it." I demand.

"I want it, I need it." She pleads.

I reach below me and spread her apart with my hand. A stream of her wetness coats my middle and index finger. I massage her warm, inviting entrance as she accepts my touch without any uncertainty.

"You're soaked, Harper."

Bending down on my knees, it's now my chance to taste her.

She trembles as I lightly suck on her, brushing my tongue against her most sensitive areas.

As if her open, wet legs weren't an invitation on its own, her visible sign of arousal is all I need to confirm she will gladly accept my dick.

I enter her and she's tight like a virgin. It takes a few slow pumps before she finally accepts all of me.

She moans loudly as my grip on her hips tighten.

I plunge inside and out as she quivers and grabs onto my pillows behind her.

"Oh fuck, Sam."

The way she says my name makes me push faster in her wet, warm center.

She propels her hips upwards and wraps her ankles around my waist so we are practically one person.

Her lips moan my name as her body conforms to the rhythm of my thrusts.

I flip her over onto her stomach so I can get a view of her backside.

"Keep doing that. Just like that." She whimpers when I change positions.

That mouth-watering ass has been neglected and I correct that immediately. I spank her right cheek, which evokes a scream of arousal. My fingers grip into her as my headboard bangs against the wall.

The world doesn't exist at this moment. I couldn't even tell you what day of the week it is. My sole purpose is to bring this woman to absolute bliss so I can finish right after her, which is coming soon.

Without warning, Harper's breathing becomes irregular yet consistent; her body stiffens as her limbs grasp for my sheets. She's there. Two more pumps and she's done.

And when she shatters into a million pieces, I follow a few minutes later, collapsing on top of her in a satisfied daze.

———— ◆ ————

The sounds of San Francisco are like elevator music. After a certain point, you barely even notice the police sirens, car horns or drunken people as they walk home. It's all background noise.

The clock reads 4:16am as a headache silently creeps in.

I shouldn't have had that fifth drink.

Before I can remember where my Tylenol bottle is, something moves next to me and I practically piss the bed.

Harper.

She's still here.

Sleeping next to me.

How did I not send her home?

Do I wake her up now and call an Uber?

It sounds like a great idea, but fucking her in the morning sounds even better.

My squishy, alcohol soaked brain is too exhausted to determine a polite finale for our night, so I fall back asleep.

———— ◆ ————

A noise startles me and I rub my eyes as a blurry figure emerges.

Harper has her clothes on and purse in hand.

"I'm sorry to wake you!" She whispers.

"It's cool. I'm up at this time anyway." I lie. It's 7:10am. I never get up before 8am on the weekends.

"I didn't mean to stay." She admits, putting each shoe on. "I've uh… never done this before."

"Fuck a stranger?" I ask, getting out of bed, still naked.

"Actually, yeah." She admits with a hint of embarrassment.

When she realizes I'm still naked, she gets a better view of my physique in the daylight. She releases a puckered breath of air through her lips. Those lips... that were on my dick hours ago, saying dirty things and kissing me like no other woman has.

"Sam, your body is…"

She doesn't know how to finish the sentence. Maybe the word she's thinking of hasn't been created yet. I'd like to think I'm worthy of that.

I noticed her red thong and a piece of paper sitting on the foot of the bed.

"Forget these?" I have one finger laced through the strap as I smile at her.

She tucks a piece of hair behind her ear. It's wild and untamed. Her lips are puffy and she looks like she was just fucked. I beam with pride because I made her look like this.

"I wanted to leave my number, just in case… you'd ever want to… do this again." She is slow and precise with each word like she's afraid she'll say the wrong thing.

I practically memorize her number.

"I'd love to do this again." I say.

Wait, do I?

Yes, now, if I'm being honest with myself.

"I- I can see that." She giggles.

Her face is drawn to my erection that is begging to be sucked, stroked, touched, anything.

"And as much as I'd love to do this right now, I have early plans."

She turns out my bedroom door, rejecting my dick and me.

That… fucking sucked.

I slip on some sweatpants to shield my deflating boner.

"I had a great time." Harper says at my front door. "Thanks again for the drinks. Text me if you ever get stood up again."

"Yeah, for sure."

Before I open the door for her, she gives the bulge in my pants one last look.

Instead of turning the door handle, she pulls my sweatpants down and takes me in her mouth.

It's so unexpected; I rest my body on the wall, close my eyes, and let her work.

Her mouth is too much. She works me with her lips and hand and I'm slightly embarrassed at how easily she can get me there. It only takes me a few minutes and I explode. Down her throat.

CHAPTER TWO

———◆———

I return to my bed and smell my sheets, just to confirm Harper wasn't a figment of my imagination. Smirking at the sweet pheromones entering my lungs, I take pride knowing Harper's remnants are left in my bedding.

I text my buddies as I thread Harper's panties through my fingers.

Sam: "Thanks for bailing on me last night."

Jake: "Oh boohoo. You met a girl. Tell us about her."

Sam: "Book editor from Maine. Dark hair. Hazel eyes. Phenomenal body. Brazilian wax."

Diego: "You banged? Surprised your dick still worked."

Sam: "I'd say she was happy with it."

Jake: "*Just* happy? That's it? Ouch."

Sam: "She liked it enough to suck me off in the morning."

Diego: "Whoa, whoa she stayed the night?"

Jake: "Holy shit she spent the night? At your place???"

Sam: "It was an accident."

Diego: "Gonna see her again?"

Sam: "She gave me her number. We'll see."

Jake: "That means no."

Sam: "I said I'll see."

Diego: "That means no."

I close out the thread, refusing to confirm or deny their assumptions.

Pulling up my twin sister's info, I give her a call and see what she's up to.

Stella answers almost immediately.

"Damn, isn't it a little early to be calling on a Saturday?" She groans.

"What's up?"

"I'm in bed, where else would I be?"

"It's almost 8am!"

"Exactly, it's the weekend and Nathaniel and I are being lazy today."

"Aww how cute."

"So, what's new? What'd you do last night?"

Instead of being an immature schoolboy and saying 'a random girl', I respond with the grown up response. "I was supposed to get drinks with the guys but they bailed. I met a girl."

"I *don't* even care."

"I'm assuming nothing will come of it."

"Nothing ever does."

"Job still going well?"

"Amazing." She yawns. "It's taken me six months to clean up the mess the previous idiot left. I'm the best they've seen in a long time."

"You'll be running that place before the end of the year."

"Don't be surprised if another promotion is in my future. Senior creator?"

"Don't get ahead of yourself." I surmise.

"Well you never know. Doing anything this weekend?"

"Might hang with the guys."

"Diego the divorcee?"

"Stella…" I caution.

"Whatever. Are you ever going to stop by the brewery? Or have you forfeited your claims and I'm sole owner?"

"I know, I'm sorry. I'll visit soon. In all fairness, are you ever going to introduce me to this guy? Sounds like it's getting serious."

"Of course it's serious. I'm the best thing that's ever happened to him."

"Does he know that?" I joke, my intentions playful.

"Look Sam, just because you're single doesn't mean I have to be lonely and miserable like you. Nathaniel and I are happy. Okay? Happiest I've ever been."

"Okay, gosh, sorry."

Her random confession has me wondering if she's trying to convince me or herself.

"Anyway, the staff misses you. Mom and dad would have wanted you at the brewery more."

And there it is. The guilt trip. Of course my parents would have wanted me there to help, but I'd also like to believe they wouldn't expect me to drop my entire life to run an already profitable business that's doing fine without me.

"Mom and dad would want us working on this together."

"Stella, I'm not moving back to LA. We've discussed this."

"But why stay in dreary San Francisco?"

"I have my friends out here."

"But your family is in LA."

My silence prompts her to take it one step too far.

"I mean what if you run into Camilla out there. Don't you ever worry about that?"

My veins harden, frozen. A cold chill sweeps through me.

"A client is calling me, gotta go." I abruptly end the call.

Sometimes I wonder if Stella brings up Camilla on purpose to rile me up, to remind me of the life I could have had before everything fell apart nearly a year ago.

This thought has me pausing as I look at Harper's number on the slip of paper.

I could come to the realization right now, in this moment that she was nothing more than a one-night stand. I could easily toss her number in the trash and go about my day and chalk this up to a phenomenal sexual experience.

However, I'm brought back to last night and replay her intoxicating laugh. Her infectious energy gave me confidence I hadn't felt in a while.

From what I gathered, Harper is successful, independent, and in my age bracket.

Was that what I was missing this whole time? She wasn't like those young, eager women that latch onto men like the desperate hopefuls they are.

I decide to take a chance and see where this goes. Friends with benefits perhaps?

Sam: "Your thong is too small for me."

I don't expect her to text back right away, but she does.

Harper: "LOL! Who is this?"

Sam: "Wow, how many pairs of panties are you leaving around San Francisco?"

Harper: "What color do you have?"

Sam: "Red."

Harper: "Okay red, this must be… Sam."

Sam: "You're cute, but a little birdie just told me

you've never done this before."

Harper: "Busted!"

Sam: "Thought I'd let you know I had a lot of fun last night."

Harper: "I did, too. Probably more than you realize."

Sam: "I'm glad it was me and not Matthew that got to take you home."

Harper: "He texted me this morning! Can you believe it? Came up with a BS lie."

Sam: "Men are assholes."

Harper: "Well you were a gentleman last night. When can I buy you a drink?"

Instincts hit me and I want to say I'm busy all week. I'm occupied, unavailable, out of town. I don't know why it's my first reaction, but it is.

I'm actually sitting on my ass, all my cases closed. No plans in the foreseeable days.

Sam: "How about next Friday? I'm kind of busy until then."

Harper: "Let me check my schedule at work Monday. Pretty sure it'll work."

Sam: "Sounds good. Enjoy your weekend."

Harper: "Thanks! You do the same."

I rest my head on my pillow, take a brief inhale of her panties, and go back to bed.

CHAPTER THREE

———◆———

Sunday mornings are reserved for Jake and Diego. Instead of going to church, we meet for brunch. We've kept this tradition going and it works for us. Our heathenism is a perfect excuse to catch up and drink alcohol before noon.

The table we're sitting at faces the sidewalk and busy streets. Part of our Sunday ritual is critiquing the devout churchgoers and one-night stand victims doing their walk of shame. It's harmless but entertaining.

Our usual waitress places three bloody Mary's down.

"Anything else, gentlemen?" She gives me a hopeful, toothy smile.

"We are good. Thanks, Charity."

When she's inside the restaurant, Diego says, "Damn, did you feel that sexual tension?"

"She was giving Sam that look." Jake adds. "You know she requests us to sit in her section every weekend."

I play dumb even though I clearly saw the look he was referring to.

"Charity is sweet but not my type." I confess.

"Why, because she's a waitress?" Jake asks.

"No," I confirm, no trace of judgment in my voice. "Because she's what, 22? I'm not down for that."

"Since *when*?" Jake exclaims.

"Sam is too hot for her, is what he's saying." Diego jokes.

I punch his broad shoulder.

"Diego, shut up." I say.

"You are kinda out of her league." Diego admits.

I blow out a mouth full of hot air.

Am I handsome? Sure, yeah. I've been blessed with the face of a runway model, minus the million dollar pout and strut. I can roll out of bed with two-day stubble, messy hair and still outshine guys who spent hours perfecting their look.

Yes, I have a great body. But who wouldn't if they dedicated their time lifting weights like I do? There are guys like me all over my gym with bigger muscles and smaller dicks.

Yet somehow I manage to one up everyone without even trying.

I've been told I'm the classic boy next door, turned hunk who doesn't know what he has.

I pride myself in being an upstanding guy; not too cocky (only where it counts: in bed), and never taking myself too seriously.

I'd like to think my warm brown eyes and endearing smile are my best attributes. But I've been told my dick is the best thing about me, and I wouldn't disagree. I've had my share of women through the years and I've never had any complaints.

Diego snaps in front of my face.

"Earth to Sam."

"Sorry," I apologize, as the food is set in front of us.

Charity places a cold palm on my forearm and tells us to "enjoy".

Diego and Jake are discussing Diego's current predicament.

He's neck deep in a divorce; something Jake and I saw coming a mile away.

I remain stoic as I recall the past few months and the hardships Diego tackled with his soon to be ex-wife.

Diego and Val, short for Valentina, knew each other only three months when Diego proposed. He was in a state of eternal bliss. They had a small ceremony, despite Jake's and my protests. You'd think not having her family present at the civil union would be obvious enough.

But once married, things changed almost overnight.

Red flags popped up everywhere. Val stole from him, would disappear for days, and could never keep a steady job.

Diego loved her, struggled to do everything in his power to reinforce their connection. But a meager six months into their marriage, Val demanded a divorce when she met someone else.

She left Diego, moved back to Cuba with the new man, and never looked back.

Diego was devastated. But he's still young and has plenty of time for a second chance.

So Val, the bitch that has a hit out on her if she ever returns to the states, is still somehow in our lives.

The divorce that won't end, as we call it, has been dragged out and delayed all thanks to Val marrying this new guy in Cuba.

"How is that even legal?" Diego asks his counsel.

"If I weren't so busy with work, I'd fly to Cuba myself and bring you back her head."

"Jesus, Jake."

"Dude!" Diego gawks.

"I'm kidding. Sheesh." Jake pops some fruit in his mouth. "I'm not about to go full Sicario on her…"

"I've thought about going to see her." Diego admits. "Showing up on her doorstep… with all the things she left at my place…"

His voice borders nostalgic and Jake gives me the nonverbal cue to bring Diego back to reality.

"Dude, she stole money from you. Married someone else."

"You'll find someone else." Jake adds, slapping his shoulder with a loud thwack.

I take a gulp of my bloody Mary, watching the strangers pass in front of our table.

"Yeah, someone who won't empty your bank accounts."

As I finish my sentence a woman with a similar profile as Harper runs past us. Her ass is outstanding, one I could never forget.

"Harper?"

"Who's Harper?" Diego asks.

"The girl I met Friday night. That looks just like her."

Her brown ponytail waggles behind her as she runs past the restaurant, her face now out of sight.

"The one in those tiny black shorts? Text her. Make her come back." Jake suggests.

"No way. That might not have been her."

"If it was, her ass looked delicious."

"Text her." Jake repeats, stuffing his face with food.

"And say what? 'Hey my married friend wants to check out your ass', I don't think so."

"We want to meet this infamous girl that got to spend the night. Jake and I never get to meet them anymore."

"I need a better view of her face. Got a great view of her backside."

"If she comes this way, and it *is* her, I'll say hello."
I lie.

"Sweet." They repeat in unison.

My phone buzzes in my pants and I'm anxious to see if maybe it *was* Harper running past me, the universe possibly sending me a message.

But no, just Stella.

Stella: "Hey jerk. You hung up so fast the other day I didn't get to mention I'm flying to Vancouver. Purposely getting a layover in San Fran. Let's get a quick dinner."

Sam: "Sounds great. What day?"

Stella: "Friday. Around 8pm. Late, I know, but this is like the only time I can see you since you're avoiding the brewery."

Sam: "I'll set the night aside."

Stella: "Good. I'll send the calendar invite. You're buying."

I set my phone down and look at my two friends.

I met Diego and Jake our freshman year of high school out in LA. We bonded over our love of sports, video games, and Playboy magazines.

Stella was like the needy, annoying little sister that wouldn't leave her cool older brother alone. Diego and Jake tried to include her, we *were* twins and all the same age, but our interests were too diverse.

I remember worrying Diego or Jake would possibly hook up with Stella. I even prepared myself for that day to come. But boy was I wrong. They couldn't stand her. When they'd sleep over, Stella would turn off the action movies and change it to some romance crap. When we'd sneak out to go to a party, Stella would tattle on us because we didn't invite her. If we went to the park to hit some baseballs, she'd hide my glove.

All in all, she was a buzz kill.

We were not a packaged deal, like Stella so frequently reminded me.

My friends were not her friends and her friends... well, she didn't have any friends. But if she would have brought someone home back in our adolescent years, I would have been nice; though secretly wary of this companion and what they were gaining from her friendship.

Now that we are older and live in different cities, the only thing I have to put up with is Jake and Diego's reactions when I mention her name.

"Shit." I say as I open my calendar. I may be a scatter brained womanizer that has no sense of direction, but I'm somewhat organized.

"What?" Jake asks, not bothering to look up from his phone screen.

"I told Harper we should get dinner Friday."

"What's the problem then?" Diego questions.

"Stella will be in town."

"I'd pick Harper over Stella any day and I don't even know Harper. And at least Harper will suck your-"

"You're disgusting." I say.

"I'm kidding." Jake apologizes. "God did any of your ex's like Stella? What about Camilla?"

Camilla is rarely brought up, let alone twice in the same weekend. It's a random coincidence but I hate it nonetheless.

"Camilla liked everyone. So yes, she did like Stella."

"Hey, hey isn't that the girl?" Diego points his long tanned arm towards a brunette coming our way.

It's her. Harper's face is shielded behind big, black sunglasses, but no doubt it's her.

She has an armband wrapped around her bicep with her iPhone inside it. She's walking this time and her perspiring body glistens in the sun. Goddamn, she looks good. Her skin is sweaty, creating contours against her athletic frame that accentuate her curves hidden behind her tight clothes.

"Wave her down!" Diego yells.

Luckily she hasn't seen us yet, because Diego and Jake are on the edge of their seats, ready to wave their cloth napkins in the air like a white flag.

I'm a ghost, hiding behind Diego, unsure if I want to introduce her to my friends. I barely know this woman, and here she is, like fate is dangling her in front of me again.

Before I can decide, Jake throws a breakfast roll at her.

Time slows down and I see this all happen in slow motion. Jake grabbing the roll, winding up his arm, throwing it through the air as it sails toward her, smushing into her shin as she slowly recoils at the unknown violence.

Diego falls out of his chair laughing as she's pelted in the leg.

Harper scans left and right, wondering where this food fight is coming from.

She casually strolls up to our table next to the sidewalk, removing her earbuds, confusion stretching from her furled eyebrows to her squinting eyes.

"Excuse me sir, did you throw this bread at me?" Her tone is serious, but she's fighting off a smile as she recognizes me.

"I'm sorry, that was my idiot friend over there."

Jake and Diego are laughing so hard people are staring. Their cackles and howls are causing a scene.

"What a lovely surprise to see you again!" Harper says loudly over the maniacal laughing at the table.

"Sorry, I didn't mean for my friend to assault you with food…"

I make the fatal mistake and say "assault," and this when Diego and Jake really lose their shit.

"You live around here?" I ask.

"A few… a few miles away."

It's difficult for Harper to get a word in thanks to my moronic friends and their obnoxious laughing.

"This is Diego and Jake. Assholes, this is Harper."

"Nice to meet you. I hope that didn't hurt, sorry." Jake apologizes.

"No worries, I'm just glad it wasn't a sourdough loaf."

"I'm Diego, nice to meet you. So how do you know our friend, Sam?"

He smacks me hard once in the back and places his hand on my shoulders like he's about to massage me.

I want to kill him.

"We actually met Friday night." Harper begins. "Apparently some assholes stood him up."

Harper just gained 10 points for that one.

She winks at me and I return the gesture, offering the most enticing smile I can muster. Seeing her sweaty and hot transmits onto me and I gulp a glass of water to cool down.

"Ooh, can I have some? I forgot my water bottle and I'm dying."

Handing over my glass, Harper takes a big gulp then empties the rest over her head.

I watch the water mix with her sweat as it drips down her cleavage. I follow each drop as it disappears to areas inside her sports bra that I can't see from where I'm standing.

Out of the corner of my eye, Diego and Jake ogle her chest as well. Her breasts are so perky smashed inside that unfortunate bra. She could easily pull off the sports bra only look very well.

She smiles back at the three sets of eyes that are more than likely imagining x-rated scenarios.

"So getting your weekly brunch and mimosas in?" Harper shakes off some of the water drops.

"Actually yes, we meet here once a week and get brunch." I confirm.

She covers her mouth, trying not to laugh. "Oh, I'm sorry. I was just kidding about the brunch thing. My girlfriends and I used to do that all the time back in Maine. I didn't think guys actually did brunch."

"Their bloody Mary's are on point." Diego jokes.

"Yeah, and the bread is fantastic." Jake adds, taking a bite of a remaining roll.

"Well good for you guys." The briefest moment passes and I can sense she's overstaying her welcome. "I better get going. It was nice to meet you guys."

"You too!" They say together.

She starts to walk away and comes back, "Oh and Sam! Friday works!"

"Oh yeah about that..." I begin. Her cheerful face deflates a bit. "Can we reschedule? My sister is coming into town and we don't see each other often."

"Bitch." Diego coughs.

I snipe him in the balls and he hunches over, laughing in pain.

"Next Saturday should work, I think." She glances over at Diego perplexed, probably wondering if he was calling her a bitch or my sister. "Can I text you later?"

"Sounds good. Enjoy your walk home."

When Harper turns the corner, I snipe Jake in the balls to make it even.

"What the fuck! I didn't even do anything!" Jake shrieks.

"You threw food at her? How old are we?"

"Dude, I have a great arm, what can I say?"

Jake's laughing again and I roll my eyes.

"Do I need to get you a change of underwear? You both look like you pissed your panties."

"I'd need it for other reasons." Diego corrects. "She's hot, like really hot. You've never hooked up with her before? She looks familiar."

"Damn, Diego, I've slept around a lot but I would know if I hooked up with someone like her."

"Did I maybe?"

"No." Jake and I say in unison.

"Damn, I wish I did. She is cute, Sam. If things don't work out, gimme her number."

"I'll keep that in mind." I say, possessiveness getting the better of me.

Jake's phone beeps and he reads his text.

"Avery is waiting for me. I better get going."

"Where are you off to?" I ask.

"Avery is remodeling the living room. I think we're

on boutique #182. Can't seem to find the perfect couch."

"Sounds... fucking boring." Diego deadpans.

"I'll pay you to go for me."

"Not a chance." Diego says.

———◆———

I walk the rest of the way home to my condo trying to ignore the fact the guys brought up Camilla.

It's been a while since she entered my mind. And even though I don't have Facebook, I've thought about searching for her to see how she's doing.

Where is she living now? Does she ever think about me? How has she managed over the past year?

By the time I'm up my 22 floors, I lock Camilla away in the memory vault. She needs to stay there.

I snap open a beer and plop onto my couch.

Dinner with Stella Friday will be interesting. It's been a few weeks since I've seen her, months since I've seen the brewery.

Some relationships are better when it's long distance, and in this case, it's definitely true. We get along better when we see each other sporadically. And with our parents gone, she's grown very attached to my life and what I'm doing with it. Or not doing with it is more like it.

When she expresses snide, insincere comments or concerns about Jake or Diego, I have to ignore her. She thinks she knows what's best for me and hasn't accepted that I'm actually an adult and she doesn't need to be my mother and father.

We only have each other at this point so I can't do much but love her. Her new boyfriend, Nathaniel, must see something in her because he's stuck around. She has to have a good side; maybe I don't see it.

———◆———

I'm napping on the couch when I hear my phone ping across the room.

Straggling over to my kitchen counter, I see Harper's number light up the wallpaper.

Harper: "Your friends are cool. Hope they knew I was only teasing them."

Sam: "They are assholes, but they mean well. So you picked out a place for Saturday? Sorry about rescheduling."

Harper: "No don't worry! Family comes first. But yeah there's this cool place where you make your own pizzas."

Sam: "Sounds... interesting."

It's probably not what I would have picked out. I would have chosen a dark restaurant where we could order drinks and have some privacy. This sounds like a cooking class for first dates and I normally don't like to cook my own food if I'm going out. I immediately want to cancel.

Harper: "I promise it'll be fun. I'll text you the address and you can meet me there?"

Sam: "Perfect. Let me know what time and I'll be there."

Harper: "Awesome! Have fun with your sister."

Sam: "I will. Talk to you soon."

———— ♦ ————

Friday arrives and I'm calling Stella as I wait for an Uber.

"Hey, are you on your way?"

"Yes, just landed and getting a taxi. Can you leave now and grab a table?"

"Already am. See you when you get there."

Stella and I meet frequently when she travels to Vancouver. She purposely books her flights to stop in San Francisco with a long enough layover so we can see each other. Sometimes she'll stay the night, other times she goes right back to the airport. She could easily take a straight flight from LA but chooses to add a quick trip so she can visit her irresponsible "baby brother."

Stella always says I can choose the restaurant, but I know her too well. I really only have three options. They are very expensive, classy and close enough to the airport and my place without putting me out.

I'm sitting at the table only a few minutes before she arrives.

"Hey!" She spots me and sets down her briefcase.

Getting up from my chair, I wrap her in my arms and hug her tighter than she can take.

"Okay, okay, I can't breathe."

"Let me get that." I pull out her seat for her.

"What a gentleman."

Stella dramatically shakes out her cloth napkin and sets it in her lap with a loud huff.

"So, what's new Sammy?"

"Nothing too exciting."

"There has to be *something* new?"

The waitress comes by and before she can even introduce herself, Stella demands, "Belvedere martini. Dirty."

Stella doesn't even give her the courtesy of eye contact.

"And when I say dirty, I mean filthy. Last time I was here I sent it back because the waitress didn't listen."

No please or thank you. Typical Stella.

If we were at Chili's, the waitress would probably spit in her drink. Luckily, we are at a classy place where that sort of thing hopefully doesn't happen.

"How's Nathaniel?" I deflect.

"He's great. Gosh, he's amazing. I am so lucky to have him and he's so lucky to have me."

If this was your first time meeting Stella, you'd think she was embellishing to be funny, except she's serious.

"You met at work?"

She nods and takes a sip of water.

"How has he moved in already and I haven't met him?"

"Well if you came to LA more you could have…"

Touché.

"And besides we've been friends for a while before we took it to the next level, okay?" Her tone is defensive and I quickly change the subject before I hit a nerve.

"How's the brewery doing?"

"You need to come by. I redecorated. It looks great."

Now *she* hit a nerve.

"You redecorated?" I confirm.

"Yeah." Her martini comes and she doesn't even say thank you.

"How much did you change?"

"I mean, a little here and there."

"How much is a little?"

"I didn't spend that much money, if that's what you're concerned about."

"Who cares about money? It's the fact that mom and dad decorated that place themselves. Everything was original and vintage. How much did you change?"

"God, Sam. Give me a break. You're never around and I decided this on my own."

"We own it equally. You technically can't change anything without my say so. It's in the contract."

"Equally? Where the hell have you been lately? I didn't think you'd care."

"You should have consulted me. Big decisions like that need to be discussed. Did you change the name, too?"

"Fuck off." Stella chides.

"You know what? I *will* come by. Maybe next week and I will see just how much you changed."

"Whatever."

Her standoffish behavior has me wondering why she even asked me to come down in the first place if it comes with stipulations.

"Let's order." I snap.

———— ♦ ————

Dinner doesn't end as ugly as it started. Stella can't handle anyone being mad at her. It's unacceptable for her to appear anything less than perfect. So my job is to forget this happened as quickly as it started because that is the only way we can move on.

I pay the bill and leave the waitress a bigger tip than necessary. My way of apologizing for my rude sister who treated her like trash the entire night.

"You don't have to come." Stella concedes.

"What? You've been guilt tripping me for weeks and now that I offer, you say no? I'll take Jake and Diego with me."

"Great." She mumbles under her breath.

"Headed back to the airport?" I ask.

"Yeah, I'll sleep in the lounge this time. My flight isn't until the morning."

A yellow Prius pulls up and we say our goodbyes.

Our two hour encounter was almost too long this time around.

CHAPTER FOUR

———— ◆ ————

I'm buttoning my jeans when my phone buzzes.

Harper: "Meet me on the corner of Broadway and Notre Dame. See you in 15?"

Sam: "I'll be there."

Even though it's less than five miles away, I schedule a driver so I don't have to worry about leaving my car or driving home drunk.

Giving myself one last critique, I examine myself in the bathroom mirror.

Brushed teeth? Check.

Cologne? Check.

Wallet? I pat my pants. Check.

Condoms?

My nightstand drawer holds an almost empty box. It's lasted me a while.

It's presumptuous of me to assume we'll hook up at the end of the night, but after seeing her last weekend in such little clothing, sweaty and wet, she's all I could think about.

In the shower jerking off, at the gym wishing I was jerking off, and now, examining the box of condoms, wanting to jerk off.

I grab one anyway just in case.

Running my fingers through my hair, I exhale and head out the door.

The Uber pulls up to the curb and I get out.

Turning my head in all directions, I double-check the address. I don't see any restaurants.

"I might be calling you back here in a few minutes." I joke, wondering if Harper is going to stand me up in the middle of nowhere.

I pull out my phone to text her when someone taps me on the shoulder.

"Hey!" She announces.

"Hey!" I'm shocked to see her, expecting a homeless man instead. "You look great!"

She's wearing a pair of dark wash jeans and a top that exposes a bare shoulder. No bra. Her hair is pulled back and her face is flawless and fresh. She's barely wearing makeup and definitely doesn't need it to look as beautiful as she does.

"So where is this make your own pizza place you were raving about?"

"Actually, it's up in my condo." She points to the building in front of me.

"Oh," I say, the tension in my fists dissipates as I realize she's not setting me up to get mugged.

"Yeah! It's a little more intimate. I love cooking so I thought this would be kind of fun. Come on." She wraps her arm in mine and leads me through the intricately designed steel gate.

"You showed me yours, so I thought it was fair if I showed you mine." Her voice is playful, teasing. I want to rip her shirt in half as we ride up the elevator, but instead, I bite the inside of my cheek to suppress the boner growing in my pants.

When we arrive at the top floor, yes, the top floor, the elevator pings open.

Even though my sky rise condo building has me at a higher level, Harper is closer to the water and has impeccable views.

"That's Alcatraz!" I admire, sprinting toward her huge windows that provide a panoramic view.

"Yeah, that's why this place cost so much. But I'm new here and want to soak up all San Francisco has to offer."

"Damn well your views are definitely better than mine."

"You have a great place, too. I had a decorator come in and do everything but it doesn't feel personal. I'm still trying to make it home."

She leads me to the kitchen where a bottle of Vodka sits on her counter, the kind I was drinking when we met last week.

"Look at you." I compliment. "You have a good memory."

She has an amazing spread of various toppings and cheeses laid out in front of us.

"Can I do anything for you? Open a jar? Chop... anything?"

"No! Relax those muscles. I have everything ready. Go snoop while I make you a drink."

I walk towards the living room with floor to wall windows and porcelain floors. Maybe they're marble. I don't know stones, but I know they are expensive. She has a spacious balcony off the side of the living room.

Her place is decorated nicely, but there are zero pictures of her anywhere. The only one she has is framed over her beautiful fireplace. She appears to be in kindergarten and she's sitting on her dad's lap, her mom's hand resting gently on her knee. The picture was obviously done in a studio and looks very 80's.

"Drinks are ready!" She calls from the kitchen.

Her condo could be featured in a magazine, it's that perfect.

"I didn't know what you liked, so I kind of got everything. Pepperoni, olives, mushrooms. I already made the dough and it's been sitting out and ready to go."

I set my drink down and ask, "What can I help with?"

She watches me as I strip off my military jacket, rolling up the sleeves of my flannel shirt.

I accidentally, okay intentionally, flex every muscle in my forearm so my veins and tendons bulge from the fabric.

Words and complete sentences are a struggle for her as she glares at me, trying to roll out the pizza dough.

"I- I uh…" She stutters, laughing at how ridiculous it is that she's speechless.

I know exactly what I'm doing. I don't know why women find something as simple as rolling up your sleeves so sexy, but right now she's devouring me with her eyes. I'm irresistible.

My sleeves hit my elbows and I come up from behind Harper as she grips the rolling pin. My erection hits her in the ass as I press up behind her.

She stops rolling the dough and acknowledges the obvious.

"Is that the sausage I feel?"

I spin her around so her chest smashes into mine.

She inhales sharply and her body reads like a book. An electric current buzzes through her skin and conducts onto mine. Her face is flushed and I swear I can hear her heartbeat increase.

My hand slides up between her thighs until I can't go any further.

Dear God, the heat between her legs is unbelievable. She trembles as I cup her in my palm, her jeans warm and hopefully ready to be ripped off.

Pizza is the last thing on my mind. The only thing I want to eat is Harper.

———— ◆ ————

We're on the floor of her kitchen when I finish, her hair tangled and messy, both our jeans tossed aside.

She's out of breath as I momentarily clean up in the bathroom.

My reflection in the mirror reveals a taut, vascular physique, dark green veins popping out like roadmaps across my chest and forearms. Pleasure consumes me.

Harper is good. Better than good. She's the best sex I've had in a long time.

When I return to the kitchen, Harper has an apron on but no clothes underneath.

The little bit of fabric hiding her chest is wrong and I walk over to her and tear off the apron, revealing everything that was hidden during our recent affair with her shirt.

She's bare ass naked now as I fondle her in my hands. I taste and lick her skin, sink my teeth into her right nipple. I missed these babies all week.

"You're too sexy for clothing." I tell her.

She moans an, "mmm" as I continue ravaging her chest.

"Seriously, you should never wear clothes ever again."

"I'll keep that in mind." She says.

She runs her hands through my hair as I'm slumped over caressing her breasts. I'm about to get hard again when my stomach rumbles quite loudly.

We both start laughing and get dressed.

The simple pepperoni pizza is almost gone as we eat on her living room floor.

Harper takes a sip of her red wine and asks, "How was your week?"

"It was good! I live a pretty simple life. I'll meet Diego and Jake for mimosas tomorrow."

She doesn't eat her pizza crust so I grab her leftovers and eat them.

"Your friends seem super cool."

"Yeah, they're awesome. We grew up together in LA. Jake made his way out here to start his own law firm. Diego came next and then I followed."

"That's awesome. Do either of them have kids?"

"Jake is married but no kids and Diego is going through a divorce actually."

"Oh how horrible."

"Yeah, it's a shitty situation. I feel bad for him."

She plays footsies with me and if I were a guy turned on by feet, I would let Harper step on my face with those cute toes.

"Tell me about your job." I ask.

"Basically the publishing company I work for sends me books that need to be edited. Whether it be grammatically, cutting out unnecessary stuff, pointing out plot holes, I take lots of notes and send it back to the author for revisions."

"It doesn't get boring?"

"Not at all! I actually love being one of the first to read it. I feel special. Especially when it gets published I get to brag, 'I read that already.' "

"Is it a busy job?"

"It can be. Sometimes authors want it back by a deadline; sometimes others give you a few weeks so you can take your time. It's not exactly stressful but it can be."

"And you love it?"

"Yes! I was blessed to get paid to read. I love my job. Don't you?"

"Eh."

"Eh?" She repeats.

"I won't lie... and you'll have to forgive me for coming off as pretentious, but I don't actually have to work. I'm helping Jake when I can but... I don't know. I do love law. I just don't love it enough to work full time."

"I get that. If that's the situation you're in and that works for you, that's awesome!"

She seems to understand me on a level I didn't expect. Maybe because we are similar in age and she can appreciate that fact because she, too, is successful.

"Well you could always become an Instagram influencer on your downtime." Harper jokes.

"Oh God, don't get me started. Jake's wife, Avery, has a fashion blog. I don't know how she does it. It's so time consuming."

"I got rid of all my social media when I moved out here."

"Really?" I ask, shocked. "No sexy selfies floating around in the Facebook universe?"

"Ha! No way. I'm not about to ruin my career by getting caught posting something stupid and x-rated."

"Fair enough. But if you get the urge, you can just send those pictures to me."

She slaps my leg as we lean against her couch, my ass slowly becoming numb.

I stare at the clock on her wall and it reads past 1am.

"Shit, it's late." I admit.

"Wow, you're right. I didn't even notice the time. Need to get going?"

"Yeah I better head out."

The room is quiet as we grab our plates and clean up.

I'm still not sure where we stand. She knows I don't want a girlfriend, right? Did I clarify that yet? Is that even what I want? Is that even what she wants? I don't know. I had a great night and I don't know how to end it.

I'm lacing my shoes and Harper changes into a long, oversized t-shirt.

"I had a lot of fun." Harper admits.

"Likewise."

Likewise? What am I, 80?

I have no freaking clue what to say. Is now a good time to tell her she's great but I don't want anything more than this?

These last two dates, if that's what you want to call them, have been fun. But I know most women, especially Harper's age, want to settle down, not sleep around.

"Look Sam, I know this is awkward to say aloud but..." She pauses and her jaw muscles clench, biting down hard on her teeth. "You're the first guy I've hooked up with since I've been single. I got out of a toxic relationship a while ago and it's been rough moving to a new city. I'm not exactly sure what you want from this... from me."

"Let's have fun. Why label it?"

"I don't normally do these things... sleep around."

"Are you sleeping around with other guys?" My eyebrows rise in curiosity and I drop them immediately so she doesn't sense my envy.

"Well, no. I wasn't even sure I was ready to date again... not that these were dates." She quickly corrects herself.

"I know where you're coming from, I get it." I continue. "I am kind of in the same boat. I'm not looking for anything serious."

It's been a while since a woman made it to round two. In the past year, I had a handful of one-night stands that meant nothing to me. But Harper is actually in my age bracket, and I see the appeal of this. She's confident, self-sustaining, and charming. But I don't want to promise anything more than what we are doing.

"Okay, Sam. Text me later... if you want. Thanks for coming over."

"Have a good night, Harper."

"Goodnight."

I leave without kissing her. Only a boyfriend would do that and I just made it clear I'm not interested in filling that spot.

———◆———

The next morning the smell of champagne makes me dry heave.

"Hung-over, are we?" Diego asks.

"A wee bit." I lower my baseball cap so the sun isn't my face. I've been drinking way too much lately.

Charity, our usual waitress, comes by and refills my water.

"Thank you." I gaze up smiling, but my eyes are hidden by the brim of my hat.

"So, how was Harper?" Jake asks.

"It was good. She has her shit together."

Diego dramatically covers his mouth with his fingertips, gasping.

"Why is this hard to believe? You guys act like I was celibate and this is the first girl to come along that has a full time job."

"Umm, you basically were celibate." Jake states.

"And no cool girls did come along because by the time you ended it, you barely got to know them to find out."

"And you won't find quality girls that blow you in bathrooms."

"That was LA." I correct. "And speaking of LA, do you guys want to come with me to check out the brewery?"

"I'm down!" Diego is on the verge of ditching us now so he can go pack.

"Let me talk to Avery…"

"It'll only be a few days! Stella redecorated and-"

"Whoa wait, will she be there?" Diego interrupts.

"Obviously. She lives there."

"But yeah, she has a life and all, right? She won't be with us the whole time?"

"I- she might be? I don't know."

Diego hangs his head. "I'll be there. Would be nice if *she* wasn't but ya know."

"Count me out, in case I commit then back out."
Jake surrenders.

"Fine. Diego, when are you free?"

"During the week? I could go anytime. I'll work from the hotel and flight. It'll be quick?"

"Yeah, we'll check it out. Four days max. I'll check flights."

———◆———

When I get back to my place, I open my laptop and book two flights. Diego could afford the fare, but I invited him so I decide to pay.

I unlock my phone to text him the flight info, and in the same moment, I receive a text from Harper.

No words. Just a picture.

It's a risqué shot of her perfectly flat stomach and a piece of her lower breast. I can almost see her nipple.

My phone chirps again.

Harper: "I got the sudden urge to take a selfie. Figured you're the lucky recipient."

A devious smirk widens across my face and my lap aches.

Her selfie doesn't actually show her face at all. She's smart, unlike most women who stupidly flaunt it all with no hesitation or concern.

Sam: "Thank God you're not on Facebook."

Harper: "Now it's your turn."

My laugh echoes my empty condo. I never send nudes. Ever. Granted, she wasn't completely naked, but still.

What the hell am I going to send? My half erect cock? My bicep? I never do this shit. But I feel obligated since she asked. Most girls in the past sent them and expected nothing in return.

I do a few pushups and crunches, then take off my shirt.

Walking to my full-length bathroom mirror, I flex my muscles and feel like a tool.

Sam: "I can't do it. It's not the same."

Harper: "Aww come on. I'll send one more if you take a picture of your abs."

Sam: "Get your entire chest in the picture and we might have a deal."

Harper is silent for a few minutes, then my phone lights up.

Another picture, and this time, those glorious babies made the frame. Her plump lips managed to sneak in and she has a sultry pout that turns my lap to stone.

I grip my phone tightly in my fist and admire her body.

Sam: "Come over."

Harper: "LOL seriously?"

Sam: "Yes. Now."

————— ♦ —————

When Harper arrives, she's wearing workout clothes. "I'm sweaty." She admits.

I grab her wrist and haul her over my shoulders as I carry her to my shower, her laughter and screams following us down the hallway.

I start the water and peel her out of her damp clothes.

I'm naked within seconds, joining her in the shower.

I pin her palms flat on the tile wall, like I'm a cop about to frisk her.

Lathering a generous amount of soap in my hands, I trace my palms over her small frame and watch her react to my touch.

I'm standing behind her, cupping her breasts in both hands. I pinch her nipples and give her a tight squeeze; my arousal fierier than ever. Her body stoops in response, her ass pressing into my groin.

Flipping her around so we are face to face, with a husky voice I whisper, "I want to see you when I finger you."

I slip my lathered fingers inside her and her knees almost buckle.

"Ohhhh." She groans.

She wraps her arms around my neck as my fingers

glide in and out of her. My other arm is wrapped around her waist, supporting her as she trembles.

When she's almost there, I stop and rinse her off.

She can't breathe and through scruffy gasps, her irritation is obvious.

"Wha- you can't do that! I need more." She begs.

I set her on the tile bench, her butt barely on the edge.

My cock is in her face and I know she knows I'm expecting her to put me in her mouth, but instead I crouch on my knees and spread her wide open, tasting her, licking her.

Her moaning is loud and magnified as it bounces off the bathroom walls, filling my ears with satisfaction.

I circle my tongue against her, using the right amount of pressure and speed that forces her to take a chunk of my hair in her fist.

She's gyrating against my face and I take pleasure knowing she's letting me fuck her with my tongue, letting me lick every sweet inch of her.

I grope her left breast and she seizes with a painful pleasure.

"Don't stop." She demands. "Oh, oh my god Sam… don't fucking stop."

I contemplate doing exactly that, winding her up like a clock with this excruciating teasing… but instead she's on a timer, and I know the very moment she's ready to ding.

Her thighs close around my head and she comes against my mouth.

She… sounds… incredible.

I'm blaming the acoustics of the shower because I did not hear these satisfied cries the previous two times.

I give her a quick moment to recover as I put a condom on.

Before she can catch her breath, I lift her with ease and position her in the angle essential to enter her.

She's light to carry and easy to slide in and out of due to the moisture all around us. She may get hexagon tile imprints in her back, but hopefully it'll be worth it.

I slam her and her body against the shower wall, each thrust wreaking havoc on the endorphins swimming through me.

My entire body tightens as I use every single muscle and ligament to fuck her brains out.

Maybe it's the ambiance of the steamy shower, the sounds she's making that I've never heard from a woman… could be the way I'm controlling her entire body in my arms, forcing her to move as I want to move her. All that put together creates the most intense climax I've ever had.

"Goddamn, Harper you feel so fucking good. Too… fucking… good."

Harper had to have been with one guy her entire life and some dude with the tiniest dick alive because I can feel her stretching open to fit me inside her. I'd like to believe no one has filled her up like I have.

And with that thought, I finish.

———— ◆ ————

When I wake up, it's déjà vu.

Harper and I are back in my bed, except this time, it's still light out.

She's sleeping soundlessly next to me as the clock reads 5pm.

Harper's bare back is exposed and the sheets barely cover her exquisite ass.

If I were a photographer this would be a picturesque moment to capture: the lighting, the angles, her body.

I take a mental image instead and find a clean pair of boxers.

When the waistband is around my torso, my stomach growls.

Risking a bold move, I grab my phone and order some take out.

The food arrives pretty fast and I gently shake Harper's shoulder to wake her.

"Oh crap, what time is it?" She asks in a shock.

"It's Sunday, like 5:45pm."

"Oh thank god. I thought I slept through the night somehow."

"You have big plans tomorrow?"

"Yes, an important meeting with my publishers. I thought I slept through... what is that amazing smell?" She sniffs the air.

"I ordered some food. Didn't know if you liked Chinese. I took a chance."

"Well you, my friend, guessed right. I love Chinese food."

We eat in my bed, Harper wrapped in my sheets, and I contemplate if I did the right thing; I'm giving off the vibe that I want nothing serious but eating food in bed after a hookup resonates as a relationship gesture.

"Tell me more about yourself." Harper asks, fingering her chopsticks like a pro.

"What do you want to know?"

"You said you have a sister? The one you got dinner with?"

"Twin sister, actually."

"No way! You never said she was your twin! Do you look alike? Stupid I know, since you're a guy and a girl..."

Grabbing my phone, I pull up a picture of the both of us the last time I was at the brewery.

"She's gorgeous." Harper says, coughing on some noodles.

"Chew!" I demand.

"Sorry, I tend to inhale, I love this stuff." She wipes

her mouth. "She's older? Younger?"

"Oh, she's older."

"She more mature or something? Boys don't mature as quickly as girls do." She pinches my cheek and I wince in fun.

"She's five minutes older. And she's just... different."

"Different?"

"I might as well tell you now." I wipe my hands together to prepare. "She doesn't have a lot of friends, if any actually."

"In her defense, I get that. It is not easy making new friends. Girls are vicious."

"Oh, you got that right."

Harper looks at me bemused.

"Any relationship I didn't manage to ruin on my own, Stella did it for me." I confess. "My previous girlfriends *hated* her. I can't explain it. We are close but I have to set boundaries. It's almost like she's jealous of my girlfriends."

"Well luckily, I'm not your girlfriend."

She playfully nudges my bare leg with her toes.

"What's her name?"

"Stella."

"Cute. Wait." She sits up and our eyes lock. "Stella and Sam? Like beer names?"

"Yeah, my parents loved beer. My dad's favorite was Sam Adams, my mom's Stella Artois."

"That's probably the cutest thing I've ever heard. Your parents sounded adorable. What were they like?"

"Gosh, I rarely talk about them."

"You don't have to if you don't want to, I'm sorry. I should have known from experience how difficult it can be reliving the past, talking about it again. It opens up old wounds."

"It's different. You don't have to pretend to understand what I went through because you did too."

She nods her head, letting me continue, and for once, I do.

"Gosh, they were awesome parents. Everyone would always want to come over to our house because my parents always had the fridge stocked with the best snacks. They were the cool parents everyone wanted. Left us alone and trusted us. They also owned a brewery and had some of the best food around. This was back before most places served food, so that really set them apart and helped their success. Friends would always want to be there and hang out. I miss them so much."

"May I ask what happened?"

I exhale loudly, raking my hands through my hair. I can do this.

"It was an ordinary night. Stella and I were seniors in high school, a few weeks from graduation. We were working at the brewery, learning the ins and outs of running a company. This was back in LA, before breweries were on every corner and underage servers weren't completely frowned upon. But my parents were so trusting. We were responsible kids and knew the consequences of underage drinking."

I pause, not on purpose to sound suspenseful, but so I can figure out the words to say without getting emotional.

"One night it happened. Two police officers showed up to the brewery as Stella and I were closing up. We thought they were there to finally bust us because 17 year olds shouldn't have easy access to alcohol like we did. But they were there for other matters.

A drunk driver killed my parents as they drove home from a dinner party."

Harper covers her mouth with her knuckles. "Oh gosh," she whispers. "I'm so sorry."

"It was so surreal. The officers actually knew my parents. Most of the city did. They let us down gently, but once I heard 'parents' and 'killed', I lost it."

Harper shimmies her body next to me as I continue.

"It was so hard on us. We contemplated shutting down the brewery. We felt responsible handing out alcohol to negligent people, irresponsible people like the guy that killed my parents. Want to know the shittiest part? He was completely fine. Not a scratch on him. How does that even happen?"

"Well, I'm sure he's in prison right?"

"Yeah, but the sick part of me wanted him to suffer like my parents did. For the longest time I wish he died in the accident. Life was never the same. He didn't have insurance and somehow their life insurance tripled. Either way, Stella and I were set for life, with or without the income of the brewery."

"But you decided to keep it open?"

"We did. If we shut it down, we'd be letting go of a lot of friends. Diego's dad was a cook there. We couldn't upend their lives and force them to start all over because of what happened. They became our new family. I stayed in LA and went to law school during the day while I would serve and bartend at night. Stella did her own thing and helped when she could."

"That's so responsible of you both."

"I think my parents would have wanted it that way. It's their legacy."

Harper caresses the nape of my neck. Her gesture is so intimate and she must not realize how much it's putting me at ease.

"Luckily you have your sister to support you and vice versa."

"Stella has been through a lot with me. My ups and downs. And even if she's a pain in the ass, she's my twin sister and she's all I have left."

"I'm glad you two are close. It's the way it should be."

"Close enough to strangle her sometimes."

We both force a laugh after such a solemn conversation.

"The brewery sounds amazing. I'd love to see it one day."

"I haven't been in a while. I'm going in a few days to check it out. Apparently Stella changed some stuff without telling me."

"Oh?"

"Yeah, could be a disaster."

"How long are you gone for?"

"A few days. I'll be back by next week's mimosa date."

"You won't miss too much work during the week?"

"No, I don't have any open cases at the moment. How about you? What will you do this week?"

"I'm sure I'll sneak out one of these days and go to a yoga class. Maybe go to happy hour with some girls from work. They're always inviting me but I felt like it was an obligation since I'm still the new girl, not because they liked me. But they keep bugging me so maybe I need to give myself some credit."

"Yeah, you seem pretty cool."

Harper's endearing smile lights up the room as she hops out of my bed.

She's still not wearing any clothes and by now the sun has set and casts a shadow across her flawless skin.

"I better get going."

"Alread- all right." I correct myself fast. I'm a bit relieved the conversation has ended.

She grabs the Chinese boxes and walks to my trash.

Harper is dressed and holds her keys in her hand as we linger at my front door.

I'm hoping she'll pull my boxers down and give me the goodbye she gave me last time she was here, but it doesn't happen.

I get the feeling she wants a kiss, maybe even a hug goodbye, but instead she opens the door and wishes me a great week.

CHAPTER FIVE

Diego and I are sitting in first class as we depart for LA.

"You nervous?" Diego asks. "Scared she changed too much?"

"Stella better not have… if she knew what was good for her."

"But what if she did…" Diego presses.

"Then I'll deal with it as it comes."

"You're too nice. You've always been too nice to her. She doesn't deserve it."

"And what does she deserve?" It's slightly rhetorical but he answers it anyway.

"She deserves a dose of her own medicine. No one affects her the way you do and I think she'd learn a lot if you treated her how she treated other people."

"I can't do that."

"Even after everything that happened?"

I say nothing, hoping my silence will be obvious enough to end the conversation.

"You *know* what I'm talking about." Diego warns. "I don't bring it up anymore but you know what I'm talking about."

Clenching my fists, I can feel the skin tighten to the point it might rip. We agreed we'd never speak of this again, but Diego must have forgotten that promise.

"Why can't you let that go?" I request. "I have. You don't even know if you saw what you saw."

"I know what I saw." Diego confirms.

I punch my tray and then apologize to the person in front of me, this rare act of violence not in my nature.

"Don't go there, Diego. I mean it."

Diego surrenders his hands up, not wanting to argue anymore.

"Sorry, man."

———◆———

When the plane lands an hour later, we step out with our carry-ons and the baggage of my past is weighing heavy on me.

"Let's get lunch at the brewery." I suggest.

"I was going to buy you lunch but that's easier if you don't care."

We rent a car and drive the fifteen minutes from LAX to the brewery.

Pulling around the corner, I see it.

"In A Draught" still stands.

I exhale loudly, releasing my grip on the steering wheel.

"She kept the name the same at least." I profess.

Diego chooses to stay quiet. Probably best.

We park and approach the entrance.

The manager sitting at the hostess seat exclaims, "Sam!"

"What's going on?" I say casually.

"It's been forever! How are you?" She gives me a platonic hug, but her body is flush against mine.

"I'm doing well. Just checking up on a few things. How's it going?"

"Things are great. Stella hasn't been in for a few days…"

"This is my friend, Diego. Diego, this is Carrie."

"It's a pleasure to meet you. How long have you worked here?"

"Only a year. Sam hired me. Sorry." She corrects. "Mr. Evans."

"I bet he did." Diego bumps his shoulder into mine.

I can already read his mind: attractive, young and hopefully single.

"Carrie is one of the managers." I add, as if this means off limits.

"The lunch rush will come any moment. Someone called out so I'm hosting today."

"Well I already notice the menus are different."

Pulling one out, the menu isn't just different in design, but we have new food on there.

"Who the hell would order duck tacos?" I ask.

"They are pretty popular. Stella wanted some 'rare cuisine' on the menu. We also added some cool appetizers. Didn't you know?"

"Nope."

"Let me show you to a table before it gets crazy."

Some of the fixtures on the walls are different and I can see Stella slowly revamping the tables and flooring. Chandeliers are new and the lamps are trendier.

I curse under my breath, "Shit."

"Let me know if you need anything." She gently rests her hand on Diego's.

When she disappears, before Diego can even say anything, I say, "She's too young for you."

"What? She's like mid-20's?"

"And what have you said to me about hooking up with women younger than us?"

"Come on. It's been so long. Don't make Val be the last girl I hooked up with."

"I can't stop you from sleeping with my staff. I

just highly insist you don't. Besides, what makes you think she'd stoop to your level?" I tease.

Diego has the Cuban thing going for him, attributes that Jake and I fail to own. He's the tallest between us three, but he's without a doubt the most self-conscious.

Diego's wavy dark hair is on the longer side and he has a permanent five o'clock shadow, regardless of how many times he shaves his face. We joke about his bushy eyebrows, but it's his reminder to stay humble, because in reality, he's one handsome looking man.

Once in a blue moon, when we are out on weekends, Diego's overly gracious, drunk accent emerges, turning women into pools of lust. But when it comes time to perform, he gets stage fright.

"God, it's been so long, I hope he still works." Diego admits, never ashamed to cross the sexual line with me.

"I'm sure if you do hook up with Carrie, you'll last your usual 10 seconds."

"Gimme some credit, Sam. It's 30 seconds."

———————◆———————

When we're back in the rental car, full from those surprisingly delicious duck tacos, I pull out my phone. It's dead.

"Son of a bitch." I curse.

"What?" Diego asks, putting his sunglasses back on.

"My phone has been shutting down lately. Not sure why."

"From the new update? Go replace it. There's an Apple store nearby."

"No, it's fine I'll do a hard restart. It always works after that."

When it finally turns back on, Stella has texted me.

Stella: "Are you in town yet? Don't eat lunch! I want you to come meet Nathaniel. Stop by my place for some food."

Stella: "Did your plane crash?"

Stella: "Why aren't you texting me back?"

Stella: "Fine. Nathaniel didn't want to meet you anyway."

Shit.

Sam: "Sorry. My phone died. Dinner tonight."

A few minutes later...

Stella: "Fine. 6:30pm."

We check into the hotel a few blocks away from the brewery.

"Have you heard from Harpa?" Diego pronounces her name as if he were from Australia.

"I have not."

"Do you care? How long has it been since you saw her?"

"Only a few days. I saw her Saturday night. Wait, no Sunday she came over for a quickie."

"Ugh, screw you."

"She already did."

He throws a phallic looking pillow at me and I take it from the floor and hump the end right in my crotch, the other end hitting Diego in the face.

"Oh Carrie, you're so hot for me." I playfully moan.

Diego doesn't find it as funny as I do.

"Knock it off! She actually gave me her number if you even care."

I toss the pillow aside. "Good for you. Maybe after dinner you can take her out. Her shift better be over though. I'm not about to pay her for sucking your dick on the clock."

"Dude, could you imagine how great a story that would be?"

"No." I say with no trace of humor.

"What's the plan for dinner? Want to go to In & Out? I'm craving a burger."

"I was thinking of the brewery again, if you're down. It's free."

"Count me in!"

"Stella will be there."

"Count me out."

"Play nice? If you do, I'll let you have the hotel room to yourself."

Diego contemplates it, spinning the tube shaped pillow. "Deal."

My phone buzzes and I momentarily hope it's Harper, but Diego's lights up at the same time, which can only mean a group text from Jake.

Diego, Jake and I rarely text each other individually; anything said to one we can say to all.

Jake: "Hope you guys are living it up in LA. Do me a favor and bring back those cookies Avery loves."

Diego replies for the both of us while I click back to the rest of my text messages. Pulling up Harper's thread, I see we haven't spoken for a few days. Which isn't strange.

I text her something simple. Easy.

Sam: "Well the brewery hasn't changed too much."

She doesn't respond right away.

Not even for an hour.

Diego takes a nap around hour two of silence. Working from the hotel, my ass.

Deciding I'm not going to sit on *my* ass waiting for a reply, I head to the hotel gym.

She usually texts back right away, so of course I think something's wrong when I'm done working out and it's still silent.

I wrap a rolled up towel around the back of my neck so it can catch the sweat.

My phone sits in the cup holder on the treadmill and I'm still overanalyzing why she hasn't texted me back.

I put my phone on silent and decide to get ready for dinner.

I am nowhere near as critical with Stella's love interests, mainly because not a lot come along. Her previous boyfriend dumped her and disappeared. We never heard from him again. Diego insists Stella killed him and buried his body somewhere.

She's sitting at the same table we were at earlier for lunch, dressed pretty casual. I finally get a glimpse of the boyfriend.

Nathaniel is tall even as he's sitting down. He's in great shape, a bit long and lanky, but I can see Stella's requirements already: nice smile, dresses well, and looks rich.

He reaches out his large hand. "I'm Nathaniel. It's so great to meet you."

I shake it graciously. "Sam! It's a pleasure. How are you tonight?"

"Great!" Stella answers for him. "We already ordered some appetizers. Hi Diego." She already has her back turned when she greets my friend.

Nathaniel doesn't notice as Diego pretends to blow his brains out.

I whisper, "Chill out."

The four of us sit down and Stella orders the strongest beer on tap.

"I didn't plan on getting wasted tonight." I admit.

"I did." Diego says.

"You're such an alcoholic." Stella says to Diego.

"It's the only way I can stand to be around you, Stella."

I start laughing obnoxiously, not ready to defend Diego from Nathaniel, who might want to beat his ass, and he definitely could.

"They are practically like brother and sister, too." I defend.

He must think their banter is playful and not malicious, because Nathaniel laughs along with me, which is a good sign. He seems cool so far.

"So remind me how you met." I ask.

"We work together." Stella rubs his back. "We've been friends for a long time. I think he was just waiting for the perfect time."

"Cool. And you're already living together? Wow!" I can't help but throw a dagger in there.

"Yeah, I lost my apartment. Didn't renew the lease in time so I was kind of stranded. I think it was headed this way anyway; it came sooner than we thought. Stella was sweet enough to take me in."

Nodding my head in acknowledgment because my mouth is currently full of appetizers, I notice my phone light up on the table.

I unintentionally start smiling when I see the name and Stella notices my changed expression.

"What?" She asks.

Diego snoops on my phone. "Ooooh it's his new

girl." He says this like it's nothing, knowing wholeheartedly this will turn Stella's mood foul.

She's so sensitive when it comes to my dating life. Maybe she's scared I'll miraculously be happier than she is. I'm so used to being in the backseat while Stella takes control of her own life.

"New girl?" Stella repeats, clarifying. "You didn't mention a girl when I came last week. Are you seeing someone? You haven't seen anyone for a long time."

"It's not anything serious." I admit. "But she's cool. I'm seeing where this goes. Casual for now. Very casual."

"What is she like?" Stella swallows her judgment faster than Diego can finish his pint of beer. "Do you have any pictures?"

"Um, none of her face." I confess.

"Ooooh!" Diego jeers loudly. He lays out his palm for a high five and smacks mine at least five times. I didn't mean for that to come out the way it did.

"You guys are disgusting. Aren't we too old for nudes?" Stella disciplines.

"Never too old." Diego disagrees.

"Typical for you. You act like you're 10." Stella continues.

Diego ignores her.

"What's her name?" Stella asks.

"Harper."

"Harper? Sounds stupid."

"Stella? Not tonight. I'm not in the mood for this."

"Yeah, it's cool Stella." Nathaniel agrees. "What's the big deal?"

"Sam is always making mistakes and I have to clean up the pieces."

Diego gives me a look that says he's had enough.

"Well tell me about her." Stella keeps pushing the subject.

"Jesus Stella, it's not even serious. I'm still getting to know her. I've hung out with her literally three times."

"I want to know about her."

"She's a book editor that moved here from Maine."

"And?"

"And she has great tits. I fucked her, too. Is that the stuff you want to hear?"

Diego starts heckling obnoxiously.

"You're sick. I only wanted to know how you're doing." She gets up from the table and I can see Nathaniel mentally contemplating following her or staying to give her space.

"Sorry, Nathaniel. I didn't mean for it to turn into this."

"She'll come back." He says.

"And she wonders why I only come out here once every couple months." I say under my breath.

I leave Diego and Nathaniel at the table to pursue my sister.

Stella is outside the restaurant, sitting on a bench looking like a rejected first date.

"I'm sorry, Stella. I know you were being nice. But you're so aggressive. You don't know how to back off."

"Mom and dad aren't around anymore." She says this as if I don't know. "And no one else is here to protect you. Just me."

"Shouldn't it be me protecting you? Even if you are five minutes older than me, I'm the man."

"But you've always been a basket case. I've always had my shit together. I'm the responsible one. It's a lot taking on your stress."

"I'm not asking you to do that."

"We're twins, we do it without realizing."

I hug her to end this never-ending conversation. It always turns into her being the perfect one and me being the reckless piece of shit that doesn't know how to settle down.

"I'm sick of you calling me wondering where things went wrong." She says into my chest.

"I know. Believe me, I know."

"When will I get to meet her?"

I release her slowly. "I'm not even sure I'll see this girl again."

She's at a loss for words, which is rare.

"Come on, let's go back inside."

Dessert comes and I'm stuffed. My belt loop needs to be loosened after that big meal.

"What's the plan for you lovebirds?" I ask.

"Going home. I have a big day tomorrow." Stella says.

"Working toward senior creator?"

"You know it!"

"You're one tough mega-bitch." Diego's masked compliment goes unaccepted.

I realize I haven't even checked my text from Harper. It's been about an hour since I received it.

Harper: "I'm going to need one of those I♥LA shirts I see everywhere. That is, if I'm allowed to wear it around you."

Turns out it was a text and a picture.

She's naked in her bathtub, bubbles placed in conspicuous places, but not well enough.

Her light pink nipples are popping through the bubbles, as the rest of her body is hidden.

I instinctively bite my fist at the sight before me and Diego notices.

I show him. A quick flash of guilt hits me, but at the same time, you can't see much. It's tasteful but oh so boner inducing.

"Damn, she's hot." Diego says under his breath so no one can hear. The last thing I need is a lecture about scandalous selfies.

Dinner is free so I leave our waitress a $1,000 tip so she can split it between the others that worked tonight.

Stella and I make our rounds to the servers, cooks, bussers, and hostesses. People react like I'm back from the dead. They are so excited to see me.

By the time we are walking outside, Diego is kissing Carrie in the parking lot near her car.

Stella scoffs. "So unprofessional, if you ask me."

For once, I agree with her.

I offer my goodbyes and tell Nathaniel it was great to finally meet him. He invites me to the gym tomorrow and I accept. Guy time will be the perfect opportunity to show him I'm not an uptight bastard. Also gives me an opportunity to feel him out more.

Diego jogs up to me as I'm getting in the rental car.

"Sam, Carrie is incredible."

"Get a room, dude. You can't suck face in the parking lot. Go back to the hotel."

"Really?"

"Yes, let me know when it's safe to come back."

I drive back to the hotel but I go down to the empty pool and get comfortable on a padded lounge chair.

I can't help it. I pull out my phone to send Diego a text.

Sam: "Old grandmas. Chlamydia. Rotten fish. Your mom. Stella."

I know that last one will be a huge turn off and I laugh at Jake's immediate response.

Jake: "Is Diego about to bone? Dicks, big veiny dicks!"

I close out the thread, doubtful Diego even saw our good-natured boner repellent visualizations. If Carrie really is going all the way with him, I'll be surprised. I never got the easy vibe from her, and the double standard of loose women and slutty men tends to be unfair.

LA can be pleasant at night. When all the smog in the air has dissipated, you can actually see the stars. Sometimes.

My phone lights up. Diego snuck a picture of Carrie's thong on the floor of our hotel room, with the words "fuck off" in a text bubble below it.

"Oh Jesus." I laugh, hoping Diego has a good night. He deserves some fun.

Speaking of fun, I look back at Harper's text and realize I never responded.

Instead of texting back, I give her a call to kill some time.

It rings a few moments and then she picks up.

"Hello?"

"Hey, Harper, how are you?"

"Hey, I was starting to think you didn't get that picture."

"Oh I got it." I practically moan into the phone.

"And?"

"I got you a shirt!" I joke.

She scoffs and laughs sarcastically. "Wow, thanks!"

"I'm kidding. I saw that picture in the middle of

dinner and had to bite my fist so my sister wouldn't see my napkin pitching a tent."

"I don't know if I should be flattered or feel bad for you."

"Sympathy is always nice."

"Well, how was it?"

"My hard dick?"

"Haha, no you freak! Dinner!"

"It was good. Got to see my sister and her new boy-friend."

"How was that?"

"He's okay."

"Was he nice to you?"

"Yeah I mean he seems like a good guy. I didn't talk to him much. She seems happy. What are you up to to-night?"

"Watching some TV. So exciting for a Tuesday night."

"I get in Saturday morning if you want to do some-thing later that evening?"

"That sounds great! Any ideas of what you'd want to do?"

"I have lots of ideas of things I'd love to do to you right now…" A couple walks by and nods hello as they walk towards the Jacuzzi. "But I'm currently outside at the hotel pool on a lounge chair and can't get into it right now."

"A lounge chair?"

"Yeah, Diego is hooking up with one of my employees in our hotel room."

Harper bursts out laughing. "Oh my god, I didn't need to know that."

"He needed it."

"I need it." Harper insists.

And dear God I want nothing more than to be inside her.

"If you can hold out a few days, I'll make it worth your while."

"I can promise you that." Harper breathes.

"Well I don't want to keep you from The Real Housewives…"

She giggles. "Actually it's Keeping Up With The-"

"Oh god, no!" I cry out, laughing. "Anyone but them."

"Haha, sleep well, Sam. Text me later."

When I hang up, Diego has texted.

Diego: "Dude…"

Sam: "I hope you at least used your own bed."

CHAPTER SIX

———◆———

When I wake up in the morning, there is a note next to my phone.

"Hey man, Carrie's off today and we are going to the beach. Don't wait up. I'll check with you later. D."

Wow, he works fast for a man that has no confidence.

My phone is dead so I plug it into the charger.

It pings so many times I lose count.

I walk over to it and see it's charged at 30%.

Wonderful.

It died again.

Luckily there are no important, threatening texts this time around, but I do pull up Harper's picture again.

I'm so horny I'm about to call up an ex-fling that lives in the area.

But I decide to wait. I can wait. I'm trying to settle down and even though Harper and I agreed this would be casual, I have a feeling she wouldn't be too pleased if I was hooking up with a slew of women. Or maybe she wouldn't care. Maybe she's hooking up with other guys.

Either way, I jerk off in the shower.

———— ◆ ————

I'm headed to Equinox where Nathaniel is meeting me on his lunch break.

Apparently, he's a gym freak and works out instead of eating lunch like a normal human being.

When I arrive, I spot him. Oh god, he's one of those guys.

He's wearing a t-shirt, except he split the sides so low you can see his ribs. It's also torn at the neck and at the chest. His nipples are showing and I suddenly realize how cold it is in here.

"You're ripped." I say, pun intended.

"Wait til you see what I have to show you." He exclaims, telling me to follow him to the locker room.

I suddenly worry he's about to whip out his dick or something and I quickly rehearse last night to see if I missed the signs that he was into me.

But luckily, I'm wrong.

He unzips his gym bag that is full of various supplements. He looks like a drug dealer for steroid addicted freaks.

"Ta-da!"

Caution tape, bombs, and explosions are printed all over the various tubs of drugs. And I say drugs lightly. I can barely understand anything.

"Dude, what are these? I can't read the label."

"My cousin from Russia ships them to me. Pre-workout supplements, creatine, human growth hormones. They are the best I've ever had and I've tried everything. Been using them for years."

There's a fine line between performance enhancing supplements and drugs. These look borderline criminal. I see HGH and can guarantee those are illegal in the US.

"Are these FDA approved?" I ask.

"I mean, not exactly. Sure, I can't read some of the ingredients… but trust me, the pump is phenomenal. It's unreal. Want to try some?"

"I'm good but thanks."

———— ◆ ————

Later that evening, I meet Stella at the brewery as she studies financial reports.

"Hey! How was the gym?"

"It was good. Nathaniel is a cool guy."

"He's the best, right? I think he could be the one!"

I never get jealous of my sister, hardly ever. But a whip of envy hits me in the face. We are in such different stages in our lives, but for her to say she might marry this guy makes me feel like I'm behind in life.

Camilla pops up into my head, the only girl I ever contemplated marrying.

"Uh oh. I know that look. What's wrong? Talk to me." She asks.

"Been thinking about the past year. How my life would be completely different right now."

"You can't think about that. There are so many what if's in our lives."

"I know, it's just, so much has changed."

"Well you need to settle down. Stop sleeping around."

"This Harper chick might have potential."

Stella is quiet and I know her well enough to assume she's silently disagreeing with me that this girl won't be the one, let alone so soon.

"It's okay to be alone." Stella reminds me. "There are worse things."

"I'd say it's worse to be alone because I was too scared to move forward."

"True. Don't do anything crazy. If this does get serious, I want to meet her. I have the final approval."

I ignore her statement and rearrange the pencils on the desk.

"So you like Nathaniel?" She asks.

I'm quiet for a moment, choosing my words with

precision. "Did you see all that crap he takes before and after his workout?"

"Oh I know. It's the worst. He gets so crazy on it sometimes. He keeps talking about this 'pump' thing and I have no idea what it's like. He's nuts, but he loves the adrenaline."

"Some of the side effects can be wicked. He doesn't get physical with you, right?" My brotherly instincts kick in.

"God no, he wouldn't hurt a fly."

"Some of that shit is illegal, Stella. I looked at the ingredients, the ones I could interpret. Keep an eye on him."

"Gosh, Sam you act like he'll turn into the Incredible Hulk and beat the shit out of me."

"Watch him. That shit messes with you."

"I will be fine. I can take care of myself."

———— ◆ ————

When Diego and I reach the airport, it's Saturday morning and I desperately need coffee.

Diego reads my mind and grabs us some once we are through security.

When we are settled in the terminal, Diego pulls out his phone and shows me his screen.

"It's Carrie!" He practically giggles.

"Wow, you two hit it off."

"Yeah, she's cool. She wants to come visit." He replies to whatever text she sent; a smile igniting his face.

"You're hooked already, aren't you?"

"No, man. She's just really cool."

"Not too young for you?"

"I think that's what I like about her most. She seems so real for her age, it's crazy."

I don't believe in love at first sight, so I'm reluctant to believe Diego and Carrie are soul mates or any of that bullshit. But as long as she makes him happy, I'll support whatever relationship they have. I just hope he doesn't make the same mistake twice.

———◆———

We land in San Francisco on a dark, rainy Saturday. Typical.

When I'm back in my condo and sprawled across my bed like a starfish, I sink my face into my feather filled pillows.

There's nothing better than coming home from a trip and being in your own bed. The familiarity is comforting.

The rain pounds loudly on my windows and I wrap a pillow around my head, covering my ears.

It doesn't do its job as I hear my phone buzz underneath me.

Harper: "This rain is nuts! Did you still want to go out?"

If my dick could answer, it would say yes. But right now I don't feel like doing anything.

Sam: "Do you care if we reschedule?"

She doesn't respond right away and I'm on the verge of falling asleep.

Harper: "Sure. Next week?"

I fall asleep before I can answer.

———◆———

It's Wednesday afternoon when I realize Harper's text has gone unanswered.

I'm not purposely ignoring her, but I kind of am.

Harper doesn't seem like the type of person to come across as needy, so when my phone dings and I see it's my sister, I'm thankful I don't have to deal with Harper getting too attached.

Stella: "Nathaniel might be headed up to SF for a work thing and I said he could stay at your place."

Sam: "Thanks for asking me before offering. Depends on the day. Let me know more details. Don't do that again."

Stella: "Calm down I didn't offer for a week. It would only be like a night or something."

I pitch my phone onto the bed and it bounces on the floor.

"Ughhh!" I snarl loudly.

I'm not one of those guys that offers his place to friends and visitors in town. I would rather pay for your hotel. I don't know why, I just really like my space. My two-bedroom condo doesn't have a guest room on purpose. It's my home office that is neglected most of the week.

I decide to go into Jake's law firm to see if he needs help with anything to distract myself from Stella and Harper's unanswered texts.

"Dude, great timing. A stack of cases landed on my desk. Pick one. Or two. Or five. We need the help."

I'm rifling through each folder and laugh.

Jake sits at his desk while I'm sitting in a clientele chair with my feet up. "These are pretty stupid disputes if you ask me."

"I know, but I need a smart guy that can actually find clear and convincing evidence with this shit."

I wave a folder in my hand.

"A woman is suing a nightclub... because she was out in the cold waiting to get inside, and she got pneumonia?"

"She claims they were only letting the 'skinny bitches' in first, and she's overweight. Might be discrimination."

"Jake, come on."

"Just look some over, will ya? How was LA?"

"It was good. Got to meet the boyfriend. I've had some ideas going in my mind about possibly expanding. Haven't vocalized them to Stella quite yet."

"Is she still acting like it's her decision that only matters?"

"Of course."

He sighs and I change the subject.

"Are you still working crazy hours?"

"Sam, you have no idea. I won't get out of here for another five hours. Avery hates when I get home any time past 7pm."

"How has she been?"

"Aside from being pissed that I'm constantly coming home at 10pm, she's good. We're trying to get pregnant."

"No shit?" The mention of a baby causes spider webs of electricity through my brain waves. Memories come flashing back.

"I don't know if we're ready for that. I'm already hardly around now."

"Well you better figure that out! Didn't you discuss this?"

"Of course, but I didn't think it'd be this soon at this time in our lives. I'm so busy!"

"Communication, man. I can't say it enough."

"Excuse me, Mr. Davis?"

Jake and I turn our attention to his assistant. "Your 5pm appointment is here early."

"Thanks, Lila."

She disappears and I mouth, "That's Lila?"

"Yeah, she lost a lot of weight. Got a nose job, too."

"Wow, she looks amazing."

"She took some time off to travel. But she came back and apparently had some work done."

"Wow."

"Sam."

"What?"

"Don't."

"Don't what?"

"We all know you slept with her back when she got hired. I overheard her talking to her friends that you're in the building. It's rare when you come in anymore and it's a big spectacle when you do."

"I'm not doing that anymore."

"Yeah well you get all the girls riled up when you come by. Make yourself useful at least." He waves his fingers over all the files on his desk.

Jake leaves and I walk up to Lila's desk. She has thick black rimmed glasses, as if she got a secretary starter kit that included the glasses, a tight pencil skirt, and low cut top.

Back when we hooked up once, she was average pretty. But now she's a new person. She wears heavier make up and gets her hair done.

"Hey Lila."

"Hey Sam. It's been a while." Her perky breasts are staring at me and I'm not even trying to be inconspicuous. They must be new because I don't remember them being this voluptuous.

"It sure has." I continue. "Last time I saw you, you were…"

"Naked, bent over your couch?"

Lila licks her lips with intent. Her attempt at promiscuity is so obvious, not even a bit subtle. She pushes her elbows together, strengthening her cleavage. That wasn't even the last time I saw her, but I see the message behind it.

"What are you doing right now?" I ask.

"Nothing. Waiting to take a dinner break. I'm starving."

———◆———

When I leave the men's room, I confirm my zipper is up and no one is wandering the hallway. A few seconds pass and I give Lila the go ahead that she can leave without being seen with me.

I guess it's much harder to shake my 20's behavior than I realized.

———◆———

Folders are gathered under my arm as I walk back to my condo. Time I start working and contribute to society.

When I enter I throw the stack on my kitchen counter. My phone buzzes in my pants.

Jake: "Did Lila give you a blow job? Either that or she went for a quick trip to the plastic surgeon to get her lips done. They are so red and puffy. You son of a bitch."

Sam: "She was hungry. I couldn't say no."

Jake: "You are a sexual harassment case waiting to happen."

Guilt consumes me for a brief moment, but I remind myself I'm not tied down to anyone.

I return to the list of text messages. Harper's name stares at me ruefully in the face.

Sam: "Sorry, I took on some new cases these past few days. Been a bit busy."

Okay a little white lie.

Setting my phone aside, I open some files and read them over.

"What was I thinking?" I say aloud.

I wipe my forehead and eyes with my hand and wish I didn't even go to Jake's firm. I'm starting to regret that blowjob, too. Stella's voice of reason shouts inside my head and I can hear the nagging.

Pulling out my phone again, I text Harper again.

Sam: "Want to go out Friday? I still owe you."

She remains quiet and I shove the files in frustration.

The rain has returned and the stillness in my living room is being overthrown by the storm pounding outside. All I want is silence right now and instead I'm burdened with howling wind and a freezing living room.

I turn the heater on and return to a black screen; no text back yet. I could suggest a date tonight, but 1, who wants to go out on a Wednesday, and 2, who wants to go out in this weather?

The screen lights up.

Harper: "Friday doesn't work for me."

Sam: "Saturday?"

Harper: "Maybe!"

Harper is too mature for games, but I can't help but feel played. Is she punishing me for canceling our plans and practically ignoring her for a week? It's not like it was a date.

I don't say anything because what do you say to maybe? I'm not about to beg her for another day so I decide not to respond right now.

I'm already playing enough games with my sister; I do not need this from another woman.

20 minutes later, my phone pings.

Harper: "Are you busy right now?"

I glare at the stack of papers that are shuffled around and now in a huge mess. They are taunting me.

Sam: "Not terribly busy."

Harper: "Want to come over and watch a scary movie with me? I love doing that when it storms like this. I'm all comfy in my PJs."

I want to ask if her PJs entail a see thru, lace nighty, but I go against it. And despite the brief hint that she's toying with me, I don't want to review these cases.

Sam: "I'd be down to watch a movie. Want me to bring anything over?"

Harper: "Just your most comfortable pajamas."

———◆———

Thank god I can go from my parking garage to hers and avoid the rain completely. It's coming down so hard I can barely hear the music in my car on the drive over. It splatters the roof and windshield with a vengeance, making visibility difficult.

Harper texts me the code to park underground and as I enter, I'm greeted with a plethora of Rolls Royce's, Porsche's, and Bentley's. My modest Benz feels out of place.

"Should have brought my Ferrari." I quip searching for a free spot.

Harper answers her door in a black pull over hoodie and unsexy gray jogger sweatpants, the exact opposite of lingerie.

But despite her boyish clothing choice, she is blessed with natural beauty. Her hazel eyes pop in the light as pieces of her messy bun frame her face.

If I could see the outline of her body, I would be pleased. But she's a blob under those clothes.

"Glad you made it over okay."

She offers me a sideways hug that is very awkward.

I haven't seen her since I came back from LA and I forgot the t-shirt I got her.

"How have you been?" I ask.

"Pretty good. Staying busy with work. I'm helping a friend from Maine plan her wedding, which isn't easy with the distance. You?"

"I took on some cases and I wish I hadn't. I forgot how much I love not working."

"Don't we all?" She pours herself a big glass of wine. "Want a drink? I have vodka, wine, and some nice whiskey that I'll never drink."

"I'll try some whiskey. Just a little though. The last thing I need is a DUI. And whiskey hits me strong."

She pours me a considerate amount that I know I won't finish.

"Sorry, I just know I'll never drink this. Please take the bottle home with you."

We both hold our glasses and head towards her living room, setting our phones on her padded ottoman.

"Take charge!" She offers, handing me the remote.

I start clicking through different genres until I find the horror category.

"What kind of cases did you take on?"

"Some stupid ones. I regret going."

Thunder briefly explodes and shakes the room like an earthquake.

"Jesus Christ!" I yelp.

"Haha, you're not used to these crazy storms?" She wraps herself in a large, lavish blanket that was folded next to her. "Are you sure you're up for something scary?"

"Give me some of that." I grab some of the blanket and snuggle next to her, hoping it can shield me from any other unexpected eruptions.

"You're adorable." Her statement is simple yet filled with meaning. I appreciate her honesty and the fact that she doesn't need to hide her feelings about me; even if I'm worried that sex might cloud her judgment. Let's be real, women and men don't always have the same understanding for what we have going on right now.

The blowjob earlier today has me feeling shitty. I forgot I liked Harper. And even though I keep saying this is fun and casual, when I'm around her I don't have to impress her.

Does it help because I know she's also financially stable? Is that selfish? A lot of women salivate when they find out I'm loaded. Money can turn a sweet, innocent woman into a gold-digger.

Her phone buzzes and I glance over at it.

An iMessage from Ethan.

Who's Ethan? I'm not compelled enough to ask.

"What's lookin' good?" She asks.

"Not sure. Let me keep browsing."

Her phone buzzes twice and I see Ethan has now texted two more times.

Who the hell is this Ethan?

It could be her boss. But it's 8pm and not necessarily appropriate work hours. But she does work from home.

"Do you need to get that?" My tone is as indifferent as I can force even though I'm very curious now. I take a swig of my whiskey.

She hunches over her lap and reads the name.

"No."

No. So flat it has no connotation. Doesn't sound bitter, happy or pissed.

Her phone buzzes again. She now has what... five text messages? I'm losing count.

"Could be important?"

She shrugs her shoulders, watching as I scroll through the horror selection.

An obnoxious, continuous buzz comes from her phone again; this Ethan asshole is calling her now. I take another huge swig.

"Will you excuse me?" She gets off the couch and takes her phone to another room, a room with a door.

I'm tempted to get off the couch and listen to her conversation through the wall. I've never been this nosey in my life. Do I have competition? Not that there's anything to fight over. Harper and I are keeping this casual. We are friends.

God, thank you Stella for creating this competitive side in me that I've never had.

I choose some stupid scary movie that will most likely be parodied in the next year just so I can give the impression I'm disinterested in whatever this guy wants.

She returns briefly as if she was checking on food in the kitchen. Doesn't even acknowledge what that was about.

"Oh great choice! I've been meaning to watch this one."

She shimmies down the couch. Our shoulders are touching and I can see out of the corner of my eye she's actually watching the movie.

I'm watching her with one eye and the rain with the other, wondering if I should say anything. I don't want to act weird but I need some kind of reassurance that she isn't sleeping with all of San Francisco.

"Was that call anything important?"

"Oh, no. It was this guy that wanted to come over tonight."

"Guy?" I emphasize because now my interests are piqued.

"Yeah, I've been reading his book and he's interested in what I have to think. Wants to know if it'll get passed through. Wanted to maybe get a drink and talk about it."

My guard comes down. Thank god. He's probably some old, fat guy that writes thrillers. I finish the rest of the whiskey. Should have paced myself but too late now.

"Oh cool, anyone I would know? Not that I read a lot."

"Maybe? His name is Ethan Miller. He's a fiction crime writer."

Nodding my head as if I could possibly know him, I say, "Oh cool."

"He's talented. I think it'll do well."

An era passes, just enough time that it looks innocent enough that I can grab my phone without being obvious I'm going to Google his ass.

Ethan Miller.

Harper is so close to me I have to tilt my position so she can't see my screen.

His biography is already summarized on the front search page and he lives in the city and he's a handsome motherfucker. His picture lies right next to where it says he graduated from Princeton and later received his PhD in creative writing at some other prestigious college. Ethan has dirty blond hair and a perfect white smile.

He's 32 and loves living in the Bay Area. His first book made it to San Francisco's best-sellers list. I didn't even know that was a thing.

Before I can read more about this dreamboat, my phone turns black and dies on me.

"What the…"

"What's wrong?" Harper asks.

"My phone has been dying on me lately. For no reason. I'm too lazy to get a new one."

"Is that why you didn't text me back?" She's smirking.

"No, sorry. I really was busy."

"It's okay, I understand."

Instead of hurling my phone across the room with jealousy, I set it lightly next to hers, hoping Ethan can feel the resentment radiating from my phone onto hers. Of course he wants to come over tonight. His book is the perfect segue to come to her place late at night, raining no less, where she probably needs male protection from this big, bad storm.

Luckily, I'm here to fill that void, and instead of staying pissed off, I attack her mouth with mine.

She doesn't see it coming; draws back at first at the ferociousness, but soon her lips relax. I don't pull away because I want her to know this is not going to be an innocent peck. This isn't going to be something casual and quick. I'm going to kiss her so long and so hard that Ethan will be a figment of her imagination.

She's the one to enter my mouth first and god I've missed this, her tongue, the sweetness in those lips. Her wine and my whiskey blend together as our tongues connect.

She climbs on top of me, our lips not separating once. A sense of surprise is apparent in her body language when she sits onto my hard lap. Even with the blanket on me, I can't hide the stimulation buzzing inside me.

My hands glide underneath her hoodie, across her braless back.

She's kissing me aggressively, her breath jagged and wild. Her hips twist and grind into me, making this make out session difficult to withstand.

Harper doesn't like the label "friends with benefits." She won't admit it, but I know it's true. We've had three amazing times together. Will the passion fizzle out or keep igniting? We're both adults that have needs. And it's clear we've been able to fulfill each other's desires. But at the same time, I don't want her thinking I want nothing else from her.

If it were up to me, I'd already have us both naked, her ankles near my ears as I held onto her thighs. But for now, her lips are doing enough to stabilize my arousal.

Minutes pass and I wonder if this is all we are going to do. I'm fine with it, I am. But I can't take the pressure in my lap much longer. I want to explode with her body on mine.

She stops kissing me so she can take off her hoodie. She's bare underneath, as I suspected. Thank god she's progressing this.

She gets off my lap and I immediately miss the weight of her on me.

Her fingers grasp the elastic waist and sweatpants have never looked so sexy. She slides them down her legs, stepping out of them. She's completely naked and I watch her move as I sit on the couch completely clothed.

Fucking hell, she is too much. She is bare everywhere. Waxed smooth and perfect.

"Want to continue this in the bedroom?" She suggests.

"No, we can do this here."

I eject from the couch and attach her warm body to mine.

While she yanks my pants down, I pray to God Harper has condoms because I didn't bring any.

The whiskey hits me as I stand up, my head a little fuzzy, but a good buzz flowing through my bloodstream.

She's on her knees and I'm quickly in her mouth.

I groan, "Do you have a condom?"

She stops and glowers up at me, her eyes wide and doll-like, "No, I thought you would?"

"Shit you don't?"

"I'm sorry! I've never needed them until now."

"Shit."

"I'm on the pill though."

Caution flashes as bright as the lightning bursting outside.

I'm on the pill echoes in my head.

"Umm, shit…" I trail off.

"It's okay, let me at least solve this problem for you."

Eventually I sit back on the couch because standing is proving to be difficult.

The scary movie playing on the TV changes scenes to a loud, violin shrieking murder, and I nearly jump.

My nerves are on edge. I'm buzzing from the whiskey and I am forcing myself to stay hard as she satisfies me. Christ, add that blowjob I got earlier and I'm basically willing the blood to travel south rather than swim in my brain.

I'm starting to go soft.

No, no!

My entire body clenches and I demand my dick to stay solid.

Get hard, you son of a bitch!

He barely cooperates and it takes longer than normal. So long Harper has to take a break, but she finishes the job.

I apologize, blaming the strong whiskey. Jake and Diego will never let me live this down, if I decide to tell them.

"Your turn?" I offer.

"Believe me I wish, but I have to get up early tomorrow. My friend is picking me up here at 6:30am and we are flying to Florida for a book signing."

"Oh." My response is so short. I'm a little offended she turned down my offer and I think she's shooing me out of her place because I'm a limp dick son of a bitch. Who says no to oral? Especially after last time. She knows I can get her there.

"You can stay and watch the movie with me! I'm not kicking you out. I have to get up early and it would be awkward if this hot, naked guy was over. Everyone at work knows I'm still single."

"You're allowed to fuck anyone you want, single or not."

She laughs, putting on her clothes. "I know. This is … so unlike me. Hooking up."

Relief empties out my pores as I can almost guarantee this Ethan asshole is no one to worry about. If she's having a difficult time processing our escapades, I doubt she can juggle two men in her bed.

"Well, I don't care for scary movies anyway, I wanted to see you." I hear the confession escape my mouth quicker than I can take it back. I did want to see her, but she didn't need to know that.

"Well I'm glad you came over."

"I'll pick up some condoms for next time." Since she's obviously not using them with anyone else.

For now.

CHAPTER SEVEN

My hair is frazzled; I don't know how many times I've run my fingers through it. I'm ripping chunks out and by day's end, I will be bald.

I've had so many cups of coffee and I'm still exhausted.

It's Saturday morning and I'm working. I'm working on a Saturday.

Jake is so appreciative, which is what keeps me going. I'm not even charging him, which is why the stress is worse. I'm not even getting paid for this shit.

I text Stella so I can think about something else.

Sam: "Tell me something. Anything interesting to keep me from working."

She doesn't reply right away and due to my exhaustion, my patience level has vanished.

I'm pulling a Stella, putting my needs and my

life as a priority. She isn't treating my text with high importance and I'm getting annoyed.

Finally she texts back, after an extensive two minutes.

Stella: "I'm kicking ass, Sam. I really do think I'll get another promotion."

Sam: "I said interesting. I don't want to hear about you excelling at work while I'm drowning in disputes, breach of contracts and other nonsense."

Stella: "You're working on new cases?"

Sam: "I am. I hate it. I hate life right now."

Stella: "You're such a baby."

Sam: "I don't care. I can't take this shit."

Stella doesn't reply. She's obviously bored of my venting.

I open Harper's thread; my next victim.

Sam: "How's the book signing? It's only 9am and I might just crack open a beer."

Luckily, Harper sees my text as a priority. I'm borderline needy and all I really want is some recognition.

Harper: "Poor guy! I wish I knew law so I could help you."

Sam: "I could use an assistant. Can I hire you?"

Harper: "You couldn't afford me ;)"

Her humor is distracting and it's exactly what I need.

Sam: "Having a good time?"

Harper: "A blast! I love going to book signings for debut authors. It's such a surreal experience for them."

Sam: "I bet! And you're a piece to their success. Coming back today?"

Stella finally texts me back and I open her change of discussion.

Stella: "I found out Nathaniel will be in town on Monday. Could he stay at your place?"

Her timing couldn't be worse and if I hadn't organized all the papers, I would slide my hands across the table and violently shove them on the floor.

Sam: "He can't get a hotel? I'll pay for it."

Stella: "He wants to stay with you! Get to know you a little better."

I whine like a child and suck up my pride.

Sam: "Fine. Please don't tell me I need to pick him up from the airport?"

Harper texts me back and I read hers.

Harper: "I haven't decided yet. I might take a detour up to Maine if I can swing it."

Stella: "He will get an Uber. I'll give you his number so you can coordinate. He arrives Monday around noon and leaves the next day late in the evening."

I don't bother responding to Stella. The two conversations are making my head hurt.

Sam: "I bet the weather is way nicer in Florida than it is here. Wish I could meet you there but some of us have a job to do. We don't have time for fun parties and mimosas by the pool."

Harper: "LOL! I thought those pictures would be fun! I didn't mean to make you feel bad!"

She sent me a few photos of her lounging poolside, her tanned legs shimmering in the sun. Her bikini bottoms cut low and barely had enough fabric to cover her. It damn near made me drop everything to meet her out there.

I tell myself it was the welcoming sunny skies, and not the other picture I received of attractive males swarming like wasps on a rooftop bar. The scenario was perfect: the setting sun over the water, mood lighting, and plenty of alcohol. Envious? I would never admit it.

Sam: "I'm kidding. Have fun. Let me know when you're back. My sister's boyfriend is going to be staying with me for a night next week, and unless you like threesomes, I might be busy, too."

Harper: "Not a big fan on threesomes ;). But have fun!"

Sam: "Not a big fan as in you've had a threesome and didn't like it or…?"

Harper: "Get back to those files."

One case I can't ignore is Diego's. Sunday morning at brunch Diego brings all his paperwork so Jake and I can go through it one last time.

"Sam and I have revised the paperwork. It's all legit and I think you'll finally be done once you sign where it's flagged."

My stack of pancakes and side of fruit are delivered to our chaotic, disorganized table.

"On a side note, how are things with Carrie?" I inquire.

"Great! She's coming into town this week."

"Did she get her time off approved by Sam?"

I throw a packaged butter at Jake's chest. "She can do whatever she wants on her time off."

"Maybe the six of us can get drinks?" Diego suggests, so hopeful. Tiny red flags are popping up already but I'm staying positive for him. Carrie is nothing like Val.

"Yeah! Avery would love that. She's been jumping all over me to actually take her out."

"Who is this sixth person?" I ask like an asshole.

"Well I definitely don't mean Lila."

"Are you back with Lila?" Diego asks.

"God, no. It was just a quick hook up."

"I thought you were seeing Harper." Diego continues.

"That's... casual. More casual than friends." I correct.

"You're always texting her! We aren't blind. Plus

Avery wants to meet her."

"Not to be an asshole, but Harper isn't anyone special for Avery to meet. I don't even know where this is going."

"Isn't it time you think about that? You know eventually she's going to get attached. If she's not already…" Diego reminds me.

"I know, I know. And hate to break it to you, but she's in Florida anyway."

"When will she be back?"

"Not sure. Couple more days?"

"Well this week is busy for Avery. Some product line is coming out and you know."

He doesn't finish his thought and Diego and I pretend to actually know what the life of an influencer is like.

"Next week we are pretty open." Jake adds.

"Let's rain check then? Not sure if Carrie can come up twice in two weeks. Maybe she really will not get the time off approved."

I contemplate being difficult and telling Stella to tell Carrie no so I can somehow get out of this dinner.

"Let's try next Friday anyway?" Diego asks, hopeful Carrie is willing to use PTO to come see him.

"I don't know." I mutter begrudgingly.

"It's dinner." Jake reminds me.

"Yeah, no shit. But I don't usually invite girls I'm sleeping with to friendly gatherings."

"I'm inviting Carrie."

"Yeah and how's that going? Friends with benefits? Doesn't this seem a bit soon to be introducing her to your friends?"

I'm trying to defend my point, but Diego is oblivious.

"She's already met you, you're her boss."

"Dude, you know what I mean."

"We haven't gone out in a long time." Jake adds.

"I'll go regardless, but if I'm a fifth wheel then I'm a fifth wheel."

"Pussy." Diego says as he pays the bill.

"Where are you guys going now?" I ask.

"Home." Diego answers. "Going to mentally prepare for tomorrow."

"Yeah, home for me, too. I have some cases I could catch up on."

"All right, well I'll be around if you guys want to get a drink later? Watch the game?"

"What's wrong Sam," Jake begins, "got nothing to do since Harper is out of town?"

"I have loads of shit I could be doing right now."

———— ◆ ————

What the hell else is there to do but go to Target? I wander the aisles and pick up a few things to make my place a bit more livable. I know if it's a disaster Nathaniel will tell Stella and I'll never hear the end of it.

Sam, how could you have the love of my life sleep in such a pigsty?

And speak of the devil, Stella is calling me.

"Sis! What's up?"

"Nothing, confirming Nathaniel is good to stay over tomorrow."

"Of course, I didn't forget."

"Great, he's excited to hang with you."

"Cool. What's he doing in the city?"

"Some photoshoot out there. I don't really know details."

"Okay, well I'll be expecting him."

"Sam?"

"Stella?" I mock.

"What if he's coming over to…"

"To?"

"To… ask your permission to marry me?"

It takes every ounce of my soul to not burst out laughing. Her presumptions could be true, but damn isn't that a little soon?

"I mean seriously, you're the only other man in my life. He needs your permission. Will you tell me if he asks?"

"Stella, if he even asks, which I doubt, I wouldn't tell you."

"You're no fun." She's quiet for a few beats then asks, "Are you still seeing *that girl*?"

"Sort of. Haven't seen her for a while."

"Don't be sad if it doesn't work out."

"Thanks for your optimism. I have to go now."

————————◆————————

Nathaniel and I meet for dinner Monday night, and even though I'm 10 minutes late, he arrives even later with no warning.

"Hey man, I'm so sorry. I was in the longest meeting, sorry." Nathaniel apologizes.

"It's cool, don't worry."

He sits and orders a beer, two shots, and an appetizer without even looking at the menu.

"How have you been?" I ask.

"Great! It's good to see you again."

"Look, Nathaniel, I have to get this out of the way…"

He gulps the now room temperature water, unprepared for my question.

"Are you here to ask me if you can marry my sister?"

His reaction would have been mine if I didn't have to restrain myself.

"Oh Sam, seriously? I bet Stella asked you to ask me, huh?"

"Guilty."

"Oh man, I love her, but no I'm not ready to be married yet. I mean don't get me wrong, if I did I'd probably never have to work again and that would be awesome."

"You've never thought about marrying her?" I ignore his odd comment about never working again.

"Maybe? I like to take things slow. I *just* got out of a relationship when I met her."

"Really? Like how soon after Stella?"

"Umm... relatively soon..." His demeanor goes from confident to panicky and a red flag waves high.

"Remind me how you and Stella met again."

"Well we worked together for like two years. I always thought she was smoking hot, sorry dude, but it's true."

His tactless comment about my sister's good looks falls on deaf ears.

"But I was seeing someone else at the time. Eventually it didn't work out and I started seeing Stella."

"God, please don't tell me Stella was your rebound." It's none of my business, but I'm shocked when he answers my rhetorical question.

"She was more than just a rebound."

His silence says what words he's too ashamed to admit.

"You *cheated*?" I ask.

"I'm not proud of it. I should have broken it off. Stella promised she wouldn't say anything. I eventually told my ex when I realized Stella was better for me."

Dick. I should have known their relationship didn't start off like a fairytale. Of course Stella omitted those facts. Stella creates this picturesque, ideal life in her head. Nathaniel must not realize the line he just crossed admitting the truth to me.

"But things happen for a reason. Stella is a wonderful woman and I'm happy with where I'm at. And if and when the time comes that I do want to propose, I'll get your permission first."

"I appreciate that."

"How was it growing up just you two?"

"You know about our parents?"

"I do, I'm so sorry, man. That's rough."

"It's not something either of us talk about a lot."

"I understand. That's why you two are so close."

"Yeah, I would die for that princess."

Nathaniel starts laughing, nodding his head in approval.

"Don't even get me started! I knew moving in would be a big step, but damn she really is a princess. Her place is a castle. I didn't realize how loaded she was. So lucky."

His comment almost makes me punch him across his thick, square jaw.

"Yeah, we're *so lucky* both our parents died so we could get our inheritance."

"I'm sorry, I didn't mean it like that. That came out wrong."

"It sure did."

"I meant... Stella was a lifesaver letting me move in."

"Yeah, how has that been going? I know in the beginning it can be a bit rough. Learning each other's habits and whatnot."

"The beginning? I've been there for like six months now."

"What?"

"Yeah, my ex kicked me out when I broke it off and I had no place to go, so Stella took me in. I told you that in LA."

"Yeah, you did, but I didn't realize the timeline was off. Stella said you *just* moved in."

He waves his hand, "Oh Stella does that. Worried people will judge us."

The waiter interrupts us and requests our entrees for the night.

We order and I take a moment to check my phone.

Harper: "Hey you! How's your night going?"

"Sorry Nathaniel, one moment."

Sam: "It's been better. Eating dinner with my sister's boyfriend."

Harper: "Oh text me later then! I don't want to keep you."

Sam: "He's actually pissing me off a little. I can't wait for him to leave tomorrow."

Harper: "Haha too bad I come in later this week or you could blame me for needing your bed."

Sam: "We will NOT be sharing a bed. He can have the couch."

Harper: "LOL! Get back to dinner. Text me later."

"Sorry."

"Stella?" Nathaniel assumes.

"A girl Harper I've been hanging out with."

"Just hanging out?"

"Well, hooking up too."

"Any pics? Is she hot? How's her body?"

What kind of man would ask that, let alone someone who just told me he has openly cheated, who is now dating my sister.

"She's pretty cool. Does well for herself."

"Stella said you were a playboy. I love it!" His odd show of support is overshadowed when he chugs his pint of beer in one huge gulp.

I'm trying not to look at him in disgust, but it's difficult.

"Whatever happened to that one chick? Stella told me about her."

Camilla?

"Something about how it ended badly." He continues.

The pain is coming back in waves and I can't talk about this right now. The fact that Camilla has been brought up so many times this past week is ripping my heart apart.

"I'd rather not talk about that right now."

"That's cool."

"Do you come to the city a lot?" I ask. Please say no. And if yes, please say you're a Marriott Rewards Member.

"Not really. I travel to New York, Chicago, San Diego. Next time I come out I'll bring your sister! Maybe we can double date."

"I might not even be seeing her anymore." I admit.

A bubble of annoyance bursts in my chest. Why does everyone want to meet Harper? What's with the sudden interest? And why is it every time I try to change the topic it still comes back to her.

"Hit it and quit, huh?" Nathaniel laughs alone.

We both sit in an awkward silence that can't even be broken when our steaks arrive.

Nathaniel orders more drinks and another appetizer after he's done with his meal, as if he hasn't eaten in days.

Just when I think he couldn't eat anything more, he orders a huge slice of chocolate cake.

The server asks, "Two spoons?"

"One!" Nathaniel bites back quickly. "I'm a growing boy."

Not that I wanted any anyway, but the fact he only asked for one spoon makes me want to shove that cake up his ass.

"You're dangerous!" The waitress in the tight dress says to Nathaniel. They are flirting, outwardly, obviously flirting.

"I'm harmless!" He laughs with her. "But seriously, you're the best. Why do you think I keep ordering more food? You're so… attentive."

When the bill comes, Nathaniel doesn't even reach for it or suggest splitting it down the middle. Doesn't even ask how much he owes when I slip my card inside. He could probably expense most of this anyway!

Either he's so used to Stella paying for everything or he's a cheap ass.

We walk out of the restaurant but I have to wait because Nathaniel forgot his jacket on his chair.

I wonder if he's going to try and order more drinks on my tab, but he comes back quickly.

I drive us back to my place, bitterness boiling in my lungs. I don't mind paying for things, I really don't. But more so for people who deserve it. It would have been nice if he offered.

This better not be the life he's accustomed to with Stella because I can see her supporting him and not telling me.

"Daaaamn! Your place is even nicer than Stella's. Ballerrrr!" Nathaniel screeches as he walks through my front door.

Stella has the beach house vibe that is relaxed and cozy, which is opposite her personality. My condo in a sky rise is sophisticated and posh, also opposite of my personality.

He walks into my bedroom as if he owns the place, setting his small luggage on the edge of my bed.

Following closely behind him, he adds, "You don't mind giving me your bedroom?"

What in the hell?

"I was going to make up the couch for you." I point to my living room.

"Stella told me she told you about my back problem."

"Back problem? No she didn't."

"Yeah, I can't sleep on couches because the cushions don't support me evenly."

I'm too exhausted to argue.

12 more hours of this douchebag.

"Thanks." He responds to my silence.

It's a little past 10pm and when I'm settled on my very comfortable sectional couch, I pull out my phone and text the guys.

Sam: "This asshole."

Jake: "What happened?"

Sam: "He's like a completely different person when Stella isn't around. Total asshole."

Diego: "I knew it. He looked like an asshole."

Sam: "He's in my bed!"

Diego: "OMG kick him out what the fuck?"

Jake: "I didn't know you were into that shit."

Sam: "I'm on the couch."

Jake: "Shut the fuck up."

Sam: "Yeah, he took my bed."

Diego: "Did he take your nuts, too?"

Sam: "It's not worth it. Causing a fight would escalate to World War III if Stella found out."

Jake: "You're such a pussy. Don't be scared of your sister."

Sam: "I'll say something in the morning. I'm too tired now."

When I do fall asleep, which is pretty fast considering the couch is extremely comfortable, despite what Nathaniel would think, I wonder what else Stella is keeping from me.

———◆———

The rumbling from my coffee machine wakes me as soon as the aroma of bitter grounds enters my lungs.

Nathaniel is drinking from one of my ceramic tumblers.

"Hey man!" He greets, chipper and awake.

"Hey, how'd you sleep?"

"Great. Your bed is awesome. Your sheets are like heaven."

I raise my eyebrows at him and ask, "Off to work already?"

"Yeah, I'll be reviewing the pictures from yesterday and I fly home later tonight. Thanks again for letting me stay here."

No appreciation or thank you for your expensive dinner, but okay. I guess I can't be picky. He did thank me for something.

"Yeah." I keep it short.

"When are you coming to LA next?"

"No clue."

"Going to be busy today?"

"Not really."

I think he can sense my frustration by my short answers, so he adds, "Well I better get going. I packed kind of quickly."

He gives me the bro hug, our hands clasped together at our chests as we pat each other on the back.

When he leaves, he takes my tumbler with him.

Instead of immediately texting Stella, I decide I'll take a few minutes and calm down before I say something I'll regret.

Walking to the coffee pot, I notice not only did he take my tumbler, but the rest of the coffee *in* the pot.

I begrudgingly pour more water and coffee grounds and wait for it to brew.

I strip my sheets and wave out the comforter and see a piece of paper fly out.

It can't be from when Harper left her number, because I have that saved in my wallet.

I pick up the receipt from last night.

Grumbling, I crumple it up, pretending I didn't spend

over $300. But something is scribbled on the back that I didn't notice before.

"To Sam, my most generous customer. Call me, we can get a real dinner. ♥ Jenny."

My eyes search the ceiling as if it'll explain the confusion bouncing around my brain.

Then it hits me like a tidal wave.

This asshole went back for his jacket and instead got her number. Probably told her his name was Sam so she'd think he paid for dinner and left the generous tip.

I pull out my phone with a vengeance, this time unable to suppress my anger.

Stella's name appears on my favorites list and my thumb smashes her little face in the circular icon.

It rings.

And rings.

Voicemail.

"Hi, you've reached Stella. I'm not here right now. I'm too busy enjoying my wonderful life. Leave a voicemail and I'll get back to you."

"Stella. Call me back. Now."

I gather the sheets in a rumpled pile and wash them in extra hot water.

Three hours later, after my brain has pooled out of my ears and eye sockets from actual work, I grab my phone that has been on silent. Four missed calls from Stella, three text messages and one text message from Harper.

I open Harper's first.

Harper: "Hey you! Just thought I'd text you good morning!"

Sam: "It's definitely better now that Nathaniel left."

Harper: "Uh oh, that doesn't sound so good. The boyfriend?"

Sam: "Yep. He's a lying, cheating asshole."

Harper: "Oh my. What happened?"

Sam: "I'll tell you later. I need to call my sister."

Harper: "Yikes. Text me later!"

Sam: "Will do."

Stella's texts go overlooked and I immediately call her. She answers on the first ring.

"Sam? My god is everything okay? What's wrong?"

"I'm fine." I don't sound fine.

"You nearly gave me a heart attack!"

"Well what I have to say is important!"

"Oh my god. Oh my god he's going to propose isn't he?" Her incessant shrills force me to pull the phone away from my ear. "I can't believe it!!!"

"Stella."

"When is it going to happen?"

"Stella…"

I can't even get a word in.

"Holy shit I can't believe this! Did he show you the ring? Was it big? Oh my gosh how many carats?"

"He's not proposing!" I nearly shout.

She doesn't say anything, so I ask, "You there?"

"So what the fuck is it?"

"What the fuck it is, Ms. Stella, is Nathaniel is kind of a douche bag."

"Sam, why would you say that?"

"Why? Oh I don't know… maybe because he cheated on his girlfriend with you? Might I add he had like seven drinks? Is he an alcoholic? And he didn't even offer to pay for dinner! Does he have money of his own? He even took my bed."

Okay that last one is pretty juvenile but I had nothing else to close with. I'm keeping the waitress's number in my back pocket for now. I don't know if she's ready to hear that yet.

"Where is this coming from? Are you trying to get back at me?"

"Not at all!" I change my tone to protective now. "You've been strangely spot on with some of the girls I dated in the past. The one that came from an abusive relationship? I wasn't prepared or emotionally ready for that. The one that lied and said she was 26 when she was 21? Way too immature for me. And who could forget the one who didn't tell me she was a married woman! You gave me so much shit for that when I had no clue! And you *knew* Nathaniel had a girlfriend. That's so hypocritical! How could you be with a man like that?"

Silence shrieks on the other end and I check the screen to see if the seconds are still passing or if we got disconnected.

"Stella, hello?"

"Mind your own fucking business."

CHAPTER EIGHT

My screen turns black and returns to the main screen.

"Shit!" I grumble as I put both my fists to my eyelids.

Stella didn't mind her own business when it came to my life. She made damn sure I knew every flaw about the women I chose in the past, no matter how miniscule.

But now, when I give her hard facts, she can't accept it?

Why are my choices up for critique but hers aren't?

I open Harper's text and finally respond.

Sam: "Well, that didn't go well."

My phone clatters on the kitchen counter and I run my fingers through my messy hair.

Her text appears a minute later.

Harper: "Oh no, what happened?!"

Sam: "I told her some of my concerns after he left. She hung up on me."

Harper: "I'm so sorry Sam. I'm sure she'll come around. Maybe give her some space. He can't be too bad if they are living together, right?"

Sam: "It's not even that. I don't understand why she can judge me and I can't judge her?"

Harper: "In her defense, women are more emotional than men and she probably likes this guy, faults and all. No one is perfect."

Her last sentence hits me hard. No one *is* perfect and I have to remind myself I have my faults, too.

Sam: "Oh really? What are your imperfections?"

Harper: "Give it time, you'll see sooner or later."

My heart does a weird spasm, a cross between a palpitation and excitement shocking my system.

Give it time.

The fact that she's assuming this situation will continue makes me wary. It makes me want to end it right now, but I just can't do it for some reason.

———— • ————

It's Thursday, and even though Harper is back in town, I make myself busy so it doesn't look like I'm waiting for her knock on the door.

Diego and I are at a Giant's game, his feet propped up in the empty seats in front of us.

"You've been glued to Carrie I'm shocked you were free for me."

"I know, sorry. It's been so great having her around. She still has her life back in LA and I have mine here so it's not like my private time is compromised. Just being around her makes me laugh again."

"That's awesome, man. So you're going to propose tomorrow?"

He smirks at me and I can still see his eye roll behind his sunglasses.

"It's very early, yes, but it feels different with Carrie. I can't explain it. I won't mess this up. And she knows about my divorce, in case you were wondering."

"Hey that's cool. I'm all for it. She doesn't mind long distance?"

"She's younger, so you know how that is."

"What's that supposed to mean?" I laugh as I snap open a peanut shell.

"Well she's young and might not want to settle down yet. This might be perfect for her. But on the other hand, women are so quick to fall hard for a guy, it could go either way."

A nod my head agreeing with him, realizing Harper might be on the same level, except she's not as young as Carrie and might *want* to settle down.

"How's Harper?"

"She's good. Traveling but coming back sometime

today I think. We might see each other this weekend but if not it's okay."

Diego senses my apparent aloofness and calls my bullshit. "Dude, shut up. You know you want to see her. You don't have to pretend with me. Or Jake. We both know you like this girl."

"And how did you come to that conclusion? I try not to talk about her around you."

"Well the fact that Lila sucked your dick and you didn't go back for more was a huge sign."

"You're basing this off a girl giving me head?"

"Blow jobs are your weakness."

"You make no sense. Are you and Jake talking about this behind my back?"

"Fuck no, whatever we'd say we'd say to your face. We thought you would have worked your way through a few girls by now, but you haven't. You got a taste of someone else and you're still seeing Harper."

I can see his stance, but I still resist.

"I'm taking this very slow. Can we not make a big deal? You know how I get when things get serious. I'm fine with how things are. We're hooking up, having fun."

"Will you at least- run you piece of shit!" Diego yells at one of the players who hit a ball into a gap in center field. "We're never going to win if we keep hitting fly balls."

I pop another peanut in my mouth.

"Will you at least ask her about dinner next week?"

"Sure, if I see her soon, I will ask her."

"Please, you know you will. You're probably going to text her the second you get home."

By the time I'm home from the game, Harper and I have already discussed dinner plans.

Am I that predictable?

———◆———

Thursday is not my typical choice for date nights. I usually try to avoid weekday dates, but it was her idea and I never say no to sushi.

When I arrive, Harper already has a table.

"Hey there!" She gets up from her seat, practically jumping out so we can hug.

I sneak a quick sniff of her hair and whatever scent it is brings me back to the night I was at her place, the last time I saw her.

"How was that book signing?" I ask, sitting in my chair.

"It was awesome! Huge turnout. He's going on a nationwide tour to promote his book, so I obviously picked the one with the best city."

"It wasn't Ethan's was it?" I ask reluctantly.

"No?" She looks confused; completely unaware I'm slightly jealous of this mysterious guy. "This one is a biography. It's intriguing. If you want to read it, I have a signed copy."

"Not a big reader."

She whacks me with her plastic trifold menu.

"Sam-u-el! You don't read?"

"I read enough law books in college to last a lifetime."

"Fair enough."

"It doesn't get old for you? Not as enjoyable?"

"It's weird, I can still read for work and read for pleasure. I think I can differentiate the job and the hobby pretty well."

"Going on more book tours soon?"

"I would love to but lately they want me more in the office so we'll see."

I order a bottle of wine to share and the waiter asks for our ID's.

Handing mine over, Harper mumbles, "Of course he asks for ID."

"What's up?" I ask her, putting my ID back in my wallet.

She tucks a piece of hair behind her ear and admits, "I probably should have told you this before dinner, but my wallet was stolen in Florida. I didn't think they still card people these days."

She gives our waiter a hopeful look.

"No ID, no alcohol."

He leaves with the cocktail menu and takes his bad customer service with him.

Harper guffaws. "Well, I didn't mean you couldn't drink just because I can't."

"Jeez, sorry want to go somewhere else?"

"No, it's totally fine. I'm good with water."

"Someone stole your wallet?"

"Yeah, on my second to last day. I left it on a signing table and got preoccupied with the event. Someone took it and I didn't even realize it until the end of the day. Thank god I left my passport back in my hotel room so I could fly home. I knew taking that as a backup would come in handy one day. But all my credit cards were in there. I had to borrow cash from my boss to hold me over until I went to the bank. So embarrassing."

"Wow, that's shitty. Especially since it was your turn to pay."

Her face turns white with humiliation.

"Holy shit I'm so sorry." I laugh, realizing I have the worst sense of humor.

"Sam, no I feel so bad. I should have said something."

She looks like she's about to cry and I'm overcome with this overwhelming feeling of providing for her.

"Don't worry," I tell her. "I got this."

———— ◆ ————

My jeans and boxers rest at my ankles as Harper climbs off my wet lap. The windows of her Porsche Cayenne are foggy and you can smell the aroma of wild sex and salty sweat in the condensed space.

"Goddamn," I huff. I'm flooded with sensation overload.

I shimmy up my pants, the perspiration lingering on my legs creating resistance. I feel like Ross and his leather pants but I eventually get them on.

Harper keeps her panties on the floor but adjusts her dress as we both fix ourselves.

She opens a door and a whoosh of cold air filters through.

We both step out, her legs wobbly and unsteady.

"Whoa, you okay?" I ask, catching her.

"Riding you like that made me use muscles I didn't know I had."

I slip my hand under the backside of her dress and cup her butt cheek in my palm. I smack her hard and she presses her body into mine.

We kiss against her car, both unaware if people are around.

Inconspicuously, I move my hand to the front of her dress where she's bare, warm, and oh so wet. She's ultrasensitive to my touch as I hover my thumb right there.

"What are you trying to do to me?" She moans in

my ear. "I won't be able to finish again, it's too soon."
She warns me.

I take that as a challenge and I continue pressing into
her, massaging and thrusting until I know she *will* suc-
cumb to my touch. My pressure and speed varies as she
backs her ass against the car door. Our embrace is tight
as I resume sliding my fingers against her.

She squeezes her legs shut while she squirms under
my hand.

She smacks my forearm, stifling a moan that resembles a cry.

Harper comes quietly, her face pressed into the
shoulder of my jacket.

"How the hell did you do that?"

"I have my ways." I boast.

"I'll need an Uber home after that."

I zip up my jacket and adjust my shirt.

"Want to come back to my place?" She asks. "I can
open a bottle of wine we weren't able to drink tonight."

The thought of coming over, possibly staying the
night, has my decision swaying. While it sounds like
it could be fun, I don't want her thinking I'm going to
spend the night every time we go out. I never want to
give someone the wrong impression, and I'm still unsure
of what we both want at this moment. I'm not her boyfriend and I hope she remembers that.

"I think I'll head home. I'm kind of exhausted."

She's disappointed and doesn't hide it as well as she thinks. "Oh, okay. Well," she pauses and I feel like an ass. "Thanks for dinner. I'm sorry again about my wallet."

She feels rejected, I know it.

But the last thing I want is this becoming a routine. We hook up. One of us spends the night. Then next thing you know she's always over and then one day we'll be living together-

"Have a good night, Sam." She gives me the most platonic kiss on the cheek I've ever had and gets inside her car.

No typical "I'll text you later", or "what are you doing next week?"

And shit. I didn't even mention dinner next week, though the timing is suspicious.

Thanks for the fuck. I don't want to go back to your place but how about a triple date next Friday?

She exits her front seat and walks towards me. I get the sense that she wants to plant a giant wet one on my mouth, but instead she hands me my keys I left on her center console.

"You might need these to get home."

"Oh, yeah, right. Thank you. I'll talk to you soon, okay?"

Her insecurity might as well be printed words on her skin. I can read the thoughts in her dejected eyes.

"Okay, goodnight!"

When I stroll back to my car, I hold my keys tightly between my fingers, the fingers that were just inside Harper, and I realize how stupid I'm being.

CHAPTER NINE

---•◆•---

When I wake the next morning, I'm halfheartedly expecting an apology text from Stella. But I receive nothing.

I keep envisioning both of us growing old until we can no longer walk, bound to wheelchairs, neither wanting to take the first step at a reconciliation.

Eventually I'll cave and text her, but Harper's right. Maybe we need some space.

I'm always paving over the speed bumps that are inevitable in all relationships and families. I know one of Stella's prominent flaws is losing her shit if she doesn't appear perfect, and my easiest flaw is willing to forgive any wrongdoings without actually fixing the problem.

The gym is calling my name, so I put on my workout clothes and take advantage of the distraction.

Before I head back to the weights, I ask my buddy who is the owner of the gym, "Hey have you heard of some supplements from Russia called Pumped Up? I couldn't translate the ingredients but some were printed in English and looked intense."

"Yeah, I think I've heard of those. They're illegal man."

"I figured."

"Stick to American suppliers, Sam. Everything made overseas you can't trust. I can give you some recommendations if you need them."

"It's not for me. A friend of mine is taking it and I wanted to make sure he wasn't going to grow a third nut sack."

"Suuure. Well tell your 'friend'," he does air quotes. "There isn't a ton of testosterone enhancing ingredients. So if he's hoping to grow his baby dick, it ain't happening."

"Ouch, you really think I'd need help in that area?"

We both laugh and he suddenly turns serious. "But no really Sam, if you are taking them, be careful. That shit puts a lot of pressure on your heart. It filters through your kidneys and you can fuck them up royally if you're abusing the limit. It can create erratic blood pressure and a slew of problems internally that you wouldn't even see."

This confirms my suspicions.

"Thanks, dude."

———◆———

It's Tuesday morning and I haven't heard from Harper since Thursday night, which is odd. I'm not *trying* to read into it, but something might be up because usually she texts me on Monday so we can bitch about it being Monday.

I also haven't heard from Stella. Are all women ignoring me? Am I in denial and I'm the common thread to all these disasters?

I'm giving both Stella and Harper space for now. After our sushi night, Harper seemed to be getting attached. Is that something I want right now?

I'm drinking my morning coffee and looking over some paperwork.

I've been thinking about building another brewery closer to me. It's all speculation; haven't even voiced my ideas to Stella. But it's distracting me and keeping my brain stimulated.

When I have a moment to digest all the financial quotes and estimates, I think of my parents doing this exact same thing decades ago, getting ready to open up their own place.

I miss them terribly. It's been so long since I heard their voices, I can barely remember them anymore.

Back then, we didn't have cell phones glued to our hips and we didn't upload every single insignificant moment of our lives to Instagram or Snapchat. I don't have any videos of my parents, just photographs that don't do justice. I would give anything to hear them tell me they love me, to tell me I'm doing a great job with my life, but right now it's like a cloud evaporating in the sky.

A twinge of stubbornness causes my hands to take control as I pull up Stella's thread. I want to say something, anything, but instead I close it out. If I don't hear from her by this weekend, I'll go out to LA and see what's going on.

———— ◆ ————

When Friday rolls around, Jake reminds me of the reservation he made.

Do I really want to be a fifth wheel? Will I get more shit if I come alone or bring Harper?

Cringing at my phone, I summon the strength of a greater man and text Harper.

Sam: "Hey stranger. How are you doing?"

It's been a solid week since we spoke and I'm worried there will be apprehension on her end.

Twenty minutes later, she replies.

Harper: "I'm so sick of reading. My eyes can't take it anymore."

Sam: "Ouch. Want me to call instead? My texts that bad?"

Harper: "Ah no I mean with work! I've read way too much these past few days. I need a break."

Sam: "How about dinner? Tonight?"

Harper: "Yeah! What were you thinking?"

Sam: "Jake and Diego wanted to go out. They told me to bring someone but it's very casual."

She doesn't respond right away and I know in that moment I'm giving her mixed signals.

Harper: "Okay…what time?"

Sam: "Let's say 7:30pm?

Harper: "Sure!"

The second she agrees, I wish she hadn't.

———◆———

My ears are buzzing with anxiety and luckily it drowns out the rain that beats on my car like a bad omen.

What was I thinking?

I'm 20 minutes late and I'm shocked Harper hasn't texted me to remind me how rude it is to be tardy. Then I realize she's nothing like Stella.

A large birthday party is taking up most of the restaurant and I'm surprised we even got a reservation.

"Harper in the bathroom?" I ask, checking my watch one last time.

"She's not here yet!" Jake tells me.

I expected her to be here, maybe even one drink in. A cold wave of panic crawls up my back and latches its claws into my shoulders.

Pulling out my phone as I sit, I text, "Everything okay?"

She responds quickly.

Harper: "Yes! Sorry I was stupid and stopped by the office for the first time in a while. It took longer to escape. Be there soon, sorry! Don't wait to order drinks!"

Sam: "Can I get you something?"

Harper: "I'm dying for a Pinot Grigio. Thank you!"

I set my phone face up on the table and stare at the two couples across from me. Despite my hesitations, inviting Harper was the right move. I couldn't last two hours of questions like, "Why are you still single? Why haven't you moved on? Why are you being such a limp dick asshole?"

"Did she stand you up?" Jake jokes.

"No, she's on her way. Running late."

"I hope she's not nervous." Avery coos, brushing back her auburn hair.

Avery and Jake have been married for six years. She's an Instagram influencer, if that even counts as a real job. Their home is immaculate and plastered all over social media. She's tall, stunning, and comes from a wealthy family. I've always loved Avery. She's great to Jake and has always been down to earth, even if her privileged upbringing rears its head here and there. She's classy and sophisticated. Exactly what Jake needs to balance out his wild side.

"Nervous? No way." I say.

"Let me get this straight," Carrie starts, "She's not your girlfriend? We don't call her your girlfriend?"

"We don't have a label." I confirm.

"Label or not, this is a date. You're dressed nice and Jake and Diego are in ties!" Avery points out. "This is a *glorified* double date where you're introducing her to your friends."

"This is a friendly get together, nothing more." I say, feeling judged for skipping the tie.

The party near the front of the bar is continuing its loud charade and serenades of "happy birthday." I'm missing most of the conversation with my friends, wondering how they can carry on with the rambunctious group.

On top of the stress of the night, I also continuously check my phone to see if Stella has texted to apologize. Even a simple "sorry" would put my qualms at rest. I don't want to call it a fight, but I know we are both upset with each other. Why she's mad at me I'm still trying to understand.

"Hey! Sorry I'm late!" Harper struts up to the table and takes off her coat. She's wearing a pair of strappy wedges and a tight dress underneath that shows the right amount of leg. The neckline is a deep plunge and it's only human nature that my eyes fall to her chest.

I get up from the table and give her a gentleman's hug and brief kiss on her cheek.

When Harper sits, Carrie and Avery fawn over her dress.

"Is that the new Monique Lhuillier? You've got great taste. It's so good to meet you!"

"I bet I can't afford it but I want it! You're gorgeous." Carrie swoons.

"You are both so sweet, thank you."

"I'm Avery! Married to this handsome fella over here."

"Hey, Harper! How have you been?" Jake asks, sliding the breadbasket away from her in case she wants to retaliate.

She laughs and takes a long sip of her wine. Gratitude fills her face. "I've been good! Sorry I'm late."

"I'm Carrie! While Diego and I have only been dating a while, I've heard a lot about you."

"All good things," Diego adds, right as I'm about to bonk their heads together like the Three Stooges. Diego probably hasn't even mentioned Harper!

The conversation flows just fine without me and I wonder how long I can sit here wondering what the hell I'm doing.

I'm paying more attention to my drinks that keep appearing. The waitress must read my mind. I take a large gulp of my second drink, feeling the alcohol slip down my throat and hit my bloodstream with a vengeance.

"So, Harper," Diego begins. "Now that we have you here, tell us about yourself."

"Oh god, this is going to feel like a job interview." She jokes, adjusting herself in the booth. "Well, I'm originally from Maine. I moved to the city when I accepted a new job at a publishing company. I work from home but travel occasionally for book tours. It's seriously my dream job."

"How do you like our boy Sam here?" I kick Jake under the table.

Harpers cheeks flush, embarrassment practically searing off her skin. "Sam's great!"

I wait for her to elaborate, to say I'm a sweet guy, handsome, sexy even, but she doesn't. Her answer is so short and meaningless I'm almost insulted. I finish the rest of my second drink in one huge swig.

"He's such a great guy, huh?" Carrie contributes to my lack of praise. "All the girls at work love him. He's so handsome, so nice, so polite, so caring."

If I were an outsider, I would assume Carrie liked me more than Harper and that stings.

I guess my only noteworthy attribute is being "great." Even as friends, she could enlighten us with more.

"Have you made up with Stella yet?" Diego changes the subject quickly.

"Not yet. I might call her in a few days."

"Has she reached out at all?" Harper seems more interested in me again because she's actually looking me in the eyes.

"Of course not." I snap, immediately regretting my tone of voice.

"Don't reach out first." Jake suggests. "You always reach out first. Give her some time. Maybe you need to take a month off."

"This isn't like a vacation from a job, Jake. I've never gone that long without talking to her. How has she been at work, Carrie?"

"She hasn't been coming in a lot actually."

The waitress understood my previous head nod and brings me a third drink and that too is quickly inhaled. She comes back 10 minutes later and I order four fingers of whiskey, neat.

Everyone judges me like I'm a recovering alcoholic that fell off the wagon; shock smeared across their faces as they watch me ungraciously throwback my drinks.

"Might want to slow down?" Diego suggests. "4 fingers? Are you trying to die tonight?"

"What's it to you?" I snap.

"Well, I need to use the powder room." Avery says, getting up from the table.

"I'll join you." Harper grimaces like my alcoholism is airborne and contagious.

"Me too!" Carrie adds.

When they're gone, I ask, "What is Harper's problem?"

Diego answers first, "Look in the mirror, dude. What's *your* problem? How about you leave for the bathroom instead and not come back? Why are you drinking so much?"

"I don't know. Nerves I guess. I'm starting to think she came out of obligation. She doesn't seem to want anything to do with me."

"Why are you being so touchy?" Jake chimes in. "You said you've been honest with her. I'm sure she would tell you if she didn't want to come. Yet she's here. Enjoy it and stop being such a little bitch."

The alcohol is hitting me harder and faster than it normally would. My empty stomach latches onto the only thing filling it: vodka and olives from my previous beverage.

When the girls return, they have an air of mischief following them.

"What's wrong?" I'm a rabid dog sniffing for information.

"Oh nothing. Something funny happened on the way to the ladies room." Avery tells her husband.

"What?" We all ask.

Harper is laughing to herself and shrugs it off like whatever it was was no big deal.

"Tell us!" Jake demands, pounding his fists on the table, laughing.

"A guy asked Harper for her number!" Carrie exclaims, as if this is so scandalous.

It's not, but on the other hand, I don't necessarily like it.

"What did you tell him?"

I'm glad Diego asks because had I asked, I might have encouraged it.

"Well, he asked if I had a boyfriend, and I said no. He asked for my number and I said I wasn't interested, so he gave me his number instead."

"He shoved his business card down her top!" Avery squeals, like she would support Harper leaving with this prick. Whose side is she on?

"Which one is he?" I ask, ready to size up this asshole.

"The one in the gray suit. At the bar." Avery says inconspicuously pointing.

Right as we all look in his direction, he stares at our table.

He looks right at me.

"He's got some balls." Diego states.

The jerk takes a sip of his drink, still surveying me.

"Ignore him!" Harper says, rubbing my inner thigh.

"He's no one. And I think he's drunk."

I think I'm drunk. "I don't like the way he's staring at me."

"I think he's staring at Harper." Avery points out.

I'm not even tied down to Harper, yet here I am ready to pick a fight with competition. I'm normally not a jealous person but for some reason I feel territorial.

Luckily, the guy in the suit leaves when he realizes, sure she doesn't have a boyfriend, but she's here with me tonight.

———◆———

I'm six drinks in, maybe seven, while everyone else is still on their second, maybe third. The girls are sharing a bottle of wine and I'm eating all the bread because I'm hungry and our food hasn't arrived.

What's the holdup?

"Dude, if you're not gulping your drinks you're taking all the free bread!" Diego murmurs in my ear. "Leave some for us!"

My earnest stare gets him to back off. I'm an animal in the wild who found scraps and isn't willing to share.

Thankfully, our food arrives shortly after.

The steak enters my stomach, adding to the toxic mixture of whiskey and vodka, a decision I'm going to regret later.

"Do you and Jake have any kids?" Harper asks.

"We've been thinking about it. Waiting for the right time. Jake is so busy but I really want a baby."

"One of my best friends from Maine just had a little girl. She's so precious." Harper says.

"I don't want kids." I blurt it out without thinking. It's not even true, which is why I'm so confused I say it.

"Umm, okay?" Diego mimics my abnormal tone.

Harper's body stiffens in perplexity. I'm another person, someone she didn't agree to go out with tonight.

"Do you have any brothers or sisters?" Carrie asks Harper.

"Nope, only child."

"Are your parents still back in Maine?" Avery asks.

My knife clatters on my plate. Shit. I should have warned them that her parents are dead.

"They passed away when I was little." She says without an ounce of sadness. She's more familiar with admitting her tragedy than I am.

"How sad," Jake says, totally oblivious I never told them that fact. "Are you managing okay?"

What's with the fucking interrogation?

"Umm, yeah I'm doing okay. It's so rare to lose a parent at such a young age. And I lost both of them. Sam and I discovered that unfortunate connection the night we met. The grief never goes away but it gets easier as the years pass."

"You poor thing." Carrie is one blink away from sobbing all over our cloth napkins.

"But you know I think I'm doing okay for the most part. It sucks not having them here to share in the celebrations. There have been so many times I wanted to call my mom up just to tell her about my day. The holidays are always the hardest. They won't be here for the big milestones. My dad won't be around to walk me down the aisle…"

Diego whispers, "Is this when you tell her you don't want to get married?"

"Shut up." I sputter loudly to Diego, but everyone thinks I'm talking to Harper. God I need to stop drinking.

"No, not you, sorry. Diego. He's being insensitive."

Harper shakes it off and ignores me, disliking the drunken side of me. And I don't blame her. I don't like it either but fuck, my mind has a mind of its own.

"It's a lot different from Maine, but I'm finally opening up and meeting more people."

More people? Other guys?

I'm so drunk I'm taking everything out of context. I know for a fact she told me the first night we met how hard it is to meet guys. Has that changed? Am I ruining a good thing?

———◆———

Diego, Jake and I split the bill three ways, regardless of what we ordered or didn't order. I should probably pay more considering I drank the entire bar empty.

On a scale of zero to drunk, I'm stuck between "I'll fight you for looking at me funny" and "one more whiff of alcohol and you're about to see what I ate for dinner."

The girls hit it off so well that Harper and Avery exchange numbers.

Inside I'm cursing because her becoming friends with my best friend's wife can get awkward. If things don't progress with Harper, which after tonight I guarantee they won't, she will still have a connection to my friend and I don't know if I like that.

Everyone is quick to leave the awkward dinner all thanks to me.

Harper wraps herself in her jacket and we are left standing outside the door.

"Sooo…" I slur, unsure if she can tell I'm barely able to stand.

"You're obviously not okay to drive home."

"I think I'm alright."

She laughs at me and I take no offense, because she's right. "I don't think so, Sammy. Let me drive you home. Come walk me to my car."

When I sit in the front seat, I cross my arms over my chest.

"What's going on, Sam?"

"Nothing." I dribble.

"Why are you making it seem like I did something wrong?"

"You were *great*."

I emphasize great and she doesn't catch on.

I'm mostly hurt that she didn't take this opportunity to admit to my friends how amazing I am. But maybe I'm not. Maybe she truly just wants a fuck buddy and I'm nothing more than that.

God this is exactly why I shouldn't have started anything. The back and forth of trying to read her mind is exhausting.

When she pulls up to my street, she parks out front.

"You're not coming up?"

"I think you need some time to recoup. Thank you for such a nice dinner. That was so sweet of you to invite me last minute."

The "last minute" comment sounds like a dig, like she was an afterthought or sloppy seconds.

My adrenaline has worn off completely and loneliness is setting in.

"I'm okay, really. I'm fine." My last attempt at getting her up to my place.

"I'm sure you are, but it's late and you look like you're about to pass out anyway."

I nod my head, accepting defeat.

Chapter Ten

———— ◆ ————

I wake up in the middle of the night when my stomach decides to eat itself. It churns in ways that make me wonder if I'm about to shit out my intestines.

"Oh fuck." I murmur and I jump out of bed and head toward the bathroom.

Somehow, I'm at the toilet bowl just in time as all those disgraceful drinks come up my throat, scorching my esophagus.

"Oh dear god." I preach to the toilet that now holds the remains of my bad night.

Another bout of nausea hits me and I spew more alcohol and food.

I had to get the steak, didn't I? It tastes horrible the second time around.

This happens for the next twenty minutes, expelling everything I ate and drank for the past 24 hours. I flush when necessary and wipe the sweat from my forehead, the bathroom spinning in a whirlwind of blurs and blurbs of light. My stomach is still writhing in pain but it's beginning to subside as I rid it of the poison.

My strength has been flushed down the toilet, along with my pride.

When I think I'm in the clear, another surge of pain contracts and I throw up even more.

And then I'm hit with an excruciating pain elsewhere. My brain billows against the lining of my skull, creating the worst migraine I've ever experienced in my life. Pain swells throughout my limbs, through my muscles, in my bloodstream, and deep into my nerves.

Now is when I wish Harper had stayed the night because I don't know if I can reach my fridge to get a bottle of water. I'm so dehydrated I can feel it in my skin.

The color has drained from my face and the room is spinning.

I stagger out of the bathroom, my head expanding to twice its size when I fall back onto the floor. My only option is a pathetic army crawl that barely gets me out the door. I'm sweating everywhere yet I'm freezing.

Images play in my head of me lying dead on the floor shirtless, in puke stained boxers, shriveling up due to alcohol poisoning; no one finding me until morning when it's already too late.

I'm able to reach for my phone and I pull up Diego

and Jake's text thread, barely able to see what I'm texting.

Sam: "I'm think dying. Can downtown practice come over? I'm seriously."

Five minutes pass and the guys don't respond to my jumbled text that makes no sense.

Groaning, as if I have to call my parents and tell them I'm in jail, I text Harper.

Sam: "Awake?"

Any respectable woman would ignore my text after how I treated her, yet she answers immediately.

Harper: "I am now. You okay?"

I choose speech text this time because I can barely see anything in front of me.

Sam: "I might have alcohol poisoning. I can barely move. My vision is blurry and I'm throwing up everywhere."

Harper: "I'm coming over."

Luckily I equipped my condo with some high tech amenities. It takes me five minutes to figure out how to send Harper an invitation to access my front door. When she arrives and her phone connects to the lock, it will open. I'm so disorientated I don't even care if I've never given my code out to another woman besides Stella. Now is not the time to be petty.

Light-years pass and I hear the door click open.

Embarrassment nearly sweeps me up off the floor,

almost causing me to throw up again, but I manage to keep the heaves intact.

She's about to witness the second most unattractive thing I've ever done, within 12 hours, no less.

I hear her set her car keys and purse down and she enters my room with zero judgment.

"Oh, Sam."

"I'm a mess. Don't smell me." I mumble in a fetal position on my carpet.

"Sit up. I grabbed a Gatorade from your corner store. Drink this."

I'm basically her child as she leans me up against the wall like a doll, tilting my head back so I can get some much needed electrolytes in me.

She forces me to drink more than half and the coolness slides down my throat like ice water. I'm in such a stupefied daze that I picture myself in a video game; my health rating in the top left corner would add a giant beating red heart. Only three more to go and I'm at full strength.

"Feel better?"

"A little." My vision returns, thank god.

She sits next to me but keeps her distance. I smell disgusting.

"So, on a scale of 1 to 10…" I begin. "How turned on are you right now?"

Harper sniggers a bit and it feels like it's been forever since I made her laugh.

"I give you a solid four considering you're shirtless." She jokes. "Drink the rest. Do you have any crackers? Can I make you some toast?"

"Food is like the last thing I want right now."

"I know, but you should get something easy to digest in your stomach to soak up whatever might be left inside slowly killing you."

I give her a halfhearted laugh and shrug.

She gets up and returns with a cold rag and some Ritz crackers that I know are stale.

"Those are so old. Probably been up there for years."

"Eat a few."

"But now I'll have food poisoning." I muse.

She huffs and sets the cold rag on my forehead, instantly cooling down my fever.

Another beating red heart appears at my health level.

"Should I take you to the ER?"

"No, I think I'll be okay. I don't feel as nauseous anymore. It might have passed."

"Let's shower you off."

She pulls me up under my armpit and it takes me a moment to get balanced. Harper leads me to the shower and starts the water.

"Don't get any ideas." She tells me as she slides me out of my boxers. She uses the very tips of her fingers to avoid touching any vomit left on my shorts.

Once I'm completely naked, I get in the shower and

sit on the bench. My body hits the tile wall behind me and I relax my useless limbs.

The steam enters my lungs like a medicinal cloud. Each inhale leaves a therapeutic imprint in my chest as I can feel my body begin to soothe itself from the liquids and mist.

A few minutes later, she returns.

"I'm coming in to help you, but like I said, don't get any ideas."

She enters in her bra and boy shorts and takes some soap in her hands, mixing together until she has a giant, foamy lather. Her fingertips feel amazing as they glide over my skin. Her delicate hands slide over my back and chest.

"You're too nice to me. I was such an asshole." My confession, along with all my preceding nausea, leaves my mouth faster than expected and without struggle.

"Don't worry about it." She keeps washing and doesn't continue the conversation.

Her bra and panties are soaked and I take the last remaining gulps of the Gatorade.

"Thank you for this. You are so prepared. Stella is right. I am a disaster."

"Stop. You had a bit too much to drink. We've all been there."

Harper fans her hands under the water, rinsing off the rest of the soap.

I'm starting to feel better as the minutes pass, but I want to rest my head because I don't think my headache is going away anytime soon.

I groan and Harper notices. "What's wrong?"

"Would you mind getting me some Tylenol? It's in the cabinet next to my fridge."

"Yeah, I'll be right back."

I turn off the water and manage to get a towel wrapped around my lower half.

Harper is back in her jeans, borrowing one of my t-shirts. Her wet undergarments sit on my messy bathroom counter. Normally I would be turned on knowing she's not wearing panties, but my heart can barely filter blood, let alone produce an erection.

She hands me three Tylenol and a glass of water.

I take them like the idiot I am and swallow all three with ease.

We walk to my bed like I'm a cripple.

Atop my dresser is the candle I bought for Nathaniel's visit, the flame burning bright and releasing a fresh cotton scent into the air.

"Get some rest. You'll feel better in the afternoon."

I don't know if she's leaving for good or if she's going back to the kitchen, but I grab her hand anyway and hold onto it like I only have a few minutes left to live.

"Thank you. I don't think you know what this means to me. I could have died."

She gives my hand a gentle squeeze and kisses my forehead. "You're so dramatic Sam Evans. And warm. Let me go get another cold rag."

By the time she returns, I'm already asleep.

———◆———

When I wake up at 1pm, the sun is nowhere to be found, and neither is Harper.

Groaning as if I awoke from a 20 year slumber, I emerge from my coffin like a pale vampire and set my feet on my soft carpet.

The candle still burning smells like a Laundromat on steroids. My senses are on overload and I'm tempted to dry heave, but I manage to swallow it down.

When I walk to my bathroom, I notice her lace boy shorts are gone, damnit, and I pee bright yellow. I need to hydrate some more.

Bits and pieces of last night flicker in my mind. Boxers. Gatorade. Harper washing me.

I cringe when I imagine how unattractive I must have looked. I return to my cool bed and cover myself with blankets in shame.

There are 20 unread texts.

I reassure Diego and Jake I'm not dead.

But the next text doesn't come so easy.

Harper.

God, what do I say?

I start typing things in and then delete it. I write something else and erase that, too.

Finally I say what I feel and it's the truth.

Sam: "I can't thank you enough for being there for me last night. Especially after the way I treated you. I'm so sorry. I have no excuse for that behavior. I understand if you don't want to see me again."

I turn my phone on silent and set it next to me. I don't want to know when she responds, if she does at all.

Her answer comes 10 minutes later.

Harper: "I accept your apology. It takes a lot to admit you're wrong and I appreciate it. As for taking care of you, I would hope you'd do the same for me. We're friends. That's what I'm here for."

Her response is sweet and cryptic. We *are* friends. But what she did goes beyond the call of friendship. That is boyfriend/girlfriend status. And I'm glad she hasn't brought up that we are borderline acting like we are in a relationship even if we aren't.

Sam: "Can I buy you dinner? Tonight? Anything you want. On me."

Harper: "Might want to settle those abs of yours before you think of food LOL!"

I instinctively flex my abs and my stomach is sore from all the crunching I did over the toilet.

Sam: "True, but I need something greasy."

Harper: "How about I come over tonight? You should probably take it easy still. I can pick something up and I'll be over around 6:30pm?"

Sam: "Sounds great. Let me know if you want any ideas. There's a great burger place around the corner. I like the #3. With extra cheese and shoestring fries. And Dr. Pepper. I have cash."

Harper: "You sure know what you want."

I wish more than anything she didn't mean about the food.

———————◆———————

Something chimes loudly, fighting the clatter of the pouring rain outside. It rings in my ears and I crawl off my bed that I don't even remember getting into, and onto the floor where my phone lies.

Not only is it 6:45pm, but I also see Harper has called and texted.

The doorbell rings and I realize that was the noise that woke me up, not my phone.

Oh shit, Harper is here already.

Running towards the door, I answer in a huff, out of breath and smelly as fuck.

Harper is surprised to see I'm alive.

"I got worried you might have gotten sick again. You okay?"

"I'm so sorry, I fell asleep."

She runs her soft hand over my cheek.

"I can tell. You have sleep marks still on you."

She's dressed in a blazer and jeans with some sexy knee high boots.

"Can I come in?" She has a paper bag of food and wine and an umbrella in her other arm.

I'm blocking the entrance on purpose.

"My place looks how I feel."

"I saw it last night, it's okay."

She passes through the door frame smiling and I cringe.

When she walks past me, I can tell my stench has crept up her nose.

"Jesus I thought I washed you well enough! I think you forgot to put on deodorant."

She's pinching her nose and I want to jump out the window. I do smell.

"I feel like a jackass. You look great! And I'm in," I pause and review my casualness. "Sweatpants."

"Stop worrying. It's raining. You're allowed to be lazy. Plus you're recovering from a hangover. Maybe go put on a new shirt." She laughs as I run out of the hallway.

New shirt and deodorant on, I emerge feeling better after seeing her face.

We both sit at the table and I devour my #3 within minutes. It's amazing, as expected, and to have food in me feels spectacular.

When we're done eating, I tell her to follow me into my room.

"I have a gift for you. It's nothing special."

She waits in excitement, hopefully not expecting a Tiffany blue box.

I open my bedside table drawer and pull out the bag. A piece of paper falls to the floor.

She sees the t-shirt I got her and claps in excitement.

"Oh my gosh, you didn't!"

"Of course I did. It's only been a year since I've been holding onto this."

"You are too sweet. Seriously."

My eyes ogle her as she quickly strips off her sweater and puts the simple LA t-shirt on.

The receipt from my night with Nathaniel lies face up on the floor.

Harper picks it up before I can discreetly hide it under my foot.

"What's this?" She asks.

I don't need to explain. I don't need to answer her, yet I feel inclined.

"I know this will sound crazy, but that's not mine."

"Uh huh." She states in disbelief but with a hint of scorn.

"No seriously. When I went out to dinner with Nathaniel, he went back and got her number. But he must have told her his name was Sam because I paid.

He wanted to impress her. And then he left it here when he spent the night."

I'm rambling and judging by Harper's face, I don't think she believes me.

"Whatever." She says undismayed. "It's not like we said this was exclusive. We agreed it would be casual. I can't imagine you wouldn't be taking other girl's numbers."

"I'm not though." I take it and crumple it up again, showing how inconsequential that is to me. "Swear to god. This is one of the reasons I hate this asshole's guts. And why I'm not talking to Stella."

My words hold truth and Harper might believe me.

"Okay. But seriously, it's okay if you want to take girl's numbers."

She walks out to the living room without another word and I give her a light pat on both her butt cheeks; a playful gesture, sign of affection.

Harper turns back to the kitchen and grabs her glass of white wine.

She decides to sit on my couch with the rest of her fries, wedging herself in the corner of the cushions, my favorite spot.

"How has work been?" I ask because I want to change the subject.

"It's been okay."

Her mood is so off now. I blew it and I didn't even technically do anything.

I realize I have to apologize. Again.

"I didn't want to bring it up again, but I am sorry."

"Thank you. The fact that you can even apologize is huge."

I consent, accepting that she's willing to let it all go. "I never asked where you grew up."

She takes the last sip of her wine and sets the empty glass on the table next to her.

"I grew up in Camden, a super cute coastal town with lots of boats. Seriously the most beautiful place you'll ever see. As you know, my parents owned a bookstore there."

"That sounds so peaceful! You said the other night no brothers or sisters…"

"Just me." She smirks at me, the peculiar attitude disappearing.

"How old were you when they passed?"

"I was 10."

"What happened, if you don't mind me asking?"

"No, I don't mind. I'm surprised I haven't told you yet."

The rain hasn't let up and the storm is slamming against the windows. Occasionally a flash of lightning illuminates the dark sky, creating weird illusions and patterns against Harper's figure.

"It's pretty depressing, are you sure you want to hear?" She warns.

"Death is always depressing."

"True." She wipes her hands on her knees. "Like you said for your parents, it was a normal day.

It was the first fall morning of the year. The cold weather was settling for the season and my parents turned on the heat for the first time and lit a fire. It was a Sunday and we basically lived in our PJs while eating pancakes.

The bookstore was closed Sundays and my parents couldn't recall locking it up the night before. They asked me to ride my bike to check. Also I hope you don't think less of them for that. It wasn't far and it was a safe town, so I wasn't in any danger."

I'm silent, wondering what the hell happened. Did someone attack Harper as a child and her parents intervened and got killed? Did her dad pull a murder suicide?

"What... what happened?"

"It was an accident, an accident that could happen to anyone." She starts bawling, thick, wet tears running down her face. "There was a gas leak. The heater was faulty already and when it was finally turned on, it slowly filled the house. My parents didn't even notice. Not until it reached the living room and the fireplace..."

My eyes are wide, imagining all those actions movies with such exaggerated explosions where there's nothing left but the foundation.

"Did the house explode?"

"Not completely, but there was a fire and a blast that knocked them out, thus killing them."

"God, a gas leak?"

She shakes her head yes violently, her face soaked.

"So you could have died if your mom hadn't sent you to check on the store?"

She's quiet, but I know I'm right. What a tragedy. She escaped death. How the hell does that even happen?

She wipes her face and sniffles. Clearly we both didn't plan on her crying tonight.

"It's okay to cry. This is terrible."

"That picture I have over my fireplace at home wasn't even printed and developed yet. It came after they passed and it's the only picture I have. A lot got ruined or damaged. The whole house didn't burn down, but they didn't survive…"

I scoot over to her cushion and hold her in my arms.

Harper's face is buried in my shoulder and I can feel her soft breaths on my neck and my shirt being showered by teardrops.

When she releases me first, I scoot back to my side to give her some space.

"It's so hard. Sometimes I cry and sometimes I don't. I barely remember them anymore. Isn't that so terrible? What kind of person am I that can't remember her parents?"

"You were young." I say, as if that is her excuse. But it is.

"I hate admitting I'm alone."

I'm quiet; unsure if she's expecting me to scoop her up in my arms and tell her she'll never have to be alone ever again, I'm here.

She nods her head and laughs a little. "Aren't you *so* glad you invited me over?"

"I'm shocked you even came to be honest."

She blots her eyes with her napkin, "I don't tell many people that story. My parents left me a lot of money and..." She rolls her eyes for the briefest moment. "I got a settlement due to the heater and I hate talking about money. If I could take it back, I would. I miss them."

"I know what you mean."

"I also don't like to remind myself I don't have anyone. I think that's why when I would meet guys I would fall so hard for them."

Lightning strikes outside and I feel it hit my veins at the same moment. My nervous system is as electrocuted as the air outside.

"How long was your last relationship?" I question, preparing myself with facts that I might need to decipher later.

"Four years."

Oh fuck, I wasn't expecting that.

"He broke your heart, huh?" I surmise.

"He did." She slaps her hands on her knees and releases a forced laugh. "I think I hit the depressed quota for the night."

"Was it that terrible?"

She doesn't say anything for a few seconds. "Yes. He hurt me. Another reason I left Maine. Makes me scared to start things again. And I say that with caution because I like you."

I don't know what else to say, so for now, I hold her.

———◆———

The Netflix menu is lit up when I awake.

We fell asleep together watching some documentary, her entire weight resting on my chest as I held her tight.

Yet there is coldness now. The pressure has released.

Our food has been cleaned up and it's eerily quiet.

I'm puzzled as I walk to my front door.

Her purse and boots aren't on my floor anymore either.

Harper left me in the middle of the night. Again.

Chapter Eleven

————— ◆ —————

The rain has followed into the next morning so we sit inside at our usual Sunday spot.

"She doesn't hate you," Jake says like it's completely obvious after hearing the details of the previous night. "She likes you. It's that simple. Probably more than you realize."

"Jesus then why the mixed signals? We've avoided games for this exact reason. I can't take much more of this."

Both of my friends remain quiet.

"What?"

"Seriously? 'Can't take much more'?" Diego mocks. "Dude, this is nothing. It's how relationships work. You admitted in LA you liked her, that she was super chill. And now when you hear she likes you back, you get cold feet and deny it?"

"She might have meant as a friend, because of the way I acted Friday…"

"Yeah, you acted like an alcoholic." Jake states. "And I was embarrassed for you."

"So how am I supposed to know? She just left. That's not how you go about this."

"Text her. Give her a chance."

"Did you have fun with her last night? Hanging out?" Diego asks.

"I did, I mean once I was able to keep food down."

"So there you go. If you can actually have fun with the girl and not hook up, that could lead to something, right? Would you be pissed if you found out she was fucking other dudes?"

I think hard for a good ten seconds and the fact that I need to think about it and I didn't immediately answer no says enough.

"Carrie and I are taking it slow. But unlike you, we are being honest. She probably wants more from you but doesn't know how to ask."

"And normally, any respectable woman would run for hills after seeing you Friday." Jake continues.

"Okay I get it. I was an asshole."

"Huge asshole." Jake clarifies.

"So I should text her?"

"Yes." They answer in unison.

---------◆---------

I'm walking back to my condo building when I spot her.

Lila.

What are the freaking chances? I'd turn the other way but our eyes connect and I can't bail now.

"Samuel!"

She ditched her form fitting pencil skirt and glasses. Her eyes are glossy with contacts and she's wearing tight yoga pants that accentuate her huge ass. Her platinum blond hair is slicked back in a ponytail so tight she's giving herself a natural facelift.

She hugs me, her chest pressing so hard into mine I feel like I might burst an implant.

"What are you up to?" She asks me, licking non-existent whipped cream off her Starbucks lid, her long tongue gliding over the white plastic.

"Coming home."

"So you *do* still live here. I was hoping I'd run into you one day."

Ignoring her creepy stalking comment, I repeat, "Yep, coming home."

"You look amazing."

I look like I still have a massive hangover so I know she's lying.

We're alone outside under an awning, me counting the seconds until I can politely say goodbye without being an asshole.

"Come here." She requests, grabbing my free hand, leading me around a pillar for more privacy.

"I've missed you. I can't stop thinking about you since you came to the office last week." Her voice is sticky and wet, like the air around us. She opens her umbrella with a loud pop and we stand underneath it as rain splatters the nylon fabric, dripping down the sides and onto my broad shoulders. "I think about that day in the bathroom all the time."

God, how amazing it would be to ruin her fantasy and mention the other memory I have of us in the bathroom, when a year ago I took a shit and ran out of toilet paper. I was screaming for help and Lila came in to reprieve me. I doubt she's thinking of that memory, though.

"Can I come upstairs with you?" She asks.

It's such a loaded question that I answer it carefully.

"Oh, I'm kind of busy right now."

"Tonight?"

She fondles my bicep and I will it to go limp but it's hard and tight, blood pumping through my entire body from this awkward moment.

"I don't think so, Lila. I'm kind of in the middle of something right now. Seeing where it goes, even if it's going slow."

Her tight face twitches with a swift flash of disappointment, but she hides it just as quickly and says,

"Well if you ever want to go slow, really slow, the way I know you like it with me on top, text me."

She leaves with her umbrella as the rain hammers the top of my head.

I watch her ass as she sashays down the street, telling my dick to calm down. I'm not desperate enough to hook up with Lila again.

I pull out my phone and text Harper.

Sam: "I hope you're home because I'm coming over in 10 minutes."

When I arrive at her building, I wait to be buzzed up.

The elevator takes less than a minute and I take those moments to reassure myself that what I'm going to say to her is what I truly want.

When the doors open, she greets me in simple clothes. Barefoot with joggers on and a black long sleeved baggy top. Her left shoulder is exposed and her smooth, tanned skin causes an ache in my pants.

"Hey stranger." She jokes.

"Hey, stranger."

Before she can say anything else, I grab her by the wrist and tug her towards me.

She doesn't expect it, and when we touch, I feel a spark, a flash of something that feels right, like we are meant to be embracing this way. Her cheek rests softly on my pec and she shimmies her shoulders into my solid upper body.

"Is this the part where you tell me you want nothing to do with me?" Harper laughs nervously as we separate.

"Don't be crazy. What happened last night, Harper? I woke up and you were gone."

We're sitting on her couch as I wait for an intervention.

Does she think I'm an alcoholic loser? Commitment phobic?

"Something... changed." She says instead.

"Tell me about it."

"Look, I enjoy being around you. When we met, it was by accident and I didn't even know if I was ready to get back out there. But then you suggested this fun and casual situation that I was up for. The sex was phenomenal and you were actually cool to be around. You're funny, handsome, and I kept asking myself why you're single."

"I'm not an alcoholic, I swear." I use humor to try and lighten the mood, but her seriousness is overpowering.

"But then I realized maybe you just didn't like me enough to be serious with me."

"That's not true." I cut her off before she can continue. "I *do* like you. You're beautiful, sexy... I don't feel like I have to go out of my way to impress you. You seem to like me without extravagant gestures."

"You're right."

"So why did you leave?"

"When you held me last night…" She gathers her composure, fighting the tears beginning to pool in her eyes. "It was so nice. I opened up to you in such a vulnerable way…. I didn't want to fall for you. I swear. But I did. I had to get out of there before you knew it because I know it's not what you want. You told me that on day one and I still managed to get attached."

"I'd be lying if I said I wasn't attached, Harper."

"Really?"

"Hell yeah. I hated the idea of you taking that guy's number from the restaurant. And then I made a fool of myself by getting drunk off my ass. You didn't need to see that side of me and you definitely didn't need to rescue me from alcohol poisoning."

"I care about you."

"I care about you, too.

"Really? Because I freaked out when I saw that girl's number…"

"Harper, you're amazing. I find it hard to believe you're single, too. I mean that is if you're not also dating Ethan Miller."

"*Ethan Miller*?" She shrieks.

"I might have Googled him the night he was texting you. And I might have royally fucked myself when I realized he was young, attractive, and possibly my competition."

"Sam, nothing is happening there. I promise. It took all my courage to even stay and get that drink with you the first night. I can barely do a one night stand let alone date two men at once."

"Well lucky me." I beam with compassion.

She pushes a piece of hair behind her ear and smiles, cradling her coffee.

"So what are we saying here? We don't want to date other people?"

"I don't plan on dating any other women," I say. "Do you?"

"Well women no…" Harper's left side of her mouth spreads into a wicked, naughty smile.

"Men?" I correct myself.

"Only you."

My heart wants to rip out of my shirt.

Only me.

"Good."

"Good." She repeats, her smile now filling her entire face.

We're both on opposite ends of the couch but finally in the same place, and the space between us is brimming with desire and lust.

"Well let's make this official." I suggest. "Come over here so I can tear those clothes off of you."

She sprints across the couch cushions like lily pads until she's back in my arms.

I'm captivated with Harper; fascinated and attracted in ways I didn't know were possible after my failures as a man. There's a hypnotic, almost magnetic pull connecting the two of us. I was fighting it in the beginning, as was she, but I've come to accept not being around her would hurt me more than pretending I wasn't ready for a relationship. I owe it to myself and to Harper to see where this goes.

———— ◆ ————

I'm lying in Harper's bed, her sheets crumpled and sticky with sweat.

I drop my head into her pillows, purposely smelling her sheets that are stained with perspiration and traces of Harper's more personal scent.

Harper returns in the room with two water bottles, her sexy hourglass figure literally glowing from the sheen of sweat on her skin.

"Come out to the balcony with me."

She slips into a comfy bathrobe and I put on my sweatpants and hoodie.

I open the sliding glass door and it's as heavy as a prisoner's cell door.

Luckily the rain has stopped, and thanks to all the

moisture, I'm breathing clean, unspoiled air.

"I will never get sick of this view." Harper admits.

She's sitting in a padded lounge chair and I sit in the other.

"So now that we've agreed to see each other exclusively, maybe it's time I learned your last name."

"Wow I still haven't told you?" Harper balks. "Gosh you're such a slut, sleeping with someone and you don't even know their full name."

I laugh and wrap the blanket tighter around myself trying my best to keep my body heat contained.

"Walton."

"Harper Walton." I repeat.

"I obviously kept my dad's name even after I was adopted by my mom's side of the family."

"Oh you were?"

"Yeah, it wasn't the best situation. They felt obligated because there was literally no one else to take care of me."

"You're not close with them?"

"No, my cousins were cruel. My uncle, my mom's brother, was loving and kind but his wife was not."

"Do you remember your parents?"

"Yes and no." She says quietly. "I remember the bad times, which is weird and awful. The times I messed up or where I felt like I failed. The good times are there but I don't know, maybe I'm blocking it out from the trauma.

I had to grow up so fast." Her voice is so neutral. "I was all alone. I'm so used to being alone. I didn't know a child could endure so much pain like that without falling apart. Death rips you in two pieces and I feel like those two pieces will never connect ever again. I will always feel incomplete."

"Come here." I open my blanket and she crawls onto my lounge chair and we snuggle together, her back shoulder blades resting into my chest as we both admire the same view.

She squirms against me as she places her hands on my arms that are wrapped around her. Our body heats mix and my comfort level rises.

I say nothing. I keep her in our close embrace and feel the faint regularity of her breathing against me. I'm so thankful she's here with me now. At this moment, I'm happy I get to be the one to hold her; happy I'm the one that gets to learn about her past and comfort her when it turns dark.

"Have you talked to Stella yet?"

"No. I've been thinking about what I would even say to her. She's so impossible sometimes. I refuse to say sorry this time. I know we're older but sometimes it feels like she never grew out of that sibling rivalry stage."

"Why is that?"

"I wish I knew. Being a twin, there's always competition. The unspoken game of who's doing better than the other. Who's happier? I don't think she realizes that she's in first place in a game I'm not even playing. The second I have something she doesn't she gets jealous."

"That's so juvenile. Was she always like that?"

"Always. Any girlfriend I ever brought around, they weren't good enough. At first I thought it was because she had high standards for me. But over the years, I learned it was because she hated seeing me happier than she was."

Harper's body stiffens and I can tell she's holding her breath, expecting the worst in my sister.

"Well maybe this time apart is good for you. You're twins, you'll talk soon. Don't let her boyfriend get between you."

My sarcastic laugh echoes her balcony. "Just wait until you meet him, that is, if they last. I have this feeling in my gut that he'll cheat on her. Did you know he cheated on his previous girlfriend? What a douchebag. Once a cheater always a cheater."

"I would die if I ever got cheated on."

Her confession sounds like a warning, and I clarify, "I don't plan on sleeping with anyone else but you. And if something changes down the road, for either of us, we have to communicate."

"I agree."

She snuggles against me again. But I can't let the topic go. "I just, I don't get what she sees in him. I'm her brother so I feel entitled to scold her for this. She knows better."

The city skyline is dark and ominous, only lit up by a few buildings in the distance. I soak in this moment and hope Stella somehow reaches out first.

"I know I said it earlier," Harper begins, "But, I haven't felt like this in a while. This connection, this spark; it's exciting and scary at the same time."

"I won't lie," I admit, "it's been a while since I've been in an exclusive relationship…"

"How long was your last relationship?"

"It's hard to pinpoint when it ended, if that makes sense."

"I get that. Was Stella supportive at least?"

"She rarely is."

Harper opens the blanket for some slack and rolls over so our stomachs are flush against each other. She grabs my cheeks in her cold hands and says, "I'm terrified to meet your sister."

We both start laughing again.

"I'm serious! Especially now. Knowing what I know. Will you even tell her about me?"

"Well when we are on speaking terms again, I'll tell her you and I are seeing each other."

"Are we boyfriend and girlfriend?" She has her hands wrapped behind my neck and she's giddy.

"Would you like that?" My hands are on her ass and

the energy between our touch magnifies. I have no problem calling her my girlfriend and it excites me and terrifies me to be in a new relationship again.

"Well I don't know what else to call you to my friends but my boyfriend?"

"I'm okay with that." My smile widens and her eyes are hungry as she stares back into mine.

She gives me an eager, wet kiss on my lips, her tongue opening my mouth with purpose. She breathes me in and I feel myself finally let go.

———————— ◆ ————————

Heavy rainfall pitter-patters against the towering glass walls and flashes illuminate the dim room. I lay sprawled out in Harper's bed the next morning, the booming of the disruptive thunder interrupting my sleep.

I emerge from the bedroom in boxer shorts and a t-shirt while the arctic thunderstorm continues its destruction outside.

"Hey you!" Harper's hazel eyes practically beam rays of sunshine as I enter the kitchen.

"Morning."

Her head crashes into my chest as she cloaks her arms around my lower waist and I put her neck in a headlock of a hug.

"You smell wonderful." I obnoxiously sniff her hair.

She wiggles out laughing, going back to the pancakes.

I unlock my phone to see how many missed calls or text messages I have, but the screen is dark.

"I charged it for you." Harper says.

"It's dead."

"Can't be! It's been charged for like… hours."

"No, it's this piece of shit. I really do need a new phone. Remember it keeps dying?"

"Oh yes, how could I forget?" She licks her finger of pancake batter, recalling the time I didn't text her for days.

When my phone finally does power back on, there is no word from Stella.

I run various scenarios in my head, dark ones that involve Nathaniel beating her to death, and I suddenly feel worried.

"I think I'm going to LA today." I declare.

"Oh?"

"Yeah, I can't do this anymore."

"Making amends?" She comes up behind me on her tiptoes, her breasts smash into my back.

"It's been too long and I'm starting to get worried. Can I borrow your laptop?"

"It's in my car. Want me to go down and get it?"

"No it's cool, if you don't care I might go home then and book a flight."

"One day into this relationship and you're leaving me already?" She teases, grabbing a handful of my pecs and giving them a tight squeeze.

I quickly grab my delicate chest and cover my nipples. "Hey careful! These babies are sensitive after you held onto them for dear life last night."

"How could I resist? I needed something to hold onto after you fucked me silly."

"Jesus, maybe I won't go to LA and stay here with you all week."

"While I love that idea, you need to make up with Stella."

"Fiiine."

"When do you plan on coming back?"

"I'll only be a few days. Back no later than Wednesday. Maybe tomorrow if it goes horribly. Maybe Friday if it actually goes well."

"Okay. Is it crazy to say I'll miss you? Is that too soon?"

"Yes, you're crazy." I tease.

This time she gets a good chunk of my chest between her fingers and twists lightly.

"Okay, okay I'm kidding. I'll text you, you know I will."

"You better."

I dress quickly and gather the few belongings I brought with me and linger at the front door.

"I'll text you the details as soon as I know them."

She approaches me slowly, like an animal stalking its prey.

I know what's coming, I can feel it as the space slowly closes in, and I don't back away like I thought I would.

She stands on her tiptoes, our bodies parallel to each other, and places her delicate hands behind my ears. Harper brings my face down to hers, our lips uniting in a way that feels more passionate and romantic than before.

The desire burns through me as our effortless kiss ignites into something I haven't felt in a long time. A hunger that grows inside that can only be fulfilled by one thing.

My fingers brush through her hair as I stumble forward, her back hitting the opposite wall in a loud crash. Our mouths are all over each other, messy and wet and coupled so tight we can barely come up for air.

"You better get going. I don't want to keep you any longer." She huffs, my lips moving from her mouth to her neck.

She releases a whimper when my tongue slides up her throat.

"You're right. I better get going." I threaten, my breath hot against her skin. I blow lightly on the dampness that I just left behind and her legs bounce against my knees.

"Sam, you have no idea what you do to me."

She yanks my head back to her mouth and we kiss each other one last time before I finally pull away and say goodbye.

CHAPTER TWELVE

───◆───

My flight is relatively painless from SFO to LAX.

During that time, I rehearse everything like I'm practicing for a job interview.

When I'm in the lobby of her office, I lose the element of surprise.

"Sorry, sir. She is taking a late lunch." The receptionist tells me.

Around the corner is a stylish place that boasts vegan and keto options. Their décor and hip company name screams, "we remain up to date with the latest food trends and we're not afraid to brag about it." I track Stella there since we follow each other's location.

When I spot her in the window, I pull out my phone and send a non-threatening text.

Sam: "Hey."

What happens next rips my heart out.

She checks her phone, reads the screen, then puts it back in her purse with a guise of annoyance on her face.

I resist jumping through the window like James Bond, traipsing up to her table, taking the phone out of her purse and slamming it into her face.

Instead, I take a deep breath and replay the words I planned on discussing with her, my course of action now weakened.

Ten minutes fly by and no response. I'm sitting outside, waiting for Stella to exit.

When Stella emerges from the café, I say as my father would, "Stella…"

She turns to face me, the shock still recognizable underneath her huge sunglasses.

I can see her forming incoherent sentences in her head. She's fumbling for words and I've never seen her so unprepared. She's exactly where I want her.

"Sam! What, what are you doing here?"

It's now that I realize she was eating alone. No friends. No Nathaniel.

"Come with me." I demand.

She follows and I hear her murmuring to herself. What she's trying to say, I will find out soon enough.

We find a quiet bench near a fountain across the street.

"What the fuck is going on?" I curse. "Why would you ignore my text? I saw you from the window. I'm your brother for Christ sake. How could you do that?"

I know I'm coming across defensive and placing blame, something I've learned you should never do in an argument, let alone with someone like Stella. But I'm not about to start this conversation out with an apology. Her coldness towards me changed my entire game plan.

"Sam, I didn't mean to ignore you. I just didn't want to deal with what you had to say right now."

"So, what? You were going to keep ignoring me? For how long?"

"No, I wasn't going to keep ignoring you. I knew you'd reach out." She laughs to herself as if she has everything sorted out.

"Fuck you, Stella." I've never said that in our entire lives and now I'm certain I've ripped her heart out.

"How dare you? You come here expecting an apology? Because you did nothing wrong and are *sooo* perfect?"

"Perfect? Where is this coming from? I know I'm not perfect! I was coming here to apologize, actually. But when you snubbed me just now, I realize I have nothing to apologize for."

"You *judged* me."

"And you've *never* judged me? Never once thought I was being an idiot? At least I can own up to me being a complete ass. You, however, are perfect and can't even take an ounce of constructive criticism. Whatever happened to me being the only man in your life? I thought my opinion would mean something!"

She's quiet, planning and manipulating her next sentence.

"Whatever happened to 'we only have each other'? My words count for shit now?"

"I didn't ask for your opinion about Nathaniel." She snarls.

"Well guess what, I gave it to you anyway. And you couldn't even hear me out. You hung up on me! That's no way to communicate with your twin brother."

I add that last bit about being siblings on purpose because the few people walking by probably think I'm an abusive boyfriend patronizing his weak girlfriend.

"Things are going perfect for me and Nathaniel, okay? Everything in my life is perfect. I don't need to hear any hurtful words about my future husband. Got it? If I ever want your opinion, I'll ask for it."

"You better ask your future husband to stop taking other women's phone numbers then."

Her eyes are super glued to mine.

"What did you say?"

"You heard me." I'm adding fuel to this never-ending fire, something I wasn't counting on when I decided to visit. I planned on remaining calm, choosing words wisely. Instead, I'm blasting her with anything and everything that comes to mind. I'm igniting this fire instead of putting it out.

"Nathaniel did not take someone's number. He would never do that to me."

"Well he took yours when he was seeing someone else. Oh yeah, he told me about that, too. This seems like typical behavior."

"I have to go back to work."

She gets off the bench and I follow her.

"Stella, stop! We can't keep doing this."

"Doing what?" She's so detached I actually want to smack some sense into her.

"Stella just stop!" I shout, causing a scene.

"Sam, keep your voice down!"

"No, I can't do this anymore. I need a resolution. I refuse to fight with my sister like this. I'm sorry for saying what I did about Nathaniel. You're right, it wasn't my place, but I thought you needed to know. I would like to know that about the girl I'm dating."

"You're dating someone?" Blood stops beating throughout her body because I can no longer see her pulse thrashing alongside her neck.

"Yes, since you asked. That girl I mentioned a few weeks ago… we've made it exclusive. I like her."

"Good for you. I'll be sure to dig up dirt on her so you know how it feels."

She starts to walk away and this is when I grab her arm.

"Will you stop? What is going on? Why can't you be

honest with me? I feel like you've been lying to me for the past year."

"Lying? Where did you get that idea? Everything is fine, Sam. Everything is perfect. I am happy with Nathaniel. You can have your opinions all you want, I don't want to know them. I love him. He loves me and everything is exactly where I want it to be. I'm… happy."

I keep a mental tally of how many times she just said *perfect* and *happy.*

"Stella, cut the shit. If you tell me you're happy, fine, I'll believe you. But if I find out you're lying about things and he hurts you, I will not only end him but I will be very disappointed in you; to the point where our trust may be broken for good. It's always a game with you and I'm sick of playing it."

"I'm happy Sam." She reiterates.

"Okay."

The birds serenade us with their happy chirping and I feel disgust deep down in my belly.

"I feel like things won't be the same after this." I admit.

"You're so dramatic. Things will be fine. Maybe Nathaniel and I can come out and meet this girl."

"Maybe." Now is my turn to be apathetic.

"Calm down Sam. We will always be there for each other. Haven't I always been there when you fucked up?"

She gives me a one sided frontal hug.

"Yes, but now I'm wondering if it was so you could rub my face in your accomplishments while I was wallowing."

"How could you say that?" She actually looks shocked.

"For your information, I'm actually happy too." I jab.

"You *are*?" She's in such disbelief. Where did it say in the cards only one twin can be happy at once?

"I am, believe it or not. You're not the only one that deserves to be happy."

"I know."

"So now what?"

"I go back to work and you…"

"I'll just get a hotel."

"Oh my god stop being so melodramatic you can stay with me. We are brother and sister. Bad times or not, we can always pick up where we left off."

She believes her own words but it's hard for me to feel the same. We've never had a fight like this and I've never cussed at her like I did. I feel terrible.

"You want me staying with you? After everything we said?"

"Yeah! As long as you don't take this out on Nathaniel…"

"Can't promise anything."

"Sam, seriously?"

"He better be respectful, that's all I have to say."

———— ◆ ————

I hit the gym to unload my repressed anger.

How can she just casually ignore Nathaniel's act of possible infidelity? She let that go like it was no big deal. I hope she's not used to this behavior.

When I'm in the locker room, I run into an old colleague of Stella's. We have many mutual friends and even though I haven't seen him in years, it's like old times.

"Sam! Don't tell me that's Sam Evans!"

"Jeremiah!"

We're both sweating through our shirts but we hug anyway.

"Dude, look at you! You're huge!" I tell him.

"You've gained some muscle, yourself."

"You're still at B&B?"

"I'm a lifer there."

"Still working with Stella?"

"We're in different departments now." Jeremiah wipes his face with his towel.

"How are things going?"

"Aside from my 12 hour days, I'm making six figures with no complaints."

"No kids?"

"Sure hope not. How about you?"

"I actually just started seeing someone. It's pretty new but I really like her."

"Good for you, my man. I don't have time. It's crazy

busy. This year has really launched B&B and we've had so much business."

"How's Stella doing?

"It's a hard job, man. From what I hear in the meetings, she's struggling. She's managing a lot and the guys above are thinking of pulling a few accounts from her."

"Shit, really?"

"It's a big job and big shoes to fill. Lucky she got that job when she did. I think they were desperate. And you know your sister, she practically moved into the office before it was even hers."

"Wow. I never knew."

"Well I better get going. You in town long? I'd love to catch up some more!"

"Yeah, for a few days. Hit me up, we can grab a beer at the brewery."

"Sounds good! Great to see you!"

Jeremiah grabs his gym bag and exits the locker room, both of us silently realizing we won't actually have time for that beer.

I can't fight this gut feeling like Stella is keeping a lot more from me. I've always been able to trust her, but thanks to the deceiving stories she's telling me, I'm wary about how close she and I really are.

First she changed crucial business plans for the brewery without telling me, then she lied about her relationship and all the facts surrounding it. How they met, how they started, even their connection now.

And now she's lying about her job? Is she not doing well? Jeremiah implied the timing felt rushed, was she a last resort? What doesn't she trust about me that she can't even be honest with her twin brother?

Her perfectionist attitude is strange and unchartered territory for me. We're human and we are going to fuck up, but she's so adamant that things are just perfect.

Harper's name appears on my screen and I answer the incoming call.

"Hey, you!"

"Hey, how's LA?"

"Would have been better if you came with me."

"You're a doll, Sam Evans. A 1000 page document just landed in my lap. I'm talking Game Of Thrones long. How did it all go?"

"I'm still trying to figure out what happened."

"Are things better at least?"

"Yeah, but…"

"Buuuuut?"

"I feel like she's keeping so many secrets. Maybe I never noticed but she's never been like this."

"Did you get closure at least? The fight is over?"

"I don't even know. Ooooh…" I growl at the end, wiping my eyes of the deceit lingering in my core. "I might stay a night or so."

"Okay, take your time. I'll be sitting here reading this enormous manuscript waiting for you to get back."

"Why don't you meet me out here?" It's a proposed suggestion, one I'm not sure I even mean when I'm done saying it.

"Haha, I wish I could…"

"No, seriously." I continue, reassuring myself this is a brilliant idea. "Fly out and we can drive down to San Diego for the day. Maybe stay a night or two in Coronado?"

"Wow, you're serious?"

"Hell yeah! Bring the book! You can read on the plane, I'll even let you read on the beach undisturbed. Can't promise I'll leave you alone in the hotel room though…"

"That does sound pretty enticing."

My brain flips like a rolodex confirming my schedule is wide open. "It'll only be a few days. Would your office even notice?"

"No, probably not. I'd have to work a little and answer emails though."

"I'll book a hotel right now. I'll rent a car, pick you up at the airport and we'll drive down together."

"Swear to god you're not ambushing me and making me meet your sister?"

We both laugh and I say, "Hell no. I would hate for you to meet her like this. I can tell something is up."

"I think I can make it work. I'll confirm tomorrow morning."

———◆———

When I'm in Stella's neighborhood and standing on her stoop, I suck in a gulp of oxygen necessary to get me through this deceptive whirlwind.

Stella and Nathaniel are actors in a movie and I don't have the energy to be a cameo right now. I forbid myself to pretend things are fine even though Stella said they were.

When I walk into her house, Stella's plastered smile resembles the Jokers. She even has the deranged personality to boot.

"Hey Sam!"

"What are you cooking?"

"I'm making pasta! Come in!"

She grabs my bag and puts it on the couch.

"Take your shoes off! Relax! Can I get you a drink?" She returns holding her own. "I'm drinking a martini. Want one?"

My liver withers into nothing and decides for me. "No thanks, I actually got pretty sick last weekend."

"Yeah?"

"Yeah, if Harper hadn't come over I would have had to call 911 I think."

"Sam, seriously? Why didn't you call me? That's horrible. I could have lost you?"

I love how she immediately thinks about *her*self and *her* loss.

"Would you have even answered?"

"This is different! That's serious. Shit are you okay?"

"I'm fine now. I threw up a lot and was severely dehydrated."

"Did you go to the hospital? Get an IV or anything?"

"I probably should have, honestly. But no. Harper showed up prepared and nursed me back to health."

She raises her eyebrows, an emotion transcribed on her face that I can't quite figure out.

"But anyway, I'm fine. I'm not dying, but I'm not drinking that's for sure."

"Well I have plenty of water so help yourself."

"Where's Nathaniel?" I ask, popping a grape in my mouth.

"He'll be here any minute. Went to go workout."

And like clockwork, the door slams open.

"Honey, I'm home." He croons.

"We're in here, babe!"

He steps through the door and is shocked to see me.

"Oh hey, what's up, Sam?" He looks guilty of something, and little does he know, I know more than he thinks.

"Not much just came into town for a few days."

He sets his gym bag on the chair next to me and pulls out another tub.

"Post workout." He states, grabbing a glass and filling it with water. "Glutamine, Amino Acids, tons of shit to keep my metabolism going but prevents tenderness in my muscles the next morning. It rocks."

"Do you get massive mood swings with that stuff?"

Stella and Nathaniel recoil, as though I just asked if they've done anal.

"Why would you ask that?" Stella questions.

"Just curious. A guy I know at the gym said that stuff is insane."

"I'm a teddy bear." Nathaniel confesses. "Don't you worry about me."

———— ◆ ————

"Can you believe it'll be 16 years that mom and dad passed away?" I announce, as Stella and I wash dishes.

"Makes me nauseous thinking about it."

"Harper lost her parents, too."

"Harper?"

"The girl I'm dating."

"Oh yeah. What happened?"

"There was a gas leak in the house."

"Is she covered in burn scars?"

"No, she was out when it happened but had she

stayed, she would have died, too."

I almost see Stella's rock hard heart crack.

"Wow, that's terrible."

"Yeah, no dad to walk her down the aisle." I smirk at her, implying I'm going to marry this woman, when honestly I haven't thought that far ahead.

"Stop. Seriously? You already want to marry her?"

"What if I did?" I egg her on, though seriously, I haven't even pictured this scenario in my head, and I probably should at my age. If I miraculously proposed before Stella was engaged, it would be the end of her world as she knew it.

"You've been together, what? A day?"

Little does she know she's actually accurate on her harsh guess.

"Tell me what's new these past weeks you've ignored me."

I'm purposely testing her, ready to see just how truthful she's willing to be.

"Work is stressful, not gonna lie." She admits.

The poison that was mixing into my bloodstream, creating a hate filled Molotov cocktail, filters out.

Honesty. Finally.

"No way, really?" I prod for more information.

"Yeah, it has… but I'm doing great. Nothing but praise. Everyone is happy with what I've done lately. All the departments say so. I can handle a little stress."

My heart deflates.

"Oh yeah? So you're doing even better than the girl before?"

"Sam, if we're being honest, I think they fired her on purpose so they could promote me."

"Is that so?"

"Well, that's what I think."

I nod my head and say nothing else.

"We're thinking of taking some time off and traveling."

"Could you do that? With how busy you are?" I ask.

"I think so. I submitted the request."

"Where are you thinking of going?"

"Nathaniel has always wanted to go to Thailand."

"Have you?" I accuse because I know for a fact Stella loathes foreign countries.

"I'll go anywhere with him. To the moon and back."

Her corny confession unleashes a competitive side that usually stays dormant.

"Harper is flying out here in a couple days. We may go away to Coronado for the weekend."

"Do I get to meet her?"

"Not yet. This is serious for me, truly. But when it gets really serious, I'll introduce you."

"Do you mean when it's love?"

"Yes, I mean when it's love."

We're in her guest room as she says, "Well knowing you, it probably won't get that far." She quickly adds, "Let's get breakfast tomorrow morning. Just us?"

"That'd be nice!"

"Perfect. We'll go before work. Sleep tight."

Chapter Thirteen

———◆———

The next morning, after our semi-normal breakfast concludes, I take a peaceful stroll along the strand.

Harper's name appears on my phone and I answer with excitement.

"Did you get the time off?" I ask in lieu of a greeting.

"I did! We are all set! I land tomorrow at 11:35am."

"Perfect! Are you all packed?" I ask as I take off my shoes and bury my toes into the warming sand.

"I haven't even gotten out of bed. I made all my arrangements from my laptop."

"It's almost 11am! I'm impressed."

"Well sometimes I like to be a bum, too. How's LA?"

"Good, just ended breakfast with Stella."

"Oh cool, is she there with you now? Tell her hey from your new girlfriend!"

She sings 'new girlfriend' and I smile into the sun as

a wave crashes behind me, spraying a mist of salt-water speckles on my face. I taste the sea when I lick my lips.

"She's already off to work. So how are you doing this morning?"

"I'm great! What's on your agenda today?"

"Walking on the beach on my way back to Stella's."

"Oh, how boring." She drawls sarcastically. "Did you make amends with Nathaniel?"

"Not really. I don't think he knows I have a crutch against him right now. They are so fake, Harper. He came home last night and did this corny 'honey, I'm home' bit."

She's quiet and I say, "Hello?"

"Sorry, I just, Sam she's happy right?"

I feel horrible immediately. "Yeah, so she says."

"So maybe let her be? It's not up to you to ensure she's being honest. You know what I mean?"

"I do, but I don't like the guy. They want to go on a trip to Thailand."

"Wow, Thailand? That's exotic! When? Did she invite us?"

"Ha, yeah right. Stella is going to pay for it all. I'm about to get to her house. Should I snoop Nathaniel's laptop when I get inside?" I'm half serious, but if Harper supported my idea, I probably would.

"Samuel no! Don't snoop!"

"I won't. It's probably password protected anyway." I sulk.

"Good, that's for a reason."

"Maybe he's one of those weirdos that uses 'password' as his password."

"Samuel!" She scolds me but laughs. "Don't give her fuel against you. You're better than that."

"You're right. Well you better start packing missy. Text me later."

———— ♦ ————

It's early when Stella drops me off near the airport the next morning so I can rent a car. By the time Harper lands, I'll have the car waiting outside arrivals.

"Text me later." She says. "I love when you come down and see me. I'll come up to San Francisco soon, kay?"

"Anytime! Pick the place and I'll be there."

We each give each other a quick kiss on the cheek and I step out of Stella's Model D Tesla and wave goodbye.

It's only 8am and Harper should be on her way to the airport. She hasn't texted, which isn't a big deal, but I follow up with her anyway.

Sam: "Hey what's your ETA?"

I finally get the car and I buckle my seatbelt as her text comes in twenty minutes later.

Harper: "Sam, I overslept and had to pack like a madwoman. I probably forgot a lot of stuff."

Sam: "Hopefully you forgot panties."

Harper: "I love where you're going with that. But I'm 99% positive I forgot the effing book that's sitting on my table."

Sam: "Oh shit, will you get in trouble?"

Harper: "Ummmmm... not technically. I'll have to read a ton of it when I get back and fake some edits that I haven't turned in."

Sam: "You don't have time to go get it?"

I'm in line for Starbucks now, desperately needing more coffee.

Harper's response is delayed again.

Harper: "Sorry got through security. No it'll be fine. Just gives me more time to devote to you without my panties."

Sam: "Well text me when you land. I'll be circling the arrivals. I'm in a white Mustang convertible."

Harper: "Oooh fancy."

Sam: "I know. Can't wait to get that top down."

Harper: "Mine or the cars?"

Sam: "The cars ;)"

Harper: "LOL!"

———◆———

When 11:45am comes, I'm parked at the curb outside her airline.

Harper: "Walking out."

The arrival doors open in slow motion as I see Harper waltz out like a damn movie star. The air blows through her hair with elegance, as if the god of wind conjured up a breeze just for her. She struts like a runway model and dear lord, she looks delicious. I half expect a hoard of paparazzi to show up wondering who this stunning woman is.

Her destroyed low-rise jeans hug her curves perfectly. Her white shirt is cropped just high enough to reveal a sliver of her toned and tanned stomach.

"Hey!" She squeals already opening up her arms.

Our embrace is one that is familiar yet so new. Our connected bodies create warmth that ignites my flesh. Our passion is a palpable wave of desire, consuming us both. I would gladly drown in this feeling.

"You smell amazing." I say as I sniff her neck.

"So do you. You smell like the beach."

Her lips are gentle and sensual as she kisses my neck, an act too intimate for an airport welcome.

"Let me get you to the hotel." I say roughly as I give her a quick smooch on the lips.

———◆———

The hotel door is barely locked shut as Harper strips me from my clothes.

She's feisty and clawing at my pants before I can even set my phone and sunglasses on the table.

"Where do you want it?" I ask her, reviewing the various places in the hotel room I could bend her over, spread her open, hold her against a wall.

"Sam, do you mean in the ass?"

We both start cracking up at the innuendo, but I stifle her laugh with my mouth.

I'm disorganized as I rip her clothes off, a seam tearing on her shirt.

Her bare breasts are soft and cool against my warm, hairy chest.

Harper's ass and back press into the striped wallpaper as I keep her parallel, pinned between my body and the wall.

My finger easily slips in between the warmth of her legs, my other hand restraining both her wrists above her head.

She pulsates against my hand, swollen and hot. She fights to move her wrists, maybe to guide my fingers to go harder, faster, but I keep her firmly in place.

She fidgets and squirms beneath my hold.

"Why are you resisting?" I ask.

"I want to come from your mouth." She says between exasperated breaths.

My finger glistens in the light and I bring it to my mouth and slide it through my lips.

"I will gladly taste more of you."

I bury my face in her. I can feel every ripple of pleasure hit her. My lips and tongue pinch and suck against *her* lips until she's erupting with satisfaction.

She finishes loud and hard, her fingers digging into my shoulder muscles as she hits the peak of her orgasm.

I wipe my mouth with the back of my hand as Harper forces me back onto the bed.

My dick might shatter from so much pressure and no physical contact.

Harper crawls over my body, her mouth hovering over my bare lap.

I drop my head back onto the bed and guide her head gently with my hands, the tips of her long hair tickling my stomach and legs.

She adds her hand to the motion and I feel like the bed might swallow me whole.

"God that mouth of yours…" I huff, unable to finish my sentence.

Her tongue teases the tip of my cock and I grasp at the sheets to control the climax building deep within me.

Harper's mouth is impressive and I grow more rigid and erect. My body tenses. My muscles contract.

My brain is swimming in pleasure when Harper lowers herself onto me, reverse cowgirl. The sight before me nearly makes me propose marriage just so she can be mine forever.

Her ass is all I see, bouncing on me up and down.

The loud smack that cracks the air is satisfying as my hand connects with her ass. I direct her hips at various speeds, my grip becoming more intense as I get closer and closer.

Harper's dirty talk and casual declaration about how badly she missed "my cock" makes my world detonate. I'm so deep inside her I wonder if it'll ever feel this insane again.

She's all mine and I relish in the fact that I'm the lucky one taking her to heights like this.

She grabs my thighs for support, her back curving and arching so I hit all the right spots.

Her second orgasm pierces the air with magnitude, so loud our neighbor pounds on the wall as I finish pounding her.

I hold onto her hips as I thrust into her with all the energy I have left. When my orgasm hits, it smashes through me like a relentless force. Every inch of my skin puckers and swells. I'm breathless like the wind got knocked from me.

It's only after she falls onto the bed next to me when I realize I just came inside her without a condom.

CHAPTER FOURTEEN

---◆---

"Fuck." I say out of breath.

"I know." Harper pants, her hand resting on her breast to feel her heartbeat.

"Fuck." I repeat, my tone less ragged and filled with fear.

"You okay?"

Harper props her head up with her resting elbow and tickles circles into my laboring chest.

"Fuck Harper... we... we didn't use a condom."

She stops circling her fingers and lies still.

"Ooh shit. I'm clean, I've been tested."

"Are you on the pill?"

"Of course." She concedes, wondering why I care less about the likelihood of gonorrhea and more about the probability of pregnancy.

"Do you take it religiously?"

"Of course." She repeats.

I run my hands through my sweaty, damp hair. My blood pressure is rising as I play out various scenarios in my head. I'm always so careful now, how did I do this?

Her voice is so calm. "Want me to go get Plan B?"

"No!" I bark, scaring her.

She removes her hand from my chest altogether.

"I'm sorry, Harper. It's just…"

She's quiet, worried she'll say the wrong thing.

"I just… I hate talking about this."

"What's wrong?"

I say the next sentence with extreme caution. "I got a girl pregnant a year and a half ago."

Her face is a combination of trepidation and acceptance. Like she just *knew* this couldn't be a perfect relationship and I'd have a secret child that I never told her about.

"Oh." She mumbles.

"She lost the baby." I add quickly. "My ex-girlfriend. And it was one of the worst experiences I went through after my parents."

"I'm so sorry."

I cover my face with my palm, willing this sensation of dread to pass. Harper doesn't say a word so I know it's time I finally tell her.

"We weren't together long. I was taking it pretty slow and casual. She was on the pill. I used a condom, she took plan B when the condom broke, and against all odds, she still got pregnant."

What I omit to Harper are the long nights I spent researching every possibility imaginable: from adoption to abortion. Neither of us was expecting to become parents due to a few months of no strings attached sex. We took every precaution and now we'd have this burden of raising a child for the rest of our lives.

Abortion was against Camilla's religion and morals, so that was not an option. She told me she was going to have the baby with or without me, but she wouldn't hold it against me if I didn't want to be a part of his life.

"Stella was furious with me." I continue, "She berated me on how I could be so irresponsible, which was a complete paradox considering I was everything but that in this situation."

"Sam, that's awful."

"Mistakes happen. Things like this happen every day. Condoms aren't 100% reliable. I didn't want this, but I was willing to be the responsible man she needed."

"She miscarried?" Harper whispers.

"She..." I begin, on the verge of tears. "She had an accident."

I rub my forehead, realizing aside from Stella, no other woman knows what I went through. Maybe Jake told Avery but this isn't something I talk about often.

"She was in her last trimester when it happened. She fell down some stairs. It was that simple. Nothing dramatic. No rhyme or reason. It just... happened. A freak accident like our parents."

"Oh Sam." Harper squeezes me, thinking she's heard the end of this nightmare.

"She was rushed to the emergency room. With the pressure and trauma to her abdomen, she was bleeding profusely. She wasn't even conscious. I arrived in time for the doctor to tell me the worst of it all. There was a placental abruption so the baby wasn't getting the oxygen he needed. He was alive but they'd have to do an emergency C-section for him to survive. And he... we found it was a boy after the fact... he would have..."

I choke out a sob.

"He'd have a handful of health issues from the lack of oxygen and brain damage. He'd live, but his quality of life was questionable. She had already lost a lot of blood but could recover if necessary steps were made. The doctor told me point blank I could only save one of them."

A lone tear cascades down my cheek. I was put in an unthinkable situation and I still feel like I'm judged for my decision.

"We didn't even have that talk." I say. "We didn't think we'd need to, you know? Save her or the baby? How do you make a choice like that?"

I remember the blank stare of the surgeon. I'll never forget it. He was so unsympathetic, no nonsense, all business. Time was running out for Camilla and I knew whatever choice I made would change both of our lives. How was I supposed to know I made the right one? My body broke into pieces and I wished they'd just take my life instead so our baby and Camilla would live a normal, happy life.

"I chose her." I state. "He had to save her. How was a guy like me capable of raising a special needs child alone without any experience or help? He was already premature and had so many disadvantages. The doctor warned me his survival rate past six months was questionable. I wasn't prepared for any of that. And... I loved her."

"You probably did the right thing." Harper consoles me.

"It didn't feel like it. After the surgery and she found out what happened, she didn't blame me, but I know she probably wished I had saved our baby, even with the disabilities I would have had to handle alone."

I tell myself any relationship facing those obstacles would deteriorate. Camilla's resentment and my guilt was a recipe for failure.

"We didn't last much longer." I tell Harper, my tone flat and emotionless. "I knew when the doctor told me to choose, no answer would have saved our relationship.

It became too much. We weren't the same people after. Our happy ending wasn't meant to be. Devastation and loss filled us to the brim and there was no room for love anymore."

Harper holds me tight, so tight I can feel her muscles straining but she suffers through it so I can feel her connection.

"Tell me what to do, and I'll do it. Anything."

"I don't think God would be so cruel to put me through this all again. We need to be more careful. I would hate for us to be put in the same position."

She nods her head against my skin as my heart beats like a drum against her cheek.

"You can tell me anything. I would never judge you, ever." Harper says, adding a delicate kiss to my fingers to seal her promise.

———— ♦ ————

Later that night, when I can finally breathe after that huge weight has lifted off my chest, Harper turns on some fun, lively music and dances around our hotel room in her bra and panties.

"This is the only other pair I brought so you better enjoy them while they last." She jokes.

"I'd prefer you take them off." I say from the bed, watching her bounce and sway to the music.

"Come take them off me."

I accept her request and walk over to her, my only clothing my boxer shorts.

When my hands reach the elastic trim of her lace thong, she grabs my hands in hers and dances with me.

"Tricked ya!" She laughs, forcing me to move along with the music.

I only dance when I'm drunk, so maybe it's the song choice or how Harper is so carefree and happy, but I oblige.

Our balcony doors are open and the music booms its melody onto the beach. The moon sparkles in changing shapes against the indigo tinted ocean waves, bursts of salty air drifting through the doors.

We both dance like fools, high with infatuation and absurdity.

I dip Harper graciously and she giggles when I bring her back upright, my hand in hers, leading the way. She's lucid yet drunk; letting go of all the strange emotions she and I were keeping from each other for so long.

I've never seen her like this before, so free. We are both laughing like idiots at the simplicity of the moment.

The music changes from fun and upbeat to a club song. Harper takes a big gulp of her champagne and does a seductive dance against my body. Her moves are more impressive than mine, and she can drop it low very well.

I grab her in my arms and we both fall hard onto the bed, laughing in our embrace as her chest bounces onto mine.

"I'm having so much fun with you." She admits.

"I am too."

Her nose is inches from mine and I can see the reflection of my face in her eyes. They gleam and sparkle with hope, hope that just because there was no room for love in my previous relationship, doesn't mean it won't happen again. Harper is slowly repairing all the damage from my past, creating a stronger heart that can love again, and more than likely, love her.

———— ◆ ————

When we land in San Francisco, I feel the excitement of the weekend slowly fade, as we have to get back to our lives.

"This was the most fun I've had in a long time. No technology, just relaxing, it was amazing." Harper tells me.

We both tilt our faces towards one another, eyes closed and lips pursed.

Harper licks her bottom lip when we disconnect, her forehead on mine.

"I better get up there. That manuscript won't read itself."

"Yes, get up there and read. I don't want you to get fired." I pause. "Or do I?"

She bonks her forehead lightly with mine and I laugh.

I take out her luggage and we kiss once more before my eyes follow her steps back into her building.

———◆———

The next day I'm thankful Jake and Diego could find time to sneak away for lunch so I can brag about my amazing weekend.

"I can't believe I flaked on brunch yesterday!" I exclaim.

"We texted you!" Diego informs me.

"Figured things didn't go well with Stella and you broke your phone."

"I contemplated calling the cops. Thought Stella might have killed you or something."

Jake rolls his eyes at Diego and I do the same.

"Dude, really?"

"We didn't hear from you! So tell us how it was."

"Things with Stella are fine. I mean, as fine as they can be. Things with Harper are... awesome. I can't believe how stupid I was to think I wouldn't want to settle down with someone."

"So when will Stella get to meet Harper?" Jake asks.

"It'll be a while. I already told her once it gets serious, then maybe she can. Harper is scared of her."

"Dude, I'm scared of her and I've known her my whole life." Diego claims.

"Be careful. Soon enough Stella will be bugging you to meet her. You won't realize how quickly the time goes when you're happy again."

———◆———

Harper's period arrives three weeks later.

And when it does, I can feel the weight of the world lifting off my shoulders. That was the final release I needed so I could give myself over to her completely.

Seeing her still excites me and I can only surmise the honeymoon stage is getting stronger as each week passes.

Weeks feel like days and I consider myself the luckiest guy alive. How on earth am I so fortunate to call this woman mine? Harper is fun, spontaneous, so intelligent, and brings out a side of me that was dormant for so long.

I know fairytales don't exist and that love develops over time, but there is something about her that makes this so different. No games, no devastation. Real life can't be like this forever, right? Things will eventually calm down?

———◆———

Week 7. That's when things finally begin to feel like real life and not some fantasy.

Snotty tissues create a blanket of snow on my counter-top as we discuss the facts.

"It's not even about the income." Harper cries. "It's the fact that I've never been *fired* before."

"Laid off." I correct. "It's not the same thing. Don't beat yourself up about it."

"It's practically the same thing!" Her tone is snarky and I chalk it up to embarrassment. "I feel like a loser. Who gets fired like that?"

I want to correct her, yet again, but I don't have a death wish.

"At least you didn't steal from them or burn the place down. They'll still give you a good reference, right?"

"They better. I did so much for them. This sucks!" She shouts burying her face in her used tissues.

"Let's go out. Let's do something." I suggest. "If we sit here you'll fall into that hole and it'll be a mess climbing your way out. Let me distract you for a bit."

Harper nods her head lightly and accepts the invitation.

———— ✦ ————

I'm the most unoriginal idiot ever to suggest taking Harper out with no real plan. I text Avery on the sly and she suggests the new spa that opened near the Bay.

Avery: "It's a girl's fantasy to go there. She'll love you for it."

Tittering with nerves at the mention of the L word, Harper asks, "What's so funny?"

"Oh, nothing." I lie, plugging the address in my phone with fidgeting hands.

When we park at the San Francisco Bay Spa, Avery wasn't kidding.

"Oh my God Sam, you are amazing!"

I check in at the reception desk, only now realizing this place could be booked. That would really win me points.

The young lady is very accommodating and patient as she looks for availability.

"If she hurries, we could do a facial in 15 minutes. And we could do a couples massage later tonight at 6pm, if you wouldn't mind waiting."

"Excellent!" I finally breathe.

"Great, I need a credit card on file and we'll set you up to get robes in the back."

Harper and I meet in the lounge in our robes.

"You look so cozy." I compliment.

"This is so sweet, thank you. This is just what I need."

"Don't think about anything while you're in there, okay?"

"I'll try not to, no promises." She huffs. "Now I can be a bum like my boyfriend."

Her smile is a little forced, but I appreciate her trying to make light of the situation.

"Hey, that title is reserved for me only, missy."

"I've never not had a job, Sam. Do I stick with the publishing industry or branch off? I don't even know what else I'd do."

She plays with the fringe on a pillow in her lap.

"Take it easy. If you're financially secure, take some time off. Don't rush it. Maybe we can go away for a weekend?"

"Anywhere with you sounds perfect." Harper snuggles into me and I hold onto her.

After her name is called, I pass the next hour checking emails and getting caught up with texts.

Stella texts to inform me she plans on coming into town next Friday. One of her last San Francisco stops before she leaves for Thailand.

Stella: "Think you're ready to introduce Harper to me yet? I'm dying to meet her."

Sam: "I'll think about it."

Stella: "Let me know. I come in around the same time. I'll text you the night of what restaurant I'm in the mood for."

Sam: "You got it. I'll let you know if I'll be coming alone or if Harper will be with me. She just lost her job so I doubt she'll be in the mood to socialize but maybe she'll need it."

I get another text and Harper sends a picture of her face covered in mud and two cucumber slices over her eyes.

Harper: "This is the best day. I love it."

She adds a kissy face emoji and immediately my heart goes into tachycardia. It's the same sensation I felt from Avery's text but overblown.

I take a screenshot of the tiny picture and the words Harper included.

I send it to Stella.

Sam: "Explain this to me."

Stella replies instantly. "She's falling in love with you. I told you."

She confirms my suspicions. Harper has been dropping subtle hints like this recent text; saying she loves something about me or something that I do, but refuses to say she loves *me*.

My phone is back in my locker with no response. I forgo going nude like a few other gentlemen walking around the spa, and keep my boxers on when I get in the jacuzzi.

I mull over my emotions as I slowly sink and relax into the scalding hot water, the jets massaging my back, as if hammering me with the shove I need to accept the reality I've been ignoring.

Harper and I have been together, whether it was friendship or relationship, for just shy of four months.

All relationships are different, and while it may take weeks for some, a year for most, falling in love is a process only you and that significant other can experience. Not everyone is alike and no two relationships will ever be the same. Love stories aren't black and white and right now nothing is gray about the situation I'm in.

I knew this was coming. Love. But I didn't think Harper would show signs now. I can't compare this situation to Camilla, or how Stella and Nathaniel became a couple, or how Diego and Valentina got engaged after three months.

Love can be accidental, intentional and for most, inevitable. And deep down I knew loving her was possible back at the hotel weeks ago. I didn't think I felt it until now when I realize how much I'd be willing to do for her just to make her happy. And whether Stella is right in her assumptions that Harper most likely loves me, too, it doesn't change my opinions of her.

I'm commando behind my robe as I approach the front desk.

"Would it be possible to get some champagne when my 6pm massage ends? I know it's last minute and I understand if you're booked after…"

"That is definitely doable, Mr. Evans." She confirms after looking at the schedule. "There is of course a charge, but we can bring a nice bottle of champagne and some chocolate covered strawberries. Are we celebrating anything special?"

"No, just trying to make a memorable day."

"Understandable. Would you like anything written in chocolate?"

———— ◆ ————

After I've had the best massage of my life, my mind is clear and my body is relaxed. Harper surfaces with sheet marks on her face.

My massage therapist places the tray and champagne on a small table and tells us we have the "Harmony Suite" for the next hour.

"Sam you didn't!" Harper removes the sheet to expose her naked body. She opens the sliding glass door that reveals a private Jacuzzi just for us.

The champagne is chilling in an ice bucket and I take the moment to scoop her up in my arms before she can grab a glass.

I'm naked as well, sitting on the massage table with Harper cradled in my arms.

"I'm sorry about today." I tell her. "But I want you to know, despite the misfortunes earlier, this is the happiest I've ever been."

She kisses me with such force we both fall back onto the massage bed, our lips still connected as we breathe each other in.

I didn't bring a condom and fear doesn't even enter

my mind as she straddles me, sliding down my erection, wet and ready.

Harper doesn't move and lets me rest inside her for a moment, neither of us speaking. She leans forward a little to kiss my lips, so sensual and soft.

She arches her back and slowly lifts her hips a little so I slip in and out of her, only a few inches.

I grab onto her to help but she stops me.

"No, let me do everything." She's soft and persuasive, so I don't argue.

Her movements are slow and steady, a rhythm so measured and exact that with each motion of her hips, I feel the pleasure strengthen.

I can feel everything, all of her, rubbing up against me as she holds onto my chest.

My hands are on her hips and the more I thrust into her, the louder she moans. She stifles it well, hunching over to my face where she buries her mouth into mine.

The fluidity of her on top of me is prolific, beautiful. I'm not sure what I did in this life to feel such happiness, but I *do* love her. I've never come so fast from movements so slow.

When we're done, the massage bed is a tangle of oily sheets.

"That… was… amazing." I'm panting, the pleasure still lingering on my fingertips.

Harper nods her head in agreement, unable to speak.

I yearn for the champagne and strawberries sitting near the door and I'm about to climb off to get them, but I'm stopped.

"I have to tell you something." She says with severity in her tone. She holds onto my face so our eye contact doesn't break. "We told each other we'd always be honest with each other, right?"

"Yes." I say, worried where this might be going.

"I have to come clean about something."

She's pregnant.

She wants to break up.

She really did get fired?

"Regardless of what happens after, I have to be honest with myself and with you." She pauses and I can't take the suspense. "I'm in love with you." She declares. "I've loved you for a while now. I know it's soon, and I know you might not love me back…"

"Give me a second," I say, realizing how terrible this looks, like I need time to process something so absurd.

I grab the tray of strawberries and bring it over to her.

"Look." I tell her, tears already forming in her eyes because who the hell could be this cold and walk away after a profession of love.

She peeks down. "I Love You" is written in chocolate on the metallic tray. Truffles and strawberries adorn the platter.

"What?" She's speechless.

"Harper, I love you too."

She laughs through her tears.

"Sam, really? You love me?" She cries, astounded I could love this adorable woman in front of me.

"You crazy?"

Her tears surprise me as they spill onto both our cheeks through our kiss.

"I don't know what to say now." She giggles.

"You've already said what I've wanted to hear the most. I love you. I can't resist you."

The sincerity and gratitude on her face is something I will never, ever forget.

"I love you, Sam."

CHAPTER FIFTEEN

———— ◆ ————

"Look, Stella, I'll talk to her, but if she doesn't come at least you'll see me there." I chastise over the phone.

"She's already making you choose between us. I don't like it."

I roll my eyes and choose my words with precision. "That's not it. You know how you are."

"And how am I?"

"Aggressive!" I remind her. "You scare people when you first meet them. I'll talk to Harper, I promise."

"You love each other already, I know it. You promised when it was love…"

Stella sounds like a damn whiny child and I release the phone from my ear.

"I will talk to her. Where do you want to meet tonight?"

"I haven't decided. I'll let *you* know when *I* feel like it."

She hangs up and I stare at my phone to confirm she really did end the call.

"For fuck sake!" I curse to no one in particular.

I rest my elbows on the window, peering down the multiple floors below me, willing the glass to crack and let me fall through. Plummeting to my death sounds more appealing than convincing Harper to meet my brat twin sister.

It's Friday night and Stella only has a brief window for dinner, which is a great excuse in case it goes south. I'm using Harper as *my* excuse because I'm sure she'd go willingly. It's me that's rehearsing different scenarios in my head.

What if Stella hates her? What if Harper realizes my sister is an evil witch and does force me to choose between them?

I bang my head on the freezing cold glass and try to think positive. What if they hit it off? What if they like each other?

Stella's face buzzes on my phone and I read her text.

Stella: "Come with Harper or not at all. I mean it."

My chest collapses inward and I instantly feel the panic creeping in.

I'm not about to let what I have with Harper become tainted due to my sister's cruel judgments.

I text Harper and close my eyes when I press send.

Sam: "Hey you, Stella is coming into town for a couple hours between layovers. She insists she meets you. How do you feel about that?"

Harper: "Aaaand that's a huge bomb to drop on me. LOL!"

Sam: "I know I'm sorry I kept hoping she wouldn't show up but she's coming. Tonight."

Harper: "Oh Jesus tonight?"

Sam: "Yes."

Harper: "Ummm…."

Sam: "If I sense any animosity upfront, we can leave."

Harper: "You think she'd be so upfront about that?"

Yes.

Sam: "No, she's probably very excited. I would love for you to be there."

Harper: "You want to go out in this storm?"

Sam: "Stop finding excuses!"

Harper: "LOL! I'm sorry, I just started sweating, I'm so nervous."

Sam: "It'll be okay. Stella hasn't chosen where yet or the time, so want to come over to my place and I'll drive us?"

Harper: "Oh Sam…"

Sam: "I'll warn her to be on her best behavior."

Harper: "Okay, I'll go. When should I be there?"

My chest swells back to normal and I'm grateful Harper is such an angel.

Sam: "Let's say 6pm just in case she lands early. Love you."

Harper: "Love you."

———————◆———————

I haven't heard from Stella all day, even after I sent her a non-threatening text message saying she better not screw up at dinner because I can't handle another disaster.

I could see her manipulating Harper into divulging something secret and private to use against her to prove Harper is incapable of making me happy.

She hasn't responded and I haven't a clue where we are meeting.

We switch between three restaurants and I have no idea which one she'll be at.

Harper knocks on my door right at 6pm.

When I open it, I'm instantly hit with a whiff of her sweet, pungent perfume.

"Well hello." I stare at her modest dress that still manages to showcase her hourglass figure.

"Hello." Harper walks in with her long legs that are propped up four inches higher.

She has a white pea coat draped over her arm and I'm thankful we can valet the car so she doesn't have to wear rain boots.

"You smell amazing." I grasp her neck and drag my nose from her collarbone all the way up to her hair, inhaling her scent.

She breaks out in goosebumps and I give her a quick nibble on her neck.

She pants, her body temperature rising already.

"You smell and look…" I slip my hand in the front of her dress and I can't finish my sentence when I realize she's not wearing panties.

"Are you trying to kill me?" I cup her skin and she backs against the wall for support.

"We don't have time for this." She giggles.

"It's fine, I haven't even heard from her yet. My phone is over on the table waiting for her to land."

"You're going to wrinkle my dress." She laughs again, not as aroused as I am.

"You'll look amazing no matter what." I shut her up with my lips so she can't protest any longer.

We make out in my entry but Harper pulls away a few minutes later.

"Let me at least put my stuff down. I got her a little gift and it's heavy."

I groan and bang my head against the wall next to Harper's head.

She walks into my place and sets her phone next to mine, draping her coat on the back of a chair. Her purse clangs loudly on my glass table.

"What did you get her? A brick?"

"A bottle of wine we can share at dinner and a cute little passport holder for when she goes to Thailand."

"That's so thoughtful."

"I'm so nervous. I need a shot. I'll drink anything right now."

"I have some gin?"

"Repulsive. That'll work."

I walk into the kitchen and pour us each a glass. When I return Harper is on the couch and I can physically see her apprehension.

"Hey, it'll be okay." I bend down on the floor and gently rub her thighs.

"I just, I love you so much. I want her to love me, too."

"She will."

"And what if she doesn't? What if she hates me like all your exes."

"Well I'll have some things to think about."

She takes the generous shot I poured her in one gulp and swallows with disgust.

"Oh, shit that's terrible." She wipes off the remainder on her lips.

I sip mine and check the clock on my wall. Stella should be landing around 6:30pm but I wonder if with this storm her flight might be delayed.

"Come here." Harper says, opening her legs as I kneel in front of her on my knees, her full and mouthwatering chest invading my sight.

She hugs me and trembles, poor thing.

"I promise, it'll be okay. Now kiss me."

Our lips connect and finally I'm able to continue the kiss from the hallway.

My hands run over every inch of her back, behind her head, and through her soft, curly hair.

My erection presses into her leg and I know we don't have a lot of time, but shit.

"We have time." I moan and lie between the brief moments our lips aren't smooshed together.

Harper sneers but doesn't react to my advancement.

"I'm serious." I say again. "Take off your dress."

She realizes I'm not kidding and looks at me in disbelief.

"If you want me so bad, take it off me."

She lifts her arms up and I slip it over her head and place it nicely on the arm of the couch, avoiding wrinkles. Although I'm horny as hell, I'd hate to ruin her nice dress.

She keeps her heels on and fuck. Her long, lean body being propped on those pumps is almost too much to take.

She releases my belt, grabbing the buckle and yanking it free from the belt loops around my waist. She's unhurried and methodical when she frees the button and undoes the fly, slowly reaching inside my pants.

"Is this what you want?" She caresses me in her one hand, her other slipping beneath my shirt, grabbing my chest like she knows I love.

"Yes."

"Do you want my lips?"

"Fuck yes." I demand.

My pants drop altogether and fall at my ankles.

She kneels down and takes me in that wet, hungry mouth.

Her red lipstick doesn't smudge and the sight below me is remarkable. Her savory lips devour me over and over and over again.

I grip the back of her head, guiding her mouth at a speed faster and more assertive. My fingers interweave within her loose curls and I can feel my knees buckle.

She keeps up well and I'm so, so close.

And then she stops. She gets up off her knees and shoves me roughly on the couch behind me. I recoil backwards, the pounding of my heart relocating its beat to the head of my dick. I feel like someone poured ice water all over me. The sudden halt has me speechless.

Dropping my head back on the top of the couch, I can feel blue balls looming. Harper leaves for the kitchen to get who knows what.

But soon enough, she's back, taking another revolted swig of the alcohol.

And finally, before I know it, she's wrapping her legs around my waist as I glide into her.

"Holy fuck." I roar.

She's on me, working those hips, letting me guide her as I lift her at her underarms with ease.

She's resisting an orgasm, letting the pleasure build and build.

I refuse to finish before her, so I let her enjoy it, willing her to lose so I can hear that sweet voice of hers scream my name.

She's a determined one; I'll give her that. She never takes this long and for a split second I feel like I'm losing my touch.

Harper rocks her body in my lap and I realize I need to change positions so I can get her closer.

"Oh Jesus." Harper shrieks, completely taken by surprise at my strength.

I stand holding her at the hollows of her knees, forcing myself to fuck her like I never have, maneuvering my technique with vigor. I'm carrying her entire weight and she's still not there.

"Stop fighting it." I order, realizing she might outlast me and I can only hold her up for so long before my arms will lose feeling.

She must have been waiting for my permission, because moments later she cries, "Oh, oh... I'm going to come, Sam."

And when she does it's the most rewarding and satisfying moment.

To feel her entire body quaver in my arms, knowing I hit her g-spot just right that I made her burst like a water balloon, spilling all over my groin, is gratifying.

I'm not ready yet, also fighting it, as I push into her over and over. I don't want this moment to end and I'm not about to back down now. I'm going to make this memorable.

Sitting back on the couch I let her grind into me, working her hips like a stripper.

She's pulling off moves I've never seen in my life and my breath is lost along with every thought going through my head.

"Just like that." I demand. "Yes, just like that."

By the time I realize it's too late, no going back, I force myself as deep as I can go, practically weeping to get this intense of a release.

"Fucking Christ, Harper…"

I grab hold of her and dig my fingers into her as I finish.

When I can think again, comprehend time and life, I seize her in my arms.

I leave small imprints of my lips into her damp, sweaty neck, feeling guilty her hair has lost some of its curl.

"You look amazing."

"I'm sure I look like I've just been fucked." She breathes loudly.

"You have a dirty mouth, young lady."

"You seemed to like it tonight."

"I loved everything about you tonight."

She gets off my wet lap, gleaming with all kinds of moisture.

"Where are you going?"

"I need to clean myself off."

"Let me come with you."

I splash some cool water on my face and pat the back of my neck.

I keep an ear out for my damn phone but get silence in return.

"Where are we meeting tonight?" Harper asks.

"No clue. You going to be okay?"

"Yeah, that little romp helped settle my nerves."

"*Little* romp, huh?"

"Yeah, little." She winks at me.

"Fucking you for 30 minutes is little?" I say as I check the clock again.

I do a double take.

"Jesus Christ it's 6:45pm already?" I shout.

Rushing to the kitchen where my phone is, I press the lock button over and over.

Nothing.

"No, no, no." I repeat.

I can hear Harper approach behind me.

"What's going on?"

"How did we fuck for that long and I didn't notice the time?"

"Your phone never pinged. She probably hasn't

landed yet because of this storm."

A miniscule piece of me is relieved, she's probably right, but that doesn't change the fact that my phone is dead.

I silently pray for the next minute that when my phone finally does turn on, there are zero text messages.

"Can you check her flight? See if it was delayed?" I request.

Harper's fingers work in a frenzy and she pulls it up instantly.

"Which airline?"

"Alaskan Air."

"And what time was she supposed to land?"

"She always takes the one that lands around 6:30pm, why?"

"One landed at 6:15pm and another is landing at 7:55pm."

"Well she can't be on the 7:55pm, that's too late."

"The previous says it was ahead of schedule…"

"Oh mother fu..!" I blast obscenities but stop short when I sense Harper's trepidation. I don't think she's quite up to speed with the ramifications we are about to face.

My phone finally lights up, the Apple logo frozen for centuries.

When my home screen appears, I feel like I'm in the clear when seconds pass and nothing pops up.

But I spoke too soon.

My phone pings so many times I throw it across the room.

"Oh shit."

"Did- did we mess up?"

I nod my head as she walks over to my wrecked phone.

Half of the top is protruding out, and from what I can see in the spider web cracked screen are multiple notifications.

"3 voicemails and 10 text messages." I want to cry, a tear threatening to escape from the corner of my eyelid.

Harper is clothed and trying to console me.

"Is it too late? Can we go to the restaurant?"

"I don't even know which one she's at."

I open the text thread and close my eyes in fear.

Stella at 6:10pm. "About to land. I see my previous text didn't send. We took off early. Everyone boarded on time. Can you believe it? Where do you want to meet?"

Stella at 6:15pm. "Well since you can't decide let's go to Flannigan's. I want a burger. Getting a cab now."

Stella at 6:20pm. "I just called you and it went to voicemail. Where are you?"

Stella at 6:30pm. "Okay what the fuck? Did Harper back out and you didn't want to tell me?"

Stella at 6:40pm. "I'm at Flannigan's and you're not here. I've left you another voicemail. Sam where the fuck are you guys?"

Stella at 6:44pm. "Please don't tell me your pathetic little girlfriend got cold feet and you're running late."

Stella at 6:47pm. "I'm kidding she's not pathetic but fuck you where are you? Text me or call me back dammit!"

Stella at 6:50pm. "Don't even bother showing up, it's too late. I can't believe you. You made me look like an idiot."

Stella at 6:52pm. "You better be in the hospital, I swear to God."

Harper and I read them together, her eyes glossier than mine.

"Can we, can we like meet her at the airport?"

"It's too late." I say pessimistically. "She's going to kill me for this."

I dial her number and it goes straight to voicemail.

"She's already on her flight or she turned off her phone."

I feel sick. I've been on this emotional rollercoaster for too long, sending my stomach heaving over hills of sadness and regret.

"Sam, what can I do?"

"Nothing for now. I'll call her in the morning."

"Sam, I…"

"It's okay. I'm going to take a shower. Can you stay by my phone and answer if she calls or texts?"

"Of course. Take your time."

When the glass walls in the shower are fogged up and ambiguous enough to hide my frustration, I let out a disparaging snivel under the running water.

This night was supposed to be perfect. Stella and I are finally on good terms, I'm in a love with a woman that makes me happy again. Yet right now it feels like a step backwards.

Stella is going to be furious with me. I *could have* gotten in a car accident and she'd still be upset with me. When I tell her my phone died she's going to tear me a new asshole.

I told you to get a new phone. You're so stupid, Sam. So unreliable.

I dip my head low and let my chin hang near my chest, the pressure of the water beating against my back. Droplets trickle into my eyes and I let them mix with the tears fighting to break free.

"Sam," Harper enters and I bring my head up. "Hey, I thought maybe you should text her since it won't show she got a missed call. I don't want her worrying about us."

"Good idea. Can you tell her we are fine and I'm so sorry? I'll make it up to her."

"Of course." She walks halfway out the door but turns back. "She knows this was a simple mistake, right?"

"She won't see it like that. She'll think I did this on purpose."

"That's horrible! Who would be so cruel…" Her sentence ends early. She covers her mouth to prevent any other damaging words from coming out. She already read the nasty texts. I can't imagine what negative judgments are going through her head about my family.

"I'll handle it, don't you worry about a thing."

———◆———

It's been two weeks and I haven't heard a word from Stella. Nothing.

No call, no text back, no email, nothing. She could have gone to Thailand already and I would have no clue.

The only thing keeping me distracted is that Harper is currently in Texas for a job interview. Luckily, this is keeping me preoccupied because my mind is running from a million questions.

Is this when things get really serious? So serious that she might need to move in? Or worse, relocate with her? What does this mean for me? For us?

Stella is purposely ignoring me, but that won't stop me.

I open up Nathaniel's text thread and as much as I don't want to do this, I text him.

Sam: "Hey man, how has Stella been?"

He replies instantly.

Nathaniel: "We are kind of fighting right now. Things haven't been so magical if you know what I mean."

Sam: "Oh? Anything I should be concerned about?"

Nathaniel: "Just life. It'll work itself out. You know when she gets in these moods."

Sam: "Oh yeah. Should I come down?"

Nathaniel: "No. Give her some time. Work has been up her ass about every little detail right now. She's kind of a wreck. Thailand is in a few days and we're just trying to get through the drama."

I can't bear knowing my sister is hurting and I can't do anything to pacify her. But then again, I've reached out. I've done what I could. It's her choice to keep rejecting me.

Sam: "I refuse to let this continue with her in Thailand. I won't allow it. I'll come down there if I have to."

Nathaniel: "Sounds coo. Take care of yourself bruh."

I don't dignify that odd text with a response, so I set my phone down.

Stella is a wreck. I knew it. I send her one last plea before I give up for the week.

Sam: "Stella, this is the last time I'm reaching out. We can get past dinner. You know it was an accident. This is not the worst we've been through. Text me back."

Of course there is silence, deafening silence.

Later that night, when I know Harper is settled in her hotel room, I call her up.

"Hey, what's shakin' in Texassss?"

I hear her adorable laugh echo in what sounds like a bathroom.

"Are you in a bath?"

"You know me too well. Yes, I unpacked and I'm soaking in this giant tub. You should be here with me."

"I wish I was."

"Any word from Stella?"

"Nope, I spoke to Nathaniel today. They are fighting and work is a nightmare."

"Poor girl. She needs her brother!"

I hear splashing on the other end and I tell her to get some sleep. "It's late so I'll let you go. Call me tomorrow if you need help studying interview questions. We can do a mock interview. I'll be your boss. You can say 'yes sir' to me. I think I would like that."

"I bet you would... sir."

"Miss you, love you, Harps."

"Love you, Sammy."

The next morning I reach my hand over the bed to rub Harper's bare back, but I realize it's empty. I grab nothing but cool sheets.

It's odd when you're used to a routine and that routine is interrupted. Harper's interview is tomorrow morning and I'm not familiar with her being gone. I sit up in bed lost for a few moments.

As I'm buttoning up my jeans, ready to head out for the day, I hear my phone ringing.

I'm not as eager as I should be, but when I see Stella's name appear, I run for my phone.

"Stella?"

"Sam!" She cries, and I can instantly tell it's not an excited cry. Something is wrong.

"Stella? Stella what is it?"

She's sobbing hysterically on the other end, and if she were capable of speaking, I don't think I could understand her anyway.

"Stella, breathe. What is going on?"

"Sam, Nathaniel…" She stops.

Nathaniel? What did that fucker do?

"Stella, did he hit you? Were you fighting? Talk to me!" Flashes of rage enter my mind, Nathaniel hyped up on those supplements, beating the shit out of my sister. I go into panic mode, steam coming out of my ears like a cartoon character. My fists clench on instinct prepared to kill anyone that gets in my way. I'm sweating everywhere. A cold sweat that has me freezing and melting with hot anger inside.

Her wails have intensified and I can't understand her, "No… Nathaniel he…"

My sweat turns to droplets of ice and I calm down. I don't have to kill him. I can breathe again.

"What is it? Did he break up with you?"

She's hyperventilating now. The quick inhales coming so fast I don't think she's exhaling anything. Her breath is so inconsistent I fear she might pass out.

"Oh shit did he propose?"

"No!" She screams.
"Stella what is it?!"
"Nathaniel is dead!"

CHAPTER SIXTEEN

---◆---

I blink rapidly hoping this will somehow reset my brain. "What do you mean he's dead?"

"He… he…" Stella releases a bloodcurdling scream and goosebumps break out in a rash all over my skill.

I'm outside my body watching this happen; it's surreal and frightening.

"Stella?"

I hear muffled screams in the background, like she's screaming into a pillow, possibly suffocating herself. Someone else picks up the phone.

"Hello?" A gentleman asks.

"Who is this?" My voice is so rough and sounds nothing like me.

"This is Officer Lims. I'm here at Stella's residence. We just gave her the news that Nathaniel Teague was found dead in his car."

I refuse to believe it.

"No, I spoke to him yesterday." I disagree, like me speaking to him yesterday can't possibly mean he's dead 24 hours later.

"I'm sorry sir, but there was a car accident this morning and he was inside."

It takes all my strength not to let the phone slip between my fingers and crash onto the floor.

"No." I repeat, covering my mouth with my other hand as I shake my head. "How?"

"He crashed his car into a light post. We will investigate but it appears to be accidental. No other cars were involved or skid marks of other tires, just his. The paramedics that took his body out said there was vomit inside the car. I know it's early to say, but I'm guessing a heart attack hit him? We will know more when…"

"Sam! Sam! A fucking heart attack? This isn't happening!" Stella steals the phone back and I can finally interpret a fraction of what she's saying. "Sam, I can't deal with this, I'm going to die."

"I'm on my first flight out. I'm coming to you."

She's still crying and I hope that the police officer is comforting her somehow because I know all too well that inherent loneliness creeps inside her soul.

"Sam, fuck what if I did this? What if I made him have a heart attack?"

"Stella, that's impossible. You didn't *make* him have a heart…"

"We had sex this morning. Right before he left for the gym." She's whispering now, like the cops might hear her confession and arrest her on the spot. "He was so out of breath I have never seen him like that. Doesn't that happen in the movies? What if I did this to him?"

"Stella, have a friend come over. Can anyone stay with you until I'm there?"

"I have no one!" She bellows. "Oh Jesus Christ I have no one."

"Stella," my voice cracks and I try to keep my composure. "Ask the police officer if he can stay with you for a few hours. I will be there soon."

"He has to take me to identify him. Oh god, Sam what if it's not him? Oh please say it's not him." Her tone changes from suicidal to hopeful.

"Take your time, if you could wait a few hours for me to get there, I'll go with you."

"What if it's not him?"

"Wait for me, okay?"

———— ◆ ————

I miraculously get the last seat for a flight leaving in five minutes when I arrive at the airport. When I get through security, no luggage or carryon, I run to the gate and see two flight attendants waiting for me.

As I trip and stumble through the narrow aisles, passengers shoot judgmental and curious looks my way.

Who is this asshole holding up our flight for 20 minutes? Who doesn't travel with any *baggage? A terrorist? An air marshal?*

I'm at the very back of the plane sandwiched between two portly men whose elbows dig into my triceps. They could be sitting on top of me or I could be strapped down to the left wing in a harness for all I care. Any discomfort that would normally piss me off is nonexistent in this moment.

I pull out my phone, the only thing I brought, and realize I never told Harper. Crouching low like I'm tying my shoelace, I dial her number.

"Hello?" Harper sounds groggy and I'm sure I woke her up.

"Nathaniel is dead." The bluntness of my words crush me.

"What?"

"Stella called me. Nathaniel crashed his car. I'm about to fly out to see her."

"Sam, hang on. Did you say dead?"

"You heard me." It comes out nastier than I intended.

"No. No, how the hell did he crash his car?"

"I will know more details when I land. I'm sorry I told you, I don't want this news to ruin your interview tomorrow…"

"Screw my interview. Do you want me to meet you out there? What can I do?"

"No, you need to go. I would hate for you to miss it and realize it was a waste of time coming out here. Let me figure out what's going on and I'll get back to you as soon as I know."

"Oh Sam, I'm so sorry. Just…" I think she's crying and it rips me apart knowing there's nothing I can do for anyone. I'm useless. "Tell Stella I'm thinking of her. I know they are empty words but hold her tight."

"I will. I gotta go the plane is moving. I love you."

"Love you, too."

I'm jittery the entire flight, bouncing my knees up and down, stomping my feet into the cabin floor. We hit turbulence, but in reality, I think it's me shaking the plane.

I pound a few water bottles and prepare myself for what's about to come.

When I land, LA is a haven of sunshine and blue skies. I think I pass Justin Bieber and hordes of paparazzi in the airport but I run past him and hail a taxi.

When he arrives at Stella's in record time, I pay him extra because he ran multiple red lights and risked a speeding ticket for this.

There are two cop cars with flashing lights and I swallow the giant lump in my throat.

I'm two steps up her entrance when the door bursts open and she runs into my arms.

Our embrace is depressing. She's as light as a feather as I carry her inside, her legs dragging below like a limp ragdoll.

Two police officers sit at her table with cups of coffee that I'm sure they had to make for themselves. Stella would never have the decency to offer a beverage even in her right mind.

Stella crumbles onto the floor, slipping from my grasp quicker than I can catch her.

"Oh god Sam, this has to be a dream." She cries in a heaped mess.

I scoop her into my arms and carry her onto the couch. The police officers are completely immune to the grief filling the house. They deal with death every day; this is nothing new.

When we are all sitting in the same room, I prepare myself for the hard facts.

"I'm sorry for your loss, Ms. Evans. I am, but we have a few questions to ask." An officer begins.

Stella is comatose, barely conscious with a voided stare in her dark eyes. I've never seen her eyes so black.

"Please tell us what happened before he left. We want to establish a timeline. Did he seem okay? Did he normally leave at that time of day?"

She's deaf and mute. I wrap an arm around her and give her a nudge.

"Stella, what happened? Tell me what happened. You said… you said…" I don't want to outright say they had sex just in case it's not relevant.

"Ms. Evans, was he acting weird? Having trouble breathing? The EMTs suspect a heart attack but it could be anything. Brain aneurysm, fell asleep at the wheel. We aren't thinking suicide only because there was vomit in the car. And his pants were soiled, which isn't always a rare thing when people pass. The body gives up and…"

She has dissolved into nothing. I've never seen tears form and fall so fast.

If I could assault a police officer without ramifications, I would. Stella did not need to hear that last detail.

"Oh God, why? Why would you do this to me?" She wails. "Take me instead. Take me now."

"Stella," I remain as calm as I can handle.

She refuses to answer any questions. She can barely breathe.

"We can get information later." The officers are impatient and annoyed. "But we need you to identify him down at the hospital."

"I can't, Sam, I can't." She acts as though the officers aren't even in the same room. She talks to only me.

"We'll go now." If Stella does have any hope this

might not be Nathaniel, we need to end that immediately.

I have to drag her into the car like my child. Stella won't stop crying and it brings back memories of when our parents died. I'm fighting everything I have not to cry with her. If she sees me break down, she'll know it's over and he's really dead. If I can prolong this for another 15 minutes I will. I don't want her to accept her new reality just yet.

She's glued to me. If I move, she moves with me. If I wipe my forehead, she clings onto my wrist. If I stop walking, she stops right beside me, our hips joined like Siamese twins.

We're in the basement part of the hospital where the morgue is. It's everything I expected it to be: cold, morbid, and dreary.

The white tiles shine gray due to the lighting and Stella can barely put one foot in front of the other.

When the police officer stops us behind the double doors, Stella turns to run, but this time I grab her.

"Stella, I'm sorry this is happening. I am, but we *have* to do this."

"You do it. I can't. I can't face seeing him dead. I can't."

I let her go and tell the police officer, "I'll do it."

When the white sheet is pulled back, a swollen, distorted face stares blankly back at me. I want so badly to say it's not him, but it is.

I nod my head dejectedly, the tears stinging my eyes.

The pathologist covers his body and the other police officer with me asks, "So you confirm this is Nathaniel Teague."

"Yes. It's definitely him."

They both jot notes on a clipboard, making check marks and weird scribbles that make my brain ache.

"I'll pay whatever it costs to find out what happened."

"Sir," the pathologist begins, "There are protocols and tests to run. Most times it takes a month or longer if there are additional tests and that's if the state forensic examiner even approves this autopsy. Most are done for homicides or victims of violence."

"I don't care." I shout. "She needs closure. Find out if he had a preexisting heart problem or brain aneurysm or whatever else it might be. I'm sure he had insurance."

I leave the room with haste before they can tell me no.

Stella's in the women's bathroom when I exit the double doors. I can hear her wails and cries from where I stand.

I walk in anyway and see her huddled in the corner of the last stall.

I open the unlatched door and her face has become

unrecognizable as well. Her skin looks so saggy and ragged from crying.

She knows based on my face the answer to her nightmare.

———————◆———————

Stella passes out on the ride home and I gently place her upstairs in their bed.

When I'm downstairs alone, I don't know what to do. My first instinct is to passionately remove all his pictures from the house so she's not reminded of this terrible day, reminded of the great life she once had.

But was it great?

When I texted Nathaniel, he told me they were fighting the day before.

I'm hoping she'll come down with a case of amnesia because I know the second she wakes up she'll wish she never did. I experienced this for years when my parents passed. The pain never goes away, but as you continue to live out your days, you begin to notice the hurting lightens. But Stella has already accepted and dealt with our parent's death. Nathaniel's is a new wound that may never heal.

I'm sitting in her empty, quiet kitchen, the two dirty mugs of coffee sitting on the counter. The least I can do is clear her dishes.

Her calendar is on the fridge and I see all the plans they had for the rest of the month. Thailand.

It's then that I realize she might not have called work to tell them what happened.

When I find her phone, I dial Bateman & Busey and ask to be connected to her boss, stating it's an emergency.

"Larry speaking. "

"Hey Larry, it's Stella's brother, Sam."

"Sam Evans! It's been a day. How are you?"

"I'm sorry to call you like this, but Stella's not doing well. Nathaniel died this morning."

"Nathaniel Teague?"

"Yes, sir. I doubt in her frame of mind she called to let you know why she hasn't been in today. I'm guessing she'll need the rest of the week off. Maybe longer. What's your bereavement policy?"

"I'm sorry, son, I'm not following."

"Well, she's going to need some time off to grieve. Use up her PTO."

"No son, Stella doesn't work here anymore."

If my heart was intact enough to rip in two, it would.

"What do you mean she doesn't work there anymore?"

"Well, neither of them do." Larry continues. "Stella was recently terminated and Nathaniel took an unpaid leave of absence."

"What do you mean she was terminated? Fired?"

"You better ask her the nasty little details. Please send our condolences to Stella. I'll update HR with Nathaniel's passing. If they need anything else, I'll have them call you. Gosh, I'm so very sorry, son."

I hear an abrupt click of the line.

Her home screen reappears and I'm left stunned.

Fired from her job?

Everything has been a lie. All of it. Her perfect relationship. Her advancing career. Nothing was real. How was it so easy for her to lie about it all?

With her phone still in my hand, I open her and Nathaniel's text thread and read.

Their words are ice cold. The act they play in front of me dies as I read their true selves from last night's conversation.

Stella: "Where are you? I can see your location and you're not anywhere near being home like you said."

Nathaniel: "Spying again?"

Stella: "I wouldn't have to if you'd just talk to me."

Nathaniel: "You never have anything nice to say to me. I've had it."

Stella: "Oh stop, like you even notice me anymore. You're so preoccupied with other shit. No wonder you were forced on a leave of absence."

Nathaniel: "Oh and like you weren't fired a week ago? Did you think I wouldn't notice? I still talk to people there, you know. Nice try pretending they forced you to take vacation."

Stella: "Wow, so you do have a brain. But unlike you, I have money in the bank."

Nathaniel: "At least I'm rehireable and got letters of recommendation out of this."

Stella: "And to think Thailand would have been a good idea."

Five minutes later.

Stella: "Why does it show you near apartments? Who are you with?"

Nathaniel: "My ex, Liz. Where the hell do you think I am? The gym!"

Stella: "You're such an asshole. Don't ever bring up her name again."

Nathaniel: "You started it."

Stella: "*You* started it."

Nathaniel: "I don't have the energy for this right now."

Stella: "Ya sure? You take so many supplements I'd think you'd have the energy to last all night. And I don't mean sexually."

Nathaniel doesn't respond.

Their last words are harsh and cruel; I find it hard to believe they had sex this morning. Was she lying about that, too? *Should* I be worried?

The house feels dead and empty. Stella could float

down the stairs like a ghost at any moment and catch me going through her phone, so I set it down.

I'm lost now. I can't accuse her of compulsively lying over and over when she's dealing with this tragedy. It'd be insensitive of me to question her about being fired while she's grieving.

Stella's happy life was all an act.

———————◆———————

The next morning I wake up first.

When noon rolls around and I haven't heard so much as a floorboard creak or the toilet flush, I peak my head in to see if Stella is hungry.

"Stella? Can I make you any lunch?"

She's awake but not conscious if that's even possible. She's lying on her side, her face a blank expression.

"What can I do?" I ask.

I sit on the edge of her bed, putting my arm around her shoulder. She's dressed in the clothes she wore yesterday, as am I.

"Sis, tell me what to do. What's the next step? Should I call his parents?"

Her silence is maddening. I'm doing my best here and it's barely getting me by.

My warm hand cups her frail shoulder and I shake her lightly. "Stella…"

I picture her splintering into a million pieces, like shards of a broken mirror.

"Don't call his family. I'll do that." Her voice is flat and detached.

"Let's eat something. You need to eat."

"I'm fine."

She won't even look at me.

"Stella I called your office…"

This wakes her up faster than a double shot of espresso.

"What? Why!"

"I told your boss what happened and figured you'd need some time off. But then I found out you don't even work there anymore."

"Sam, I… I can explain."

"You don't have to explain. But why wouldn't you tell me? I'm your brother. I'm here for you."

"My life is falling apart." She bursts into tears and she finally lets me hold her. "Nathaniel and I were going to break up. He was doing something shady at work, but they couldn't prove it. They said if he left voluntarily, they'd give him letters of recommendation. Just as long as he didn't bring about a wrongful termination lawsuit. I was let go a little after. I couldn't keep up."

I hold her tighter, probably more than she can take, but she can't feel anything right now anyway.

"I was messing up so much." She sniffles and wipes her nose. "I ruined a huge account. I don't even know how it happened, I sent them the wrong contracts and it was a disaster. They were competitors and saw what we were offering the other in terms, incentives and stipulations. They were both pissed and backed out. It got out of control out of nowhere. Nathaniel is dead and I'm going to be alone forever."

"You won't be-"

"I forced him to have sex with me!" She shouts. "I knew it would probably be one of the last times. He was so unhappy with me. Do you think he killed himself?"

"I don't, but we'll see what the autopsy says."

"I'm going to be alone forever." She repeats. "Who would want a psycho like me?"

"You're not a psycho…"

"I'm on medication."

"What?" I say, stunned.

"I've been on meds ever since we were 20. But I haven't been taking them every day like I should."

"What kind?" I took sleeping pills when my parents passed so I wouldn't be surprised if Stella was taking something to ease the pain or depression.

"Mood stabilizers. I was diagnosed with depression, anxiety and cyclothymia. I never wanted anyone to know. After mom and dad died a school counselor told me to go and get help. I'm fucked up. So fucked up in the head. I stopped taking my meds because I just wanted to be normal like everyone else."

My chest is heaving like I got the wind knocked out of me. "But why couldn't you tell me? I've told you everything. Everything, Stella. What I went through with Camilla, the shit relationships I ruined, the depression with mom and dad. How am I supposed to support you if I know nothing but lies?"

"I wanted to have the perfect life. I had to have something to hold onto, even if most of it was exaggerated. I made it that way. And now it's all disappearing. I have no one. I'm so unhappy, Sam."

She's hopeless, her eyes the same shade of black as yesterday.

"Stella we have to figure out what to do. I don't know what to do."

My phone buzzes in my pocket and I ignore it.

"Just let me sleep. I don't want to wake back up." She dramatically throws her duvet over her head and hides from her problems. And for now, I allow it. She needs to go through the steps, and if anger is the current stage, then so be it.

"I'll check on you soon."

I go downstairs and return Harper's call.

"Hey, I'm so sorry I haven't called."

"How are you doing?" Harper asks.

"Terrible. I feel horrible for Stella. Nothing I say helps. I'm sorry I never called back yesterday."

"Sam, don't. Never apologize for something like that."

Gratefulness blooms in my heart. She is so understanding.

"She's a zombie, Harper. I don't know what to do. I'm giving her space but I'm so scared she'll hurt herself. She's not speaking."

"I don't even know what to say."

"Stella was fired." I profess. "I feel like I don't even know her anymore. She has lied about so much. Nathaniel was cheating on her with someone at work. He was suspended and forced to leave the company."

"She told you all this?"

"I looked through her phone. Their last exchange was terrible."

"Oh, Sam. I wish I knew what to say to make this better. I feel awful."

"I'll call you later, okay? I can't even think right now."

Chapter Seventeen

---◆---

Stella's bedroom door creaks open when I stick my head inside. Her blankets slowly inflate against her body as she breathes.

She's still alive.

I'm a cop overseeing a prisoner on suicide watch. Do I take away all sharp objects? Hide the bottle of Tylenol PM in case she wants to overdose? Never leave her out of my sight? The moment she wakes up for good I'm going to force her to eat.

Stella's phone is still sitting on the kitchen table and I open it again.

This time there's a new text. From a number not saved in her contacts.

But the second I see it, I recognize it as a number I'll never forget.

Camilla.

Why is Camilla texting Stella?

I'm going to need a heart transplant when this is all over. How it's even pumping blood and functioning is a giant mystery.

My hands shake when I open the thread.

Camilla: "I just heard about Nathaniel. I'm so very sorry, hon. I'm thinking about you. We've been through a lot but I care about you. I don't hate you like you think I do. I forgave you a long time ago, for everything. If you need someone to talk to, I'm here. We've both experienced accidents and loss, and if you need someone to talk to, I'm here."

And now my heart has burst into a million pieces. It's destroyed.

What is there that Camilla needed to forgive? What is she talking about?

I nearly knock the door off the hinges when I burst into her room.

She jolts awake and waits for the aftershocks.

"What the hell, Sam?"

"No, what is this?"

I throw the phone at her and it lands perfectly in her lap.

I watch her eyes scroll through the text. Her face is a Rorschach test, blending from confusion, to shock, to fear.

"Sam, I don't even know who this is."

"It's Camilla."

"Camilla? I don't know what she's talking about. I don't even talk to her! How would she know about Nathaniel already?"

"I don't care. What is she talking about? She forgives you for what?"

"I don't know!"

"Stella, I'm not stupid. What did you do to her? What don't I know?"

The stranger crumpling in front of me is foreign. She can't be my sister, my twin, my other half.

"Sam, I don't know what to say."

She's shaking terribly, my typically assertive sister now disintegrating before my eyes.

"What did you do to her?" I repeat.

Stella starts crying. Ugly crying. Snot is dripping out of her nose and I'm ripping in two. I want to console her; she just lost her boyfriend for Christ's sake. But she's lying about something big and I can't take it anymore.

"Tell me!" I roar.

"Camilla…" Stella begins hyperventilating. "Camilla she… when she fell… it was at Bateman & Busey."

My blood turns cold. "What was she doing there?"

"She came to see me because I was planning a surprise baby shower."

"So what is there to forgive?"

"I don't know why she'd say that! I didn't push her!"

The fact that Stella has to specify that she didn't push her suggests something suspicious.

"What *did* you do?"

"Sam, please..."

I launch towards her, my face an inch from hers. "Tell me what happened."

"You heard what happened. A guy tripped into her and they both fell down the stairs."

"Why does there seem to be something missing from the story."

"Sam... please."

"You tripped him on purpose, didn't you?"

The world stops spinning and everything is in slow motion.

Her silence confirms Jake and Diego's suspicions.

"I fucking knew it!" I shout.

"I'm sorry! I didn't think. I wasn't thinking! But why would Camilla text me? I haven't spoken to her in forever and why would she even say that?"

"How could you do that to us?"

"Sam, I'm sorry!" She uncovers herself and begs on her knees, literally begs. "Please forgive me. I'm so fucked up."

"Do you know what I went through? What if I would have chosen the baby? You would have killed Camilla! You basically killed my baby, Stella!"

My insides are scorching with rage and despair as

Stella continues sobbing on the floor.

"I have to get out of here." I declare.

Stella runs after me as I run faster than her down the stairs. Her skinny legs can't keep up.

I grab my phone and head for the door.

She's already standing in front of it blocking my escape.

"Please don't leave me, too." She cries, her arms and legs spread like a railroad crossing.

"I can't do this!" I shout. "You're crazy. I always defended you, but how can I now? Everyone that has left you had a good reason. You're toxic. All you care about is *your* life. I'm finally happy and you manage to ruin everything whenever this happens."

A vibration in my pocket brings me back to reality.

"Now I know why my friends hate you. They suspected this, did you know that? When Diego and I showed up at the emergency room, when I was busy choosing who to save, Diego heard the guy saying he got tripped out of nowhere. He kept repeating it. I refused to believe a thing."

Taking out my phone, I see Harper's face smiling at me from an incoming call.

"Harper is calling. I have to go."

Stella grabs my phone from my hand as I go to turn the knob.

"This, this is your girlfriend?" She shows me the

phone, Harper's adorable face filling the screen waiting for the call to be accepted or denied.

"Yeah?" I go to grab it from her but she's quicker than me and guards it with her life.

She swipes right and answers.

"Liz, is that you?"

Liz?

"Stella, give me my phone!"

"Liz? I know it's you! How did I not see this coming?"

"Stella you're fucking delusional. That's Harper. Give me my phone!"

"This isn't Harper!" She shouts, finally looking at me. "Her name is Liz! She's Nathaniel's ex. She just so happens to *also* be the girl I got fired so I could have her job. What the fuck are you doing dating her?"

INTERMISSION

———◆———

Liz

Well fuck.

Yes, it's true.

All of it.

You might need to go back to the beginning to better understand where I'm coming from.

———◆———

My parents didn't die in a gas leak like I said; as much as my heart wishes they had.

No, they are alive but I like to pretend the lies are indeed my reality.

Theodore and Clara, aka mommy and daddy dearest, are the kind of people that should have never procreated.

My conception was a complete accident.

To be honest, I'm surprised they didn't terminate the pregnancy. They had a hard enough time keeping themselves alive. Who knew they'd take the challenge of a small, innocent baby?

I learned at an early age I was different, regardless of my living conditions and upbringing. Teachers told my parents I was highly intelligent but lacked empathy and social skills. I wasn't like the other kids in my classroom.

I lied. A lot. Especially about my home life.

No one knew my parents were abusive. It was a game for me to see how long I could survive without getting CPS called on us.

And it never happened. Not once.

A bipolar mother and alcoholic, drug addicted father was a recipe for a not so perfect offspring. I carried the weight of mental illness with me as a looming shadow my whole life.

I was great at manipulating my situations and I became accustomed to taking care of myself.

As far back as kindergarten, I remember getting ready by myself, making my own lunches, and walking the mile to school every day.

Teachers had no clue I was living with abuse.

But I adapted.

When you're like me, you learn to adjust to your surroundings and make it work.

In spite of the neglect, I didn't want foster parents.

The system would probably see right through me: the vulnerability, the lying, the inability to form friendships. I'd be put on medication and forced to see therapists and that did not sound appealing.

As long as I kept up my good grades and *appeared* happy, I flew under the radar.

The mind games and mental abuse taught me to never trust anyone. Everyone was capable of destroying you. A liar became easy to spot thanks to paying attention to people's behavior, quirks, and tells.

As I got older, I refused to see a physician about the mistreatment I suffered as a child. Though the physical abuse was rare, it happened. It made me who I am today.

I'm calculated and careful, but not afraid to take risks.

I'm not violent by nature, but I'm not against seeking revenge.

I have a fucking conscience and I do feel emotions, but falling in love isn't easy.

As I grew into an adult, I discovered these traits carved out a successful future if I knew how to apply them accordingly.

Financially I did really well, but I wasn't accountable with my money and didn't know how to save or pay bills on time.

I excelled with all my responsibilities, but pushed colleagues away in the process.

And when I met Nathaniel, I saw narcissist qualities within him, but I knew how to control him.

People like me get bored easily. And I knew I wasn't cut out for a boring, typical relationship. I needed stimulation and excitement. Passion and fire.

Nathaniel kept things interesting and he was the first man I ever fell in love with.

We were dating for six months when an opportunity within his company presented itself.

He was reluctant in the beginning. He didn't love the idea of us working together, but when he found out the salary, he was suddenly very supportive.

Bateman & Busey was the company you always dreamed of working for. And miraculously, Nathaniel put in a good word and I got an interview.

I charmed the pants off those fortune 500 fucks.

My experience, education, vision, and creativity was exactly what they were looking for. Internal candidates couldn't captivate them like I could.

And one of those hopeful employees was Stella Evans.

Little did I know, that promotion was all she ever wanted. And since I inadvertently stole it from her, it was a formula for instant adversaries.

I didn't go there looking to make friends in the first place, but I knew from her spiteful and envious tendencies there was no point winning her over.

I knew a fellow psycho if I saw one.

But let's start with Nathaniel.

Was our relationship perfect? Of course not.

Nathaniel liked to brag that he was head photographer at B&B. He was an assistant. He embellished his salary and could barely keep up with our bills.

He was arrogant, self-centered, and suffered from severe mood swings.

By the time this foreign feeling came over me, I didn't realize it was love.

Honestly, I think he saw me for who I truly was. Though we never talked about it, there was an unspoken agreement that we were both damaged goods.

He was supportive at first.

My 60 hour work weeks were unbearable, but I had a lot to prove in my first 90 days.

But Nathaniel didn't like that he was no longer my priority. My attention was elsewhere and I was too busy to notice him beginning to stray.

I found out later on that he was cheating on me behind my back for weeks.

And who was it with? Stella.

When I found out, I assumed we'd work through it. I could handle infidelity. I've had my share of mishaps throughout my life. No one's perfect.

Stella must have gotten inside his head during that time, because when he finally got around to talking it out with me, he told me he didn't love me.

He said things that would make any woman cry.

I was cold hearted. Bitter. Negative. A liar (that was rich, coming from him). I was impossible to love.

I did not cry. Not even when he packed up his stuff and moved in with her.

So this was why people suggested never working with your boyfriend. Because when he inevitably becomes your *ex-boyfriend*, you still have to see his face every fucking day.

I contemplated handing in my resignation. But I wasn't a quitter.

Stella and I still had to work around each other. She would intentionally make easy tasks 10x harder. She'd set me up for failure and I had to be on my toes constantly, waiting for the next hurdle to come at me full force.

She'd lie to other departments about my ideas and then take credit for things I implemented.

Rivalry to this degree was tolerable. I handled it like a champ.

And then the bomb happened.

I remember it like it was yesterday.

———— ♦ ————

I'm sitting at my desk, finishing up a new contract when the page comes in.

"Liz, will you come to my office? It's urgent."

"Sure thing." I say, noticing a hint of command in my boss, Larry's, voice. His tone is different. This must be important.

Entering his office with curiosity, it's peeked when I'm met with Marcia from HR and Tom Busey, the CEO.

"Hi everyone." Their severe expressions are impossible to read.

"Take a seat, Elizabeth." Larry says.

My boss calls me by my full name and at that very moment my sweat glands flood. This isn't good. His jaw is clenched and his posture is very tight and erect.

"What's... what's this about?" I stutter but ultimately keep my cool.

Marcia speaks up. "Ms. Baker, as you might be aware, Larry has been receiving some unwanted attention by an anonymous coworker."

I suppress rolling my eyes at such a trivial topic.

"I know." I pause. "Is this about my work on the Simmons account?"

"No," Larry grumbles.

"I'll be asking the questions for now, okay Ms. Baker?" Marcia continues.

I want to rip her tarantula eyelashes off her face.

"What do you have to say about the unwanted attention, Ms. Baker?"

"It's distracting for the team. Especially when he finds love notes in the middle of a meeting."

"And what happens when he finds those notes?"

"I assume he reads them and throws them away?" I question. How the hell would I know? "It's not my business."

I try to remain calm and ignore the bubbling rage waiting to surface. This is wasting my time.

"Really?" Marcia rebukes. "So why did you send an inappropriate picture of yourself to him?"

"What?" I shriek.

Marcia flips over a few papers, revealing an x rated picture and accompanying text thread.

Back when I was with Nathaniel, he asked me to send him a picture of me touching myself at my desk. I was working really late, the office was practically empty, and so I did it.

My dress was pulled up, my thong to the side, and my fingers touching myself. My stupid fucking name badge was visible but I didn't think anything of it at the time. Because I'm looking at it now on an 8x11 piece of paper.

Marcia glares at me like I'm the office slut.

The exchange is one text bubble: "Thinking of you." Sent this morning.

I feel the atmosphere change as the pieces begin to fit. He wouldn't.

"I never sent that to you, Larry." Immediate denial. Good, Liz. "You think I'm stupid enough to do that?"

"We never said you were *stupid*." Marcia chastises.

"But this is you in the picture. You admit that?"

"Yes but…" I'm cut off.

"And you think this behavior is professional?" The revulsion in her voice is infuriating.

Marcia is searing a scarlet letter into my chest with that lazy eye of hers.

"Excuse me," I snipe with the hostility I've been doing so well at hiding. "Now is my turn to ask the questions. Larry, have I ever been inappropriate with you when we've been alone?"

"Don't answer that." Marcia holds the reins.

I now see my final paycheck poking out of the stacks of papers.

"I'm sure this is a fireable offense, but I swear to God, I'm being set up. I would never do something so careless to jeopardize this amazing opportunity." I'm yelling, unable to control my temper, the beast emerging. "This is bullshit!"

"Don't raise your voice to me, Ms. Baker. We've already confirmed this is your cell phone number. Don't deny it." Marcia sanctions. "We do not tolerate sexual harassment of any kind."

"I never sent it! I swear! I don't even have the original message in my phone! Someone must have done it!" I sound insane. "You have no other proof I was sexually harassing Larry!"

"You're telling me you didn't send him a dozen white roses with a note saying, 'Fate brought us together. I need you more than you realize. I just want you to love me.'"

"You think I'm *that* desperate for a man I have to send ambiguous messages? If I wanted Larry I'd just tell him, and I don't."

"You say that, but we investigated the order and the florist said it was purchased by Beth B."

"So what!" I shout. "So my name is Elizabeth Baker. So fucking what!"

I will never, ever beg for anything in my life, and I'm not about to start now.

"She's not going to admit it." Larry hisses under his breath.

"We don't need much else. In a case like this, the picture is enough proof." Marcia states. "Your employment contract is terminated."

When I reach over the desk to accept my final check, I receive it with a shaking hand.

My body is betraying me and alluding to my apparent shock.

I search for Larry's reprieve. He didn't truly believe I did this, right?

"You will pay for this." I amend. "I will fight this."

"Yeah, yeah, wrongful termination. You can go ahead and try." Marcia mocks me. "Sexual harassment cases are very hard to win."

I'm speechless for the first time in my life. No

witty comeback. No vengeful plan immediately taking shape.

That bitch Marcia actually has the audacity to have security watch over me as I pack up my desk.

What little belongings I brought are instead thrown away in my wastebasket.

I don't want to ever remember this place or the few possessions I collected while being here.

As I'm escorted out, I pass by Stella's empty office.

She's probably rejoicing in the break room, no doubt the rumor mill already spreading that I was fired for indiscretion.

Nathaniel set me up. There's no other way around it. Fucking coward.

This morning while I was in a department head meeting, I bet Nathaniel went into my office, took my phone, and sent the picture. I knew I should have gone back to get it. And even more so, I knew I should have changed my passcode after we broke up. I have no way to prove this. Even if I could, what little evidence I have no one would believe me.

"One second," I tell the security guard. "I'm just leaving my cell phone number."

He assumes nothing and I'm in Stella's office alone.

I rip off a sheet of paper with malice and leave her something else.

"I know what you two did. This isn't over."

I fold it up and leave it on her corkboard amongst the pictures of her and her brother in front of a brewery.

"Bitch." I mumble under my breath.

When I throw her pen back, it lands on her huge desk calendar.

Taking a closer look, there's tiny scribbling on the right corner of the paper.

"125698", my passcode, is written in chicken scratch.

That fucking bitch.

———————•———————

I tried to get past it. And I almost did, until I realized I was blacklisted from any job I applied for. The #metoo movement worked against me. I was labeled a sexual predator in the industry and was unhireable, despite the confidentiality of the termination.

Everyone knew what I supposedly did. Larry was labeled a victim of harassment and played into it for sympathy. Everyone knew my name and what I had done. I was finished.

Larry had to get therapy to deal with the destruction I brought to his life and marriage. His wife showed up at my apartment and threatened to "take me down." Larry was the least of my worries. A pawn.

I was after the Queen.

Stella.

She ruined my relationship, my career, and fucked with my livelihood.

So here I sit. Six months after being wrongfully terminated in a new city with a new name.

My appearance has changed. I've lost some weight, dyed my hair and formulated my plan.

I never imagined Stella and Nathaniel would last. I *definitely* didn't think Stella would indeed get my job after I was fired.

They must have been desperate.

These six months weren't wasted.

No, I spent my time drilling into Stella's behaviors and trying to figure out how I didn't see her coming.

We both toe the line of crazy, so how did I manage to let her fuck me over twice?

Revenge has been on my mind for what felt like years.

My life was obliterated.

Nathaniel said I was impossible to love.

I'm about to prove them both wrong.

ACT I - HARPER
CHAPTER ONE

———— ◆ ————

I grip the white porcelain sink, both hands squeezing the edge as I look at myself one last time in the mirror.

Hair, perfect.

Makeup, flawless.

Cleavage, strong.

This is your last chance. Don't screw this up, Liz.

I flip my hair back and give myself a giant fake smile.

"Here we go."

When I exit the bathroom, I clutch my purse with white knuckles.

There are so many people here that I'm worried I'll never find him. This place doesn't have a dance floor, yet idiots bounce together like an orgy as I make my way through the bar.

My high heel punctures someone's toe and I hear her screech but I keep on walking. I don't have time for false apologies because there. He. Is.

I stop abruptly as I take him in, drinking alone at a table.

I'm standing from afar, watching, waiting for my moment. His look of impatience confirms he's waiting for someone. If it's a date, which I doubt because he hasn't been on an official date in months, then I'm screwed. I've already waited long enough to go this route. It's now or never.

He's on the verge of leaving and I know this is my only shot. Whoever he's waiting for isn't showing up and his drink is almost gone.

I make my move.

"Are you Matthew?" I ask hesitantly but with flirtatious inflection.

"I can be Matthew?" He flirts back, so cocky right off the bat. But he has earned that right.

He guesses about my blind date, like there would be any other reason I'm asking a stranger for his name. When he confirms he's not Matthew, I look into my purse, making sure my cleavage is in line with his eyesight so he can get a view of my goodies.

Ask me to sit down already!

"Have you called him?" He asks instead.

No! What the fuck? You're not supposed to suggest

me calling him! You're supposed to invite me to sit with you. Shit!

"He's not answering my texts." I lie, because there is no Matthew.

"Well hey wait a minute. Have a drink with me. I have this entire table to myself. Let me buy you a drink. Not all men are assholes like Matthew."

I bite my lower lip so I don't burst into creepy, maniacal laughter that would likely scare him away.

"You're not waiting for your girlfriend?" I ask, ensuring some whore doesn't come and ruin everything.

"No, I can assure you, I do not have a girlfriend."

Fucking. Perfect.

But, I mean, I already knew that. I know more than he realizes.

I accept his offer.

"I'm Sam, in case you didn't hear me earlier."

We shake hands as I tell him my name, my fake name. The contact of his skin on mine feels like a dream. I've envisioned this moment so many times and it's finally happening.

"So, Harper what do you do in San Francisco?"

I pull out my mental script and rehearse it perfectly.

Our conversation is flowing easier than expected. Even though it's small talk, Sam regales me with things I've already known for weeks.

I purposely order the nicest vodka this place has, just to see if he'd balk an eyelash. Nope. He is rich and doesn't mind spending money to get what he wants. And hopefully, that's me tonight.

He's eating up my words like a hungry, horny animal.

I realize now is a good time to light the fuse.

"I grew up around books my entire life. My parents owned a bookstore so I would spend all my days reading while they worked."

"That's so cool. Do they still own it now? Back in Maine?"

"No, unfortunately they passed away when I was young. I used some of my inheritance to buy a condo here in the city. Otherwise I'd never be able to afford to live here."

I wish I could take a photograph of his face. It's a blend of shock and disbelief.

"My parents died when I was a teenager." He tells me, a detail I'm already well aware of.

Kind of sad he doesn't suspect anything.

For this to work, I had to ensure this tragic, fabricated detail would reveal itself on day one.

We both have heartbreaking, broken pasts. Not many our age experience such a tragedy. He doesn't know it yet, but I'm creating a world where this chance encounter will turn into everything he's looking for.

———◆———

My drink is now room temperature as I let Sam get pretty intoxicated in case this doesn't go as well as I'm playing out. He might be too drunk to remember this in the morning.

Sam's glass is empty and I wonder what our next step will be.

"Hey, maybe that's Matthew." Sam points to an unsuspecting man at the bar. He's alone and I want to burst into distrusting laughter.

The bill is left on the table and Sam grabs it. I try to pay anyway, even though I only have a five dollar bill and maxed out credit card in my fake Louis Vuitton wallet.

We're outside and if it were even possible, all the oxygen has left the area. I'm taking short breaths in hopes he doesn't realize I'm silently praying he takes me home.

And he does.

———◆———

Two hours.

That's how long I last before I almost completely ruin everything.

Sam is driving us to his condo, a district of San Francisco I'm familiar with. My place isn't too far from him, and I've taken many trips past his elaborate skyscraper in hopes of getting further than the lobby.

There's so much traffic for a Friday night and he's taking all the wrong streets.

"It would be faster if you took Fremont to Folsom", I practically confess like the deranged stalker I am pretending not to be.

I bite my tongue before the words depart my mouth.

How am I supposed to know where he lives?

We've never met before. Everything is new to me. I'm a stranger.

I'm concentrating on the other cars because the last thing I want is for Sam to get a DUI or kill us both.

I'm tempted to jump him in the parking garage, give him the element of surprise, but I hold out until we're out of the elevator.

By the time he unlocks the door, I'm already entering his mouth with my tongue.

His body language reads unsuspecting, but his frame immediately hardens in all areas: his muscles, his posture, in his pants.

He lifts me with ease as I wrap my legs around his waist.

His lips and tongue are delicious and his kissing style is so aggressive that I have my work cut out for me. I'm supposed to be in control, I'm supposed to be the one setting the tone. But the way he grabs onto me and lowers me to his bed, spreading my legs open, I'd bend backwards for him.

I didn't think I'd be enjoying this as much as I am. I can see how much he wants me. I can feel how badly he wants me now that he's in my mouth.

My heart is beating so loud I'm scared he'll sense my apprehension and call it all off. I'm still fully clothed but that is quickly rectified.

I'm vulnerable as I stand here naked and exposed. He scans my body and his expression mirrors the face of a man that just saw the Mona Lisa in person. He stares at me like I'm a work of art. He wants me. Needs me. Craves me. It's a lovely feeling being desired.

He pushes me back on to the bed and wraps his impressive dick in a condom.

The heat swelling between my legs grows as he yanks me to the edge of the bed.

He makes me beg for it, and I do.

For a split second, before he enters me, a million scenarios run through my head. What if he lasts 10 seconds? What if he's absolutely terrible in bed? What if he's into kinky shit I'm not comfortable with? What if he doesn't even finish at all? What if I have to fake an orgasm?

That last one is quickly redacted within three minutes. Holy shit. Sam got me off so hard and so fast that I'm nearly incapacitated. I don't know if he was showing off or that's how he normally performs, but fuck.

All the other what ifs disappear, too.

Of Life

I hate myself for even thinking for a second that my experience with Sam would resemble my time with Nathaniel.

Men like Sam are gifted with the stamina, girth, and moves that would impress any porn star. He has every right to be cocky, confident and then some.

We both fall asleep right after but I'm suddenly awake and turned on just thinking about what transpired hours ago. I lift the sheets with caution and gently step each foot to the floor.

Sam is breathing lightly beside me and I have to be extremely vigilant now that my time has come to snoop.

I tiptoe to the nightstand.

His phone.

I double-check that it's on silent before I unlock it.

No pass code.

"Thank you, Jesus." I mouth while doing a Hail Mary.

I turn the brightness to the dimmest it goes and I take it into the bathroom.

It's dark yet the intensity of the dim light is still extremely risky. If Sam got up to take a piss I would have no warning. Unless he breathes like a bear when he's drunk, he could stumble in here and find me spying. Game over.

I give myself a full minute to go through his texts to Stella.

Most of it is boring. They talk about the brewery, Sam promises he'll visit soon, Stella brags about how amazing work has been.

It takes all my strength not to purposely drop the phone in the toilet. I feel my skin turning bright red with fury and I scroll through more of her bullshit lies.

Onto contacts.

Camilla.

She's still there. In a perfect world, he would have deleted her and their past.

But this isn't bad news, per se. If I see her as an eventual threat, I'll just block her.

I check his apps to make sure he isn't hiding a Facebook profile or Instagram account that I don't know about. Nope.

I'm not a contact on his phone, yet, so it's not like I can share his location to spy on him. That will have to wait.

I close out all his apps and charge it, you're welcome, and set it back on the nightstand.

Contemplating my next move, I realize I'm still bare ass naked.

Where are my things?

I spot my dress in a rumpled pile on the floor, next to his boxers and pants.

His pants have a bulge in the pocket and I immediately pull out his wallet.

I would never stoop so low to steal from him, but I do count the cash.

Who the hell carries $578? It's like you're begging to get robbed.

Aside from this being a one night stand, he didn't treat me like one. Sure, maybe he wanted to impress me so he could go all the way tonight, but I genuinely felt like he was interested in me. And the fact that I had an orgasm out of this speaks volumes. He's not a selfish bastard. He wanted to please me; though it didn't take a lot of effort since he knows where a woman's clit is.

Plus, he didn't kick me out, which has me guessing if he has ulterior motives.

Please don't suffocate me with a pillow in the middle of the night.

Unwrapping the sheets, I climb back in bed just as a siren erupts in the city. The weight of my body hitting the mattress harder than expected causes Sam to shift in his sleep.

My body lays frozen solid, my lungs turn to concrete, unable to breathe.

He's awake.

I'm facing the other way on my left shoulder, but I can feel his eyes on my back.

What do I do? Is he going to finally kick me out? Choke me with the sheets?

Before he can decide, I can hear his head relax back onto the pillow.

Hopefully the sex was good enough to ask me out again.

———————◆———————

My internal clock has me waking up at 6am on the dot.

Sam is still sleeping and I realize I better get the hell out of there. One-night stands don't usually end with the woman's makeup smudged into his pillowcase.

I find scrap paper in his kitchen and write a quick note on it, along with my number.

My panties are torn but I wrap the note inside it anyway and place it under the duvet near his feet. I know easy women don't usually make it to another date, but I have plans in place.

By the time my dress is back on and my shoes are in hand, Sam rustles awake and gawks at me as if I might be a figment of his imagination.

He's probably thinking "did this bitch really just spend the night?"

"Oh, I'm so sorry to wake you!" I say.

"It's cool. I'm up at this time anyway."

Lies. I bet he sleeps in until 11am every morning.

Sam emerges from the wrinkled sheets and I see his full, naked figure in the light.

His body is incredible. Better than Nathaniel's and I never thought that'd be possible.

His muscles are so proportional and trim. I want to rub my hands all over him until I can memorize every inch and curve so I can mold him from clay. His chest is hairy but it's not wild because he probably trims it. His abs are so well defined and I don't think he's even flexing them right now.

His dick is hard again and the ache between my legs throbs. He fucked me so good last night and I don't think I could physically have sex again. It's been so long and I'm already sore.

I foolishly reject him and if I was able to feel any guilt, I would for him now.

No one has probably ever said no before.

When he walks me to his door, I need to leave a lasting impression.

I swallow my pride... and more of Sam than I ever thought I would.

CHAPTER TWO

———◆———

An Uber is waiting for me as I step onto the sidewalk.

Sam knows my name, has my number, and so far things are working out well. The fact that we've already slept together is a given, but it was a must in cases like these.

By the time I'm dropped off at my car, my phone lights up.

I already have his name and number programmed, so when I finally read it as a notification, I nearly faint.

We chat back and forth and I choose my words wisely. Playing hard to get just a bit but still adding flirtation to keep him interested.

The playful banter is all I need to prolong my killing spree in case this goes terribly.

Between the mindless chit chat going on, I finally ask when I can buy him a drink.

Sam: "How about next Friday? I'm kind of busy until then."

Next. Friday.

Why not say next year? Why not say never? I have to wait a week?

I know for a fact his social life has tapered off after his breakup with Camilla. He sees his friends weekly, barely works, and rarely goes to LA anymore to visit Stella.

Whatever. At this point, I'll take what I can get.

CHAPTER THREE

———— ◆ ————

Stalking has its perks. I've discovered so many good restaurants thanks to Sam. But this one, however, has never been on my radar.

Every Sunday Sam and his two best friends get brunch at this two star café.

It's cheap, the menu is bland, and the waitress's look like hopeful fives surrounded by hung-over eights and nines. It's also a tiny place that makes it difficult to scout without getting spotted.

One of my plans that backfired tremendously was literally eye fucking him as I walked by his table one morning. I went by twice, each at different angles, staring him down, willing him to come ask for my number.

It didn't work, obviously. He barely noticed me.

And it caused me a three-week delay just in case he remembered me.

Luckily San Francisco is full of thousands and thousands of faces and he didn't have an epiphany at the bar like, "Wait, haven't you been following me around for weeks now?"

So here I am, Sunday morning, eavesdropping on my impending boyfriend and his best friends. They put in their orders and it's go time.

I tighten my ponytail, smash my breasts together in my sports bra, and do a quick hop before I leisurely jog past his table like I'm the most in shape, fit bitch he's ever seen.

Maybe they noticed me, but he didn't call me over like I was hoping. I guess I have one more chance coming back the other way.

Instead of jogging like I probably should be doing, I buy a water bottle using the dollar I stuck in my shoe and take a seat on a bench around the block. I pour a little over my head and shake the rest on my arms and chest, giving the impression that I'm a sweaty, hot mess.

I give myself twenty minutes and walk back the way I just came.

When I'm around the corner, I already see his friend Jake pointing right at me.

Yes, wave me over-

What the hell?

A spark of pain hits me in the leg. What the fuck was that?

I bend down and grab the breakfast roll that made contact with my shin, trying to comprehend why this grown ass man would throw food at me.

"Excuse me sir," I say as I approach their table. "Did you throw this bread at me?"

My impatience is trying not to rear its ugly head because they're laughing like hyenas and I can't get a word in.

But eventually they tell me all about their weekly mimosas, yeah I know already buddy, thanks, and I engage with them like this is so fascinating.

I don't want to overstay my welcome and make it look *too* obvious, so I say, "Oh and Sam! Friday works!"

"Yeah about that," Sam pauses.

I've blown it already, haven't I? He recognizes me. He caught on that I said I'd check my schedule Monday and it's only Sunday!

"Can we reschedule? My sister is coming into town and we don't see each other often."

"Bitch." Diego coughs.

I glare at him with curiosity. His friends must hate her, too. How could they not?

"Saturday should work." Of course it'll work; I'll make any day work for you.

I'm huffing and puffing the few miles back to my place. When I enter the building's front doors, I spot Ethan grabbing his mail with his boyfriend.

If I could, I would hide behind a pillar, but he sees me immediately.

"Ethan!" I squeal in a valley girl cadence.

"Hey, girl!"

He gives me two air kisses and I can't tell who the faker bitch is at this moment.

"How are you?" I ask just to maintain appearances. "How's the book coming along?"

I watch the clock behind him wondering how many minutes I'm going to be stuck talking to him. While it's difficult to connect with people, I can be charming when I want to be, or in this case, when I *need* to be.

"It's done! Can you believe it? I sent it to my editor."

"That's amazing! You're going to be on the top best sellers in no time."

I stroke his ego because he is merely an instrument to be played.

"You'll have to read it! I'll send you a copy."

I'd rather go blind, but I need it.

"Thanks!"

CHAPTER FOUR

───────◆───────

So the condo isn't exactly mine.

It's my Uncle Arnold's.

Arnold is letting me live here while I pick up the pieces after an abusive ex-boyfriend nearly killed me.

He has no clue what kind of nightmare he just let into his life.

For the longest time I didn't even know I had an extended family. My parents never talked about siblings and thanks to them holding onto grudges, I never had grandparents to save me from the abuse before they died.

I don't feel comfortable calling Arnold my Uncle because I didn't grow up with him.

I only learned about him by accident when my mom, during one of her drunken stupors, called me asking for money.

She kept calling me Arnold and when I corrected her, she said, "I think I know my own brother."

She must have been super trashed because she didn't even acknowledge the voice she was speaking to was female.

Imagine my surprise to find out she had not one, but two brothers!

They were just as shocked to find out about me, too.

I found it strange that my mom was riddled with mental illness, yet they were highly successful businessmen operating a reputable luxury rental company.

Not bothering to go through mommy Clara, I found my Uncle's information and laid on the tears.

I'm not a crier, but I do it out of necessity and when it suits my needs.

Let's just say he was filled with so much guilt after I told him about my childhood. I didn't even have to lie for once!

Arnold owns a highly regarded rental company for wealthy clients looking to stay in luxurious cities across the globe.

Most rentals go for one to three weeks for family vacations.

Occasionally, he'll rent out places for the month if it involves traveling for business short term.

So when I brought up the prospect of staying anywhere close to San Francisco, he offered me his own personal penthouse that he hadn't visited in months.

Rich people. They have too many houses and not enough time to enjoy them.

I moved in with the intention of rebuilding my life.

Once I received the keys, I went through all his personal items that he left and locked them in the office.

Any photo albums of his adventures or knick knacks collected over the years were boxed up. I pawned a few of his Audemars Piguet watches for extra cash so I could have some spending money. If he hadn't worn them in months, like he stated, he wouldn't miss them.

His money was spent at the classiest spa I could find.

My hair was colored and perfected by celebrity stylists.

I got a dose of Botox and minor facial contouring procedures to make my hidden qualities pop.

The weight I gained from the breakup had to go.

I had to be thrifty. Food or fillers?

The weight melted off.

Even now, looking in the mirror, ready for my date, I look pretty damn good.

I've been stuck at a size six for months. I'm curvy where I need to be and Sam seemed to like my body just fine.

I do my third and final walkthrough to ensure everything is in place. No magazines with Arnold's name on it, no random pill bottles in the medicine cabinets. I think I'm good.

I meet Sam downstairs as his Uber drops him off.

Our hug is quick as he realizes we are going up to my condo. I can sense his relief as his body language relaxes. I link my arm in his as we ride up the elevator, his skin is warm and electric and buzzing with desire.

I made the effort but without being obvious about it. My hair and makeup are classy and simple but I have to admit, you get what you pay for. My designer clothes look good on me.

Sam walks around, enamored over the luxury and views. Even though I'm positive this looks like I live here, my chest constricts. No single woman my age has a four bedroom condo. It's preposterous if you think about it. Unmarried. No kids.

I make us drinks as he returns to the kitchen. He has that look on his face, the one I saw outside the bar. I was hoping we'd round the bases tonight, but I didn't think it would happen five minutes into him coming over.

He rolls his sleeves up, as if whatever he's about to assist with in the kitchen has to have his bulging fore-arms exposed.

Puh-lease. He's doing it to entice me... and it's working. I can feel my organs thawing, liquefying as it travels down south.

This part, the desire and lust, is not hard to fake like I anticipated. It's been so long since I've had male contact of any kind, it's refreshing to see Sam lust after me.

Nathaniel wasn't overly affectionate. He had an average dick that was never worthy of praise. Sam, however, I would tell anyone and everyone just how fucking perfect his dick is if they'd listen. And I've only had it once. *Once.*

Sam puts his flat palm between my thigh gap and I feel the distinction of his cold hand against my warmth.

And just like that, I'm flooded with arousal.

Pizza won't be happening anytime soon, if at all.

He spins me around so my ass is pressing into the bulge in his jeans.

He unbuttons and unzips his pants from behind, slowly. I'm aching to be touched and his movements are intentional.

He doesn't slide me out of my pants. He can easily fuck me and leave, so the fact that he runs his index finger against my lace thong has me trembling with anticipation.

He lifts the edge of my thong away from my skin and guides his hand from my lower belly button into my panties.

I drop everything I'm holding and grip the countertop as he slowly massages between my legs.

The space in my pants is limited and his hand occupies most of the room.

"Moan for me." He whispers in my ear.

And I do. I buckle and bend against his body as he pins me against the counter, his right hand still inside me, his left cupping my breast from the bottom of my shirt opening.

I reach behind and tilt his head towards mine so our lips connect. Everything changes when our tongues find each other. The speed of his fingers becomes urgent, his hand gripping my chest becomes greedy, and our kissing is interrupted when he asks, "Can you come like this?"

I shake my head yes, how the hell can I not when he's working me like this.

"Say it." He demands.

"Sam…" I pant his name as his speed increases. Words are impossible.

"Say it." He asks again.

"I can come like this." I moan, about to implode.

I'm tender, warm, and ready to come at the top of my lungs. I hit my peak. A few more circles of his fingers and I'm a goner.

I've never orgasmed standing up, and I realize this when my body collapses forward onto the countertops, unable to keep my posture upright as I ride the waves.

I hear Sam's lips part as he smiles, his amusement and satisfaction obvious, as I'm left writhing and screaming for the longest 10 seconds of my life.

I'm still catching my breath against the cold, hard counter, when his shimmering fingers drop a condom next to my head.

My pants are yanked off and Sam kicks my ankles apart.

He tosses the empty condom wrapper on the floor as my senses finally return.

The tip goes in and I shudder in pleasure.

"Can I fuck you now or do you need a second?" He asks, as he dips another inch inside me.

"You can do whatever you want with me."

I'm pulsing around him. We both feel it.

"Fuck, you can't say shit like that, Harper." He groans, delving the deepest he can go. "I've been waiting to fuck you since last week."

Heat blooms in my chest. He's been thinking about me.

"Ugh what the fuck do you do to me?" He exclaims as my torso pounds into the drawers.

Blood rushes to all extremities at his confessions as he fucks me from behind.

"Can you come like this?" I repeat back to him.

He releases a loud gruff and grips my hips harder. "All I need is a few minutes with you. Jesus Christ."

I'm rocked with yet another orgasm and Sam gets off on hearing me.

Sam keeps repeating that I'm "fucking amazing" and I want to agree with him.

"Fuck I wanted to give you three but I don't think it's going to happen." He admits.

And before I know it, he shudders and pumps a few good ones into me before he's done.

We end up making the pizza and drinking quite a bit. I was hopeful once he stayed past midnight he might decide to sleep over, but he doesn't.

And as we say goodbye at the door, I admit something, which isn't exactly a lie.

"You're the first guy I've hooked up with since I've been single. I got out of a toxic relationship a while ago and it's been rough moving to a new city. I'm not exactly sure what you want from this... from me."

"Let's have fun. Why label it?" He says, like any guy would.

"I don't normally do these things... sleep around."

"Are you sleeping around with other guys?"

It's a loaded question and I sense intrigue.

Would he care if I *was* sleeping around?

I'll have to test that theory at some point to gauge his jealousy.

———— ♦ ————

The next morning I expect to wake up to a text from Sam describing, in detail, just how perfect we are together.

But my phone is silent.

And I must be delusional because that won't happen for a long time, if it even happens at all.

Had I woken up early enough, I could have spied on Sam and the guys again at brunch, but I don't want to press my luck. Some flags have risen in suspicion.

When Diego saw me outside brunch I could sense the recognition flash in his eyes.

Apparently neither Sam nor Jake remembers the night they almost died of alcohol poisoning.

They were wasted at a bar and I ordered Sam a drink. He was so far gone by the time he drank it, he forgot someone even bought it for him. But Diego was kind, sort of sober, and he kept staring at me like Sam wasted a precious opportunity that Diego would have been willing to fulfill.

My plan didn't work and Sam did not pick me up that night, let alone thank me for the drink. Asshole.

And thanks to that, I had to wait another two weeks until my next plan just in case Diego remembered me. Hopefully that doesn't come back to haunt me.

CHAPTER FIVE

———— ◆ ————

I need to know Sam's weaknesses, his faults.

What worked for him while he was dating Camilla and what didn't?

What mistakes did she make that I won't?

Befriending his ex wasn't exactly on my agenda, it just sort of happened.

Chalk it up to boredom that I wanted to find Camilla. I knew so little of her that it became a game.

And I needed something to challenge and stimulate me during the down time.

Tracking her down was rough.

It was hard to even get a start to my stalking without her last name.

With Sam hating social media, I couldn't look at his Facebook friends list.

Stella had Facebook but she wasn't friends with a

Camilla. Shocker.

I contemplated stealing Sam's phone one time while he was at the gym so I could find her name in his contact list, but I chickened out. Too many factors that could have been bad for me.

I knew she lived in San Francisco with Sam, but not *with* him.

I got so desperate I searched all the Camilla's in the San Francisco area. Page after page looking for a gorgeous brunette on Facebook. The only thing I had going for me was I saw her right around the time I got axed at B&B. Had I known how important she was back then, I would have memorized her visitor's badge.

Considering I knew nothing about this girl, it was hard to get a start. I'm talking damn near impossible. Where do you go when you have no beginning?

I dedicated my days like it was a full time job.

I finally caught a break with Venmo of all apps. Freaking. Venmo.

Going back months, almost a year, I looked at Sam's Venmo history once I confirmed his cell phone number and created him as a contact.

No transaction history with Camilla. But when I looked at Jake's, and then Avery's, I found one measly exchange.

Camilla isn't a common name, so before I did back

flips, I wanted to make sure I had the right one since she didn't have a picture on her profile.

Typing her full name in the search engine and "San Francisco", an article appeared right away.

San Francisco's Favorite Sous Chef Making Waves In Monterey

I clicked the article title frantically, reacting like I found my birth parents after being left on the stoop of a fire station.

The main picture filled my vision and I nearly fainted.

There she was. It was her.

Camilla stood behind a kitchen line in a chef's coat. She was a goddamn European angel.

I pictured a burst of balloons emerging from my closet door, confetti exploding from the ceiling, raining onto my laptop and into my hair. A party and parade played in my head and my devious smile resembled the Grinch.

Sous Chef Camilla Bianchi is moving on from the San Francisco crowd to follow the footsteps of legendary restaurant owner, Vladimir, as he prepares to open a brand new location in Monterey, California. Specifics are unknown at this time, but Vladimir intends to give free reign over to Bianchi for menu creation...

Blah, blah blah...compliments I don't care about...I had a name.

Camilla Bianchi.

The article was about three months old.

I found her instantly on Facebook and started from there.

Unfortunately her profile was extremely private. But a unique name like hers was all I needed.

I befriended her with my fake profile but she declined. Okay, so she wasn't one of those desperate wannabes that needed a high follow count.

She hadn't used Twitter in years, so no help. All her posts were from three years ago and she only tweeted pictures of food and random things that had nothing to do with Sam. She probably didn't even know him then.

I couldn't find her on Instagram by her first and last name, so that was a dead end.

Things were drifting towards inevitable doom.

I was stuck.

Until one hopeless night, at 3:08am to be exact, I thought of something.

Who uses Facebook and Twitter, but not Instagram?

I looked at her twitter handle "karmakarmacamilla", which was probably the stupidest username in the entire world. I gagged at the obvious reference to Culture Club's stupid song.

I searched that username in Instagram and bingo!

A match.

I nearly passed out. It wasn't private.

Suddenly, Karma Chameleon was my jam and I was blasting it from my speakers as I scrolled and scrolled.

While I was hoping for 2000+ posts, the 300 she had were enough.

She didn't add her name in her bio. A public profile but unsearchable by name? Smart.

I immediately found the most valuable images and screen shot them, just in case she felt her ears ringing and decided to go private.

Camilla bought a house. #NewHouseWhoDis

Camilla loves Pilates. #ReformMe

Camilla goes to a café frequently. #ButFirstCoffee

Camilla's restaurant had finally opened up. #Exqui-siqué

Judging by the looks of her staged pictures, Camilla had the life. She had moved on from whatever messy break up she had with Sam and looked blissfully happy in Monterey helping Vladimir create a new five star restaurant.

I inspected the classic picture of Camilla holding her "sold" sign outside her house.

6783 was showing in the picture, which was all I needed.

Her name did not pop up in the site I use that basically gives out everything but your blood type. She hadn't been in the system yet and would probably appear in a few weeks once her house went through the network.

Thanks to her tagging the studio she goes to for Pilates, I saw it was located in a neighboring city, Carmel.

Upon looking at the coffee shop she *also* tagged, they were around the block from each other. She had to live close by.

I searched Zillow for sold homes that coincided with the date she posted her picture.

A house matched the address numbers and the outside stoop.

It only took ten minutes to find her house, an hour to get to know what kind of person she was, and a day for me to finally get the courage to drive out to Carmel and see her for myself.

My initial drive down included a detour to Monterey so I could take a look at this fancy restaurant.

Exquisiqué was way out of my price range. I'd probably be turned away at the door when they did the mandatory credit check.

So instead, I spied. I followed Camilla for weeks, learning her routine and work schedule. She went to the 8am Pilates class Mondays and Fridays, always treating herself to a coffee afterwards. She mainly worked the busy nights, Thurs-Sun. I became obsessed.

I finally got the guts to join one of her Pilates classes when I knew there was nothing to lose. Sam wasn't even aware we were living in the same city, let alone I existed at all.

I parked early and got another coffee at the café I'd be visiting again in the next hour and a half. I chugged it because all the caffeine in the world would have to get me through this Pilates class.

When the studio opened up, I chose a reformer and waited.

No one was overly friendly.

I noticed that about people. As I got older, women were set in their circles and not proactive about making new girlfriends, which was fine by me. I was used to being alone.

The class started in two minutes and my hands were sweating. Camilla wasn't there.

No, no, no. I did not get my ass up early, drive over two hours, pay a shit load of money for a Pilates class bundle, to not have her be here.

The instructor told everyone to get ready and just as I was about to demand a motherfucking refund, Camilla walked in the door.

———— ◆ ————

The class was an eternity and I was sweating harder than all these bitches combined.

An 80-year-old grandmother beat me in the planking

contest and that did not sit well with me. I strive for competition and when I lose, I do so ungracefully.

Level two was challenging. And despite the instructor suggesting me go to level 1 for beginners, bitch, I wasn't about to let that ruin my mood.

I casually followed Camilla across the street to the café, my demeanor calm and imperceptible. When we both ordered our drinks and waited for our names to be called, I approached her slowly.

"Hey, weren't you in Pilates this morning?" I ask.

"I was! Fun class today. I love that instructor."

"Yeah she was great," I lied. I hated her. She was too chipper for 8am and kept correcting my form. "It was my first class in a while."

"It's the best. So much better than the gym."

And so much more expensive, too, I thought.

"I forgot how much I enjoyed it. I need to go more often."

"I go twice a week! Mondays and Fridays."

"I was thinking of the Friday class also. Same time?"

"Yeah, I'll be there. I'm Camilla."

She reached out her hand and I shook it.

"I'm…" I had a momentary seizure. I couldn't tell her my real name. And I couldn't tell her my fake name just to be safe! "… Sophie. You're in great shape."

Compliments are the easiest way to win someone over.

"Thanks, girl! I'd go more than twice a week if I could, but you know… life."

"Yeah it's beautiful here."

What am I, new to the English language? Why is this so hard?

"We are truly blessed to live here." Camilla adds.

Like my bond with Sam, it's easiest to form a connection when you mirror the past of your current subject. As I always say to myself, compliment, ask questions, act interested.

"What made you choose to live here?" I finally spit out.

"Well I work in Monterey. I'm the head chef at Exquisiqué. Have you heard of it?"

"Oh my gosh, the amazing white Spanish style restaurant right on the water?" My enthusiasm is so believable.

"That's it!" She confirms, practically jumping up and down. "That makes me so happy people know of it by word of mouth. The first few months are always the hardest but we are doing what we can to promote it."

"I have to admit though," I begin. "I've never actually eaten there. I just drive by and gawk at it."

"You'll have to come by!"

And this is why I set up the conversation to end here. Camilla is sweet enough to invite a stranger by the restaurant. I'll take her up on that eventually.

"That would be amazing!"

Our drinks are called and I break out in hives because she didn't even notice the barista call for Liz instead of Sophie.

I wanted to keep talking with her, build a friendship, but when you have the personality of Ted Bundy, it's quite difficult. I'm pleasant and agreeable, but I have a dark side that comes to light.

"Well enjoy your coffee, Camilla. I'll see you Friday!"

"Have a great day, hun!"

———◆———

It's been a slow burn. That was two months ago and we've met for a quick coffee every Friday since. She's slowly opening up more and more.

With men, you can win them over with sex.

But with women? You have to be kind, interesting, funny, all things I'm not.

Each day I drive out of my way, I cross my fingers that Camilla will tell me something useful about Sam. So far, nothing has happened and I feel like I'm wasting my time.

CHAPTER SIX

——◆——

My inner thighs are sore as I emerge from bed. Last night, Sam went down on me in his shower and then fucked me unconscious. To whoever is keeping score, Sam is phenomenal with his dick, hands, *and* mouth. I fell asleep yet again and he was sweet enough to buy us dinner.

But now, as I wake up early, I remember I am meeting Camilla for our weekly Pilates and coffee.

Luckily Camilla has my number and she's really good about letting me know if she can't make it to a class. Only once was I halfway there and had to turn around because she had a restaurant emergency.

But today is different. I can feel it.

I'm very selective on details and let Camilla talk most of the times we meet for coffee. Friday has become a ritual and each week I learn a little bit more about her.

Where she went to college, her family life, what it's like running a business as a woman. But everything is G rated and I don't know a single thing about her love life.

That ends today.

We're sitting with jackets on after a sweaty class. I must say, Pilates might just help me lose those pesky pounds.

"What are you having today?" Camilla asks.

I always get their cheapest drink because who the hell has the budget to spend this type of cash on coffee?

"The usual." I say.

She gets something fancy, like always, and takes a brief picture of our cups next to each other.

"Are you on Instagram? I'll tag you!"

"I'm not, actually." I admit truthfully.

"No social media? Who are you hiding from?" She jokes but I take this opportunity to knock her down a peg.

"Actually my ex-boyfriend. He became a bit obsessive when we broke up." I continue the narrative I told my uncle so I don't have too many storylines going at once.

"Oh my gosh, Sophie, I'm so sorry to joke like that."

"No it's okay. I just figured now would be a good time to tell you since you brought up social media. I'm just trying to look out for myself. You never know what people can find online about you." This is yet another dig because how could she be so stupid to post so many private things on a public domain?

"Are you okay?" She asks.

"Oh yeah, I'm fine now. I'm just overly cautious about dating and men now." I take a pause. "How's your dating life?"

"Nonexistent at the moment." She chuckles to herself.

I don't know jack shit about her relationship with Sam. He could have been abusive for all I know. I guarantee he wasn't, but he could have all kinds of skeletons in his closet that I wouldn't know about and I want to see those bones of his.

"Hopefully your exes aren't crazy like mine." I say.

"Ha, exes, no. But one guy…"

I nod my head, urging her to continue.

"Well one guy… actually it wasn't even him. It was his twin sister."

I have a lump in my throat and I hold my breath hoping it disappears.

"What about her?" I manage to say.

"She was a bit much. I can tolerate a lot, and I refuse to say a bad word about her, but she was difficult. I don't think she liked me very much and she made it impossible for things to progress."

I'm gripping my coffee cup, realizing the only skeleton in Sam's closet is one I'm already familiar with.

"Did you date long?"

"Yeah about a year. He was amazing. So thoughtful. So sweet."

A burning rage ignites every hair on my body. If she compliments him one more time I'm going to scream.

"What was so bad about his sister?"

"She just got way too involved in our business. She lied a lot and it was a bit frustrating because Sam never chose to see it."

Hearing his name leave her lips with such nonchalance makes me quiver with jealousy. She got to heights I haven't yet and I hate that she knows him more intimately than I do.

"But enough about me. Tell me more about this ex."

She's looking out the window so I roll my eyes and continue with the lies.

———◆———

Saturday morning approaches and I'm counting the minutes until Sam returns. His quick trip to LA felt like forever and we have a date tonight.

But when I look out the window, I wonder if his plane will even be able to land. A torrential storm blankets the city and in typical fashion, I initiate the line of communication.

Harper: "This rain is nuts! Did you still want to go out?"

Sam: "Do you care if we reschedule?"

An imaginary knife guts me. I do care. Of course I care. Why did I even ask? Rookie mistake.

Harper: "Sure. Next week?" I suggest as I scoop my intestines back into my torso.

He doesn't answer.

No answer for hours.

By Sunday morning I've received radio silence. Where did I go wrong? Was I coming on too hard too fast? What the hell did I do?

———— ♦ ————

I meet Camilla for Pilates Monday and the drive is getting to me. Four hours in the car roundtrip is making me homicidal. And that's on a good day with no traffic. I think my aggression is intensifying because Sam has not texted me back in days. DAYS!

Camilla is intuitive and senses something.

"You okay? You seemed so angry during class."

We're both putting our shoes back on and apparently I need to work on hiding my aggression better.

"My ex somehow got my number."

"Oh Sophie, no! How?"

"I think an old friend gave it to him. She had no clue about our past."

"That's terrible, especially after all you told me last week. Let's get breakfast and you can tell me all about it. My treat."

I'm taken aback by her sweet gesture and accept it graciously. Usually we don't have time on Monday's but I have no life and no job, so I'll take any time she gives me.

On our walk to a nearby café, I elaborate on my false predicament.

"He's not violent. I just don't think he understood we weren't meant to be, ya know?"

"I do. People are in your past for a reason."

This... is good. She understands Sam is in her past and won't be reconciling any lingering feelings anytime soon. I think.

We're sitting at a quaint little place and we both order eggs and toast. I'd really like the full stack of pancakes and a mimosa, but she's not drinking this early so I won't either.

"So what aren't you telling me?" Camilla's quizzical look has me shaking in my knockoff LuluLemons.

"Umm, what do you mean?"

"This ex! Why can't he just let you go? You said he wasn't abusive, right?"

She's so sweet and genuinely seems to care about me and this ex problem of mine. Most women just want to talk about themselves, so I'm not prepared to elaborate.

"We only dated a year." I sip my water to allow a realistic story to come to mind. "Things were going well but in the end we just changed."

"How so?"

I grit my teeth and want to tell her to lay off the fucking questions.

"Well, I noticed him changing a lot. He became insecure. I don't know why. I never gave him the inkling things weren't going well."

"Hmm…" she says, waiting for me to continue.

What is she a fucking detective? I feel like I'm being interrogated.

"He became possessive. Didn't like when I hung out with my girlfriends."

"That's definitely odd." She agrees.

I use the info she gave me about Stella and give her an opportunity for her to share her experiences.

"He just kept sabotaging the relationship. Things never progressed."

She's quiet, still letting me talk. What the fuck, do I have to tell her my whole life story? The guy was bad news. Why can't she offer her own memories so we can commiserate together?

"And the biggest issue was he wanted kids and I didn't."

"Kids…" Camilla whispers and I realize I've unintentionally struck oil.

"Do you want kids?" I ask cautiously.

"I do. Well, I did. My ex and I got pregnant but I lost the baby."

"Oh my god, I'm sorry."

I'm reeling, trying so hard not to volley her with a fuck load of questions like she just did to me, though it's only fair.

"Is this the same guy with the sister?"

"Yes, umm, we should probably change the subject."

She has tears in her eyes and I'm wishing I can rewind time so I can go back two minutes and figure out a better way to approach this subject. Now that she jogs my memory, I do remember her being pregnant when she came by B&B. How the hell did that detail escape me until now?

"I'm sorry I brought it up."

Apologies are easy for me, they are just words. It's what you say when you hurt someone's feelings, even if I don't mean them.

"Don't!" She dabs her wet eyes with a napkin. "I'm just really emotional lately."

"Should we get mimosas?" I'm dead serious. I need a fucking drink.

Instead she laughs, so I take that as a no.

"You're too funny. A mimosa at the spa sounds divine."

I'm salivating at the thought of alcohol so early in the morning that I barely register her when she says,

"Let's do it!"

"Huh? I ask.

"Mimosas at a spa! Let's do it!"

"Really?" I ask again, considering we've never adventured past coffee dates.

"Yeah! We deserve it. It'll keep you distracted from your ex. And let's be real, I'm always down for a relaxing massage."

"I'm not exactly relaxing, I don't want to ruin it for you."

This gets her to laugh and squeeze my hand.

"Sophie you are *too* funny. That's what I love about you. Heck yeah, girl. We'll go Friday instead of our Pilates class."

Her eagerness for my friendship is unrequited. She has no clue who I am or what I'm after. I can't keep coming out here week after week in hopes of her accidentally divulging her deepest secrets in her past relationship. If I don't get something helpful out of her at the spa, Camilla is about to outlive her usefulness.

She rambles off the name of the spa she loves and instead of looking at my calendar to confirm I'm available (I am), I Google the spa treatment menu.

Their cheapest service to get me in the door is $400. I nearly pass out. And that doesn't even include the tip, drinks and lunch.

Camilla unlocks her phone and my eyes are saucers.

She enters her pass code so casually, still unaware of my intentions.

5528. 5528. 5528.

She sets her phone down and hopefully my pupils have dilated back to normal size.

"I'll call after we're done here and schedule our appointments. This will be good for you. You don't need to be thinking of that guy. You deserve happiness, and if it wasn't him, then that's okay."

She squeezes my hand, again, and the gleam in her eyes reminds me of a fucking cartoon character.

She's so sweet and innocent. She does not belong around someone like me. Because all I can think of right now is ringing her pretty neck and asking what the hell happened between her and Sam and the baby. Hopefully I'll find out Friday.

———◆———

Wednesday comes and I've been going out of my mind.

Camilla and I solidify Friday plans. She suggests bringing an overnight bag just in case we are feeling #extra and want to get a room.

I'm feeling #extrapoor but I can't really tell her that now, can I?

Sam is ignoring me and I stew with fury, shoving my phone aside trying to stave off this temper tantrum.

When I moved to San Francisco, I got a new identity and new phone number. I still have my old cell and I pull it out of the bedside table and power it on.

It's been a good month or more since I've checked in on my old life. I don't expect to see any signs of contact, but when it powers on, I show 14 new text messages.

Opening the texts first, I hold my breath with uncertainty. I have no idea what these could be about.

My mother's thread shows up for all new notifications, the first being sent six weeks ago.

Clara: "We need money. Call me."

Eye roll.

A week later.

Clara: "We need money. Dad has withdrawals. Do you know anyone who sells?"

A couple days later.

Clara: "Are you getting these? We need money. Where are you?"

I decided not to tell my parents about San Francisco juuuust in case Nathaniel ever came looking for me.

Clara: "We. Need. Money."

True alcoholism, the kind where you can't even function without a drink, is a horrible dependency I wouldn't wish on anyone. I've seen the side effects firsthand, and my mother can't go a couple hours without a drink. All remaining brain cells in Clara's dried up skull have evaporated thanks to the power of cheap vodka.

And when she *does* decide to take her medication, it's a recipe for psychosis.

Clara: "Nathaniel came through. Ran into him at Ralphs."

"You fucking cocksucker!" My voice is immediately hoarse from screaming.

Nathaniel knew about my parent's dependency issues because I told him pieces of my childhood. He only met them by chance when we happened upon them at the store; the liquor aisle of course. I would have never introduced them had that unfortunate accident not occurred.

Since when is the grocery store the place for fucking reunions? Imagining my mom running into him and probably begging him for money, alcohol, or drugs has me feeling dirty and in need of a shower.

Nathaniel wasn't a huge drug user. He used them recreationally or at parties, not all the time. But he had hook ups with some guys at his gym. They would trade illegal body supplements for hardcore drugs.

Clara: "Dad's in hospital. Drugs laced with Fentanyl. Doesn't look good."

I presume most people would be crying or experiencing an anxiety attack right about now. But I am not most people and I do not feel anything for my dad when I read these words.

A few days later.

Clara: "Dad barely made it. At rehab. Come home and bring cash."

Can't she take a fucking hint?

Clara: "Not sure where you are. Call me. Dad lost his job."

A delayed text message pops up and a spark ignites a fire in my lungs. It burns deep and hot. As I breathe, I can almost taste the smoke.

Nathaniel: "Just stopped by your parents. Your dad tried to steal my watch. He looked high as fuck. I see the rotten apple doesn't fall far from the tree. I can't keep giving them drugs. I only did it because they looked so desperate."

His damaging opinions about Theodore and Clara produce an odd reaction out of me. Yes, they might be the worst parents known to man, but only I can talk shit. How fucking dare he?

Nathaniel sent it two weeks after my mom said my dad was in rehab, which means even after my dad almost died, Nathaniel still sold them more drugs.

The fire inside me burns out of control. My chest glows a bright orange red, the heat exploding down my torso like a brush fire.

"I could fucking kill you." I mutter under my breath.

———◆———

Later that day, after many cold showers, I come up with a plan that isn't exactly foolproof.

I know where Jake works, so I decide I'll stop by his office and coincidentally bump into him. What a small world?

And then Jake can tell Sam we saw each other, thus reminding him to text. Me. Back.

In an hour I'm going to hate myself for doing this. San Francisco is such a big city; the likelihood of me being in the same building will be so suspicious.

Some of my best work is on the fly, so the fact that I don't have a cover story ready doesn't worry me. I'll think of something. Maybe ask advice about a made up legal issue.

I refuse to look desperate and text Sam again. Won't happen. But apparently I'm hopeless enough to show up at his friend's office.

When I reach the fifth floor, there's a plastic looking blond bimbo sitting behind a huge desk. Behind her are glass walls of high-end law offices.

"Hi, can I help you? Do you have an appointment?"

I read the blonde's placard.

Lila.

"Oh, no I didn't. I was in the area and I was wondering if Jake was available. I'm a friend and just wanted to say hi."

Desperation is my least favorite quality and I'm feeling it in excess at the moment.

"He's busy right now." Lila informs me, without even checking a damn thing.

I don't say anything and she's looking at me, waiting for me to speak up or leave.

Uncomfortable silence doesn't bother me so I stand my ground.

"He's not available." She repeats.

"I heard you." I smile a joker's smile and add, "I guess I'll just use your bathroom before I go."

She rolls her eyes and points left.

"Down the hall."

As I saunter toward the women's bathroom, I look at all vantage points and realize there's no way I can sneak back without Lila informing security.

As I'm about to open the bathroom door, I hear it.

Sam's voice.

He's somewhere between these glass walls, and if I see him, that means he'll see me.

I didn't think he'd be here. What are the freaking odds he's actually working today?

Instead of being smart and running out of there, I barricade myself behind the door of the single stall bathroom, thus trapping myself with no way of knowing where he is.

Dear god this was the biggest mistake ever. I will live in this bathroom until the custodians kick me out.

Only then will I know the office is closed and I can leave without being seen.

I've been in here for twenty minutes with no interruption.

Positioning myself right next to the door, I will Sam to walk down the hall and scream his goodbyes to his coworkers.

It doesn't happen.

What does happen, however, is a woman approaching the bathroom door.

Her heels click clack as they get louder and louder, probably Lila coming to kick me out.

But instead, I hear Sam whisper, "Lila, hurry up."

The men's bathroom door parallel to me opens and shuts quickly.

I put my ear to the shared wall and close my other ear with my finger.

Everything is muffled, but I hear the distinct sound of a lock being secured.

A moment goes by and then I hear it.

It's so obvious even with the wall separating us.

The familiar deep growl I've heard from Sam's mouth echoes on the other side.

Lila is quiet; no doubt sucking his dick because if Sam was giving it to her, there's no way she wouldn't be screaming out his name.

I summon the strength not to punch the tile wall. A

reformed woman doesn't have bloody knuckles.

He's moved onto the next conquest. I was nothing to him.

I run out of there and contemplate pulling the fire alarm so their fellatio is interrupted.

The entire way home, I come to terms that everything I've worked toward was for nothing. For once in my life, I'm incapable of getting revenge.

———— ◆ ————

My phone buzzes hours later and I ignore it.

I need to cancel the spa appointment. It's not like being friends with Camilla is going to get me anything at this point.

When I go to unlock my phone to call the spa, I see a text.

Sam: "Sorry, I took on some new cases these past few days. Been a bit busy."

"What?!" I screech, like a broken record. "Wait, what?! I've been a bit busy?" I mock his words and do not reply.

A few minutes later.

Sam: "Want to go out Friday? I still owe you."

Harper: "Friday doesn't work for me."

What the- why did I say that? I can cancel plans with Camilla, who cares? Why are my fingers betraying me like this?

Sam: "Saturday?"

Harper: "Maybe!"

I'm responding like a scorned bitch and I should be taking any date he offers, even if it's painting his bedroom walls on a Tuesday at 2am.

I was dead set on this being over. But here I am, pulling myself out of the bowels of hell ready to keep this act alive.

Harper: "Are you busy right now?"

Sam: "Not terribly busy."

I feel him out and see if he wants to come over for a movie. On a Wednesday night. Who wants to do that? This will be a test. We never hang out mid-week.

He says yes.

And wouldn't you know, I dart out of my bed like the bolt of lightning flashing outside my room and take a shower.

I wasn't prepared for him to say yes, so I quickly shave and tidy up the place.

Sam arrives an hour later and I answer the door in sweats; the exact opposite of sexy.

Our hug is awkward and this feels like a mistake. Too soon. Should have kept him dangling.

"How have you been?" He asks.

I answer dishonestly and welcome him inside.

His eyes undress my frumpy clothes. Had he been a bit more talkative this past week, maybe I would have answered the door in lingerie.

He wants to hook up tonight. Why else would he come over?

Normally a blowjob wouldn't take a man out of commission. But Sam is about to get a taste of the humiliation he gave me when I drown his ass in alcohol. When he no doubt wants to fuck, he'll encounter the dreaded whiskey dick.

Arnold's liquor cabinet holds some very expensive, very aged bottles of alcohol. The one I have in mind has a label that's flaking off. Does alcohol expire? This might be poison and completely unacceptable to drink. I guess we'll find out soon enough.

I pour him more than necessary and hand it over.

We sit on the couch and I let him pick a movie.

The storm creates a perfect setting and I snuggle into him under the blanket. I've kind of missed him, missed this connection, missed whatever this is between us.

Sam eventually finishes off his giant glass of venom and I swallow my fear that he could keel over in a matter of minutes.

"Piece of shit." Sam cusses.

"What's wrong?"

"My phone has been dying on me lately. For no reason. I'm too lazy to get a new one."

"Is that why you didn't text me back?" My retort has perfect timing and I mentally pat myself on the back.

"No, sorry. I really was busy."

"It's okay, I understand."

Bullshit. Busy getting his dick sucked by a blond vacuum.

His insecurity is getting the better of him, because without warning, he's biting my lip and kissing me like he hasn't seen me in weeks.

I instinctively climb on top of Sam and I'm utterly shocked to feel his hardness underneath me. This whiskey plan isn't working.

We're kissing for what feels like an hour and neither of us is making the next move. I'm grinding into him and his mannerisms are pointing towards combusting below me, but he doesn't move this along. I keep waiting for him to go soft but it doesn't happen.

I remove my top and pants and ask, "Want to continue this in the bedroom?"

"No, we can do this here."

My plan is backfiring. Sam is going to fuck me and I do not want to be sloppy seconds.

His pants fall down his broad, long legs and I see them waiver as I get on my knees. The whiskey has finally hit him. He can barely stand up.

Yes.

I'm fighting the suppression of disgust when I put him in my mouth, realizing someone has been here earlier. If I see Lila's lipstick on his dick, I might just throw up all over him.

He stops me and asks for a condom.

Assuming he doesn't have one, I lie and say I don't either.

So instead of fucking me, I work my mouth as he struggles to stay hard.

"Give me a second." He requests.

Wiping my nose upwards to mask my smile, I let this pacify the indignation within me.

He chugs some water and jerks himself off a bit to get him going again.

He's suffered enough.

Forcing him back into my mouth, I pull out all the stops and he finishes like a champ.

Sam heaves breath after breath after I swallow down his venom.

I make a mental note to gargle with bleach in case Lila left behind traces of swine flu with that snout of hers.

Through the orgasm haze, Sam doesn't notice my phone on the coffee table light up with Camilla's name.

I am that stupid, ladies and gentlemen.

Starting tonight, I'll be smarter.

"Your turn?" He asks.

As much as my body wants it, I say no. I have to start the next step in my grand plan, which is hanging out without the sex. Now that Sam shows interest again, he needs to realize we are actually great together, physical attraction aside.

I have to pretend like I have a real job here so I tell Sam I'm leaving tomorrow for a book signing in Florida. In reality, I'm going to Monterey with his ex.

"I'll pick up some condoms for next time." Sam says as he waits at the front door to leave.

The dormant butterflies somehow surviving in my stomach spring back to life and flutter their wings.

Two words every woman wants to hear.

Next time.

Chapter Seven

Friday morning my alarm screeches its 4am wake up call.

I fake sob straight into my pillows.

Why did I agree to pick Camilla up? Oh yeah, because I don't actually own a house out there and it's easier saying I'll drive.

I zombie walk to the bathroom. I need to look extra glamorous so I don't stand out at this five star resort. I can't roll up in an Old Navy swimsuit and Marshall's sundress. It's curled hair and fake eyelashes kind of day.

When I arrive in Carmel two hours later, I pick up two venti coffees from Starbucks. Camilla better not give me lip for the caffeine choice. I don't have the budget for gourmet espresso. I had to charge these on my credit card, for fuck's sake.

Buying my new identity wasn't cheap. The one credit card I was approved for has a $5,000 limit. I've maxed it out two times and I'm probably on the verge of a declined transaction after this coffee run and pit stop for gas.

As I wait for Camilla to come outside, I unlock my phone and change Sam's name in my contact list to… Sebastian. I can't take that chance if he decides to text when Camilla is around. Sam is a common name but I learn from my infrequent mistakes.

"Hey girl!" Camilla sings, slinging her overnight bag in the backseat.

Oh dear lord, she really is planning on getting a room. But the possibility of getting access to her phone all night makes me smile deviously.

"Hey, morning!" I take a giant gulp of the scalding coffee. "Ready?"

———◆———

For once I actually feel like I belong when I pull up to the valet in the Porsche Cayenne. The spa is located inside the most insanely gorgeous resort I've ever seen.

"Holy fucking shit." I whisper under my breath. I have to keep up this good girl façade because I've yet to hear Camilla say so much as "I hate", let alone the word "fuck."

The Acts Of Life

The resort is vast and luscious with dozens of palm trees. The expansive and dedicated landscaping is meticulously cared for. I could easily get lost here if it weren't for signs pointing to all the amenities this place offers. The air even tastes different here.

We check in at the spa reception and I feel like a celebrity. This place is indescribable. I guess you really do get what you pay for. And my treatment better include a diamond crusted exfoliant and gold flake cleanser for what I'm paying.

When we're back changing into puffy robes and our bathing suits, Camilla's cell phone chimes rather obnoxiously.

Every woman around looks at us in horror, like we just snapped a picture of them in their unmentionables.

One older lady even has the audacity to point to a sign that says "Cell phone use in the lobby area only", as if we are inconsiderate *and* illiterate.

"Shoot this is work, I'll be right back." She rushes out and adds, "Can you grab us some lounge chairs?"

I agree and secure my things in my locker with a four digit code.

When I make my way to the pool entrance, I grab two plush towels that feel more like luxurious blankets. I plan on stealing one or two before I leave.

This place is packed full of financially responsible adults who don't have to work for a living.

The delicate little snowflake that was easily disturbed by a cell phone ring follows behind me, also looking for lounge chairs.

We glance at each other and spot the last open chaises. I sprint faster than her and sprawl across them claiming them as mine.

When she catches up she says, "I was saving those."

I look to my left and right, glad Camilla isn't here to witness this. "Weird, I don't see anything claiming these as yours."

"I'm a member here." She tells me.

"Cool." I reply and then lean back on the chair to get comfy.

She doesn't have a witty retort, but instead huffs out a hot breath of air, lingering.

Setting my LV tote on Camilla's chair, I give her an impatient look.

Just as she's about to leave and look elsewhere to sit, the man on my other side says he and his boyfriends are leaving for their treatments and she could have his chairs.

"Thank you," she says, plopping down next to me as soon as they clear away their things. She sets the rolled towels on the now vacant chairs, waiting for her friends to join her.

"At least my purse isn't fake." She mumbles under her breath as she takes off her cover up.

"What was that?" I begin. "Your dentures shifted, I couldn't understand you."

"I said…" She says louder, "Your purse… is… fake."

"Yeah, well so are your tits." I jab, wondering how the hell she can tell it's a knock off from her vantage point.

Grandma is in a modest one piece with tiny Chanel C's and a shawl around her waist. Her nails have a French tip, typical old lady manicure, and gold jewelry adorns her sagging neck. The only perky thing on her is her paid for breasts that look very unnatural.

My bikini isn't skimpy, but I'm definitely showing more skin than any of these old biddies. It took a lot of hard work, Pilates, and starvation to get the body I have today, and apparently I'm being judged because I don't have cellulite like the rest of them.

"Mother of God." She says with disgust, loud enough for me to hear.

A bald man with a hairy potbelly waves at me from the shallow end of the pool. I'm hidden behind sunglasses so I pretend not to notice him.

I feel like I walked into a 65+ community pool complex. I search for other guests and I'm the youngest one here by at least 20 years. I'm surrounded by grandparents enjoying their retirement. Camilla needs to hurry up before the grim reaper takes me by accident.

Nana is soon reunited with her equally older female

friends and they all look at me like I'm sunbathing nude.

Have they never seen a bikini before?

A waitress approaches and asks, "Can I get you anything to drink?"

"Two peach bellinis, please." I grit my teeth when I hand her my credit card. This better be a goblet sized glass with Georgia's finest peaches and Italy's best Prosecco. "You can close me out," I add. I don't mind paying for the first round, but I can't fund the entire day with an endless open tab I no doubt can't afford.

Soon enough, Camilla returns in a whirlwind.

"Sorry!" She speed walks over to me and strips her dress in one swoop. "A big event is happening at the restaurant tonight and no one bothered to print out the preset menu. They're lucky I had the PDF saved in my email."

Grandma interrupts, "Spa policy says no cell phone use out here."

"Sorry," Camilla blushes, so sweet and accommodating. "Won't happen again."

"Let's hope not."

The waitress returns but no peach bellinis in hand.

"I'm so sorry, but your card was declined. Do you have another?" She practically shouts into a bullhorn.

My mind implodes as I register this unexpected calamity.

Well... fuck.

"Here, use mine." Camilla hands over her debit card with ease.

"That must be *so* embarrassing." The old lady next to us says to her friends as she giggles like a schoolgirl.

I'm bubbling with rage because I'm incapable of reacting the way nature intended me to.

"Sorry, I didn't even bring my debit card." I say sheepishly. I don't own a debit card. "That's never happened. I got us bellinis."

"Don't worry about it! You drove here and got us coffee, I'll get drinks!"

It takes a lot to embarrass me and I'm right on the precipice. Normally I wouldn't give a shit, but this old hag keeps niggling me.

Our peach bellinis arrive minutes later and we cheers to the "freakin' weekend." Eye roll.

She takes a boomerang and posts it to social media.

#tgispaday #bellinibabes #spadayallday

Obviously my talk with her the other day didn't sink in. She tags our location.

Camilla and I are just beginning to soak up the weak rays when she shoots up, phone in hand.

"Not again!" She panics. "I'll be right back, Sophie. Promise."

Unflappable to her drama, I readjust in my chair. At some point, Camilla has to give up her cell phone long enough for me to get some answers. I'm still on the edge of my seat wondering what the hell happened with her pregnancy. I didn't see a C section scar on her abdomen, though she did say she lost it. I need answers!

The champagne is flowing nicely with my bloodstream and I take off my sunglasses to get a better view of my surroundings.

Out of my peripheral view, I notice eyes on me.

"Can I help you with something?" I interrogate this strange elderly woman who can't seem to leave me alone.

"No, just looking." She says nonchalantly.

"Well... stop."

One of her friends whispers, "Gloria, do we know her?"

Gloria... what an old bitch's name. She shakes her head and I see the skin in her neck twist, unable to keep its form.

"Then why can't you leave me the fuck alone?" I question with a giant smile on my face.

"This impoverished tramp is exactly why I won't renew my membership here. They let in just about *anyone*." Gloria says to her friends. "Like this destitute transient who can't even afford a $20 cocktail."

Camilla returns and once again, I have to shut my mouth.

"Gosh, I'm so sorry! One of our deliveries got delayed and they are worried we won't have the proper menu for the event tonight."

"Do we need to leave?" I want to physically coil into a snake as Gloria stares me down.

"No, we are good." She pauses, sensing hostility in the air and says to the skeleton next to me, "I'm Camilla, this is Sophie."

Stop being so nice!

I force a half smile. Gloria doesn't deserve even that.

"Hi honey," Gloria's tone is more pleasant with Camilla. "I'm Gloria, these are my friends Catherine, Nancy, and Virginia."

All four of them exude wealth and class. They must be able to spot a commoner among the affluent. I'm more noticeable than I realized.

Camilla exhales deeply and I make a mental note of all the ways I could kill Gloria.

Twenty minutes go by and we order a second round.

Nancy, the short, homely looking woman next to Gloria, announces, "I'm going to go grab my book in my locker."

"Can you grab mine as well?" Gloria asks. "I'm in locker 215."

My sunglasses and earbuds give me the perfect cover. I slowly crane my neck to the left, pretending I'm trying to get more sun on my cheeks, everyone around me unaware I'm actually listening to their conversation as opposed to music. So when Gloria hand mimes her locker code, I'm able to see three of the four digits required to get in.

Pretending I have a phone call, I sneak away to the bathroom to call my credit card company. I'm always wary because I am using a deceased person's information and the last thing I need is a red flag popping up on my account. Luckily the pending payment is released and I can purchase this exuberant facial that would have cost me more than a car payment back in LA.

———— ◆ ————

My facial did not include anything gold tinted, but I do feel totally refreshed. My skin has never looked better.

When Camilla and I return to our chairs, a man is snoring on my lounge, wrapped in his own towel. His beach bag is at his side while my stuff is gone.

I turn to Gloria. "Where's my stuff?"

"Why would I know?" She answers innocently.

I take a mental inventory of what I left out here. Just my sundress, sunscreen and insulated water bottle.

Oh my god.

My wristlet that had my ID and credit card. Holy fuck I can't believe this.

The man sleeping in my spot has the face of a child molester. I bump the chaise with my leg to wake him up.

"Hey." I screech, no doubt interrupting his kidnapping fantasy.

"My things are all here." Camilla says as she goes through her belongings.

Of course they are.

"Where is… my stuff?" I snarl at Gloria.

A lady in the pool interrupts, "Are you looking for a dress?"

Turning around, I watch as she strains for something at the bottom of the pool.

She hands over a soaked dress.

It weighs 20 pounds and I accept it in disbelief.

"How odd, maybe the wind blew it." Gloria guesses, as the air remains stagnant.

Instead of sucker punching her in the face, I say to Camilla, "I'm going to the sauna."

"Wait for me, I'll get us two more drinks and then close out."

I leave anyway, stomping my feet to the locker room. A spa attendant comes by and tells me she will wash my dress free of charge. She gets my information in case my cards show up and asks if I want to make a police report. I tell her hell no.

The thought of a cop asking me questions about my false identification actually sounds worse than slowly dying in the sauna.

Gloria, that fucking blue-haired, casket-smiling old bitch.

She did something with my stuff. I'm sure of it.

I walk to locker 215 and discreetly glance around and realize I'm alone. No other spa goers, no video cameras, just me and her belongings.

"Let's see what you got in here, ya fucking dinosaur."

The four digit pass code is easy enough to guess if you have three of the four numbers.

I type in 1-3-5, the numbers I know she used, and guess the last digit to be 7.

A red light blinks at me.

So she's not as unoriginal as I was expecting.

I try 1-3-5-9 and a red light blinks at me.

I'm beginning to sweat as I realize her friend might have locked it with a code of her own. I start at the beginning and try 1-3-5-1.

Red light.

"Fuck." I whisper.

I try 1-3-5-2.

Red light.

I finally make it to 1-3-5-8 and it flashes green and I hear a click.

Time is of the essence and I rifle through her purse.

She has $900 of newly printed hundred dollar bills in her powder blue Hermes wallet.

Stealing cash is a big N-O in my book. That's bound to cause concern.

I swipe a gift card to Saks and a Christian Dior tube of lipstick.

Everything is back to its original place and I lock it back up so at first glance, nothing will be amiss.

———————◆———————

After raising as much hell as I could without making a scene, the hotel offers us a discounted rate for an overnight stay. Camilla jumps at the opportunity and I oblige, hoping the long night will finally give me access to her cell phone.

Camilla's buzz has lasted throughout the day and I've unfortunately lost mine. I remedy that quickly when we go to a rooftop bar on the resort.

I'm stopped at the entrance when I inform the bouncers my ID was stolen at the spa. The manager confirms this from a report and I'm let through.

So this is where all the attractive men in our age bracket are.

I'm not going out of my way to initiate conversation with the men here. I'm committed to Sam even if things aren't serious yet. But if they approach me, I'll enlighten them and flirt back.

The view is breathtaking. Pulling out my phone, I snap a quick picture. The sky's bright blue is being overpowered by splashes of orange and yellow thanks to the descending sun. I bet the sunset is like this every fucking night in this rich city. The inhabitants get what they pay for and they better have a stellar sunset as a backdrop to their mansions every goddamn day.

Sam gets my view via text and I intentionally include five hotties in the background just to remind him I'm around available, attractive guys. I add, "Hope you're having a good night. Terrible view, right?"

God I hate those people. The sarcastic ones that must think they are so original by posting their braggy, boastful photos accompanied with some mocking caption like "I'm obviously having a horrible time." Yeah, sure you are. You're petting a rare species of dolphin in the Bermuda Triangle. You're swimming in an ocean that is more pure than holy water. Fuck off.

I'm actually okay if he takes his time to reply. The last thing I need is another interrogation asking what bar I'm at, then I'd have to head over to Yelp and...

Holy hell. How could I be so stupid? I sent him a picture of a sunset! Sun hitting the ocean. That doesn't happen in Florida! And not just that, my "sunset" should have happened three hours ago because of the time difference.

Fucking Christ, Liz! What is wrong with you?

I can't exactly take it back and argue, "Oh did I say a book signing in Florida? I meant I'm in Monterey. And by book signing I mean I'm currently taking blowjob shots with your ex."

It doesn't work like that!

Maybe he isn't that perceptive.

What is happening? I'm slipping.

Camilla's name on my cell phone. Strike one.

The credit card fiasco. Strike two.

Now this?

Amateur.

Camilla takes an identical picture, posts it to Instagram, and adds the location.

Breathe. Breathe.

Sam isn't on Instagram. But the fact that Camilla's account is *still* public means he could check in on her at any time. We all have the curiosity bug inside us. Sam could be infected far worse than any of us and visit her profile weekly. Daily!

"Look how pretty it is!" She shows me just to rub salt in my wound.

This can't be happening. If Sam did a bit of late night reconnaissance, he could easily see the similarity of our pictures and suspect something. All that is missing in her photo are the hot guys… and me!

My blood pressure is sky high and I chug the rest of my drink, like alcohol is the cure for my erratic heartbeat.

By 9pm Camilla is feeling great. I, on the other hand, feel like Cinderella at midnight, seconds away from being exposed for her true self.

She's dancing with a few guys and I'm watching like a freak in the shadows.

"I'm getting kind of tired." I force a yawn when she and another guy approach me.

"Aww no! It's still early!" She shouts.

"Yeah, it's still early!" This stranger adds. I give him a death stare.

"Have another drink." Camilla suggests.

"I've had way too much." Lie. I'm a heavyweight champ and could drink them both under the table thanks to my alcoholic genetics flowing through my system.

"Have some water! Order some food." Camilla advises.

"I think I have diarrhea."

"Oh my gosh, Sophie!" She exclaims.

"Niiiice." The guy congratulates me with a high five.

"Go back to the room, I'll see you a little later." Camilla says.

I practically run out of there because I can't keep this up much longer.

I'm exhausted. Tired of always looking for an exit strategy in case I'm ambushed with the unknown.

If I pretend to be asleep when she gets back, hopefully she'll put her phone on the nightstand and crash next to me.

———◆———

Get me home, now.

I drop off Camilla at her place and head back to the city.

San Francisco appears closer and closer on the map.

Sam asks when I'll be back and I lie and give myself a day or two just so I can recharge in peace and quiet. It shows him I'm not willing to drop everything for him.

In reality, there's a lot for me to process.

I read his incoming text.

Sam: "Let me know when you're back. My sister's boyfriend is going to be staying with me for a night next week, and unless you like threesomes, I might be busy, too."

I swerve the car and drop my phone at the same time.

"Ugh the balls of that guy." I seethe. Nathaniel's presence means I won't get to see Sam, and that makes my blood boil.

I stop at a grocery store and stock up on food because I'm going to be housebound for the foreseeable future.

Knowing Nathaniel will be in the same town, let alone staying with Sam for the next few days, makes my guts smolder. This is one risk I refuse to take. I don't care if it's 1 in a million stepping foot outside my place. If I see Nathaniel again, I'll commit homicide.

Especially after that stunt he pulled with my parents.

I unpack my groceries with the $40 I had hidden in the Porsche for emergencies and prepare myself for a fun evening in for the next five days.

I open my laptop and log into my dummy email account.

Last night, when Camilla was asleep, I finally had my moment.

As she slept soundlessly like an angel, I unlocked her phone and pulled up her emails. I searched "Sam Evans" and highlighted every exchange with his name mentioned or as a sender or recipient, and forwarded them to an obscure email address. I then deleted all the emails in the sent folder so there would be no digital footprint of my being there.

As I wait impatiently to login to my account, I pull up my side project.

B&B was notorious for being overly cautious with their security systems. They made you log in remotely with a VPN to access the portal for my old department.

Using a VPN from home, I connect with an LA IP address to hide my real location.

In the past, they gave us designated usernames. Mine was EBAKER, first initial of my first name and my full last name.

Naturally, Stella's login would be SEVANS.

In the real world, guessing someone's password is 1 in 500 million, and that's if they don't use a special character. The odds are not in your favor.

But if you were me and already had Stella's job, you'd know you're given a temporary password first.

I kid you not; your username was also your temporary password. Some security measures, eh?

Back in the day, I changed mine immediately, like any normal person would.

Stella, however, never changed her initial password like a fucking moron.

So for the past few weeks, I've been tweaking some numbers. Nothing major yet, small tiny errors that any human could make. I imagine these small miscalculations are similar enough to the tricks she played on me. It feels amazing to get this kind of justice, even if she hasn't noticed it yet.

I close out B&B and check on the emails.

Camilla and Sam's exchanges are unremarkable and scarce.

I cipher through the hotel reservations and look for something scandalous.

There are calendar invites to a few parties but no real emails. Which makes sense, what couple of this century corresponds by email anymore?

I'm about to give up hope when I stumble upon an email between Camilla and her mother. Its contents create shockwaves as I realize this might become more useful than I realize.

"Hey mom. Sorry I haven't called you back, this is just easier without getting emotional. I'm doing better each day. I still miss him, but I've accepted it. There's just so much space between us now. I know you keep hoping things will turn around, but they won't.

And as for what I said in the hospital, we have to let it go. The random guy who bumped into me... it was an accident. Despite seeing what I saw, accusing Stella of purposely tripping him with no proof... it's just not worth it. How was she to know he'd send me down the stairs? That's a horrible thing to accuse someone of and Sam doesn't need to know this in case it's not even true. Stella might be cruel, but I'd like to think she wouldn't do something so heinous."

Accident my ass. I'd bet my life Stella tripped this innocent bystander and he inevitably sent Camilla down like a domino. I wouldn't put anything past her to get Sam back where he belongs: withering away at the bottom of the totem pole. Damn, she's more cold blooded than I expected.

I screenshot the email, unsure what I'll do with it at the moment. I'm not sure releasing a bomb this huge will protect me from the blowback.

CHAPTER EIGHT

———— ◆ ————

The credit card was easy to replace. My ID, not so much. I had to contact the same guy I purchased it from off the dark web and he gave me shit about not being careful with it. I told that dweeb he could shove it up his tight ass and offered to pay the normal price. But luckily the replacement came within 36 hours. He must like me for some reason.

Sam's silence makes me feel like I'm about to be ghosted.

When we said goodbye after our sushi date, I think he picked up on my desperation. I'm overcome with this intense pressure to ensure this works out for me. And winning Sam over, by any means necessary, is part of that plan.

But I think he knows I'm trying too hard. Why else would he not text me over the weekend?

I pull out my phone and text the only friend I have at the moment.

Harper: "Might not be able to make it Friday for Pilates."

Camilla responds right away.

Camilla: "All good! Are you at least doing something fun?"

Harper: "A couple job interviews lined up."

Camilla: "Oh you'll do great! If you wanna stop by the restaurant I'll make you lunch and we can study interview questions."

Her niceties make me question the human race. Are there really people like Camilla that exist in the world? Selfless and genuine?

Harper: "Wine sounds amazing right now ;) But I'm actually driving to San Francisco to drop off my resume in person. I thought it would be a good first step."

I can't pretend forever that I'm able to survive without a job. Okay and maybe I'm feeling her out bringing up her old stomping grounds.

Camilla: "Wow, San Fran? I used to live there with my ex."

Harper: "Oh that's right! I totally forgot." I didn't. "Watch I end up working for him ;)"

Camilla: "That'd be a small world! But I don't even know where he works anymore."

That's a good sign.

Camilla: "Want me to text him in case he knows someone where you're applying?"

Oh fuck no.

My right arm goes numb.

My chest constricts.

My breathing is pitched and shallow.

I would rather die from this abrupt heart attack than have Camilla reach out to Sam now. I've almost accepted the fact that I am yesterday's news, and I would have less of a chance winning him back if Camilla was back in the picture.

Harper: "Oh no I would never ask you to do that. I'm certain my amazing skills will land me a job ;)"

I'm using too many winky faces. I need to cool it.

Camilla: "Yeah... sometimes I want to text him though and see how he's doing."

This must be what dying feels like.

Clasping the phone in my homicidal grip, I type and erase a response four times.

Harper: "Don't listen to me but you told me once our past is our past for a reason."

That was a pretty responsible reply, if I must say so myself.

Camilla doesn't text back.

If the world doesn't end and Sam does indeed text me to make plans, the next time I'm around his phone I have some modifications to put in place.

CHAPTER NINE

———◆———

It's been eight days since I last spoke to Sam.

It doesn't sound like a long time, 8 days, but that's 192 hours. 11,520 minutes.

691,200 seconds I've wondered if this was the moment he'd finally reach out.

Eight days.

I've barely left the condo.

You'd think I forgot to pay the water bill (which I almost couldn't afford) because I haven't showered in four of those days.

That's 96 hours I've smelled this funk on me.

My hair is so dirty it hurts, and I'm pretty sure in the last 48 hours, I've gained 10 pounds.

Unless Sam is in the hospital and unable to text, I don't see this ending well for me.

In the forefront of my mind, a relationship with Sam

was the best-case scenario. He'd brag to Stella about his amazing girlfriend, and as time elapsed, I'd remain mysterious but hear any updates firsthand about her life beginning to implode.

She'd have no idea the person making Sam's life so amazing is the same person making her life so miserable.

Worst-case scenario, the one I'm in now, things with Sam would never progress. I'd have to watch from afar as I did my handy work in the shadows.

Her job would end. Her relationship would end. And finally, her life would end when Sam finds out what really happened with Camilla and the baby.

My objective has always been to destroy Stella's relationship with her brother. He's the one person in this world who loves her unconditionally. She can't just have his affection and support waiting for her at the end of this.

But during all this, I realized something.

I'll be no better than Stella because I won't have Sam either.

And even if he does manage to come back around, he'll find out who I am one way or another, right?

It's all wishful thinking because I don't think I'll be hearing from him any time soon.

It's Friday and I can picture him going out with Jake and Diego, flirting and schmoozing a bunch of hot, single women, then taking one home and replacing my number with hers.

Violence materializes before my eyes and I hurl my soggy leftover French fries at the wall.

They scatter everywhere and the stains of ketchup briefly placate the anger.

My phone buzzes under my butt and I reach below me and read the screen.

Sam!

I pinch my leg to confirm I'm not dreaming.

Oh my god, this is real.

How did this turn of events come to be?

Eight whole days of silence and now all of a sudden I'm triple dating with his friends? I'm not complaining, but what made Sam change his mind? My silence? Leaving him alone? Does he like the chase?

This is my last chance. This is it.

The highs and lows aren't new to me; and to go from 0 to 60 like this gives me butterflies you'd expect on a rollercoaster. The excitement, the stimulation, it's what gets me going.

Sam said this was casual. Ha, yeah, like that's gonna happen.

Gloria's stolen gift card has been waiting for this day. $1000 to Saks will reap the sexiest dress you'll ever see and some killer new heels.

I'm going to charm his friends like the snake I am and by the end of the night, he'll be begging me to shed my skin and be his forever.

He likes working for what he wants. Well, I'll make sure he'll work for it tonight.

My laptop is open and I pull up Craigslist.

———————◆———————

I'm a few minutes early when I approach the hostess at the restaurant.

"Hi, good evening. Do you have a reservation?"

Before I can answer, my eyes hone in on a loud party attendant that is occupying the bar with a group of maybe 30 friends.

My memory for faces is top notch and standing before me is a team leader who used to work at B&B. She's 20 feet away, drinking a martini and laughing her unique smoker's cackle.

Not everyone is good with faces and mine is a bit different from the last time she saw me. She might not recognize me at all, given I've lost weight and had a few upgrades done. But will I take that chance? You bet your ass I won't.

"Were you waiting for someone, ma'am?"

I focus back on the hostess and say, "I'm early I'll come back."

I quickly retreat to my car across the street singing, "It's A Small World" on a maddening loop in my head.

What if she doesn't leave?

Awesome, this plan I had to wow his friends won't even happen because I'm hiding in my car like a pussy.

Sam, Diego and some blond walk into the restaurant.

I shrink in the passenger's seat and wait for a plan to formulate in my head like it normally does. But it doesn't happen.

Sam texts me moments later.

Sam: "Everything okay?"

Harper: "Yes! Sorry I was stupid and stopped by the office for the first time in a while. It took longer to escape. Be there soon, sorry! Don't wait to order drinks!"

Time speeds up and for every second I spend hiding out in my car, five minutes creep by.

But lo and behold, she steps out the front door with a fucking Vape stick and walks around the block with an acquaintance to smoke.

I practically run out of my car and through the restaurant, thankful her dependence to nicotine is a reliable addiction.

"Sorry I'm late!" I exclaim as I approach the table.

Sam stands and gives me a hug, my cleavage pressing into his firm pecs. He doesn't kiss me, which feels like a huge diss. Not even on the cheek. Nothing.

Great, this is going well for me.

Introductions are done and I feel like I might come on too strong too fast, so I play it cool.

The usual questions are asked. What do I do? Where am I from?

Sam is quiet through all this and I can't get a read on him. I didn't think I'd have to charm him tonight, too. He's throwing me off my game.

Sam's on his third drink when Jake asks the ice-breaker.

"How do you like our boy Sam here?"

"Sam's great!" I say it with conviction but leave it at that.

The better part of me would feed that ego 'til he was stuffed and bursting at the seams. But the typical part of me, the side of me that doesn't listen to logic or reason, wants to blast him in front of his buddies.

He doesn't deserve praise right now.

I finish my drink and listen to the conversation, contributing when necessary but mainly taking it all in and analyzing the women. Are they a threat? What do I need to know about them?

And then Stella's name is brought up.

"Has she reached out at all?" I ask.

"Of course not." Sam's tone of voice is unfamiliar and rude.

Jake and Diego look stunned.

I bite my lower lip and wonder what the hell is going on. He's never done that to me before. And he's being foul with his friends, too.

Another drink appears before him and Diego suggests he might want to slow down.

I would second that motion if I weren't scared he'd start an uprising.

I'm scanning the room and I notice my old coworker is gone. I relax in the seat and then remember the call I made. The guy I hired for the night. Sam's competition.

I spot him at the bar thanks to his high quality headshot he sent.

"Well I need to use the powder room." Avery says.

Jumping at the opportunity to join her, Carrie does the same.

As we walk to the ladies room and past the man at the bar, I loudly shout, "I've heard great things about their steak salad here!" Our sign. Our code phrase.

Glancing back so our eyes connect, he winks at me in acknowledgment.

When the three of us enter the ladies room, Avery puts on some lipstick and Carrie pees.

"Sam is smitten with you. I can tell." Avery says to her reflection.

"Sure doesn't seem like it tonight."

"He must be nervous. He's drinking a lot. We haven't gone on a date like this in a long time. Since his last girlfriend."

"Well, I'm not his girlfriend." I correct her nicely.

"But he likes you. I know it."

I nod like I want her to continue, to feed *my* ego, but she doesn't.

"I really like him. But we both agreed this would be fun. Is it worth the trouble telling him I want more? You both know him well enough, right?"

"Do it!" Carrie squeals in support from the stall.

"I've known Sam a long time." Avery begins. "He doesn't always say what he's thinking. Sometimes we have to pull it out of him."

As we exit the bathroom, the man in the suit at the bar approaches us.

"Hey ladies." He slurs.

"Hi." We all say in unison.

"I was watching you when you first walked in and I must say, you are gorgeous."

Neither Avery nor Carrie assumes it's her he's speaking to, which just earned them a point. They aren't conceited like I expected.

"Me?" I confirm.

"Yes you. You are delicious. I want to taste you." Even though his eyes aren't glossy, we all get the vibe that he's drunk out of his mind.

"Oh well, I haven't heard that pick up line before!" I exclaim.

"Is that guy at the table your boyfriend?"

"Well, no." I admit, because when Carrie and Avery repeat this story, I have to ensure Sam knows

I know I'm not his girlfriend.

"I would love to get your number." He asks.

"Thanks and I appreciate the compliment..."

"Parker." He interrupts.

"Parker." I begin. I'm sure this guy has spent thousands on acting classes and little does he know, no conscience like mine will get you similar results. We both have parts to play and acts to complete. "... But I'm not interested right now." I finish.

"Well here's my business card." He slips it lightly between my cleavage. Oof he actually gave me goosebumps with that move. "Call me if you change your mind. You won't be disappointed."

"Thank you, Parker. You have a good night."

We all return to the table laughing.

My original plan was to have him buy me a drink before everyone got there, but that all went down the toilet. This was plan B and I'm glad he was bright enough to follow directions.

———◆———

The rest of the night is a disaster.

And I don't just mean dinner.

After I left Sam's drunk ass outside his condo, I went home and contemplated what the hell I did wrong. This was supposed to be my night to win him back. But instead, he pushed me away.

Then somewhere between REM cycle and 2am, Sam texted me because he can't hold his own and nearly keeled over from alcohol poisoning.

I don't even know what to think. He was a helpless child and I was his mommy taking care of him. The only, *only* upside to this whole night is that he's passed out before me.

Now is the time I can go through his phone.

Camilla did in fact *not* reach out... yet.

Thanks to her being a contact already, I block her ass and hope if Sam ever wonders how that happened, he'll think he did it in a drunken stupor... oh my gosh, like tonight!

I'm not about to press my luck and start following his location. That would come across on our text thread and I'm too paranoid to download an app right now.

My time is done here. I have to leave.

With caution, I place his cell phone on his nightstand.

His breathing is fine, he fell asleep on his side, and if he knew what was good for him, he'd declare his love for me tomorrow.

Who the hell puts up with this kind of behavior? A girlfriend.

CHAPTER TEN

———◆———

The apology text is waiting for me on my phone when I wake up.

I'm shocked he didn't call me out for leaving him, but I think he knows. No woman in her right mind would put up with that shit if she didn't really have feelings for the guy.

Forced or not, I can feel myself growing to truly like him. Most people would run for the hills with the way he acted, but all I saw was he's flawed like the rest of us. He's not perfect.

His confession for his foolishness is so sincere that I have already accepted his apology.

Relationships aren't perfect and I can admit with certainty that we can get through this.

———◆———

Maybe we can't get through this.

I sneak out of Sam's yet again and this is becoming a god damn routine.

Where do I even begin?

For one, I found a receipt of a dumb-fuck waitress addressed to Sam being overly flirtatious. She even added her phone number. I did not see that coming.

But then he explained that it was all Nathaniel's fault, like Sam's life depended on it, like this relationship depended on me believing him.

Nathaniel *would* do something stupid like that. Which is a great indicator that he's being unfaithful. Once a cheater, always a cheater.

So why did I sneak out like a cat burglar?

I've come to the realization that not only am I ruining Stella's life, which is fine by me, but I'm also ruining Sam's.

And while I don't normally feel guilty about this, a part of me is hoping this could still work out in my favor.

We hung out tonight like we were old friends. I knew we were capable of this. Finally I was able to tell my side of my tragic story. I even cried! Granted I had to sell my soul to the devil to get those tears to release, but I was overcome with a sense of security being in his arms.

I always imagined this would work like an arranged marriage.

When two people are forced into a predetermined relationship, they make it work. They *have* to. I figured my situation with Sam was similar to that.

I would accept every part of Sam, flaws and all, because I had no choice. What I forgot to take into account was Sam isn't seeing this through the same rose-colored glasses. He could walk away at any time. I cannot. I *have* to make this work, so I'm willing to do whatever it takes. Make sacrifices, change who I am for him, all for the sake of love.

I'm starting to wonder if there's a way around this; maybe there's a way I can get back at Stella, ruin her relationship with Sam, and still come out on top.

Sam will be over any minute and this is it.

It's do or die. He's going to agree to be exclusive or send me on my way. And if it's the latter, I will jump off my balcony... after I send that email of course. I keep that in my back pocket just waiting to pull it out if things take a turn.

The knock at my door echoes loudly in my ears and I answer with caution.

"Hey stranger." I say, because what else do I say?

You can only have one psycho in your life. Will it be me or Stella?

He pulls me in for an embrace and it's compassionate, warm, feels like a home I've never known.

We sit on my couch and I grab us a pot of coffee and he helps himself to a mug.

I tell him everything before he has a chance to tell me he's over it. This is *my* chance to stroke his ego like he's never been stroked before. I'm over the games. I actually want to see if things could progress for me. For us.

And everything falls away the second he says, "I don't plan on dating any other women."

———— ♦ ————

We're exclusive.

If I were Camilla, I would have locked Sam up and never let him see the light of day.

He's a rare specimen and does not belong among other females who could potentially steal him.

But the only woman I have to worry about now is closer than I'd like.

Too close.

Stella.

Sam will give me all the dirty details the second her life begins to fall apart, which should be soon. I'll revel in every little nasty mishap but support him whenever necessary. This is actually better than I realized. I am going to have firsthand observations at her demise.

And then I'll spill the beans about the baby.

My initial plan was to ruin Stella's life by any means necessary, even if that means I'm alone again at the end. As long as she's single, fired, and without her brother, she's worse off than I was.

But I'm thinking of other avenues. Maybe I can figure out a way to make sure we all get what we deserve.

———— ◆ ————

Sam spends the night like a real boyfriend. *My* boyfriend.

I wake up at 6am and make the quick mile drive to Walmart. I'm palming Sam's keys because this is the last piece to one of the many puzzles in my head.

I need Stella's house key, plain and simple. I don't know which one is hers, which is why I look like a janitor at the key copying kiosk in the entrance. I'm sure if I went to an actual locksmith, I could get these seven unknown keys copied for under $20. Instead, I'm paying for the convenience and accessibility and spend a whopping $60 for six keys I undoubtedly won't need.

I grab some eggs, milk, pancake mix, and bacon in case Sam wakes up while I've been out.

When I return to my condo, I set his keys just as they were and begin cooking breakfast.

When Sam does wake up, one of the first things he tells me is, "I think I'm going to LA today."

Umm, this is a bit sooner than I was expecting. I was hoping we'd be a well established couple before Sam extended the olive branch down Stella's throat.

He asks to borrow my laptop and my pupils disappear into little white marbles.

I have way too many suspicious links bookmarked and who the hell knows what's on the main browser when he opens it. I lie and say it's in my car.

As luck would have it, he leaves to go home and book a flight. I'm flooded with relief that I don't have to hand over the main tool used for stalking, but taken aback that he's already leaving me.

Looks like I'll be following him out to LA.

CHAPTER ELEVEN

———•◆•———

Sam's flight is in three hours, and while he's packing and preparing to go back to the dark side, I gas up the Porsche and drive the six hours down to LA.

Sure, I could use my Elizabeth Baker ID and get on the second flight out, but I do not want a paper trail. And I don't want to risk my bought ID going through the system, even if I was assured it would get me anywhere in the US. TSA security is a bitch and driving is much safer.

I look at my reflection in the driver's window before I leave the gas station with a water bottle and protein bar.

My appearance has changed drastically in the past year. I see the old me staring back, the reflection of an insecure, blond little butterball who tried to keep to herself. I didn't ask for any of the drama that followed me the moment I met Stella.

Only a handful of people have seen what I'm capable of. Stella will soon bear witness to the type of person I really am, if she didn't already suspect it before I left her life.

She is guilty of more than she realizes. I'm certain she persuaded Nathaniel to get me fired, to set me up. She was the ringleader and he was a measly follower, drunk on love and stupid enough to do everything she wished.

Pushing aside the past, I get in the car and set my destination.

I don't plan on being in LA long. I want to get this done so I can focus on Stella's downfall. Changing numbers in her account hasn't done shit. I need to pull out the big guns.

I'm entering LA just as Sam's name appears on caller ID.

Right after he tells me he and Stella made up, he says, "Why don't you meet me out here."

Is this a trap? Is he waiting for me to lie to him? Does he know I'm already here?

I ultimately agree and decide I will have to either sleep in my car or get a hotel. If I can swing it, I could try and stop by Stella's house to see which key works. But my window of opportunity is so small.

I'm parked in a loading zone outside B&B at 4:55pm.

As long as the same systems are in place when I worked there, this will be an easy in and out operation.

I'll barely be on the security cameras long and I doubt anyone would even look twice at me. They're too busy in their own worlds. Welcome to LA.

The courier should be picking up all the priority mail by 5pm, but I'll be getting to them first.

I'm worried I'm too late and maybe they beat me to it when I walk into the mailroom.

An unfamiliar face greets me.

"I'm here for pickups." I say confidently.

"You're new, dearie." The older lady declares.

"Just for today, he's super backed up and might not get here for the pickup." I say "he" praying their usual messenger is a male, and I'm right.

"Oh that poor Mark is always so busy." She hands over a huge stack of large, heavy envelopes and I take them with a smile. Most are your common USPS, FedEx, UPS, and DHL, but then the lesser known companies that need to go to specific destinations. She hands a clipboard and I scribble illegible words as a signature.

"Thanks. Enjoy your night."

The exchange is effortless.

How could it be this easy? She didn't ask for ID, nothing!

I hurriedly take the box and run back to my car.

While I'm rifling through the dozens of packages and express overnight deliveries, I spot two familiar items that are at least 50 pages thick. Contracts. I stare at the account number on the top of the mailing label and confirm it was once my department.

I take out the packing slip for both and replace them in the opposite package. I've never heard of either recipient's name, but it won't matter tomorrow. Because tomorrow, they will get the other's contract and realize the woman handling their accounts is a bloody moron.

Chapter Twelve

———◆———

I've been staying at the shittiest motel imaginable for the past two nights. It was the cheapest I could afford and had I known I'd need a flea bath, I would have splurged and stayed at Motel 6.

The door barely stays shut and you can see sunlight pouring in through the cracks of the dilapidated wood frame. All it would take is one broad shoulder to the door and you'd be inside my room with easy access to rape.

Los Angeles is my least favorite city now. Not because my life ended here and I have nothing but bad memories haunting me, but because of the people.

Everywhere you go there are hordes of hipsters, influencers, wannabe supermodels, or Wall Street clones invading your personal space. Everyone wants to be someone and everyone is going somewhere. No one looks at life the same out here; LA is a different planet…

one where narcissism and vanity rule everything. You can't walk a couple blocks without stumbling upon a dilettante hoping to make it big.

I hate being stuck here while Sam and Stella rekindle their relationship. They can repair it all they want. After I'm done with them, there's no olive tree big enough to fix what I'll break.

I requested more towels because I refuse to sit on the actual bed without protection.

Occasionally when I'm bored, I check all the major job sites to see if B&B is hiring for my old position. When I don't see anything posted, I go as far as calling the office to see if Stella is still employed there. When the receptionist offers to transfer me to her, I hang up before it can go through.

Fuck. Why hasn't she been fired yet? I've checked her task list. She's so behind and has so many past dues with clients and referrals.

What more do I have to do? She's probably fucking up on her own and won't need my help much longer so why hasn't it happened yet?

My boredom is broken when Sam calls me.

"Nathaniel came home last night and did this corny 'honey, I'm home' bit." He tells me.

Wait an ever-loving minute.

I'm stunned silent as I replay an identical greeting he used to give me.

Wow. He's so unoriginal he can't even come up with a new bit with his new girlfriend.

"Sam, she's happy, right?" I choke out. Of course she's not happy. She's a liar. She's probably miserable. He's treating her just like he did me.

"They want to go to Thailand." Sam discloses.

This is when I sit up fully and comprehend what this means.

"When?" I spit out.

"Like next month…" Sam says more but all I see is an imaginary calendar in my head and realize her leaving the country probably won't happen.

Her relationship won't last for them to go on a trip together.

Mark my words. If Stella does go to Thailand, it'll be alone.

Chapter Thirteen

———— ◆ ————

Why is hotel sex better than regular sex? Is it the new environment? The bed being the focal point? The risk knowing you have neighbors on the other side of the wall hearing everything?

Coronado is already proving to be amazing for this new relationship. Even if I did leave my car in LA, I'm glad this worked out. We needed this.

"Fuck." Sam says out of breath.

"I know."

Our sexual chemistry is insane, off the charts. Who knew two people could be so compatible.

"Fuck Harper… we… we didn't use a condom."

He says this like I didn't already know. I climbed on top of him, fully aware of this fact. I wanted to see how he'd react. I'm hoping this open door will gain entry into his worst fears.

"Are you on the pill?"

"Of course." And I actually am. Trapping a man with a baby is beneath me.

"Do you take it religiously?"

"Of course." I pause. "Want me to go get Plan B?"

"No!" Sam barks at me like a dog and it's unexpected.

He's going to tell me, I can feel it. I've been waiting to hear his side and I think the time is now.

"I got a girl pregnant a year and a half ago."

Delaying my reply, I take a breath, try not to react like I already know, and let worry, fear and shock all pass across my face before I finally say, "Oh."

"She lost the baby." He adds. "My ex-girlfriend. And it was one of the worst experiences I went through after my parents."

And now the floodgates open. He tells me everything; the good, the bad, the ugly, and the unknown.

"Stella was furious with me." Sam begins, like I didn't already expect this. "She berated me on how I could be so irresponsible, which was a complete paradox considering I was everything but that in this situation."

God, she's worse than I thought. This wasn't even his fault. How is he still putting up with her bullshit?

And then the blast happens. The important piece that Camilla managed to leave out explodes across my face like shrapnel.

"The doctor told me point blank I could only save one of them."

He goes into detail about what would have happened to both the baby and Camilla, but all I can focus on is my eyes not bugging out of my skull.

Why did Camilla omit that? That seems rather significant to the story! And why hasn't he mentioned that someone stumbled into her causing this accident? *Does he really not know?*

"He had to save her. How was a guy like me capable of raising a special needs child alone without any experience or help."

I'm speechless at the mystery surrounding this one event. Sam had to choose who to save? He doesn't even know Camilla suspects Stella tripped someone to cause this? Am I in an episode of All My Children? What's with all the secrets?

Acting normal after digesting all this will be rough, even for me. Would I call them all liars? Maybe? This is just so unexpected, I don't know what to think.

———— ◆ ————

We kiss and dance the rest of the night, ordering room service and bottles of champagne.

Sam's demeanor already seems better; like he finally told me every part of his past and he can move forward into this new life with me.

When we fly home to San Francisco, I take a train right back down to LA to pick up my car that was left there after our weekend getaway.

The only positive thing to come out of this extraneous, unnecessary errand was that I was able to put a GPS tracker on Nathaniel and Stella's cars when I stopped by the parking garage at work. I've been meaning to do so but I haven't had the time and I refused to do it while they were home. A strange woman poking around her ex-boyfriend's car? Perfect scenario for the cops to be called.

This tiny achievement is what's getting me by, because no less than a few days later, I'm met with obstacles I didn't account for.

The first boulder that comes barreling toward me is when Sam stopped by my place unannounced. I wasn't expecting him and I was actually in Monterey enjoying lunch with Camilla. I had to lie and say I went into the office last minute.

Which was fine; totally believable right?

Until another day I pulled the same stunt and he asked if he could come by the office with coffee because he missed me.

Sam: "What's the address? I'll bring your favorite."

Cardiac. Arrest.

Harper: "Now isn't a good time, my boss is being a dick."

Sam: "Even more reason to come by and beat his ass."

So now I need to get fired.

The second obstacle happened last week when my condo building posted a flyer for a potluck on the rooftop patio. We could all mingle and drink and get to know the neighbors.

Sam wanted to go, of course, but I'd be a fool to put myself in a situation where I was exposed for not being the actual owner.

And besides, Sam doesn't need to know Ethan is my gay neighbor who didn't, in fact, use me to edit his story.

Stella postponed her trip because, apparently, she's been so busy at work. Sounds like a fucking lie if I ever heard one, because with all the work *I've* done, she should be getting fired.

———◆———

Instead, I've been "fired."

It was impossible to fake a job with no fictitious books to read, no real office to go to, no tasks to complete. I got lucky with Ethan but my luck ran dry. This had to happen or it really would have come back to bite me in my ass.

I feel like a newbie actress on the set of a soap opera as I dramatically cry into soggy tissues.

Sam is calming me down, which is expected. He tells me everything will be okay as he holds onto me and rubs my back. Frankly, I wish he were rubbing me elsewhere because I am so turned on with the way he's comforting me.

He's such a good guy. And for the briefest moment, I feel it.

Warmth covers my insides as my hollowed out chest expands.

I love this man.

I've known deep down the strange feeling consuming me might be love. Ignoring it only made me feel it ten times harder.

This is unusual for me and as Sam suggests going to a spa, I decide I have to tell him.

Even if Stella hasn't been fired yet, hasn't been dumped, I will still be around as her life falls apart.

But I'll be his lover, not just his girlfriend. So things are working out of order. I don't care. I think he might actually love me back.

———◆———

"I have to tell you something." My words shake as I smush Sam's cheeks with my oily hands.

Our couple's massage is over and I'm hoping this moment of tranquility releases more than just toxins. I'm hoping his heart is open.

"I'm in love with you." I confess. "I've loved you for a while now. I know it's soon, and I know you might not love me back…"

"Give me a second." He says getting off me.

I'm about to fall through the massage bed and plummet to my death. Wow, did I underestimate myself. I really thought I had this; it's not like me to misjudge scenarios.

A lifetime passes and I see myself growing old alone. Probably in jail for identity theft, fraud, assault, robbery. I'm two seconds away from grabbing the sheets I'm draped in and hanging myself so I can end this nightmare.

But then Sam returns with something. What is it?

A picture of me and Nathaniel together? Is this an ambush? Are the cops going to barge in and arrest me?

"Look."

I don't want to. I want to go drown myself in the champagne that hasn't been popped yet. God, what a waste.

But then I see it. Those three little words all women want to hear. Written in melted chocolate, barely legible.

My face is soaked. I'm sobbing all over my naked body, his naked body, crying happy tears. Relieved tears. Exhausted tears. Tears I don't have to fake because he actually loves me, too.

Finally.

Take that, Nathaniel. I *am* loveable.

CHAPTER FOURTEEN

———◆———

Tuesday morning I wake up alone in my condo and the emptiness is foreign.

A few days have passed and I haven't seen Sam, which isn't concerning. But I don't want it to become a habit.

The inevitable is hitting me hard and I know this will all have to end at some point. This charade. The acting. It can't last forever.

Eventually, Stella is going to find out who I am. And as long as she ends up with nothing, I'm okay with that.

Right?

Contemplating this notion under my covers, I quake with apprehension.

I don't want this to end.

I love being with Sam. What does that say about

me? That in order to achieve that level of happiness I have to fake who I really am?

Things with Camilla have been put on hold thanks to my fake new job. I'm keeping her accessible just in case the email I stole from her phone doesn't prove as useful as I'm hoping.

Somehow, Stella has managed to survive at B&B. Those contracts I fixed didn't do much damage, so I strategize how I can get this to happen sooner.

I'm not against taking a page from her rulebook and setting her up to get fired the same way I did. But the similarity might cause suspicion. As far as she knows, I'm long gone.

And speak of the devil, a text arrives and I'm two seconds away from losing control of my bowels.

Sam: "Hey you, Stella is coming into town for about two hours between layovers. She insists she meets you. How do you feel about that?"

"Son of a bitch!" I yell.

Did I just jinx myself? No less than an hour ago I was willing to prolong this as long as I could.

There's no way I can get out of this. We're in love. We're official. I can't hide from Stella forever and I knew this would happen someday but I didn't think *tonight*.

It can't end now. I'm not done yet. I still want more time with Sam.

Nothing has really changed in her life. And I know if I had more time, I'd come up with some solution to maybe end up happy at the end of this.

But instead, my fingers betray me and type: "Okay, I'll go. When should I be there?"

———◆———

As I ride down the elevator to the parking garage, I pray it gets stuck on the tracks so I'm trapped in here for hours.

But when it reaches the ground floor, I step out frowning.

On my drive over to Sam's, I contemplate getting in a car accident. Nothing serious, but enough to rough me up a bit.

But with my luck I'd total the car.

When I knock on Sam's door, I cross my fingers that we are hit with a magnum earthquake.

Instead, a hurricane comes at me, sweeping me up with its wild force field. His horny ass is actually trying to feel me up right now.

My mind is in Neverland, wondering how the hell I can get tonight canceled as Sam slips his fingers up my legs.

I have a tiny bottle of eye drops in my purse; they are my last resort if I can't think of something else. I will mix them into my water and get the worst stomach ache of the century to get out of this dinner.

A thought enters my head.

Could I call a health inspector and claim I saw cockroaches in the kitchen?

"I haven't even heard from her yet." Sam admits as he continues molesting me. Well there goes that idea. We don't even know which restaurant we're meeting at!

"My phone is over on the table waiting for her to land."

And it's there. That simple little sentence and I know I only have one shot.

"Let me at least put my stuff down. I got her a little gift and it's super heavy in my purse."

I walk over to the table and set my phone next to his. He won't keep his hungry eyes off me.

"I'm so nervous. Do you have any alcohol? I'll drink anything right now." I ask, hoping that will distract him.

He leaves me for his kitchen.

And with that, his back is turned and I power down his phone.

Goodbye, Stella.

———◆———

My mind is on the clock as my body is against Sam's.

We're fucking like we have all the time in the world as I withhold the most intense orgasm.

It's been 10 minutes. 15. 20. We're approaching 30 minutes and I know this is enough time. I've been prolonging everything, like I want this moment to last forever. And I do.

Sam is oblivious to the time as we clean up in his bathroom.

"You going to be okay?" He asks as I put my hair up.

"Yeah, that little romp helped settle my nerves."

"*Little* romp, huh?"

"Yeah, little." I wink at him.

"Fucking you for 30 minutes is little?"

Sam is back on planet earth, a quick trip to heaven and now he'll soon be in hell.

"How did we have sex for that long and I didn't notice the time?"

We're both at his dead phone, the phone that keeps turning off for no apparent reason, the phone he's been neglecting to replace because he's stubborn. The phone I intentionally turned off.

"No, no, no." He cries.

I'm sympathetic when I need to be, secretly praying Stella doesn't show up in his apartment. I didn't think about that.

My ears open expecting to hear a knock at the door.

I check her flight as Sam's phone comes to life.

He's a madman, cursing and whining like a child, pacing the condo like some exercise might give him some answers. I almost feel bad. Almost.

Why is he acting like this is the worst thing in the world? I didn't pray for her pilot to crash her plane, even though it did cross my mind, so why is he overreacting?

He eventually leaves the room and I know he's mad at me. Over what? He's the one that couldn't keep it in his pants. It's not my fault he never got his broken phone fixed. This was the best outcome for all of us involved.

He has no idea the shit storm I have waiting in the wings.

———◆———

Two weeks go by and I'm in the dark the entire time.

Stella has been ignoring Sam like the bitch sister she is.

I've tracked her car every day this week, and Monday morning I'm met with a surprise. She's home all day. Could be a fluke. Could be working from home. Could be sick?

But on Wednesday her car is still home. She hasn't traveled to work, let alone leave to go anywhere.

Did she get a new car? Did she take an Uber to work?

The timing is suspect, which is why I immediately dial her work line.

"Hi, can I please be connected with Stella Evans."

"May I ask who's calling?"

"Myra. She'll know who I am." I say with confidence.

"One moment please." The receptionist tells me.

I'm outside on my balcony as Sam prepares lunch. It's not usual for me to take a call in private, but I told him it's a possible job opportunity.

The music playing while I hold gives me PTSD. It's the same played in their elevator and if Stella does in fact answer, I might just puke over the railing.

"Ma'am?" The receptionist is back on the line.

"Yes? I'm here."

"Ms. Evans is no longer with the company," he says, "but I'd be happy to transfer you to someone else on the team."

"Oh," I rejoice inwardly. "What happened? She never told me and she's handling my account."

"I apologize, I don't know the details. But let me get you over to-"

I disconnect the call quickly but keep the phone pressed to my ear to buy me more time. I need to process this.

Sam looks out at me and gives me an enthusiastic smile and two thumbs up.

I melt for him and his charming, supportive ways.

There's no way in hell I'm letting him go without a fight.

Stella has been fired and only I know about it. For now.

———◆———

Sam thinks I'm in Texas for a job interview. In reality, I'm taking a quick trip to Carmel then heading south to LA to execute some long awaited justice.

I'm at a drugstore buying potassium chloride powder pills and a pay as you go cell phone.

Potassium chloride sounds illegal, but surprisingly, they can be bought over the counter. They're used to treat low levels of potassium or hypokalemia, but are dangerous if you overdo the dose. They can cause severe stomach aches, vomiting, irregular heart levels, or worse.

The clerk rings me up without even looking me in the eyes.

I stuff the pills and phone in my giant purse and walk to my car.

This will most likely be the last time I ever see Camilla. She's oblivious to this fact as we both greet each other at the Pilates studio.

"Hey girl!" She gives me a sideways hug and I reciprocate the affection.

My plan will all go to shit if she doesn't have her cell phone with her. When I see it intertwined between her fingers, water bottle, and socks, I let out a five count breath.

I need her phone. It's that simple. Uninterrupted time to go through every detail in there. This isn't something that can be done while she leaves for a quick trip to the bathroom.

The only viable solution is to steal it, but not in a way that causes red flags. Which is why I bought an identical iPhone 11 that will fit her case perfectly. The only difference is it won't turn on. No matter how long it's charged or even with a hard restart. I bought it broken and it will stay that way and no Apple Genius will get it to work.

By the time she realizes this, I will be done with the real phone and it'll be smashed to bits.

20 minutes into the work out, I excuse myself to use the restroom.

All our things are in cubbies in the back of the studio, secluded from the reformers and right next to the bathrooms.

I pull out my makeup bag that has the dead iPhone inside it. Quickly, I take out Camilla's working iPhone and replace it with the broken one.

Camilla's working phone is then powered down and put back in my makeup bag. The switch is seamless and easy.

She will have no clue I have her working cellphone one cube away. Scratch that. She won't even know it got switched because nothing will look suspicious at all. The only confusion will be why her phone died, which won't be my problem.

When class is over, Camilla offers to get lunch again.

"Oh, I can't." I admit, realizing if I don't leave for LA soon, traffic will be a bitch.

"Want to get drinks later?"

She seems so needy, like she knows.

"Can we raincheck?" I ask, not adding the typical, "I'll text you later", because I do not want to draw attention to her dark phone.

"Yeah! Of course. Text me later."

My eyes bug out of my head when she turns to leave. *Ha.*

I don't feel anything when I watch her go, realizing this is the last time I'll ever see her again.

———◆———

I'm parked a block away from Stella's home, opening the package of pills I bought.

In the span of five minutes, I empty the contents of 90 delayed release tablets into a plastic baggie. I'm guessing there's at least two ounces worth of potassium chloride that will soon be mixed into Nathaniel's supplements.

Checking the GPS locator, I see Stella's car is parked at a shopping mall.

Hypothetically, if she's in the parking lot and in her car now, it'll still take her 35 minutes of LA traffic until she gets back.

Plenty of time to do what I need.

Nathaniel's car is parked in a residential area.

I'm not familiar with the location, but like Stella, even if he left now and hit every green light, it'd still take him a solid 30 minutes.

Walking toward the backyard in a diagonal shape, I prevent any possibility of being seen near her stoop. Stella has the Ring doorbell and the last thing I need is being caught on camera and sending her a motion alert.

I'm inconspicuously putting on clear latex gloves as I approach her gate. Unlatching it, I make my way through her backyard.

I've watched too much CSI, but you can never be too careful. I don't want to leave my fingerprints anywhere near her residence.

I make quick note that there aren't any flood light cameras, but I tip my hat lower just in case, making sure all my hair is still tucked inside it.

The copied keys I stole from Sam rest in the palm of my hand.

If none of these keys work, I'm screwed. I could always try to do this at his gym but gaining access to the guy's locker room is a sure fire way to get caught and thrown out.

The first key I try doesn't even fit the hole.

I'm on key five of seven when one finally fits the keyhole and turns completely. I release a breath that could have blown down the door; just like the big bad wolf. Let me in your house, little piggy.

I adjust the baseball cap one last time and enter.

Time is not on my side, so I use every precious moment to scour her house like a bloodhound.

Supplements. Where does Nathaniel keep them?

That was the obvious answer when I asked myself how I could guarantee he'd be ingesting this shit once or twice a day. He's already on the verge of a liver failure with all the crap he's mixing into his bloodstream. What's a bit more potassium to his never ending list of narcotics?

"Where are you, you bastard?"

I'm through every kitchen cabinet and I can't find anything.

I'm running out of time!

He wouldn't keep it in any of the bathrooms; it'd have to be easily accessible.

It finally dawns on me that he probably keeps them in his gym bag and I pray it's not in his car.

I search the house for that nasty sack of shit and I find it in the laundry room.

The pre-workout tub is staring at me with its German vernacular that might as well say "heart destroyer."

My hands are sweating beneath the latex gloves, creating a nasty residue that makes it difficult to twist the tight lid off.

I take out the mini plastic scoop and dump the contents back into the tub. I grab the plastic baggie of drugs and pour it directly into the scooper and add the rest of the sandy substance on the top layer and mix it up. The white powder blends nicely with the beige crystallized bits of paraphernalia. A few days of this stuff and he'll be on his way to urgent care.

Placing the scoop lightly back into the contents, I twist the lid back on and return it to his gym bag.

You don't just nearly kill my good for nothing father without suffering consequences. I'm fighting fire with an inferno.

I head towards the door but stop short. A car approaches, the brakes squealing as they come closer, tires crunching as they turn into a driveway. My skin breaks out in a cold sweat. I peak through a window and see it's a neighbor returning home.

I slide down the wall on the other side of the door, giving myself a moment to collect my breath and thoughts before I'm exiting the way I came, out like a puff of smoke.

Later that night, I'm in another cheap motel, checking my dwindling account balance.

I'm risking diseases and take a bath when Sam's face pops up on my incoming calls.

I give him some BS about the potential job, quickly changing the topic to something more interesting.

"Any word from Stella?"

"Nope, I spoke to Nathaniel today. He said Stella is upset about stuff. They are fighting and work is a nightmare."

He is covering for her? Why?

Now that I know how difficult it is to live a double life, I don't know how Stella can do it every day. How do you not get so caught up in your lies that you slip? I've had so many close calls and I have a lot more to lose if I screw up. Stella just has a brother who will accept her faults anyway.

Why does she care what people think about her so much?

Seems like her perfect little life was on its way of crumbling even before I came along.

CHAPTER FIFTEEN

———◆———

My ringing phone interrupts my dreamless sleep the following morning.

I put Sam on speaker and croak out a raspy, "Hello?"

"Nathaniel is dead." A voice tells me, possibly the voice of someone in my dream, because I'm still dreaming, right?

"What?"

"Stella called me and Nathaniel is dead. He crashed his car. I am two seconds away from flying out to go see her."

Oh fuck, I killed the son of a bitch.

It's a peculiar sensation that blankets my limbs. My body itself is calm as it registers the facts. Nathaniel is dead. I probably killed him. But I'm numb. I feel nothing.

Our conversation is so quick I wonder if it even happened at all. Sam is about to board a plane and I'm stuck with no answers.

He crashed his car? Could be a complete accident.

Maybe this wasn't my doing. But still, less than 24 hours of feeding his brittle heart a lethal bullet isn't a coincidence.

Realistically, I'd hoped the fool would suffer a heart attack. Despite all the warnings I used to give him, he'd take the supplements religiously, knowing the risks that they were terrible for his internal organs.

If only he listened to me. Maybe we'd never be here. Maybe if he stopped taking those stupid performance enhancing, testicle shrinking, personality altering drugs, we'd still be together and it wouldn't have come to this.

I'm supposed to be in Tennessee for a damn job interview, so I can't exactly meet Sam in LA to get more information.

Shit, I mean Texas. Tennessee? No, it was Texas.

Either way I collect my things, check out, and decide to lay low in another motel in case the cops come looking for me.

I scour Twitter, Google, the LA Times, looking for an article with more information.

Silence everywhere. I take this as good news because if it were a multiple car pileup, some media outlet would be showcasing the story nonstop.

Stella has been fired.

She's technically single now. Yikes.

The last piece was to get Sam out of her life.

Weighing my options, I get out of bed and pace the room.

"Sam has to find out." I declare to the silence.

He has to learn about what did or didn't happen in Camilla's accident. Stella was responsible for something and if she's gone this long without mentioning it, I doubt she'll just come clean now. And if she hasn't mentioned it, that means she's hiding something big.

Contemplating what would be the easiest way of ripping them apart but still keeping myself intact, I peer over at my phone and mull over the tidings in the email.

I can't just send Sam a text telling him there's more to Camilla's accident than he realizes.

If it comes from me, I can kiss my relationship good-bye because it'd show I know more than I should and can't be trusted.

What *did* I plan on doing with the email?

This whole time I've known Stella is guilty of something, but I have no way of actually proving it.

Even if Sam *did* see the email, or find out Stella might have done something, it doesn't guarantee he'll even believe it.

Stella could concoct some elaborate lie and claim she has no idea what he's talking about.

Then I'd have nothing.

Doubt begins to sink its claws in me.

"Think!"

The only thought that flashes in my mind is Nathaniel's funeral. I can see it now.

I'll be invited, of course. Dressed in black, hiding my face behind a gothic mesh veil. Stella would see me, recognize me, go stark raving mad, and I'd trample over freshly dug graves to escape her accusations.

Checking the news one more time, I come to the conclusion my brain has reached its maximum capacity and is of no use to me at the moment.

———◆———

The next day I wake up feeling like half a person.

Something about me doesn't feel whole.

But when Sam finally calls me and gives me more information, I perk up and inflate.

"Stella was fired. I feel like I don't even know her anymore." He tells me. "She has lied about so much. Nathaniel was cheating on her with someone at work. He was suspended and forced to leave the company."

It's a brief conversation, but nevertheless, I have to scoop my jaw off the floor.

A day has elapsed and already Stella's little life is crumbling.

What would a normal person do in a situation like this?

"Oh my god." I say.

I still have Camilla's phone.

A normal person would send condolences.

Someone like Camilla would reach out and say how sorry she was and let that person know she's there for them, despite the traumatic history they have together.

I cover my mouth with my hand.

This could work. Depending on how I phrase it, this could totally work.

Sam just admitted he went through Stella's phone. He probably still has it. She's sleeping all day!

Oh my god, he'll recognize Camilla's number and confront Stella. It'll seem so natural. He won't even suspect me in anything.

And if he decides to text Camilla, I've already blocked him in her contacts. iCloud would update if Camilla bought a new phone and she'll never actually see it.

Before I power her phone on, I write out on the motel stationery, that is as thin as tissue paper, what exactly I'm going to say to her.

I scratch out a few options but conclude on something very Camilla-esque.

Camilla: "I just heard about Nathaniel. I'm so very sorry, hon. I'm thinking about you. We've been through a lot but I care about you. I don't hate you like you think I do. I forgave you a long time ago, for everything. If you need someone to talk to, I'm here. We've both experienced accidents and loss, and if you need someone to talk to, I'm here."

Chapter Sixteen

——————◆——————

It's going to be so much better when Sam hears the truth from someone other than me. The text has been sent and I may never have to admit that I knew this all along. I could come out of this unscathed!

I pack my things, check out of the motel and drive back home.

When Sam undoubtedly hears the truth from Stella, he'll need me.

He won't suspect a damn thing. This might just work out for me.

I turn up the radio louder and actually sing along like I'm on American Idol.

Who is this new Harper?

She's light, carefree and just bursting at the seams with joy.

My ears and heart are open for Sam and I'm just

waiting for him to call to tell me the great news of how his sister ruined his relationship.

An hour into my road trip, Sam still hasn't called me.

Has he seen her phone yet?

What's taking him so long?

Instead of waiting any longer, I dial his number.

It rings for a while and instead of hearing his manly, sexy voice, I'm met with something much, much worse.

"Liz, is that you?" Stella screams into Sam's phone.

I look at the caller ID to confirm I called Sam because why in the actual fuck is Stella calling me by my real name?

"Stella, give me my phone!" Sam shouts in the background.

"Liz? I know it's you! How did I not see this coming?"

Realizing my car is now going 30mph in the fast lane, the cars behind me swerve dramatically to pass me, not without honking. I pull onto the shoulder and stop the car. Oh my god, how does she know?

I'm whiter than fresh winter snow and my breathing is labored.

Stella and Sam are arguing over the speakers of the car and I immediately disconnect the call.

CHAPTER SEVENTEEN

———◆———

This can't be happening. How does Sam know? How does Stella know?

Waiting for him to call me back, I exit the next off ramp and park in an empty lot.

Seconds feel like days and I don't know what to do. Do I call him back? Will he call me? Why hasn't he called me back? What would be more suspicious?

Risking it, I dial his number and think of a million scenarios all at once.

He answers on the second ring to a breathy, "Harper? What's going on?"

I don't hear Stella's shrill voice so I'm hoping he's in another room, away from her, maybe having her committed?

"I don't know, we got disconnected somehow. What is Stella yelling about? Why is she calling me

Liz?" I start with that because deny, deny, deny.

"I have no clue what's going on. I just ran out of her house and I'm getting an Uber. She's going crazy, Harper. She keeps rambling about a conspiracy about how you're actually her ex coworker. What the hell is going on? Do you know my sister?"

"I'm just as confused as you are."

You goddamn dirty bitch.

"Where are you?" He asks.

"I'm actually getting an Uber, too. I got an earlier flight when I found out what happened."

"Okay, good. We need to talk in person."

The hairs all over my body grow an inch thanks to the shivers and goosebumps coating my skin.

"Sam, I'm worried. Is everything okay?"

"There's too much to say over the phone. I need to see you." He chokes out.

"What can I do?"

He's crying in the silence, I can tell. But I need reassurance he's not going to show up at my condo with the SWAT team.

"I just… I just…" And now he's sobbing, the heart wrenching man sob that you witness maybe once in a lifetime. "I just need you. I love you and I miss you."

Okay, that's good. He still loves me.

"I love you, too. But I'm so confused as to what just happened in the last 24 hours."

"I'll explain it all. I'll get the next flight out. Harper... Stella did something terrible."

Don't I fucking know it! I can't tell if he's implying what happened to Nathaniel, which was my doing, or if he means Camilla.

"Sammy, what can I do?"

"Nothing. I'll send you my flight details. Come over to my place, okay?"

"Of course, anything."

"I love you."

"I love you too. Don't worry, we'll get through this."

Because we *will* get through this. I just don't know my next move at the moment.

———◆———

The drive home will just about fit with the timeline of when my flight would be arriving.

When I'm 30 minutes out, I contemplate the scenarios that consumed my brain for the past 4 hours.

Sam obviously doesn't suspect me of anything. I need to let him do all the talking before I say a word.

He knows now. He knows what Stella did and is heartbroken.

In a normal world, if a girlfriend found this out, a crime this terrible would be unforgivable. But that's his sister. His twin. Would it be suspicious of me to tell him to cut all ties? Would it be out of character if I remind him of the numerous times she was a toxic, horrible person to him? Or do I tell him to forgive her?

Obviously I don't want him to forgive her because I'm starting to think this happy ending for us could actually work.

Who's to say I have to disappear after all this happened? That was my plan all along. Disappear and leave them to pick up the pieces.

But I love Sam. I don't want this to end. But I know it can't continue if Stella is around.

A terrible thought enters my head. I even laugh aloud because it's *too* crazy.

"I could kill her." I say to my empty car.

I burst out laughing again because it's insane. Horribly, manically insane.

ACT II – SAM

CHAPTER EIGHTEEN

The entire flight home I wonder if I actually breathe at all. The stale, recycled air must be entering my lungs, because when we land, I feel like I'm coming out of hypnosis.

My brain is creating 10 million thoughts at once and I can't keep track of anything. Yet I put one foot in front of the other like a robot.

I move like I'm supposed to. Exit the plane and follow the other passengers. But I'm numb.

Where do I even begin to uncover the lies?

Stella…

Had I missed all the warning signs that she was a pathological liar?

Was I that self-involved in my own personal life that I didn't even notice the cracks well enough to know something was wrong?

Should I be worried she killed Nathaniel? We always joked about it but it's becoming clear something wasn't right.

Now that I know what she's capable of, I can't trust her.

Camilla lost our baby thanks to Stella, regardless of the reasoning.

But even Camilla kept that from me.

Why did she never say anything to me about this? Was it because we were already doomed? Would I have believed her?

Stella's reaction to Nathaniel's accident was so real.

Is she that calculated and psychotic she could fake emotions like that? She was lifeless, like she lost her soulmate, despite the strained relationship she never told me about.

But none of this explains why she's calling Harper a different name.

Stella has never mentioned anyone by the name of Liz, yet apparently she's Nathaniel's previous girlfriend and the same one Stella got fired.

Why is she important now? And why does she think Harper is this person?

Maybe the medication Stella is taking has side effects of hallucinations? She's already dealing with a lot right now, she could be imagining all of this.

My head hurts so much I'm worried the lining of my skull is going to crush my brain from the inside out.

I breathe in hopelessness and breathe out confusion.

My phone comes back to life, alerting me of text messages and missed calls.

Stella.

The guys.

Harper.

I open my group thread and read.

Jake: "Dude, what the fuck happened? Your sister is texting us saying some weird shit. Is she drunk?"

Diego: "She keeps saying we can't trust Harper. What is she talking about, man?"

Jake: "She said we have to keep you away from her. She thinks Harper killed Nathaniel. This is some insane shit. I can't figure out what's going on. Call us."

Diego: "Why didn't you tell us Nathaniel was killed yesterday? Bro, are you okay?"

Jake: "She just called me again. I had to put her to VM. I'm starting to freak out. Diego, should we call the cops?"

Diego: "If we don't hear from him soon, I will."

Jake: "I'm freaking out. Avery is, too."

Sam: "I just got back from LA. Don't call the police. Too much to explain over text. I'm alive, but things are not okay."

I open up Harper's text as I schedule an Uber to pick me up.

Harper: "About to land. Love you."

Sam: "Are you at my place yet?"

Harper takes a few minutes to respond, and when she does, I'm already out front waiting for my ride.

Harper: "Just got to your place. Can I make you some coffee?"

Sam: "Yes, that'd be great. See you soon."

The Uber driver is quiet the entire way home. He must see the misery on my face because all I get is a simple hello when I get in the car.

Stella has left me 10 voicemails.

I scan a few of her texts.

Stella: "I will prove this to you."

Stella: "I know I can't take back what I did. But I swear to you I'm not crazy."

Stella: "Please text me Sam I can't take this. I love you, you're my brother."

Stella: "Sam, pleaaaaase!!!!! You don't know what I'm going through. I want to die right now. I can't take this."

My heart skips a beat when I read the last one.

I feel like throwing up. Nausea hits me and I choke back the feeling of spilling my guts all over the backseat. Imagining Stella wanting to die kills me, but I am torn between feeling sorry for her and sorry for myself.

I'm dropped off outside and I can see my breath in the air as I exhale loudly.

Closing my eyes, my chest stills as I count to 10.

Isn't that supposed to calm you down? So why do I feel like I could rocket myself off the concrete and up onto my balcony?

Harper greets me at the door on the verge of tears and our embrace is icy, to say the least.

I'm on autopilot.

My feet are walking for me, my lungs breathing on their own, but I am not in control of my body.

"Sam, what is going on?"

She leads me to my couch where she has a coffee mug waiting for both of us.

Her entire body shakes and I wonder if she's having a panic attack.

"Stella… she… I think she caused my ex-girlfriend's accident. Whether she tripped her or not, she admitted she didn't try to help her as she fell."

"Oh god, Sam." She holds onto me, her arms looped around my neck. "She admitted that? Why would she confess now?"

"She had to. My ex texted her and I saw it on her phone."

Harper swallows loudly, she must have a lump in her throat too.

"But why is she calling me by another name? I don't get it."

"I know this is stupid, but I have to ask. Did you work with my sister? Ever? She claims you are someone else entirely different. That you were actually Nathaniel's girlfriend first. And you were the one working in the job she has now. And that she fucked you over and this is some kind of sick revenge."

I'm talking so fast that I have to stand up.

My body needs space, the freedom to roam. I can't have Harper hanging on me at the moment.

"Did you know my sister?" I ask again.

"Sam, of course not! I've never even met her. Where did she get this idea?"

"She saw your picture on my caller ID when you called."

Her eyebrows rise in shock. I can't tell if her tone is pissed off or defensive. Maybe both. I'm accusing her of something wild and unfair.

"Okay, so I might look like someone she knows. Is she even thinking clearly? What happened with Nathaniel?"

Walking over to my window, I bang my forehead into the glass.

Back when I was reviewing a case, I read up about the hippocampus. It's the part of our brain that stores our memories. Right now, I hope I'm hitting it hard enough so that it'll shake loose the memories I'd like to forget.

Harper's hand is on my back, gently rubbing me, but it feels like fire.

"You believe me, right?" She asks me.

"I don't know what to believe right now!"

She steps back and I know I've offended her.

"Harper, it's just, fuck!" I shout. "I just found out my sister has been lying to me. About so much! What the hell am I supposed to do right now? She lied about what went on in her relationship, at her job, fuck her whole life is a lie. And somehow, the only thing she seemed certain on, the only thing she admitted to not lying about, is that you are some woman that she knew last year and you're trying to get back at her through me. Like some elaborate revenge like out of a fucking movie."

"Sam…" She approaches with caution. "I love you, which is why I'm going to say this to your face. Your sister is a liar. Look at where she's at compared to us."

She motions with her hands, placing her hands at different levels in the air.

"We are up here. Happy, in love. She is down here." She wiggles her lower hand. "She just got fired, her boyfriend was cheating. She was about to lose everything. Stella couldn't bear to see you happy. She's trying to break us up so she can have you all to herself. She's manipulating you!"

I can tell she's wanted to say these words for a while because they seem so rehearsed. But I get it. She's being honest about my sister where Camilla couldn't.

"You've always warned me about her and now I finally see it. I was hoping I wouldn't but it's true. She can't bear to see you doing better than she is. Maybe it's because I'm viewing this from the outside and I've never met her, but this looks pretty textbook manipulative."

"Harper…" My voice cracks, my lips quiver and I can't hold my weight up anymore.

Dropping to my knees, I cry into my hands.

She's there to comfort me as I realize the truth in her words.

"I'm sorry." I can't find my voice but I try to say the words anyway. "I'm… sorry." Is somewhat recognizable through my sobs.

"Shhhhh." She continues rubbing her delicate hands over my shoulder blades as I remain hunched over. It no longer feels like a burning flame anymore. "It's going to be okay. What do I need to do?"

"Just don't leave me. I'm sorry I accused you. I just, I can't think right now. This is all too much."

My house phone rings and it can only be one person.

"It's probably Stella." I admit. "She's been calling me on my cell nonstop. I can't talk to her right now, Harper. Just ignore it."

"Do you want me to say something to her? Tell her she got it wrong?"

"No, I'll talk to her eventually. I just need some time."

"Sam," her voice is low in my ear. "What happened to Nathaniel?"

"They think he might have had a heart attack and crashed his car. I'm getting an autopsy done just in case something *did* happen to him."

"Autopsy?" She repeats, surprise edging her words.

"Did I do the right thing?" I redirect. "Leaving? What if she's suicidal?"

"Did she sound suicidal?"

"Kind of."

The lump in her throat is back and she swallows forcefully.

"I need to call the guys. They have no idea what's going on."

"Okay, can I pick up some food? You need to eat."

"Yeah, that'd be great."

———◆———

Two hours later, after I barely eat any of the food, Jake and Diego are up to speed on the disarray of the past 48 hours.

They are in shock about Nathaniel, but not so much surprised Stella is trying to break up my relationship.

They are on my side, regardless if they felt like they had to choose.

I'm thankful for their friendship and support. I'll need them now more than ever because they agreed that I have to cut Stella off, maybe indefinitely.

Diego said, "She's done her job making you feel inferior all this time. It's over. You have to let her go. I can't keep seeing her doing this to you."

Jake added, "She makes your life worse. I know it's hard to hear but you can't let that continue. Give her a chance to change but you can't keep saving her from herself."

And they're right. She's finally crossed a line and we can't go back to how things were.

What I have with Harper is a good thing and I don't want to risk hurting her if she thinks for a second I believe my sister.

We've moved from the dining room to the couch, from clothes to pajamas, and Harper breaks me from my reverie and asks, "Do you think you'll reach out to Camilla?"

"God, when did I tell you her name? I swore I wouldn't. It's hard even saying it to this day."

"No, it's okay. Your head is all over the place right now. It probably slipped out at some point."

"I don't know if I'll reach out. Do you want me to?"

She takes a moment before answering.

"I mean… she's in your past for a reason. Has she reached out to you?"

"No, not at all. I almost don't even care what she has to say now. The only truth I know is that I love you and I don't want anything to jeopardize our relationship."

"You're right. She might open old wounds again, and I think you're hurting enough at the moment."

"I just don't understand why Camilla didn't tell me. Why wouldn't she say she was outside Stella's office? And I stupidly never asked. I just assumed the location didn't matter."

"Would you have listened if she told you Stella was responsible?" Harper asks with caution.

"Back then? I don't know. I really don't think I would have believed her. Now? I wouldn't doubt it."

"We should get some sleep. You need to rest."

"I don't think I could even if I wanted to. My brain is working overtime. Thinking horrible, horrible things."

"About me?"

"No!" I grab her hand in mine and rub my thumb over her delicate, smooth fingers. "Not you. I'm replaying my past and figuring out all the times she wasn't truthful. It hurts. I actually feel stupid for not realizing it."

"Don't do that. That's manipulation again. This is not your fault."

Her tone is so domineering; I don't expect this side of her.

"I might send her a text. Just letting her know I need some time. I don't want her calling the police on me or you. That's just what we need."

Harper's eyes are saucers and I reassure her, "She wouldn't really call the cops."

But honestly, I don't know. I try to appease her for the time being but I have no idea what Stella is capable of now.

Harper adjusts herself on the couch. Her posture is straight as a board as she clears her throat loudly.

Grabbing my phone, I type something quick and send it, not giving myself a change to second guess my word choices.

"I need some space. I think you can manage that. Give me some time to figure out what the fuck just happened. I'm sorry you're grieving Nathaniel alone, but please respect my wishes for once in your life."

CHAPTER NINETEEN

———•◆•———

The morning after my life changed, the world goes on like nothing happened.

I've turned my phone off and I have no desire to see what lies ahead on my calendar. I don't want to think about anything, communicate with anyone except my girlfriend who enters the room with two mugs.

Harper greets me in bed with a kiss and iced coffee and I'm reacting like I just suffered a loss. That not only did Nathaniel pass, what I knew of my sister did as well.

"Here, drink some coffee. You look like you barely slept."

I take a sip and ask, "Is there Bailey's in this?"

"Yes. Figured you needed a little something extra after your last couple days."

"Good, I feel like getting drunk so I don't have to think about the next few days."

"I know this is an impossible question to answer, but how long are you giving her? A week? A month?"

"I don't really know. It's just… unimaginable. She's the last family member I have."

"I know what it feels like to be alone."

There's an uncertain silence lingering between us.

"Should I forgive her?"

Harper takes a long sip of coffee and finally says, "If I say no, you may resent me. If I say yes and she hurts you again, I'd feel terrible. I feel like there's no right answer. And to be honest, Sam, I don't trust her. I don't know her."

My worst fear has come true, and I know that despite it not being said aloud, I will have to choose between Stella and Harper.

"Fuck, do you think Stella has to plan Nathaniel's funeral?"

"Oh god I haven't even thought about that."

"I wonder if his parents even knew about her."

"I wouldn't be surprised." She says under her breath.

"What do you mean by that?"

"Oh, well, you say she lied about so much. Maybe their relationship wasn't even a great enough one he'd introduce her. He was cheating on her?"

"Yeah, and I knew he'd do it. Bastard." I realize my insensitivity and add, "I mean, may he rest in peace. But fuck."

"You really got an autopsy done?"

"I did. Now it seems pointless. It doesn't matter now. Hey how did your interview go? Did you miss it by coming home early?"

She's taken aback by the change in conversation.

"Oh my interview! It went really well. I think they want me. They said I'd hear back soon."

"Are you thinking of moving out there?"

"I honestly don't know at this point."

My heart drops into my stomach as I realize I could potentially lose my relationship with my sister *and* the woman I love.

"I love you, Sam. I never knew this selfless kind of love existed. I don't want to lose you over all this."

"You wouldn't!" I exclaim, feeling guilty that she's unintentionally settling my nerves. "I want you to move in."

The words are out of my mouth as my brain processes what I've been thinking for the past few weeks. It's word vomit, but I won't deny that it's still the truth.

"Sam, really? Are you sure? This seems like a lot in the last 24 hours. You probably need time to…"

"I want you in my life. All day. Everyday."

She laughs at me but it's endearing.

"Okay maybe not all day." I amend. "We will probably have to work and have jobs. But I don't want you moving to Texas. I want you here with me. Is that okay?"

"Living here?" She confirms.

I shake my head emphatically.

"Okay, I'll live with you!" She squeals.

And for the first time in the past couple days, things feel right again. I see a distant hurdle of peace coming at me, and knowing Harper is by my side, I think I can handle just about anything. But boy was I wrong.

———◆———

The next couple days are spent living like things are *almost* back to normal. And I have to say, it's a relief not having to think about what the hell I'll do with my sister.

Sunday morning I meet the guys and it's the first time I've seen them since everything happened. I don't know what to expect, but the familiarity and subpar food is welcomed.

"Dude, I don't know what to say. How have you been?" Jake asks me.

"I've been okay. Just taking it day by day. Haven't talked to Stella since I sent that text. Has she left you guys alone?"

"I blocked her." Diego admits. "I just couldn't keep seeing all the shit and lies she was saying about you and Harper."

"That's fair."

"When will you reach out to her?"

"I don't really know. She'll be in for quite the shock when I tell her Harper is moving in with me."

Their mouths drop open in shock.

"No way man! Congratulations!" Jake slaps my back with enthusiasm.

"I'm happy for you guys." Diego's tone is filled with uncertainty.

"But?"

"But," he adds, "What the hell is going to happen with Stella? You can't ignore her forever. She will always be coming after you. And once she finds out this news, who knows what she'll do. I can't take it, bro."

Diego is by far the more protective of the two, and I can see in his eyes the possessiveness he's built up over the years for me.

"What will you do?" He asks.

"Knowing everything I do now, she needs help. Psychological help."

"Will it be an ultimatum?" Jake asks.

"Maybe? I just know that I can't lose someone else because of Stella's actions."

"So what will happen with Harper? She'll sell her place?" Jake asks.

"She might rent it out. She doesn't have it in her to put it on the market just yet."

"Harper needs an escape plan in case Stella comes back to ruin everything huh?" Diego jokes, punching my arm.

"Dude, too soon."

"Sorry, man."

"But seriously, I'm excited for this next step in your life." Jake says. "You've never lived with a woman. Are you ready for this? Ready for all the hair clogging your showers, tampons in the trash?"

"Jesus, Jake when you put it like that…" I pause. "Of course I'm fucking ready. I lived with a sister my whole life. That's nothing new."

The ease of that sentence puts a knife through me.

Will I still live with a sister in my life? Can I really just never speak to her again?

I have no idea how Stella is coping. It's been almost a week and I haven't set a deadline.

I haven't told Harper this yet, and I don't know how she'll react, but I just can't sever ties with my sister. I'll demand she seeks professional help before I invite her chaos back into my life. But despite everything, I have a horrible sinking feeling in my gut.

"Whatever happened with Harper's job?" Jake asks, the only one of us that seems to remember the world still continues to turn.

"She didn't take the Texas job. She actually had another interview in San Diego the other day. It was kind of sudden and unexpected. She was gone for two days but she didn't like the company. It would have been a remote job where she could work from home, but it wasn't the right fit. She's just going to take things slow for now. Try and find something in San Francisco."

"If she wants a job, she can take Lila's." Jake mentions casually.

"Why, what happened to Lila?" I ask, completely unaware drama ensued while I was dealing with my own.

"I don't know. She just stopped showing up to work. Won't return my calls."

"Damn, I wonder what happened."

"But seriously, if she wants something for the time being, I can look into it. I know the front desk is probably beneath her with all the experience she has, but has she ever dabbled in social media marketing? I know one of my clients is looking for someone to revamp his online presence. I want to say he owns a magazine. Magazine and literary world are similar, right?"

"Yeah, that might be cool. I don't think she's ever done something like that, but she's really smart and can probably do anything you throw at her."

"Then it's done! I'll connect her with my guy on Monday. We can't have her moving away from you and breaking your heart."

"You're the best, man. How's Avery doing? Is she pregnant yet?"

"Not yet. We're still trying. Fucking like rabbits."

"How are you and Carrie doing?" I ask like it's been a month since I've caught up with my friends. "Have you fucked it up yet?"

"We're good! Still taking things slow because of the long distance. She might be going back to school for a few classes. Which I fully support."

"Finally getting her GED?" Jake teases.

"Ha, she might be younger than us but she's not *that* young. You moron."

"Well I better get back. Harper is moving some of her things in and I told her I'd help clear some space in my closet."

"Don't be a stranger." Jake gives me a hug goodbye and I hug Diego next.

On my way home, despite my better judgment, I send Stella a text.

Sam: "I'm ready to talk when you are."

CHAPTER TWENTY

———— • ————

I don't expect her to come rushing to my side the moment I finally reach out, but a few hours go by and I don't hear a word. Nothing.

No call. No text. No scathing email waiting for me while Harper prepares dinner.

Guilt fills my lungs and I breathe it out hoping I didn't make a mistake by not consulting with my girlfriend first.

Over dinner, I decide not to tell Harper I texted my sister and bring up better news.

"Hey Jake said he might have a contact for a job. If you're interested in social media and magazines. Not really sure the details. Can I give him your number?"

"That'd be great! Is it local?"

"Do you think I would entertain the idea if it wasn't?"

She smiles while she slurps up some spaghetti on her fork.

"So now that I've moved in, do I have to pay rent?" She gives me a teasing smile. "Because, I can always pay you in sexual fantasies."

"The condo is actually paid off. But I can think of a weekly payment plan that involves the bedroom."

My sex drive has returned and I'm suddenly not hungry.

"In fact," I initiate as I get up from the table. "Let's start right now."

————— ♦ —————

The next morning I expect to see a text from Stella suggesting the open timeframes she's available to discuss our current situation. Maybe she'll even add a Zoom meeting. But nothing.

Something feels wrong.

I know she plays games, but this is different.

I'd imagine she was waiting on pins and needles for me to finally reach out.

Harper has a few more boxes to bring over, so I take the moment I'm alone to call her.

It rings and goes to her voicemail.

Well she didn't block me, not that she had reason to.

I send another text.

Sam: "I'm ready to talk. Do you need some time or something? Text me back."

Every minute that passes, a dark cloud settles into my mind.

Stella used to call it "twintuition", but deep down I

know something is wrong.

Before I can talk myself out of it, I research the non-emergency LA police number.

When I'm connected through, I take a deep breath.

"I need someone to do a welfare check on my sister."

"Okay sir, may I get your name?"

"Samuel Evans. Stella Evans is my sister and I'm very worried about her."

"Why are you concerned for her wellbeing?"

"Her boyfriend just died. He was in a car accident about a week ago. He crashed due to a heart attack or something."

The dispatcher reacts like he knows what I'm talking about, though accidents happen daily and I'm sure there was nothing out of the ordinary to make it stand out.

"We got in a big fight." I add, hoping this doesn't arouse suspicion.

"When did you last hear from her?"

"About a week. I asked her for some time to process everything. It was a bad fight. And I finally reached out last night and she didn't respond, which isn't like her."

"Is she suicidal?"

"I… I don't know. Maybe."

"Does she have drugs or any weapons in the house we should be aware of?"

"No, no she's not like that."

"We'll need her address and a phone number to contact you."

I give him both, my hands trembling at the realness of it all.

"Will you call me as soon as you hear from her? I'm hoping this is nothing…"

"Don't worry sir, oftentimes it usually is nothing. There's no harm in checking."

His reassurance does everything but that.

"I'm in San Francisco or I'd go check on her myself."

"I understand, sir. I'll send out my nearest patrol officer and we'll give you a call shortly."

"Thank you."

———————◆———————

An hour later, I'm on the couch with a bottle of vodka as Harper walks through the front door.

"Hey Sammy, I'm home. Where are you?"

"I'm on the couch."

She enters but I see a cardboard box come into the room first.

It's large and no doubt heavy and full of clothes.

"Hey, you're drinking without me? It's not even noon!"

"Stella killed herself." I say with no emotion.

Harper drops the box with a loud thud.

"What?"

She rushes over to where I sit idle and motionless. The only action my body gets is bringing the vodka bottle straight to my lips and swallowing.

"I found out about 30 minutes ago."

"Sam, what? Stella killed herself? How do you know?"

"I called the police to do a welfare check. She didn't return my texts. I knew something was wrong."

"I didn't know you texted her. Oh God."

I'm passive and blasé as I take another huge swig.

"The officer said the front door was unlocked. He entered and found her in her bedroom. She had been dead a few days, they think."

Harper is shaking her head, unable to process what I've been stewing in for the last half hour.

When the officer called me back, I expected Stella to beat him to it, no doubt chastising me yet again for being so dramatic. I was hopeful for it. I wanted her to call me stupid. But now she'll never call me anything ever again.

The vodka swims inside my body but I don't feel anything.

Not Harper's hand that grabs mine, not the kisses on my cheek, not even the heat that turned on after sensing the temperature drop outside.

"Sam, I'm so sorry. I don't know what to say."

She holds onto me, putting me in a headlock kind of hug. I can't breathe but I don't care.

"She uh, she left a note." I spit out.

"What did it say?"

I already have it memorized. I've been reciting its ambiguous meaning around in my head wishing it to make sense. But nothing does. And in the end, it's poetic that even in her death, Stella was still someone I didn't know like I thought I did.

"Fate brought us together. I need you more than you realize. I just want you to love me.'"

Encore

———— ◆ ————

Stella's suicide has ripped me apart.

The day I confirmed her body at the exact same morgue, I finally broke down and cried.

When I flew back home and the few days after, I woke up thinking this wasn't real. I would have preferred pretending we weren't speaking, but still know she was living her own life. Keeping up with that act would have been preferable to my reality.

Even with all the lies she told me, I wanted to believe suicide wouldn't be an option for her. Instead, her mental illness took over and she decided leaving this world would be a better ending.

I didn't realize the extent of her illness and I'll never forgive myself for not intervening sooner.

She was sick and her selfish actions will live with me for the rest of my life.

I love her and I hate her; and I don't know how to feel one without feeling the other simultaneously.

My twin, the person I entered this world with, who was with me before day 1 even existed, is gone. I'll never feel whole again.

After reading some of her personal documents and researching the disorder she was diagnosed with, the realm of mental illness is all I've focused my attention on.

I now know the signs of manipulation: doubt, guilt, feeling insecure.

How you can be charming one day and deceitful the next.

But it's all too little too late.

Knowing the facts won't bring her back. Even in her death, she still has a way of making me feel responsible for not trying hard enough, for not doing more, and not being there for her in her final hours.

If there's one thing I learned out of all of this, it's knowing that a mentally deranged person can be hiding in plain sight.

We all keep secrets. We may never reveal all our faults, the mysteries we hide from someone we love most. But I can see past the lies now.

With all I've learned, I won't make the same mistake twice and invite someone into my life so mentally unstable.

And on that note, the woman I love most, who will be the last woman to enter my life, walks towards me looking more beautiful than ever.

Harper has been an unwavering buoy during this horrible storm. We've been through so much in such a short period of time. How much more can we endure and still manage to say we are going strong?

When the dust settles and she's acclimated to the new job Jake got her, I have a three-carat east-west radiant cut engagement ring back at my condo, our condo. I'm going to make her mine for good. I just need the worst day of my life to be over so I can start the best days of my life with her.

Diego, Carrie, Jake, Avery, and a few of the original staff from In A Draught come to pay their respects.

I'm glad Harper talked me out of a huge ceremony. It would have been difficult to see the list of expected attendees and realize no one was coming.

It would have broken my heart to see old colleagues or classmates have to play nice for two hours, knowing deep down she wasn't actually amazing to work with, or so fun to live with during college.

They'd come out of necessity, all with a dark cloud over them because they knew the truth: Stella was difficult to love.

This wasn't one of those services where we'd have people lining up just waiting to share their heartwarming, uplifting story of Stella's greatest moments over finger foods and punch.

No, this little group is all we need and hopefully everyone else has better memories of her at some point in her life.

We are all outdoors, under a large tree blocking most of the sunlight creeping through the branches and leaves. There are almost no clouds in the sky but a small breeze shakes the smaller limbs and dead twigs blow past our feet.

Stella wanted to be cremated, so her remains sit in an urn atop a pillar.

We are actually right next to my parent's gravesite, a surreal and gut wrenching reality that our family is down to one. Me. It's just me now.

Stella's face is printed in a simple 8x10 frame.

I inhale deeply one last time, my left hand touching the frame.

"Thank you all for coming out." I begin. "It's not easy being here. It's hard for me to even be present in this moment, because I'm not completely whole anymore. My other half is… is right here."

I touch the urn softly, a tear escaping down my cheek.

Embracing the urn within my hands, I hold onto it for too long, the silence dragging.

When I look up to continue my speech, I see an older man approaching our group.

He looks so familiar but I can't place him. He's dressed in a nice suit and I immediately think he's the owner of the cemetery.

He's alone when he meanders toward the back of the group, unsure if he should take a seat or not.

"Hi, can I help you?" I ask, pausing my speech.

He coughs first and takes off his sunglasses. "I am here to pay my respects to Stella Evans."

His voice is familiar but still, I can't place him.

Everyone looks back to see who this man is except Harper.

"Yeah of course, take a seat anywhere you'd like." I say.

We have 16 chairs divided into 2 rows of 8, and most of the second row is empty, which we expected.

Harper's posture stiffens as he selects one behind her.

Her pupils are dark and mysterious; her unwavering focus trained on something beyond the horizon.

Concentrating on her chest, I wait to see it rise, fall, inhale, something! If it weren't for the breeze blowing a few loose strands of her hair, I'd think the world stopped.

I can't fathom why she's reacting like any movement on her behalf will spark a reaction behind her.

She doesn't even look back to offer a polite smile.

"You don't remember me, do you?" He asks me.

Harper's shoulders twitch, like a cold front just swept up her spine and left her in a blizzard.

I shrug and say, "I'm so sorry. I don't."

"It's okay, son. It's Larry, Stella's boss from Bateman & Busey."

ACKNOWLEDGMENTS

If you've made your way to the acknowledgments, that means you picked up this book, read it, hopefully loved it, and I can't thank you enough for giving me a chance to write a story you chose to read. It means more than you know!

To my husband, Joe. Before I even told you what this book was about, you were my biggest cheerleader. You always encouraged me to keep writing even when I took month long breaks because I hated everything and wanted to start all over. You had to deal with me when I was excited, anxious, doubtful, insecure, back to excited, and all the emotions in between for the past 5 years it took to finish this. And you still loved me and supported me. I'm sorry you didn't get that wizard character you wanted. Maybe the next book!

To my twin sister, Stacy/Pacey. You were the first person to read this in its entirety and your praise gave me the confidence I needed to make my dream become reality. I'm grateful we have an amazing relationship that is nothing like Sam and Stella's. Because let's be real, we are both equally crazy.

To my best friend, Karli. Thank you for being the best book buddy ever and getting me back into reading so many years ago. I'm so grateful for your friendship these past 16 years. Here 'yer books!

To Ally! You are the kindest, sweetest, and most positive person I've ever met! Thank you for motivating me to finish so you can get your signed copy.

And lastly I want to thank my 3 month old son, Will. You came into our lives at the perfect time; in more ways than one. Knowing you were soon going to be my new priority gave me the final push I needed to get serious about this book and finish it. However, you are not allowed to read this. Maybe when you're 21. Maybe.

Made in the USA
Las Vegas, NV
06 January 2022

40453140R00281